STORM'S THUNDER

STORM'S THUNDER

BRANDON BOYCE

Originally based on an idea by
Derrick Borte and Brandon Boyce

PINNACLE BOOKS
Kensington Publishing Corp.
www.kensingtonbooks.com

PINNACLE BOOKS are published by

Kensington Publishing Corp.
119 West 40th Street
New York, NY 10018

All Kensington titles, imprints, and distributed lines are available at special quantity discounts for bulk purchases for sales promotions, premiums, fund-raising, educational, or institutional use. Special book excerpts or customized printings can also be created to fit specific needs. For details, write or phone the office of the Kensington sales manager: Kensington Publishing Corp., 119 West 40th Street, New York, NY 10018, attn: Sales Department; phone 1-800-221-2647.

PINNACLE BOOKS and the Pinnacle logo are Reg. U.S. Pat. & TM Off.

ISBN-13: 978-0-7860-3522-9
ISBN-10: 0-7860-3522-6

First printing: October 2016

10 9 8 7 6 5 4 3 2 1

Printed in the United States of America

First electronic edition: October 2016

ISBN-13: 978-0-7860-3523-6
ISBN-10: 0-7860-3523-4

For
Jesse A. Boyce
and
Jesse A. Boyce, Jr.,

Western spirits.

Mamma said the pistol is the devil's right hand.

—STEVE EARLE

PART 1
THE SANTA FE

CHAPTER ONE

The young pronghorn breaks from his mother and comes to a stop in a struggling patch of milkweed, just far enough from the others to give me a clean shot, my first in two days. And I am hungry. At the center of the herd, the dominant buck has been keeping his harem on the move and packed tight around him for nearly a hundred miles, while showing less and less regard for the weary juveniles. Soon his patience will end and he will run the yearlings off for good. Few will survive. The young one I have my eye on would be lucky to last a day. I don't give much thought to taking out the buck; the entire band would perish. And I would need to be stark mad with starvation to consider killing a doe. The expectant females—three by my count—will soon give birth to fawns that, a year from now, the buck will push out, as he will this lot in the coming days.

I float down from the saddle and guide Storm backward a few paces out of view. His gray coat sweated nearly black, the stallion folds his hind legs without protest and goes all the way down to the hard-packed ground, breathing heavy, welcoming a rest after the back-breaking pursuit. For all his stubbornness, Storm has always shown the sense to keep quiet when the moment calls and now is no exception. Any noise would mean more running. And while I suspect a faster and more sure-footed horse the Territory has never known, staying both downwind and within reach of the fleetest animals on the continent has proved all the challenge we care to handle. I let the Spencer fall from my shoulder and melt in behind a low outcropping of rock on a bluff overlooking the mesa where the pronghorn have finally taken a moment to graze.

The juvenile, with his nubby excuse for antlers, has not looked up once—too ravaged with hunger—and has strayed beyond his mother's realm of comfort. The doe lifts her head, throwing her large, rear-arching rack—every bit as impressive as the buck's—high in the air. Even through the cool breeze I hear her chirping at her offspring. But his head stays down, greedily devouring the tender young shoots that had tried to get a jump on spring.

I bring up the rifle and slide it down the glove of my left hand to keep it from chinking against the boulder. My bare right palm silently throws the bolt and finds the trigger. Peering down the barrel, I settle my pulse to near stillness with every breath. The yearling takes a cursory step toward his mother, but still has not looked up. *I know your hunger, friend.* My belly tightens at the reminder of it. Only when I have him sighted to the heart do I close my eyes and say a prayer to the Great Spirit, thanking him for this young brother who will sustain me. And for good measure I throw in a prayer to the White God too, but my eyes snap open to a faint buzzing behind me. I pray it is only a mosquito, but I know it is not, not in this cold.

The yearling has shifted now, turned three-quarter so his rump faces me. I need him profile for a clean kill. What I do not need is any ruckus out of Storm. The buzzing grows louder, and I know I am in trouble. *Settle down, Storm. Just a horsefly.* The words are more thought than sound, but he gets the message, and by the second snort, I know he does not care.

All at once, the yearling lifts his small head. It is not much to work with, but will have to do. Storm hates horseflies and cannot be trusted to ignore one now. I let out half a breath and then hold, the gentle action of the trigger succumbing to the pressure beneath my finger. And then in one bursting moment—the trigger in mid-journey—everything splinters. Storm uncorks a wallop of a squeal. The rifle cracks. And a dozen startled pronghorn find full-speed in a single bound. I see the yearling's knees buckle, but then recover, and he is off with the others, gobbling up ten yards of sagebrush with every leap and doing his best to keep up.

I scramble up from the rock. Storm is on his back, kicking wildly at a pesky, minuscule adversary that has probably not even bitten him yet. At the sight of me, the stallion rolls over and springs to his feet. I sling up and heel him straight toward a steep embankment better suited for mountain goats. And just like that, we are off chasing antelope again. This time I make sure he hears me. "You got no one to blame but yourself, on this one!"

Against the beige floor of the mesa, the entire band of pronghorn is little more than bobbing flashes of white, rapidly vanishing in the opposite direction. Hardly a spray of dust betrays the retreat. But then a flutter of movement, unexpected, fractures from the herd. The yearling. His mother is there too, compelled to encourage her offspring through his injury and if not, at least away from the band. Emboldened by their scent, Storm makes quick work of the embankment and, stunned to find pronghorn growing larger in his vision for a change, needs no urging as the ground levels out.

The yearling picks up the sound of Storm's thunder and scrambles to mount an escape. But his movements have lost their precision, his strides now guided only by panic. With nothing but open country to one side, the doe nudges her charge toward a rising formation of sandstone, hoping to lose us among the towering spires that jut abruptly from the mesa floor. The remainder of the herd is but a speck on the horizon. I veer the stallion right, cutting off any sudden jailbreak.

The doe, desperate for alternatives, starts up the slope—into the jagged outcrops—but such unsure footing is bighorn domain, not antelope. The yearling wants no part of the rocks or of me or Storm—bouncing a stride or two in one direction and then back the other—deeply distressed by all options. The doe lowers her head and chirps. Only then does the yearling turn for the rocks. He takes one uncertain leap and then falters, his neck and head grazing the stone surface before he rights himself and bounds up to his mother. A dark, wet smear colors the rock where his head touched, and when he turns back, I see the red-soaked fur down the side of his neck. He might even be blind in that eye. I am surprised he made it this far. But bounding over the sagebrush comes as natural to an antelope as telling lies to a White Man; it is what they do, even when they don't know they are doing it.

The yearling vanishes up into the rocks, yet his mother remains. She stands there, defiant, willing us to move along, but there is resignation in her breath—as if she knows nothing can be done to save the yearling. All at once, Storm rears up and unleashes a mighty blow. I squeeze my thighs tight against his flanks and toss my weight forward to keep from being thrown. Something about this place has him all twisted up.

The doe has seen enough. She scampers down the slope, giving the fuming stallion a wide birth as she reaches the flat ground and in no time is striding off after the herd.

"Since when you spook at a few drops of blood?" I say to Storm. "Ain't like he's bleeding out." True that no horse rushes toward the scent of fresh blood by its own accord, but Storm's sudden refusal to take another step is bullheaded even for him. "You been pampered too long. Lost your taste for battle." I swing down and drop the ground hitch. "You stay put."

Storm nickers a brief response and I give his ear a scratch before returning my thoughts to the pronghorn. He is up there, hiding somewhere, and I do not want him to suffer more than he already has. I draw my knife and palm the blade against my forearm as I start up the slope. I follow the droplets along the red rock, but my mind falls back to Storm. I have charged that stallion headlong into horrors a hundred times worse, up in the Sangres, where fresh blood coated everything and squirted from the necks

of dying White Men. So his behavior now sits funny,
for certain. Cresting the rise, I stop and sniff the air.
Death lurks here—a faint, unmistakable whisper of
decaying flesh.

"Dang it," glancing back at Storm. "Burns me to
no end when your nose is better than mine." I start
to think the doe's course up to the rocks was more
than coincidence. Humans have graveyards. Animals
have theirs. Sometimes the only thing we can give
ourselves is a quiet place to die. The pronghorn has
found his against the base of a striated point of rock,
out of view to all but the most determined follower.
He lies on the ground, his head lolling sideways to
find me with his one good eye. But there is no protest
anymore, only exhaustion. His thin legs twitch as I
kneel beside him and stroke his flank. "Easy, friend."
I keep my voice soft and slide my left hand gently
up his neck to the prongs, making sure I get a strong
grip. The prongs may be stubs, but could still cause
plenty damage. And when I have his head firmly in
my hand I ask his forgiveness—for choosing him—
for the sloppy kill that I now promise to finish clean.
I whisper the words, a secret between the two of us.
Then his eyes flutter and with a quick, sure thrust, I
let the knife do its work. It is over in an instant. Even
the steady breeze takes pause to mourn. And in the
stillness, the stench of death finds sturdier footing.

It radiates from the cracks and hidden recesses of
the rocks. I cast a look skyward, expecting to find the
slow, circling glide of condors crisscrossing the bright
sun, but there is nothing, not even a cloud, to inter-
rupt the blue vastness. To this day—writing about a
time so many years gone—I do not know what compelled me to keep walking. I could have thrown the

pronghorn over my shoulder, field-dressed him a mile from here along the bank of the Great River and—if we rode all night—been in Santa Fe by breakfast. The property-agent fellow told me to call on him in a week, and that he might have a little money for me, not that I care much either way if he don't. That was nine days ago, maybe ten. Our goal is California—all the way to San Francisco. I aim to get Storm and myself there in one piece even if we have to walk, or book his passage on a steamer around the Horn—with him in the hold and me toiling in the bowels of the engine room to pay for it.

But instead, I step over the yearling and follow the scent around a corner of sandstone to a row of shadowy openings in the rocks. The hard sunlight cuts through the recesses as I slide along a narrowing ledge, revealing the dusty, inner depths of the hollows. The ledge dwindles to half a boot-length, and I have to shuck off my gloves and feel along the rock face for the tiniest handhold. After several yards, the ledge widens out into a small landing, made smaller on the left side by a pile of stones laid against the sheer cliff face. The right side falls off in a steep, unbroken drop down to the mesa floor. I look back at the pile of stones, their blacked hue in stark contrast to the orangey colors of the sandstone. These rocks were placed deliberately, in the style of the Apache. When the *Inde* bury their dead—under a stump or in the hollow of a tree—they lay small boulders around the grave to ward off coyotes. I see no sign of coyote up here, but peering over the edge of the landing, directly below, I spot a frustrated patchwork of coyote tracks, where they tried to solve the riddle of the sheer cliff before eventually giving up. Whoever took the effort to haul these stones along the edge did so at great peril. I kneel down and pluck a greasy condor feather from among the stones. Looks like the carrion birds took their shot as well, but came up as empty as the four-legged scavengers.

The stone pile comes up to my knee. Above it, wedged into a wide crack in the cliff surface, is a caked confection of dried mud and grass. I pinch off a bit, rolling the stuff between my fingers until the dirt crumbles away, leaving only the browned fragments of once-green river grass. We are miles from where it grows, which means this displaced mixture—the kind used as mortar in the hogans of the Navajo—was also hauled here and slapped into the rock by hand. And there is plenty of it. I follow the trail of muddy concrete up the crevasse to where it turns horizontal and then extends another few feet before descending back toward the landing. Just above the rock pile, the crack expands to the width of a man's fist, every inch of it packed with the homemade mortar. I give it a firm shove and my fist goes straight through, into an empty space behind. When I withdraw my hand I uncork a hellish gust of such putrid stink and decay that I am retching over the side before I can catch myself, my empty belly coughing forth nothing but bile. Turning my head, spitting out the taste of my own insides, I gulp down precious breaths of clean air before pulling my mascada up over my nose and mouth. I suck the dust from the coarse fabric into my lungs, but it is better than ingesting the unspeakable foulness of what lies dead beyond this improvised tomb.

My heartbeat quickening in my ears, I claw away at what is left of the mortar, chunks at a time, until the shape of the crevice becomes clear. A door. A stone door, well matched in color to the surrounding sandstone. I kick away the small boulders piled against it, shuttling rocks the size of melons across the landing. Sweated through, my blood pounding, I put my back into the work, as the boulders get larger closer to the door. At the bottom, wedged against the sandstone, lays a sturdy rock twice as heavy as the others. It takes all my strength, but with a final push, I feel the squat boulder start to budge. All at once there is a low scraping sound. I look up. Dirt—the mortar from above—rains down, blinding me as the noise builds to a solid rumble. I steady myself against the stone door and feel the great slab falling toward me.

Nearly blind, I hurl myself sideways—into the air—toward what I hope is the ledge that brought me here. My aim is only half right. I crash hard into the lip of the ledge, my hip and forearm taking the brunt of it. I bounce off the ledge and feel gravity sucking me downward. I throw my arm up—flailing for anything more than a fistful of air. Somehow my fingers find the lip and I brace for impact against the side of the rock. The falling slab booms like a shotgun as it slams into the landing—its momentum kicking it end-over-end as it flips upward and slides twenty feet to the ground, where it cleaves in two and spews forth a canon shot of dust and caliche. Hanging midair, my arm and hip stinging with hot knives, I can only marvel at how a mule-headed stallion is longer for this world than a curious fool. But I am alive and—pulling myself back up to the ledge—rest fairly certain that none of my bones have broke.

When the dust clears, I hear Storm whinny and I call out to him that I am all right. Rising slow to my feet, I steady myself against the rock wall and turn back toward where the door had been. My heart sinks. The sweat that soaks my shirt, in an instant, goes cold. The face of a white man, what is left of it, stares back at me. And where his eyes once were, pits of dried blood buzz with flies. His mouth sits frozen open, revealing the viciousness that saw his tongue get hacked out and most likely eaten. The naked body leans against the inside of the cave, supported by a steel-tipped lance that juts upward out of his chest. It was the weapon that killed him before someone snapped it in half to make room for the body next to him. I want to turn and run far away from this place, but somehow my feet defy my brain and propel me forward.

The second man, taller than the first, suffered a similar—but not identical—slate of horrors. His ears and nose have been chopped off, along with his arms below the elbow. The fatal blow came from a sharp knife that carved out his heart. My mouth goes bone dry as I move closer, the afternoon sun cutting through the cavern to display the carnage in all its stark harshness. A third man appears shorter, but only because his head lies at his twisted feet. His ribs, nearly all of them, extend outward where the shotgun tore him through from behind. Stepping to the entrance of the cave, though, the full scope of the carnage registers with unfathomable clarity. The dryness in my throat gives way to a knot that sinks to the pit of my stomach. My legs grow weak as twigs and I drop to my knees.

The butchered bodies of eleven White Men fill the small cave. I count the torsos because it is the only way to be sure. Some of the heads are missing, or discarded about the ground, or smashed into pieces among the limbs and organs that litter the floor. Staring dumbfounded at the tableau in its grisly totality, there appears no conceivable torture or bodily desecration left unaccounted for among its victims. So complete the extermination that its perpetrators must surely have luxuriated in an overwhelming advantage of force, and an orgiastic abundance of time, in which to leave unturned no stone of sadistic creativity. One wretched young man, no older than myself, looks like he was roasted below the waist while his arms and shoulders played pincushion to an awl or ice pick. Yet others among his kindred became canvases for intricate blade-work. Each of the eleven seems to have suffered a unique death, but before his suffering had ended, shared one or two communal hardships with his brethren. Not one of them died with his private parts attached and more than a few took their last, miserable breaths with their manhood stuffed into their mouths. The entire lot—probably early in the proceedings—was stripped completely naked, their clothing nowhere in sight, not a single thread of it. Scanning the chamber, in fact, I cannot observe a single personal possession of any kind—no tool or weapon or artifact—which may have aided even the most meager defense. What insurmountable imbalance of power must have been in play to render nearly a dozen able-bodied White Men into such docile submission? The final commonality is the marked absence of each and every scalp.

I cannot say how long I set there on my knees, but before I could will my eyes to look away, I was certain this vile vista has seared itself into an inescapable cage of memory.

As I find my feet again, a dot of shadow crawls across the landing. I look up. The first of the vultures circles overhead, the full stench of this discovery now extending miles downwind. I have seen enough and marshal my thoughts toward leaving, but in the shifting light, something polished and gold reflects a ray of sunlight from an inner nook of the cave. Before giving myself a chance to reconsider, I push forth— holding my breath—and tiptoe into the foulness. I pluck the overlooked object from its hiding place and shove it in my pocket. Turning back toward the ledge, I am greeted by an arriving condor. The colossal bird stands at the edge of the landing, folding in her enormous wings in anticipation of the feast laid out before her. I move to shoo her off and then stop myself. Let the scavengers have at it, I say, so that the sight of this altar of evil may never poison the vision of another living soul. I blow past the condor without looking back.

By the time I reach Storm, the sky swirls black with the great birds. I drape the pronghorn over the stallion's haunches and swing myself up. "Don't ask," and he obliges by starting his walk. The sun hangs low over the mountains to the west. I glance at the ridge and see a lone rider atop a piebald lineback, watching me with great intent. And I know right away from her knee-high moccasins and the way she sits on her horse that she is Apache. Farther south, or west into Arizona, she would be among her own. But we are deep in Navajoland. And for her to be out here alone tells me she has been watching me, or this place, with vested interest. I refrain from any sudden gestures, offering only a small nod to acknowledge that I see her. She provides no response, other than turning her mount and disappearing over the ridge.

An hour later, as Storm lopes southeast toward Santa Fe, I find the courage to pull the metal object from my pocket and take a look. It is a buckle—from a belt no doubt—a polished brass oval surrounding two stout letters, U and S.

U.S.

A cavalryman's property. That some band of marauding killers could so thoroughly destroy nearly a dozen settlers, or unarmed missionaries, figures hard enough to believe, but that their victims were none other than the Indian-slayers of the United States Army resides beyond my comprehension. All at once, what I know, and what I thought I know, fall apart. The only certainty is that no good can ever come from speaking of this to anyone. Now more than ever, the Territory of New Mexico: the only place I have ever known—*the Dinétah*, the sacred homeland of my Navajo ancestors—pushes me to leave, toward a great unknown in the West. And so I will go.

CHAPTER TWO

I hitch Storm to the post and step through the low picket gate that buffers the small, white house from the dusty commotion of Palace Street. My worn riding satchel hangs low on the shoulder, counterbalancing the weight of the short-barrel thirty-two in my left coat pocket—the one I carry when my usual rig, a pair of pearl-handle Colts, would impose the wrong impression. A path of slate paving stones divides a little garden where tiny purple flowers take in the morning sunlight from terra cotta urns that flank my procession to the porch. Potted flowers—a luxury far removed from the rocky, overworked patches of the Bend, where a few scrawny beans and waist-high corn had folks dropping to their knees to thank their creator.

In the haste of my previous visit to the home of Milton J. Garber, convened well past sundown, I had not noticed what an oasis the land agent—or more likely, some woman—had fashioned among the drab adobes a short block from the main plaza of Santa Fe. A burning desire to see my business conducted that night had been too consuming. Yet now, with that mausoleum of butchery clouding the mind, my motivation finds even greater urgency. The wood creaks as I climb the freshly painted steps, reverberating with hollow echoes as I cross to the door.

I remove my glove and rap three times under bare knuckle. From deep within the house—the second floor by the sound of it—a man's voice calls out.

"Just a moment." Footsteps clomp down an inner staircase and sighs as he approaches the door, as if put upon by the interruption. The house casts a long, cool shadow across the garden. I make it just past nine, early enough to be a businessman's first call of the day, but hardly an hour to catch him indisposed. A key lock turn, followed by a deadbolt and then the fall of a chain. The door opens and Milton Garber stand there, dressed, but there is something undone about him. His ditto jacket hangs open and a missed button on the waistcoat betrays a careless donning. "Can I help you?" Garber peering at me through his wire-rim spectacles without a hint of remembrance.

"Morning, Mister Garber," removing my hat. All at once his eyes burst with recognition.

"Why Mister Two-Trees." He pulls the door open wide and, stepping aside, extends his arm toward a chair in his front-room office. "Why, you must forgive me. I did not recognize you with your whiskers. Please, come in. Can I offer you some coffee?"

"Obliged." I step past him into the office and move toward the chair, but cannot bring myself to sit.

"Xenia!" He says, shouting toward the top of the stairs. "Some fresh coffee, straight away. Do sit, Mister Two-Trees. Make yourself at home."

"Best I stand, sir. I ought not foul up your sitting chair."

"Nonsense," Garber says. When I glance back, the missed button of his waistcoat seems to have found its proper hole. Then his fingers make quick work of the ditto buttons, and just like that, he is soberly attired. "Please, sit."

"I took a splash through the Grande about an hour ago. It cut the stink, but my clothes still a mite dusty."

"You bathed in the Rio Grande?" he says, crinkling his nose. "This morning? What on earth were you doing all the way out there?"

"I amble out that way after last we talked."

Milton J. Garber, land agent, stares at me like I had switched to a foreign tongue. "Mister Two-Trees, you were here . . ." He turns his head, squinting in disbelief at a bank calendar hanging on the wall, "fifteen days ago." He gawks at me, expecting me to speak, so I just go on letting him have a right long look. Then I nod and ease down into the chair. Garber sinks slow in the leather chair behind a desk cluttered with paper and doodads. "You mean you've just . . . been out there, at the Rio Grande, for over two weeks?"

"I fell in behind a band of pronghorn for a couple days. That swung me northwest a fair piece, but I followed the river back." Some cups rattle on a tray at the top of the stairs, followed by the careful footsteps of a woman. "You said to give you a week or so. I reckon I lost track of the rest. Pronghorn is pretty quick."

"I'll take your word. Never seen one myself," he says. "Ah, Xenia, my dear."

A pretty negro girl, about my age, maybe nineteen, reaches the bottom step and lets out a breath, relieved at descending with only minimal spillage. Sweat beads along her brow and neck, and I can smell the sex on her before the aroma of coffee fills the air. She catches my gaze and darts her eyes away quick. She does not look at Garber at all. Rather, she sets the tray down on his desk, curtsies—embarrassed—as if I had caught her in the state of nakedness she had been in five minutes prior. As she turns for the stairs, I see that Garber is not the only one who missed a button.

"I am not much of an outdoorsman," Garber says, handing me a thin china cup overfilled with hot coffee. I hold it with both hands, unsure how any grown man's fingers fit though the tiny handle. "But I am most impressed at people who can just 'live of the land.'"

"You fixed up a nice garden," I say, nodding to the window. Storm's long head undulates through the wavering glass. Beyond him stretches the burnt umber balustrade of the Palace of Governors.

"Xenia's handiwork entirely. Blessed with the green-thumb of a sharecropper's daughter."

"Mister Garber, last we spoke you said you might could sell my land up Caliche Bend."

"Indeed, Mister Two-Trees. I'll confess, when you brought me your business, I did not think much would come of the proposition. But that was because I was ignorant of two very important pieces of information, the first being your identity."

"I give my full name when I called on you."

"You did, and I'll beg forgiveness that the name Harlan Two-Trees did not resonate as it should have."

The man ducks behind his desk, rooting among the stacks of paper piled on the floor. "Imagine my surprise when I opened the *Gazette* the following morning to learn that the stranger who knocked on my door in the middle of the night, granting me full power of attorney to sell eighty-five acres in Caliche Bend at whatever price the market would bear, was the same man who rescued the residents of said hamlet from certain financial ruin by returning— damn near to the *dollar*—what had been stolen in the greatest robbery in history." Garber's head pops back into view. "And, in the process, killed the most feared outlaw in the Territory, perhaps the entire Frontier." He rises to his feet and tosses a yellowed newspaper on the desk. "You killed the Snowman."

I don't make much of the headline and its jumbled letters, but I recognize at once the penciled likeness of Garrison LaForge. You don't forget the Snowman. And farther down the page, no bigger than a nickel, is another face. That sketcher from the *Gazette* never could get my chin right.

"It was someone else kilt the Snowman. I was just a witness."

"A trifling distinction," Garber sipping his coffee. He leans back in his chair. "The power of myth can hardly be derailed by something as inconsequential as the truth."

"You said there were two things."

"Come again?"

"Two things you did not know."

"Ah, yes," Garber says. "That would be the validity and condition of the parcel in question." All at once he pushes off from his desk and slides in his chair across the room to a tall cabinet. A chair with wheels.

Had Sheriff gotten wind of such a conveyance, I suspect the jailhouse back in the Bend would still bear rings around where his desk stood. "You understand, just because a man says he owns something doesn't mean he does. The will and testament you showed me had to be verified with the assessor's office, which it was, eventually. Yes, the late Sheriff Pardell did intend for his property to go to you—"

"What do you mean, eventually?"

"Well, there was the slight matter of your heritage." He trails off and waits for my reaction. When I give him nothing, he continues, choosing his words carefully. "You're an Indian . . . or half-Indian, yes?"

"Does it matter?"

"In the eyes of the law, most certainly."

"Navajo. My mother was Navajo. My father was a white man."

"Yes, well unfortunately the law makes very little distinction between Indian and half-breed."

"I don't care for that word."

"What, half—?" Garber stops himself. A knot of flesh rolls slow down the man's throat. "My apologies, Mister Two-Trees," his voice breaking. "I meant no disrespect. The point is that there are laws against Indians owning property, except in designated areas. The reservations."

"Sheriff and the missus raise me on that land since I was a spud. He leave it to me fair and square."

"The concept of 'fair and square' doesn't apply much when it comes to Indians."

"No. It does not."

"Before I could even think about a potential buyer," Garber begins, "there is the issue of title. The problem, you see, is that the clerk has a ledger, and in that ledger is recorded every sale and transfer of real estate holdings in the territory, including the names of the buyer and seller, and of each, his race." At this, the man gets up from his seat and crosses to the window, his fingers smoothing nonexistent wrinkles from his waistcoat. "You are as much white as you are red. I don't care what Washington says. Washington is not New Mexico."

"What did you do?"

"Let's just say that there are few obstacles in this world that cannot be solved by a pair of double-eagle gold pieces. The clerk had to write something down in his book. I made sure it was what we wanted."

"You risked yourself on my account?"

"You're not the only one with a connection to Caliche Bend. My sister lives there. Perhaps you know her. Alma is her name, Alma Early. She's married to Jack Early."

"Big Jack. He's my friend. 'Course I know Alma."

"I assumed that's who referred me to you."

"Nope. Had no idea. I asked around for a fella what sold property. Barkeep down the way sent me to you."

"I don't believe in coincidence, Mister Two-Trees. It was divine providence that sent you to me. Jack and Alma had their savings stolen along with everyone else's and you, sir, are the man to thank for that money's return. I consider it an honor to express my gratitude for your bravery by finding you the highest possible price for your land."

"Obliged."

"Mister Two-Trees, you signed over power-of-attorney to a man you didn't know. Had you knocked on the door of any other agent in Santa Fe, he would've sold your property, kept all the proceeds for himself and then vanished. That, or found a way to have you arrested."

"I suppose you coulda done that. But spending my money while also dead would prove difficult."

"It was never an option, Mister Two-Trees." Garber rests his hands on his hips and looks me square. "Despite what anyone says about *my tribe*, Milton J. Garber doesn't swindle heroes." He downs the rest of his coffee and continues. "With the issue of title settled, I took a trip up to the Bend to take a look at this eighty-five acres. I can't rightly sell a parcel if I can't describe it."

"You rode all the way out to the Bend?"

"Oh, with the new railroad it's an easy hour. Alma and Jack were there to collect me in the buggy. I must say, your property is a lovely spread. Plenty of flat ground, perfect for crops or grazing, with that delightful stream down the middle. I'm frankly surprised that you want to let it go."

"Time I moved on."

"Yes, California, you mentioned. Not looking for gold, I hope. I hear it's bust." I let the words hang there and he keeps looking at me, expecting me to talk. But these days I find myself less inclined to tell a man any more of my business than I need to. "I don't mean to pry. It's just that . . . they don't want you to go. There, I said it plain."

"Who don't?"

"Jack. Alma. Just about every person I spoke to in the Bend. Hell, sir, they want you to come back and be sheriff."

"Big Jack's wearing the star now."

"Oh, God bless my sister's husband, but Jack is no

sheriff. A deputy, maybe. And for you, he'd gladly step aside. Told me as much himself. You have the trust of the people. You earned it."

"If you stood on my land, then you saw what they did." A dark memory flickers behind Garber's eyes. But now my own memory flares—searing heat, a blanket of smoke, the stench of burning livestock. I feel my blood start to boil. "They burned my house down, with me in it. My barn too. Only thing survived was me and that stallion."

"Whoever burned you out should be hanged, no question. If you were sheriff, you could do it yourself."

"Folks may see the white in me when the cotton is high, like now—everybody sitting flush—but come the first whisper of trouble, they don't see nothing but red. You think White Men are gonna take kindly to an Indian stringing up one of their own, or telling people what they can and cannot do? No, sir. You pin a star to my front side, you might as well pin a bull's eye to my back. I'm not interested."

"Well, I told them I'd ask. Can't blame a fellow for trying."

It is his trying that sits funny with me. Why this man who don't know me from Adam would angle his own brother-in-law out of steady work—thus taking bread off his sister's table—while steering me toward a job that would get me shot faster than five aces, only adds to the conundrum that is Milton J. Garber. He pulls a handkerchief from his vest and dabs a droplet of sweat from his forehead and all at once the answer hits me—he couldn't find a buyer. Simple, when I think about it. Folks have been hightailing from Caliche Bend ever since the copper mines run out. I can't get myself away fast enough. And after the nasty business with the Snowman, the Bend festers in people's mind like a canker. Garber's play is to save face by selling me to myself as some kind of hero.

"If it's all the same, I'll take the ten dollars an acre you promised and be on my way."

"Now, just one minute, Mister Two-Trees, ten dollars an acre was simply an estimate, drawn off the top of my head, before I had had a chance to personally reconnoiter the parcel."

"If you couldn't unload it, you ought just come out and say it straight."

"Please understand the economic climate in the Bend is hardly robust. Granted, your bravery helped avert complete financial disaster, but still, the parcel remains too pricey—even at seven or six an acre—for most of the folks up there. And it is not as though there's been an influx of new blood. Word back East is that the frontier is closed."

"I've heard enough," rising from my chair. "I'll take my deed back now."

Garber presses his hands together and lets out a breath. "That would be impossible, Mister Two-Trees. I don't have it."

"Step away from the window."

"Why?"

I reach into my pocket and pull out the thirty-two. "Because I don't want the bullet to go through the glass and hurt nobody."

"I don't have your deed because your property's been sold." Garber backs against the wall, hands pleading. "But not at ten an acre."

"Then how much?" He hesitates and I pull back the hammer.

"Seventeen dollars and fifty cents per acre. Cash." His words fill the air like a fat thunderhead.

"But, that's more," I say.

Only then does the face of Milton J. Garber bloom into a smile. "Oh, yes it is. Mister Two-Trees, I am very good at what I do."

"I reckon so. Who bought it?"

"Your old neighbor, Bennett Whitlock, the rancher."

"Whitlock." It makes sense, now that I think of it. Richest man in the Bend. His two hundred acres just grew by nearly half. I look down at the gun in my hands and stash it away. "Apologies."

"No need to apologize. I should know better than to take a roundabout explanation with a straight-shooter like yourself. Now, how would you like your money, gold or paper?"

"Gold'll work."

And with that, Garber closes the curtain over the window, leaving the room in a muted amber light. He turns to a wardrobe and opens it, revealing a squat iron safe at the bottom. Bending down, he stops and straightens again.

"Oh, what the hell are we drinking coffee for? Xenia! Bring the bottle!" The girl's footsteps patter atop the stairs—where she has been eavesdropping—and retreat to some place directly above me. Clinking glass echoes through the floorboards and a moment later she is moving down the steps—more sure-footed this time—clutching a pair of small glasses. A brown whiskey bottle sits tucked under an arm, her free hand sliding along the banister as she reaches the landing. She passes by me, trailing a scent of lavender powder not worn in her earlier visit. She has also found occasion to fix her hair and address the alignment of her buttons. "Take a look-see, Xenia," Garber kneeling over the safe as he rotates the dial left and then back a few inches to the right. "That is one wealthy gentleman."

She nods, a shy little move that brings a smile when I meet her eye. "You want I should pour, Mister Garber?" Her soft, high drawl roots her in Southern cotton country.

"Go ahead." Garber cranks the handle and opens the safe, revealing a stack of paper money, bound tight with string. A Derringer rests on top, the barrel no longer than a thumb, but the wide-bore muzzle assures at least a forty-caliber response to any irregular business. Next to the currency sits a clutch of little cloth bags—gold dust, most likely. He reaches deep into the safe, both arms straining as he removes a small black box, far heavier than its size would reckon. It clanks and jangles as Garber labors to his feet and lugs the box to his desk, where Xenia pours whiskey for what appears to be the first time in her life. She doles a tiny splash into one glass, then tops the other off with a few drops to even it level with the first.

Garber sits down at his desk and flips his notebook to a clean sheet. "Now let's see," dipping his pen into the black goo of the inkwell. "Eighty acres and seventeen-fifty comes to . . ."

"It's eighty-five acres," I say.

A thoughtful smile spreads across his face. "Well, there is that one knoll on your property that's not really suitable for grazing. I thought it best not to give Mister Whitlock any point of leverage in the negotiation, so I exempted that particular five-acre parcel from the sale. And while it might be too steep for heifers, it sure would be a lovely spot for a house—perhaps a little garden, maybe even a barn."

"You saying you want it?"

"No, Mister Two-Trees. I'm saying it's still yours. Should you ever decide to return to Caliche Bend, you have a prime little spread waiting, which you own, legally and outright."

"Why . . . would you do that?" I feel the words form in my throat, but hardly hear them pass my mouth.

"Because I am a man of my word," Garber says. "There is a place for you in the Bend. A place as sheriff. And also a home."

"You drive a stubborn mule awful hard, Mister Garber. But my mind's made up. I am heading off to California soon as I figure how best to get there."

"I know better than to try changing a young man's mind," Garber opening the little box. "When I decided to move West, not a pack of wolves could've stopped me. That will be all, Xenia." The girl curtsies and starts back toward the stairs.

"Miss, you make a fine cup of coffee," my voice stopping her. She tries not to smile, which only makes her smile harder. I hold my gaze and give a little nod, and then she crumbles and giggles her way upstairs. The sound of clinking metal spins me back toward the desk, where he has the box open and is counting out a golden pillar of twenty-dollar double-eagles. I have seen men kill for less coin; Garber puts too much faith in that tiny Derringer. If word got out what riches reside in that safe, the floor grooves from his wheeled chair would run red with the blood of a dead estate agent and his bullet-ridden negro girl.

But as much as this man likes to tell me my business, I opt not to tell him his. Instead I ease over to my chair and pick up my satchel.

"Eighty acres at seventeen-fifty comes to fourteen hundred dollars," Garber says. "My commission of three percent—that's forty-two dollars—leaving a total of . . ."

"Make sure you minus off that hundred what you paid the clerk."

Garber dips his head in gratitude. "Very well. Thank you very much." He scribbles a few more numbers and looks up. "That leaves you with a grand total of twelve hundred and fifty-eight dollars." He divides the pile of double-eagles into two stacks of thirty, like a dealer counting out poker chips. Reaching back into the metal box, he thumbs out four ten-dollar eagles, two half-eagles, and eight dollar coins, which he stacks on top of the gold. He slides both piles across the desk.

I scoop up the money. The weight of the gold—a heft like nothing else—sits heavy in my hands. After a long moment, I deposit the lode into my trouser pocket. Garber withdraws a document from a file and lays it in front of me.

"And this is your deed for the five acres you still own. Keep it safe, Mister Two-Trees." I gaze down at the gibberish on the page, but I know enough to spot my name and the number 5—the acreage—and can see that the words, a half-page worth, are printed in Garber's careful hand. Still, an uneasy feeling dips my heart at the site of the document.

"I ain't wearing my spectacles," I say.

Garber peers though his wire frames, reading. "A parcel of five acres commencing at the southern

bank of Merriwether Creek and extending south to
latitude thirty-six degrees, five minutes, twenty-
point-two seconds North."

"Maybe you ought make a copy of this and keep it
here with you," I say.

Garber smiles. "I took the liberty of doing that
very thing." He produces a second paper from the
folder and lays it next to the first. They look the same
to me, but I pretend to give it a hard look. I draw
back the flap of my satchel and drop a bundle rolled
up in muslin on his desk. Garber's eyes go wide with
surprise.

"What is that?" he asks.

"Pronghorn."

Garber removes the muslin covering and unfurls
the roll across his blotter. "My goodness," he says,
running his fingers over the yearling's soft hide. "It's
marvelous."

"Worth good money too."

"I should never sell it. In fact, I'll have it mounted
here in the office." Garber stands and hands me a
whiskey. "They say in a good business deal, no one
goes away happy. Here's to proving them wrong."

"Hear hear," clinking my glass into his. The whiskey
goes down smooth and warm in a single slug.

"How are you getting to California?" Garber refill-
ing our glasses.

"I figure we'd make easy stages, maybe get a second
horse, take some of the burden off."

Garber's eyes narrow. "You mean ride to California,
on *horseback*?"

"Folks been doing it for years."

"And for every man who's made it, there's a dozen

who never got past the mountains. And then you have an entire desert to deal with."

"Well," I shrug. "Maybe we head down Galveston and book a steamer."

"Around the Horn? Sir, you're talking about months. Nauseating months. With your horse in a black, airless hold. The poor beast would wither to bone."

"I'm not selling Storm. He goes where I go."

"Well, then, why not go aboard the finest mode of transportation ever created, the majestic road of the Atchison, Topeka and Santa Fe. The ticket agent is just down the street here."

"Well, I can't damn well put a horse on a train."

"Mister Two-Trees, you have twelve-hundred dollars in your pocket. You are a man of means now. Money solves problems. Surely one of the stock cars can by outfitted to keep the animal comfortable for three days."

The train. It never occurred to me. My only train ride of my life has been on top of a coal car, and that was to kill a man. I have never stepped foot in one of the coaches—Pullmans, they call them. I flop open the satchel and—drawing my knife—slice off a chunk of *carne seca* and hand it to him. Garber pops it into his mouth without quarrel, his eyes brightening at the taste.

"What is that?"

"Pronghorn again."

"Delicious."

"How much you think they're asking for a ticket on the Santa Fe?"

"I don't know exactly. But I know you can afford it."

CHAPTER THREE

The door of Garber's house has barely closed behind me when I look out to the street and find a pair of men expressing an untoward interest in Storm. The stallion, left to his usual disposition, would nip at a harmless child just for sport, so for him to allow two meddling adults into such proximity can only attest to the depths to which our rigorous adventure has depleted him. He lets out a blow at the sight of me, but the strangers fail to make the connection. The tallest of the two, wide of shoulder and sporting a thick, rust-colored beard that flowers from nose to chest like an unruly shrub, runs a lingering eye along the stallion's flank, whistling approval in a covetous whine that does nothing to quell the animal's irritation.

The second man, a full head shorter and cobbled together from an afterthought of undernourished body parts, fixates on the saddlebags and the possible treasures therein. The Spencer, scabbarded behind the left fender where I now regret leaving it, juts straight up, its varnished stock catching a streak of sunlight. The rifle may be older than I am, and due for a good smith, but we have been through too much together for me to see it lain across another man's saddle, or worse, aimed at my head. I slip down from the porch onto the stone path and push my hands deep into my front pockets. My left knuckles bump against the weight of loose gold while the fingers of my right hand find the handle of the thirty-two.

"I'll be damned if this stud don't got a set of balls like a grizzly bear," the big man says. I float in behind them with only the low gate separating us.

"Got a bite like one too," I say, flipping the latch on the gate and stepping through. The big man turns, a mass of weathered buckskin rotating in my direction. His movement is slow, but his eyes are cruel and alive. He makes no effort to step aside. I continue on toward the saddlebag. One of the buckles seems to have unclasped itself since I left it—a victim, no doubt, of probing curiosity. His friend inhales a snort of air, coming around Storm's front for a better look. I am not concerned about the little one. But the big man is worthy of attention, although I pretend not give it, deciding instead to proceed as if nothing is the matter. The buck-skinned mountain holds his ground—close enough to feel his breath on my neck. The air between us bristles with tension.

"Who the hell's this, Kirby?" the little one says, switching his weight from one twig of a leg to the next. From the corner of my eye, I see Storm bare his teeth. The man called Kirby—still unable to shake his surprise at my arrival, or the perceived audacity with which I have administered it—offers, by way of response, a deep, rumbling belch. To punctuate the act—a foul regurgitation of his breakfast: eggs, coffee and whiskey—he exhales the unpleasant air pointedly in my direction.

"Dunno." Kirby's voice is graveled and spiked with a riptide of hostility. "But he seems partial to sneaking up on a man, 'stead of walking in regular."

"That sure ain't a recipe for long livin'."

"That it is not, Lem. That it is not." I refasten the buckle on the saddlebag and feel his eyes roll over me like cold rain. "Good looking horse."

"Thank you," I say, reeling in Storm's rope.

"The compliment was to the horse, not to you," Kirby says, bringing forth from Lem a piercing cackle that leaves him spitting and winded. I reach into the bag and pull out the holster belt and my pearl-handled Colts. The sight of the pistols, shining in the rising sun, ends the laughter.

"Well," I say. "I'll be sure to pass it along."

"I guess I'd give you twenty bucks for him," Kirby says.

"Thanks anyway."

"Fifty, then."

"He's not for sale."

"Shit, everything's for sale." Kirby balls his meaty paws into fists and rests them against his hip. "Fine, damn it. Make it a hundred. Got me haggling like a Jew diamond peddler."

"My answer is no. Not for a hundred, not a thousand."

"Hell, no fella turn his nose up to that kind of coin," Lem jabbing a finger in the air. "Now you're just being rude."

"Just tired of repeating myself."

Kirby edges closer, his gaze inspecting me head

to toe. "You know, Lem. I think I'm picking up a whiff of red meat around here." Kirby's eyes shrink into slits, his nose crinkling. "Oh, yeah. Sure as I'm breathin'. No wonder he comes sidling up like a snake. It's in his blood."

"Well, I'll be damned. Injun all trimmed up, trying to pass off as white."

I grab the horn to swing up and feel Kirby's paddle of a hand clamp my shoulder.

"How about I just take your horse?"

"Then you'd be a horse thief," I say. "Horse thieves get hanged."

"Ain't that a kick?" Kirby forcing a smile. "A red-blooded rustler sermonizing 'bout horse-thieving."

"Maybe next he'll be preaching the Gospel," Lem slapping his knee. He takes a rickety step backward and that is when Storm goes for him. The stallion snaps his head forward, teeth bared, and catches a bit of pale flesh behind Lem's right ear, leaving a deep, red gash where the skin had been. The man's face stares in disbelief at the speed of the attack and then contorts as the pain takes hold. Blood seeps through his fingers as he presses his hand against the wound, doubling over in rage-filled agony.

"He bit me. Bastard bit me!" Lem springs upright again, his eyes narrowed in focused anger. Lunging forward, he throws a sweeping left hook that misses Storm's head entirely. As the stallion dances clear, Lem's momentum carries him for another wobbly stride before stumbling him to the ground. Kirby stifles a chuckle behind me, and farther on, a few far-off voices let their laughter fly.

"Lem, just you set there a spell and catch a breath," Kirby says.

"Hell I will," Lem reaching inside his vest. I close the distance in two steps.

"Draw and I'll kill you." The steel of my tone freezes him cold. A glint of metal emerges from within his vest and lingers there a brief moment before a bloodied fist returns it to its place of concealment. Kirby's shadow fills the ground at my feet as he moves in.

"That horse needs to learn some manners and so do you." I turn back and meet his eye.

"Let me pass and we will have no trouble."

"Trouble has already pitched a tent. Now what you gonna do about my friend?"

"His own fault," I say. "You don't move like that near a stallion's head. Everyone knows that."

"You calling him stupid?"

"He provoked him," I say. "Like you're provoking me now." Kirby slams both his hands into my chest, knocking me back a step.

"What if I am?" He shoves me again, only now there is a crowd gathering, and I have not yet learned where I stand in the eyes of this town or its people. But when Kirby approaches a third time, he cocks his arm across his chest, aiming to back-hand me. I curl my fingers around the row of coins in my pocket. "Hell, I've raped squaws that put up more tussle than this one."

He lets fly with his open hand, finding nothing but air as I duck under it. From the crouch I spring upward, driving my loaded fist through the red thicket of hair and landing square on the bony underside of his chin. Tears squirt from his eyes as his own teeth nearly sever his tongue. Rage swiftly consumes him. I know what is coming next, but I wait until he reaches for his pistol before I snap the Colt from my right side and level at his head. We hold in tandem stillness until a stern warning echoes from the street.

"Either man shoots, he'll answer to his maker 'fore he hits the ground." Movement flickers in my periphery as the crowd parts, clearing the way for two army soldiers on horseback. They amble up easy and come to a stop ten yards short. The wide, black brim of the officer's Stetson cuts a shadow across his face, muting the green puddles that look us over with weary bemusement. He shows no interest in his weapons. His sidearm remains holstered and the sabre, dangling from a dun Appaloosa, serves as a resting place for his elbow. The lieutenant draws all the power he needs from the gold chevrons sewn on his sleeve and the unquestioning timbre of his voice—that, and the twelve-gauge nimbly handled by the infantry regular escorting him. "Stow your arms, gentlemen. Too early in the day to die."

My gaze trained on Kirby, I lower the Colt and slide it home. Kirby shows his open palms to the long-sword. "You saw him draw on me," Kirby says.

"I saw him draw after you reached for yours," the lieutenant says. "He's just faster than you."

"He's Injun's what he is. Somebody taught this red sum'bitch how to talk pretty and put on pants."

"That's exactly what we want them to do," the long-sword says. "Beats the hell out of trying to fight them." His words drip with the weight of having fought many. The Appaloosa nickers, piquing Storm's interest. He starts for the mare, but I whistle and he stops, before throwing an angry blow to make known how he feels about it. I take his bridle and lead him toward me, scratching behind his ear to cool the fire.

Lem finds cause to hop up and make a show for the bluecoats, giving Storm a wide berth as he passes. "Look what that bag of bones did to my neck." He takes a pair of ill-advised steps toward the cavalrymen.

"You, stop," the officer commands, finally compelled to draw his weapon, which he does with the speedy exactitude of a man who kills by profession. Lem halts so quick he nearly falls backward. "I saw what he did. There is no detail of this pageant I have not seen, as it has consumed my sight for nearly ten minutes. And that stallion is no bag of bones." Fixing his gaze back on me he says, "How did you acquire him, son?"

"I raised him." I say. "Pulled him out with my bare hands. Watched him find his legs. Put my family's mark on him too. Letter P in a circle."

"I see it from here. It's your horse, all right. And well trained at that."

"Thank you."

"Oh, well if this ain't a Sunday social with the gut-eaters," Kirby's damaged tongue filling his mouth with marbles. "This cherry-nigger insulted me and his damn cur nag ought have his nuts cut off." With that, he swings an arm and raps his knuckles into Storm's flank. The stallion neighs, like stung by a bee, but his eyes stay on mine, imploring permission, which I grant in silent communication.

"You touch that animal again," the long-sword begins, but his warning is cut short by Storm himself, who lowers his head and in a single motion, flairs out his back legs. Only one connects, but it connects true, just above the knee. The sound is like a reedy branch snapping from a tree. A collective gasp rips from the crowd. Kirby's eyes flutter white as any last bit of fight drains from him. He reaches out, flailing for the nearest handhold, but finding only emptiness as the leg gives way. Two men dart from the crowd, intending to catch his fall, but sudden self-preservation changes their minds. The beast of a man falls ugly and heavy to the ground, coughing a pillow of dust into the air.

"You still want to buy him?" I say. The words are out of me before I can reconsider.

The officer clears his throat and says, "You might want to be moving along, son." I swing up to the saddle and adjust my hat for the looming burst of speed.

"I'll fetch the doc," a man says, hurrying off down the street.

Hitching into Storm, I rein him back hard just as I feel him start to go. He shrieks his annoyance. I turn toward Lem, who sits on the ground in a swath of his own vomit. I dig in my pocket and pull out the first coin I come to—a half-eagle fiver. It spins off my thumb, landing dead in the mudded foulness next to him. "For the doctor," I say, pivoting Storm back in the other direction. I throw a respectful nod to the bluecoats as Storm finds his power and shows all in earshot why he is not, and will never be, for sale.

CHAPTER FOUR

Bennett Whitlock would remember it this way: *that was the day the Brown Man came to see me.* And even then, decades later, the memory would drip cold fear down his spine. He had been strolling the newest acreage of his ranch when the stranger arrived—no, make that *appeared*—as if from the ether. The clothes struck him first—a dark brown suit, impeccably tailored, with a coat fully buttoned to the trousers, allowing only a glimpse of the mahogany waistcoat beneath. A brilliant white collar floated below his jaw, broken up by a billowy chestnut tie of fine silk. Atop his head, a bowler, pitched slightly forward, had been dyed so dark that its coffee brown registered nearly black in the morning light. But the only true black about him—the only *visible* blackness—was his hair, trimmed and tapered, like an officer's. As the man drew closer, Bennett noticed hints of rust and tawny woven into the jacket that somehow broke up the sameness and produced a most startling effect. When he looked at the stranger directly, there was no doubting the man's formidable presence, even though he stood well under five-nine. A lone pistol, holstered above the left hip for a speedy cross-draw, amplified the gravitas. But when viewed in the periphery, the stranger told a different tale. Bennett Whitlock, unsure of his own eyes, turned his head slightly to verify what he could not at first believe.

The man was not there. Against the backdrop of rolling chaparral, he was simply invisible.

But of course, he was there.

Normally a man of keen senses, Bennett figured his mind was just playing tricks on him. How else to explain a stranger sneaking up on him on his own ranch? He had no more time to dawdle on the subject when the stranger extended a gloved hand and gave his name as Jacob Cross.

Cross. Easy to remember, Bennett thought, as he noticed the prominent crucifix suspended above the second button of the man's coat. It was strangely beautiful, even feminine, and hand-carved—either of stone or wood, Bennett couldn't tell—but the leather cord from which it hung lent a masculine touch. He wanted to stare at it longer, but then Cross spoke again, and when the rancher looked into his eyes—pools of hypnotic amber—he saw his own mortality.

"Your name is Whitlock," Cross not waiting for confirmation. "Tell me where I may find the man called Harlan Two-Trees."

While Bennett did not know the exact whereabouts of the young man he had known since the boy was twelve, he offered what information he had, including the details of the recent purchase of the land on which they now stood. In fact, Bennett answered every question that Cross asked without pause, omission or the slightest attempt at deceit. He would remember that the thought of answering any other way—or not at all—never occurred to him. When people spoke to Jacob Cross, they told the truth.

"You over-paid for the land," Cross said, when he heard the number.

"I know I did. That Jew fella, Garber, had a way of haggling that turned my stomach sour."

Cross gazed out at the vastness of the rancher's property, his brow furrowing. "You are no stranger to negotiation, Mister Whitlock. You do it every time your take your cattle to market."

"Yes, that I do. And darn well."

"Then to what aspect do I credit such generosity?" Even the man's skin was brown, his chiseled face clean-shaven. *Italian?* Bennett wondered. *Maybe Spanish.* Who was Bennett kidding? He'd never met any Italians. Or a genuine Spaniard. Only Mexicans, and Cross was no Mexican.

"Truth is, I felt like we owed something to that boy. After what he done for this town? He sure didn't deserve *this.*" They turned together and looked out, across the knoll, at the charred remains where a house once stood. "Burning him out like they did, t'was a blasted crime."

"A crime, yes. Just as it is a crime for any native to own or sell property. And any man—white or otherwise—involved in such an illegal transaction would himself be guilty of fraud—his assets subject to seizure."

"Now wait just a goddamn minute." Cross spun and backhanded Bennett across the mouth.

"You'll not profane in my presence, sir." Tears of stunned humiliation welled in the rancher's eyes.

"Well, I beg pardon then, Mister Cross."

"It is the pardon of God Almighty you should be begging."

Bennett swallowed hard and felt the metallic taste of fear spike beneath his tongue. Then Cross said, "Near forty White Men died in the Sangre Massacre. The only survivors were Indian—Two-Trees and the fugitive renegade, Ahiga, of the Navajo. They will both answer for their involvement."

"Some of them dead whites was criminals," Bennett said, his voice shaking.

"Some, yes. Deciphering that is not my business. But any red-blooded native who scoffs at the laws of this nation by trespassing beyond the generous boundaries of his allotted reservation is not just a criminal, but a threat to our national sovereignty. And tracking them down is most certainly my business." Cross turned to face Bennett, capturing him in the amber shackle of his gaze. "Now where will I find this land-merchant, Garber?"

Jacob Cross strode down the main thoroughfare of Caliche Bend on a horse he had purchased that morning. He didn't think much of this town, or its people, and it pleased him to soon be rid of it. He found his man, Van Zant, tending to a wagon just outside the jail. "Will that rig get us to Santa Fe?" Cross appraising the two-wheeled buggy with suspicion.

"If that's where we're going. It'll get." Cross liked that about Van Zant—no double-talk or foot-dragging. If Cross wanted debate, he'd go back to Harvard. He needed a man who could accept an order without question, and he had found that in the Dutchman.

But the thing he liked most about Van Zant—aside from his loyalty—was his lethal precision with a shotgun. As for the ten yards of rope Van Zant wore coiled around his broad chest—that skill the Dutchman was still learning.

Cross dismounted and passed the reins to Van Zant, who led the old bay to the buggy's harness. The horse wasn't a drafting breed, but once unsaddled, she loaded into the harness with familiarity—enough to put her new owner at ease about the journey ahead. Santa Fe lay a half-day's ride and it was already past nine. Cross gave his pocket watch a twist and slid it back into his waistcoat. As he turned, he saw, trudging toward him down the High Street, the Bend's sorry excuse for a lawman. Big Jack Early wore his sheriff star pinned to a leather vest that strained to cover his belly and on his head, a gray Stetson wide enough for a child to sleep under. The lawman had with him a weathered Indian who appeared to be his prisoner, though one would be hard pressed to know by the appalling lack of security measures. Cross detested dilettantes almost as much as liars. The sheriff carried a twelve-gauge—its breach open—in the crook of his right arm, and with his left, guided the unbound Indian with nothing more than a hand upon the shoulder. Cross marveled how easy it would be for the native to run or commandeer the shotgun or—producing a weapon that he surely held somewhere under that Navajo blanket draped about him—commit any number of bloody violations upon his captor.

But Big Jack Early was not the type of lawman who favored manacles. In fact, he'd have to do some digging around the station even to find a pair. Besides, it was just the drunkard, Saulito. Jack had arrested him twice already, and he'd only been sheriff for a few months.

"Excuse me, Sheriff," Cross said, "is that native in custody?"

"Well," Big Jack eyeing the little brown man with some curiosity, "why don't you tell me who's asking and I'll decide if I'm answering."

"Quite right, sir. I apologize for my impertinence." Cross produced a small leather wallet, opened it, and held it up for Big Jack to see. "I am Jacob Cross. Bureau of Indian Affairs." Jack's eyes focused on the gold badge, the likes of which he'd never seen, but he knew it was far more substantial than the cheap tin he'd special ordered for himself from the Woolworth catalog.

"Indian Affairs? Golly. You here all the way from Washington?"

Cross carried with him at all times, a second, irrefutable credential, but he would not need that, not with this hayseed sheriff.

"I am here on official business, sir, but as this man in your charge is clearly Native, his violation of the law is also my business."

"This here's Saulito. Ain't nothing but a harmless Navajo, what comes down from the hills now and then to get his drunk of tizwin. Merle found him sitting out in his vegetable patch, eating carrots straight out of the ground."

"A crop stealer. I'll note that in my records."

"Oh, it's hardly stealing. Hell, Merle'd give him the carrots if he knew how to speak Navajo." Big Jack already had a bad feeling about the stranger. But when the second man—the one wearing a noose like a bandolier—fell in behind him, Big Jack knew things had taken an ominous turn.

"Sheriff, you have in your possession a White Mountain Apache, making him neither Navajo, nor harmless."

"Apache? He don't look like no Apache I ever seen. Hair's all wrong. Moccasins all wrong." Big Jack pinched Saulito's blanket. "And I know a Navajo weave when I see it. Now what makes you so sure he's Apache?"

Cross said something to Saulito in a native language. The Indian muttered a response.

"Because he just told me." Cross had spotted the irregularities in the Indian's clothes from the first moment. But the definitive reason Cross knew him for Apache—a reason he would not share with the gathering crowd—was that he could smell the difference. The Apache have a stink all their own. Cross cleared his throat. "And as this Apache is very far from home, you may remand the prisoner to me. It shall be my duty to escort him back to San Carlos personally. I take full responsibility. You are free to keep your jail cell available for those who need it. I'm sure it sees ample use in this town. Mister Van Zant?" Van Zant stepped forward.

"Now hold on just a minute," Big Jack finding his legs. Van Zant stopped. "I'm still sheriff of this town, and I'll decide when my prisoner gets released." Van Zant's eyes narrowed, both men considering twelve-gauge options. Cross touched his associate on the shoulder and Van Zant slackened.

"You would be Sheriff James Early. 'Big Jack,' as you're known in Calich' Bend."

"Cal-EE-chi," Jack correcting.

"Apologies, Sheriff. I may be a stranger, but I mean no disrespect to your office. As I'm sure you mean no disrespect to mine. We are both public servants, entrusted with legal authority. Although my constituency is slightly larger than yours. But I leave it to you. If you wish to defy an act of Congress, and an executive order, by abetting a known thief—a savage for whom you carry some sentimental affinity—then play your hand, sir."

"Look here, we don't need to be making no federal rumpus out of this. No one's abettin' or defyin' anything. Let's just suppose we handle this all local."

"It's not some local militia his band has been attacking, it is the United States Army. The Apache chose to wage war on this nation. A war they shall have."

"Saulito wouldn't attack nobody."

"You have no idea what he would do."

"I know Saulito. He's ain't nothing but a drunk, dumb Injun. But that don't mean he deserves to be carted off to no rez."

"A good Apache scout would make you think that. The only ones still out there are desperate. They've had to get resourceful."

"Come on, Cross. He ain't no scout."

For the first time all day, Jacob Cross smiled. "Then here," he pulled a flask from an inner pocket and held it close to Jack's face. "Give him this. Ply him with liquor and invite him to your home. He'll cook your lungs and eat them, dancing to his pagan dirt-god while his brothers rape your wife and your daughters."

"Good thing I only got boys."

"His kind do not discriminate."

"I think I've heard enough," Jack said. "Hell, you want him so bad, take him then."

Cross gestured to Van Zant. The Dutchman spun Saulito around and yanked the blanket from his body. He produced a pair of iron handcuffs and bound the Indian's wrists. Then he checked him for weapons.

"Hello. What's this?" Van Zant pulled a stone spike from the man's waistband and dabbed his thumb against the razor sharp tip. He handed it to Cross.

"Well I'll be God-damned," Big Jack said. Jacob Cross hitched mid-step—the blasphemy a physical assault to his ears.

"Vain the Lord's name again, sheriff, and I'll damn you where you stand."

By eleven o'clock, the pale sun had risen as high as it would go this time of year. The buggy meandered down the trail, making terrible time, Van Zant coaxing all he could out of the bay, but the horse had slowed considerably now that the terrain had become winding and unfamiliar. And with the unexpected load of three passengers and the buggy itself, one misstep could send them all tumbling to a rocky death. Cross sat in the next seat, keenly aware that Caliche Bend stood only ten miles behind them. Up ahead, the valley floor shimmered, as if tantalizingly close, but the wheels would not touch its flat surface for another hour. Right now a thirty-foot drop of sheer rock on either side of the trail kept everyone's focus on the present and their nerves raw.

"I shoulda asked about the trains," Van Zant said. "Rate we're going, we make the run out to San Carlos, we won't get back to Santa Fe before nightfall tomorrow. Sorry about that, Mister Cross. Sorting out gettin' places is one of the things you pay me for."

"Rest your mind, Mister Van Zant. I inquired about the trains before we left the Bend. It seems the railroads don't run on my schedule. I'll have to see what I can do about that." Van Zant smiled. That was as close to humor as Cross got. But Van Zant knew that Cross was only half-kidding. He'd seen the son-ofabitch move bigger mountains than getting the railroad bosses to rejigger a few timetables.

Saulito sat with his back to them in the rear of the buggy, his arms bound behind him, his eyes skyward. The sound escaping his mouth was like nothing Van Zant had ever heard—something between a chant and the weeping of a child.

"What's he carrying on about?" Van Zant asked.

"He's praying. Would you like him to stop?"

"Far be it for me to come between a man and his maker."

"It's hardly his maker," Cross nearly spitting with contempt. "If that heathen could understand the benevolent grace of Our Lord Jesus Christ, he wouldn't be in this predicament. Instead what you're hearing is wasted breath to the Great Spirit. Waka Tana." He turned and barked something to Saulito. The Apache stopped praying.

"That's better," Cross said.

"Pretty country," Van Zant nodding toward the Sangres.

"Hmm." Cross sat back and took it in for himself. "You never saw a great buffalo run, did you?"

"Nah. They was all gone by the time I come west."

"I saw many as a boy. A sight like nothing else. A swirling sea of darkness. Like a thunderstorm. Only louder. Shook the ground for twenty miles. Even after they'd passed through, their dust would blacken the sky for hours. The next day I'd still feel the rumble in my bones."

"They didn't run this far south though, did they?"

"Oh, yes. Long time ago. Ran clear to Arizona."

"I didn't know that."

"One buffalo could pound this wagon to splinters if the notion took him. Imagine what ten thousand could do. And yet, whole generations—his ancestors," Cross jabbed a thumb toward his prisoner—"armed with nothing more than sticks and stones hunted them, and lived off them, for thousands of years. How do you think they managed that?"

"Well, if you're asking," Van Zant doing his best to answer without driving off the cliff, "I reckon they run their horses up alongside and spear 'em."

"Ah, but you're implying they had horses. Go back farther, centuries. Even before the Spanish came with horses to trade, when the Indians roamed on foot. How then?"

Van Zant shrugged, his mind too occupied with keeping the bay on solid ground to entertain a parlor game.

"I need to piss," Cross said. Van Zant halted the wagon. Cross climbed down and walked around the back of the buggy to the other side and undid himself while Van Zant stared straight ahead. He didn't much care to witness another man relieve himself, but when it came to Cross, he found a strange comfort in it because—just like when Cross ate, or slept, neither of which seemed to happen very often—it made him human. And sometimes, Van Zant had his doubts. The water splashed down the sheer rock face and then trickled to a stop.

"Well?" Cross said, buttoning himself up. "What is your answer?" Cross walked over along the edge of the trail and stopped next to Van Zant.

"I don't rightly know, sir."

"Gravity." Cross grinned, his lips curling back to expose the white of his teeth. "They'd herd the buffalo toward a cliff, until the animals had nowhere else to go but over."

"Golly."

"Such is domination of man over beast."

Then Jacob Cross turned behind him, yanked Saulito down from the wagon, and hurled him over the cliff. The Apache screamed until he hit bottom.

Cross climbed back into his seat. "We don't have time for San Carlos."

CHAPTER FIVE

The Spanish named it The Royal Town of the Holy Faith of Saint Francis of Assisi, and even though it has grown into a straggling aggregation of low adobe huts that make it the biggest town in the territory, Storm manages to gobble through the entirety of Santa Fe in all of two minutes. "Takes longer to speak it than to cross it," I tell him as the last of the buildings gives way and we find ourselves on a bluff, staring southward at a sweeping blanket of sagebrush that slopes down for miles before leveling off at the valley floor and then rising again at the foothills of the Sangres. Storm blows hard from the sprint, harder than usual. I ease him down into a canter and let him shake out his legs on a ribbon of level ground. Then we stop in earnest. Storm is tired and I need a think.

You think better when we ride.

"And sometimes I require a ponder what without my bones jangled, or you thundering my ears into deafness," I say, removing my hat to cool the sweat in the high desert air. A young shoot of milkweed within striking distance proves too irresistible for Storm and he dips for it, not minding a hoot what my thoughts on the matter might be. "I saw that." Storm gulps it, but dares not test me on going for seconds. The sky above blazes deep turquoise and the blooming sage flavors the breeze. "And as far as thinking places go, we could do considerable worse than what we find ourselves offered presently."

All at once we hear something else riding atop the breeze, both our heads turning left as the faint, lonely whine of a train whistle rolls up from the valley. I replace my hat to lessen the glare and make out a scratch of unnatural blackness cutting a line, straight as an arrow, across the valley floor. The whine comes again, softer as the locomotive charges away from us, followed by an eruption of gray vapor from its leading edge.

"Maybe it might be the best way after all." For all the vulgarity of its mechanized intrusion into the landscape—its coughing and clattering—I find myself drawn to the rhythms of the churning wheels, seduced by the Great Step Forward that is the rail. The truth is, the mysteries and riches of California lay at a distance too daunting from where we stand at present to be conquered by one man and his horse, even one as fearless as the stallion. We might just survive the treachery of the mountains and the pounding heat of the desert that lies beyond, but the third challenge—the one that stamps its bloody imprint onto my mind's eye even as I try to shunt it out—tips the scale beyond recovery into the domain of madness. Those naked, butchered bodies entombed upriver speak to a roving evil that surely has not sated its lust for blood.

I paw through my coat until my fingers find the

rounded edges of the brass buckle, the letters U.S. as gleaming as they were in the sunlight a day earlier. If a detachment of trained army cavalry, to which I am certain this hardware belonged, could offer only pitiful resistance to such an overwhelming defeat, then the considerable faith I stock in my own skill of survival would do little more than drag out my death and prolong the inevitable, as those responsible would eventually track me down. "We both managed to keep our balls this long, I 'spect we deserve to die with them still attached." Storm throws that eye he gives me whenever I'm not sure if I have been thinking out loud.

I bring him about toward town again and we start back the way we came. No sense in leaving a conversation unfinished once I start it anyway. "Good news is we both get to bed down soft tonight. Right now, the plan is we slip back into town so I can sort out this train business." Storm decides to point out the bad news by stopping dead in his tracks, giving me a chance to reconsider. I heel him forward and he blows a long one. "Yeah, I know we made two enemies already, but I don't think they will be up and about anytime soon."

Near the edge of town I dismount and lead Storm by the bridle into the alley that flanks the shops along the main drag. We creep silent in the tall weeds, one ear trained up the road for any afterclaps of the previous scuffle, or a pair of curious eyes that may connect us to it. But in the harsh glare of late-morning, the only sound in this quiet corner is the droning, relentless wind. A single line of track extends off to the left, dead-ending at a cluster of low buildings, newly erected with sturdy pine and fresh paint unfaded by the sun. A square hut in the center, closest to the track, shows an "open" sign in the window. From a pole atop the roof, the Stars and Stripes rips stiffly, just above a second flag carrying the brilliant colors of the Santa Fe line. This must be the place. There is nothing quite as still as a train depot an hour after departure. I skirt around the rear of the ticket hut, where a second window, obscured from any view of town, faces the rail line as it winnows out toward the horizon.

"You stay put." I ground-tie Storm and, not wanting a repeat of the earlier temptation, take the Spencer with me as I float up the steps of the ticket office. The door creaks open. Stepping inside, I am greeted in the close quarters by the broad backside of a man, stooped over, as he works a pile of collected dirt into a dustpan with a short-handled broom. He rights himself as the door bangs closed and, turning around, startles at the sight of me.

"We got no cash here."

"What?"

"Lock-box went out with the 10:14. All I got what's in the till, enough to break a twenty note and that's it." He is a big man, crammed into a suit two sizes too small, with orangey-red hair cropped short beneath a ticket clerk's black cap. My second ginger of the day. And my second problem. He thinks I have come to rob him.

"I'm here to book passage." The man stares at me, dumbfounded, all googly-eyed and razor-burned. "Aboard the Santa Fe . . . Am I in the right place?"

"Lordy, fella. I thought this was a stick-up."

"Sorry to disappoint. But if thieving's a worry, you might consider stocking more iron than that Derringer in your hand." The clerk shrugs and flashes the tiny one-shotter jutting from his meaty fist. It was a slick draw though. Against a slower eye, he might had a chance.

"Yeah, well, I'm not behind the counter." He says, returning through the locked door into the barred cage that separates clerk from customer and where, I have no doubt, nothing less than a twenty-gauge lays within easy reach. The robber barons of the East have seen fit to instill admirable precaution in their expansion westward. "And I'll tell you something, buster," he begins, reddening in the face and addressing me now—noticeably—as buster. "You'll do yourself a kindness to stand down on the fire power. This here's a respectable business."

"No aggression intended," my palms open now.

"You must be from out backcountry," he says, letting his contempt fly.

"Not so back. But not so settled a man don't travel armed, indoors or out."

"Well aboard the Santa Fe, gentlemen are expected to keep all weapons in their war bag. That goes for the Spencer and them pearly Colts." The clerk blows a long, imposed-upon breath before taking his time opening the ticket book. "Destination?"

"San Francisco."

"We'll get you as far as Barstow. You change there for the line north."

"How long to Barstow?"

"Four days." The clerk runs his finger down a list of numbers. "Let's see, third-class to Barstow set you back two-dollars-fifty."

"Third-class. What's that get me?"

"A seat on a bench."

The clerk scribbles something in his book. "Next train leaves here eight past midnight tonight. Is it just you?"

"Me and the horse."

"Your horse?"

"That stallion, there." I jab a thumb toward the window and Storm, sensing the attention, flutters his gleaming mane against the breeze.

"Fine-looking animal," the man says, pawing through a drawer for a second booklet.

"Don't he know it."

"He'll need a tariff for the stock car. Two dollars."

"Stock car. Hmm."

"That a problem?"

"For your stock, it is. Best for everybody if Storm keeps to himself."

"Well, only other option is a thoroughbred stall. That's how we move racehorses. Gets his own feed and fresh hay daily."

"That'll do."

"It's fourteen dollars."

I reach into my pocket and return with a stack of gold coins, riffling them slow and loud between my fingers. His eyebrow raised, the clerk says, "That rules out the midnight train. I have to wire Topeka, put in a request for a horse car. Hopefully there's one already coming through. Your new departure time . . ." the man thumbing through his papers, "is one-twenty-five tomorrow afternoon. Now that's from the Lamy Junction, not from here, you understand? The train can't get up here."

"I saw an engine rumble out of here an hour ago."

"Yeah, that's the spur. It connects with the ATSF main line out Lamy. That's seventeen miles from here."

"Seems like I'll be needing a ticket for the spur on top, then."

"If it was just you, that would be fine, but there's no car for your animal. It's a smaller gauge track. Just two cars for shuttling passengers."

"You're telling me a train everybody calls the Santa Fe don't quite make it to Santa Fe."

"You have stumbled on the great irony. The fine city of Santa Fe sits at an elevation just high enough to defeat even the brightest engineers of the rail line that bears its name. The powers that be, therefore, had to come up with an alternate solution. Hence this shiny new depot and the one at the other end, named for his holiness the archbishop. I trust you can get yourself and your stallion to the depot at Lamy by one tomorrow?"

I gaze out at the ribbon of track, straight as a rifle barrel until it gently fades down and to the right near the horizon. The gleaming rails still hold their steel-mill luster, and so green are the softwood ties that their piney scent—mixed with the acrid spike of fresh creosote—filters through the closed window with full pungency. All vegetation has been cut back from the tracks for as far as the eye can see, leaving a pleasant width on either side to pass.

"I can't follow a track downhill for seventeen miles, I might as well lay down on it," I say.

"I'll need your name?" The clerk dipping his pen.

"Seems to me, you don't."

"What?" The clerk looking up, puzzled.

"My name. I understand it, that ticket there gets me on the train. My name don't figure into it."

"No, for the ticket, you are correct. But if you ever want to see your horse again, you'll be needing this here tariff receipt to match up with the name I'll be adding to the manifest." He holds his gaze on me and I let the silence ice over like day-old snow. Finally he breaks off and rubs his neck, his breath shallow.

"Name of Two-Trees," I say. "Harlan Two-Trees."

The corners of his mouth tighten. He swallows hard—a sickening brew of castor bean and turned milk. He starts to scratch out my name, and with every pen stroke, the distaste reverberates through his fingers, as if setting the letters down in ink is to somehow lend them credence. A cold tingle curls up my spine.

He peels the ticket from his book and slaps it onto the counter as an image powers to the front of my brain. Four days on a bench, my only landscape the sad faces sitting across from me. I remember the steerage cars that would rumble past the Bend, with their tiny windows. Nothing to look at. Nothing to breathe but hot, sickly air. A thousand nights I could sleep most comfortable beneath the church of the starry sky, only firm earth for a mattress. But to willingly entomb myself with the White Man's pox-ridden, consumptive air—when I am flush with the means to do otherwise—rings dumber than a prop bet at a travelling faro game.

"Third class, plus the tariff. That comes to—"

"I think I'd rather stretch on a bed, now you've set my mind to it."

"No beds in third-class. Bench seating only."

"Guess I better splash out for second, then."

"No. Second-class is cargo."

"Cargo. Sounds like freight travel better than a man."

"It's just a term. Read no deeper meaning in it."

"I reckon I'll go by way of first, then."

The clerk eyes me sharply. "If by first, you mean the Palace Car—but I don't recommend that. It might make you uncomfortable, rubbing shoulders with the tea-and-cake crowd."

"No. Would it make them uncomfortable?"

"We don't like to upset our passengers."

"I'm a passenger."

"Not yet, you're not." And that is when the curling tingle settles cold and heavy in the back of my throat. He tries to stiffen up behind his words, but then he makes the mistake of meeting my eye. "It's not a cheap ticket," the clerk says, trying a new course. "Why, a private drawing room, that would run you twenty-eight dollars."

"I don't need all that. Just a bed."

"There would still be shared amenities with the other passengers. Common areas."

"I ain't fussed to be sharing."

"Now you know that's not the point."

"Tell me the price on the bed."

"A shared berth is seven dollars fifty. But I can't sell you that."

"My money spends, same as the next man's."

"I can't because I can't have you bunking with a— because it'd be my job. I can only sell you a double berth, and that's fifteen."

"Done," I say, no more interest in his words. I stride twice to the counter—his eyes widening— and smack some coins down in front of the cage,

"Fourteen and fifteen make twenty-nine," I say, pulling my hand back to reveal three ten-dollar pieces. "That there extra dollar's for you, to make sure there's a stall and fresh hay for my friend. Are we transacted?" The clerk nods weakly, passing his hand over the coins and pulling them through the cage. "I'll give you the tariff receipt."

He separates the tariff in two pieces and slides one half through the bars. I look at the scribbling and hold it up for him to read. "What's that say there?"

The clerk swallows again, the bitterness lingering. "Says H. Two-Trees."

"That so hard?" I say, collecting the papers as I turn away. "Use that dollar toward some gumdrops. That ought wash out that taste of bitter's got you all pinched up." I let the door bang hard as I leave.

It was the better part of an hour ago that I deposited Storm into the care of the finest livery stable Santa Fe had to offer—this according to its proprietor, J. M. Halvorson, who spent three minutes admiring Storm and then, after passing the stallion off to the stable hand, another thirty recounting the story of how he had survived Sherman's fiery March to the Sea as a Georgia militiaman, only to later lose an eye, an ear and his left arm below the elbow in a Comanche ambush passing through Texas after the war.

"The way you sit atop your mount," he said, fixing his one good eye on me, "I had you pegged for Injun." The crooked brim of his hat did its best to cover the patch over the other. "You always ride in that fashion?"

"Only when I want to get somewhere."

He fired a line of tobacco juice on the ground and seemed to accept my answer with a shrug, offering only, "Still makes the hairs on my neck stand up, I see a body grip a horse that way."

Halvorson's supervision of Storm's sponge bath mostly involved vague instruction to the stable hand and, the more he combed that eye over me, a budding interest in my affairs, from which I found no easy way to take my leave. The conversation, one-sided as it was, kept drifting closer to who I was and what my business in town might be, questions I was not sure how I would answer.

"Looking to head out on the Santa Fe, I reckon."

"That mean, you'll be selling the stallion?"

"No. He's coming with me."

"Well, I know better than to come between a young man and his horse." Halvorson jams his hands in his pockets and looks off to the west. "Used to be, every fella with a hair on his crotch wanted to make his way out to New Mexico. Now, even the West ain't west enough. Boys nowadays too young to remember the Gold Rush and every busted dream that went along with it." Halvorson spits again and waits for me to fill the silence until he can't wait any longer. "Another train'll be heading out next day or two. Rail agent in town will sort you out."

"All right then."

"That don't directly address your more pressing needs, though, do it? Young buck like you, I reckon is in need of whiskey, hot grub and a piece of pussy." A wheezing bout of high-pitched donkey laughter overcame him, then he added, "And not in that order."

Women. The thought of curves and softness burst,

uninvited, into my head like the full sun of daybreak.
If I had, during my recent time in the wild, ignored
the thirst that told me to drink water, or the hunger
pains that compelled me to eat, as much as I had for-
saken the natural needs of companionship that every
man feels, I would have perished in the elements
months ago. Could it be that I had not lain with a girl
since Maria? That was last fall. The tragedy of her
murder still haunts me. And the invading memory of
That Other Woman, the blue-eyed temptress, whose
fate—alone up in the Sangres—well deserved as it
was, had squelched any remnants of lustful thinking.
But the dawn of spring will thrust incorrigible growth
into the barren landscape. The seeds of the reawak-
ing trace back to this morning—to Xenia, Garber's
negro girl—when I could smell the sex on her. As
much as I hated to validate the crass ramblings of the
livery owner, I felt the flickering embers of desire
begin to warm inside me after a long, frozen winter.

The swirling awakening inside me manifested as
little more than a muttered phrase. "Girls. Huh." But
it was enough to give Halvorson license to continue.

"White, brown, red, black or yellow?" The rainbow
of colors staggered me. Here I am the son of a pros-
titute and have still never seen a working girl of any
shade beyond the first three. Madame Brandywine
had always attracted a steady stream of Mexican girls
to the Bend's only brothel while managing to hold
on to a sporting corps of white veterans. There were
no negro women at all, and the only Chinese I'd ever
encountered were a raggedy crew of overworked
Coolies busting down cross ties when the first stretch
of track came through. Still I didn't need a one-eyed

gadfly making me feel anymore like a boy than I already did.

"Whichever is the most expensive."

"That would be the Chi-nee," Halvorson said. "Them uppity chink whores won't even give me time of day. Same with the white cunt. The niggra gals a sporting bunch though, keep me up to my eyeball in pussy."

I glanced back toward the paddock where the Mexican stable boy had worked Storm's hindquarters into a soapy lather. For all his orneriness, that stallion would give pony rides at a church fair if there were the promise of a warm bath at the end of it. He seemed no more cut up by our impending separation than a napping house cat.

"Your stallion'll be just fine. Two dollars a day will keep him in fresh oats and dry hay till you've sorted your stick out."

"Okay, then." I nodded to Halverson and turned to take my leave.

"You know where you're headed?" he asked.

"Reckon the town ain't that big."

"Walk east till you hit the smell of garlic and the funny writing on the windows."

I found some words forming in my throat, but decided to remain them as thought.

They all look funny to me.

CHAPTER SIX

I keep the sun in front of me and cut a diagonal course through town, where sheets of threaded chili peppers, drying bloodred in the rising heat, dangle by the doorways of each passing adobe like the city's second official flag. It is no secret, in an unfamiliar town, to finding the house where a man can lay in the soft company of welcoming arms: at every turn, opt for the narrower road. After several minutes, the chili peppers have faded into memory, replaced by strange and rooty vegetables hanging from baskets and the smell of sizzling pork, quick-fried in peanut oil.

The Chinese move with downcast eyes in straight, purposeful lines, and the ones I pass show little interest in, but a keen awareness of, my presence. A bad feeling rises up my spine. *The guns.* I am too heavily armed for the city. The Spencer weighs on my shoulder, countered with every step by the jangle of the pistols. Atop a horse and away from town, such weapons might be in any man's possession. But here, walking the streets, I forge a statement of aggression that ill-suits my intention. I flip the Spencer barrel-down and hitch the strap tight into the crook of my arm, making the rifle as unassuming as I can. The pistols I dump into the saddlebag across my back. If trouble calls, I will make do with the thirty-two riding my pocket.

I walk until the alley dead-ends and only a cramped passageway breeches the last two huts where bright paper lanterns disappear down an alley that even sunlight dares not enter. Stepping into the darkness, my shoulders scrape the encroaching walls and I have to turn sideways. Every sense of reason and propriety says to turn back, so I forge on. I duck my head below another set of lanterns while stepping over a woven hutch housing some sort of animal. The toe of my boot catches the edge and the screeching from within tells me it is chickens. Any shred of stealth vanishes in a din of clucks and fluttering feathers. I might as well beat my arrival on a drum. A few paces on, the alley opens up and I find myself in a small courtyard. A miniature fountain babbles in the corner and next to it sits a low stone bench, obscured from the view of the only door by a paper screen depicting what must be a muted Oriental sunrise. Delicate handkerchiefs of blue silk cover the lanterns, bathing the plazita in a seductive twilight, augmented only by a single shaft of clear midday sun from an opening above that beckons the bougainvillea upward along the wall.

I move toward the bench, drawn by the serenity of the setting that scarcely undercuts the genius of its practicality. How many dusty cowpokes have waited shyly behind the screen for their turn, or, having completed their business, been silently grateful for the fountain's constant din when recombobulating a belt buckle or depositing a fistful of coins into fair, yellow fingers? It is under such cover of sound that the Ears of a Buck fail me. I catch her scent before I hear her. I have hardly lowered myself into the seat when a soft voice acknowledges my existence. Turning toward the door, now opened, my first thought is not the woman standing there, but the door's hinges, so flawlessly oiled to negate even the faintest whisper of a creak. I have crossed into a world both erotic and carefully engineered, down to the splash of jasmine perfume that reaches me before I have finished turning. The Nose of a Wolf—after so many nights in the bush—misses nothing.

"Hiii." She drags out the word as her ruby-red lips curl into a smile against the powdery alabaster of her skin. Everything about her face is painted. A pair of lacquered sticks, tipped with gold and no bigger than pencils, poke from her black hair drawn tight into a severe bun. A silk robe, splotched with warring factions of bright colors, stretches over the curves of her ample frame. My hat finds its way into my hands as I nod to her.

"Ma'am."

She glides toward me, the smile unwavering, tiny embroidered slippers shuffling beneath the robe as she arrives with an outstretched hand that slips into mine. Her palm betrays the illusion of the rest of her. The woman in my grasp is at least forty, maybe fifty. Before I can protest she leads me back into the dimness of a receiving room, where her words and wrinkles can avoid suspicion. "Yes, yes, come in. You want pretty lady, okay?"

"Yes."

"Yes, okay. Pretty lady, five dollar, fifteen minute." In the low light, she turns to face me.

"Pretty lady," I say.

"You like?" I feel a languid finger trace down my chest and stop at my belly. She holds it there, expectant.

"Very pretty." The finger draws a slow circle around my navel and hovers just above the belt line. "But today," I say, placing two firm hands on her shoulders, "top girl." I give her a little squeeze and watch her shoulders slump with a sigh. Growing up in the trade has its advantages. Mamma always respected the men who spoke their minds, and were clear about what they wanted, even when the slow-death of a thousand rejections had failed to lose its sting. And in any bordello, from Peking to Pittsburg, *top girl* means top girl. But the sheriff and the missus had engrained in me too much manners to be discourteous about it, at least what I can remember of it now. Besides, offending the madam can get a fella paired with the resident sasquatch.

The madam's smile purses, a tight, hard-nosed pucker. "Top girl, top dollar," she says, her voice bottoming into the low alto of negotiation.

"Top dollar." I open my palm, revealing a double-eagle that finds just enough of the light to close the deal. Plucking the twenty dollars from my hand, she half turns, barking out some assaultive string of vowels, that, after a moment's pause, earns a reply from a delicate voice in the next room.

"Pei-Pei, top girl," the madam says, pointing behind me. I turn and from a second doorway appears a wispy, fair-skinned China doll, similarly attired as the madam, but devoid of the cakey cosmetics. The young girl's beauty needs little in the way of adornment, even the robe is too much. Deep inside me, blood begins to stir. I nod to her, but she allows only the faintest smile as she returns the gesture.

"Afternoon, miss."

The madam's hand finds the small of my back, prodding me forward. Pei-Pei, turning toward a heavy, velvet curtain, fires off a few words in Chinese, which the madam chews up and spits back at her. There is some brief argument between them. "You soldier?"

"No soldier. Just a fella." The madam relays my answer to Pei-Pei, who takes only slight comfort. Something still eats at her.

"You want bath?" the madam says, as we reach the curtain.

"Not much fussed either way."

"You take bath."

The missus Pardell once admonished me never to refuse a stick of Beeman's when it was offered. "Might just be it's you doing the kindness," she told me one Sunday, walking home from preaching. I 'spect now, staring at my reflection in lukewarm water blackened by two hundred miles of dirt and soot, the same could be said for a hot bath. I lean back against the hard copper lip of the tub and watch as Pei-Pei lugs in a second empty tub from the hall and drops it next to mine. There is nothing sexy about the chore itself, yet her movements, lithe and graceful in a short dressing gown that stops above the knees, keep the embers aflame. She rattles off in her native tongue, and a second girl, plump and dressed more for scullery than sport, hustles in with a pair of sloshing water buckets. The way her face is painted up, I'd wager even the kitchen girl gets called upon to service them what can't put together more than a dollar or two. Pei-Pei empties a whistling kettle into the second tub and then tosses in a handful of greenish crystals from a little bottle she replaces on the vanity, where a lantern, glowing beneath a pink, satin scarf enhances the mood. The only other furniture is a high, thin bed—more like a table—in the center of the room. Heavy sheets of velveteen drape the walls as well as the low ceiling, which billows down like the inside of a carnival tent.

She gives the fresh bath a whirl with her arm while the round girl heaves in the cold well water. All this activity, I am grateful I have tarred up my bath with sufficient blackness to hide my man parts, but I would just as same prefer considerable less foot traffic buzzing about when I am sitting there with my preacher and choir flopping around. The madam's voice erupts from beyond the curtain, squawking some admonition or another that Pei-Pei relays with equal vigor on down the chain to the ears of the round girl, who hustles over to the pile of my discarded clothes and collects the bundle—union suit and all—and hurries out. My coat and saddlebag remain untouched in the corner, protected by the Spencer and the rest of the guns. There is more instruction from beyond the curtain and then the chubby girl returns with a glass containing a liquid—a libation I gather, as she crosses toward me and deposits it in my hand. Then the round girl goes out for good, closing the curtain tight behind her.

As if on cue, Pei-Pei's movements lose their utilitarian urgency and she smiles at me—a shy little smile that sends her eyes back to the floor just the same. She passes behind me and graces a finger along my shoulder. Her touch against my bare skin sends my willy to full and immediate attention. I hear her strike a match, flashing a glow of orange as she steps back into my vision, dragging deep from a thin cigarillo. Holding the smoke in her lungs like a shaman, she proffers the lighted butt my way as she exhales. Tobacco smell permeates the room, but there is something with it, a sweet, sticky scent that tinges the vapor with cloying blueness. I take the cigarillo and bring it to my mouth, pulling gentle and slow until—all at once—a fire explodes from my lungs and a racking cough overcomes me. The ceiling spins, the floor lolling in in undulating waves. A cozy warmth blooms inside like a hundred downy quilts. "Oh . . . my," I say.

Pei-Pei just nods, adding a sly grin of profound understanding. Moving toward the second tub, she steps out of her slippers and taps the copper lip. Whatever she dumped in the water got it more frothed up than the head of a beer. She sticks her hand in to check the temperature and, satisfied with the result, points to the water and taps the edge of the copper. When I do not move she taps again, pointing more adamant and offering up some Chinese encouragement that I do not understand. But her intent is clear. A second bath. Makes perfect sense if you got the manpower and a preponderance of tubs lying about. I consider ruminating further on the notion for however long it takes for my stiffy to subside, but can see plain from Pei-Pei's tone that she won't be taking no for an answer. So instead I make a little circle motion and say: "Would you, uh . . ."

Pei-Pei turns around and I down the drink in one swallow. Taking encouragement from the fruity, medicinal paint that spreads warm inside me, I stand up, gray water dripping loud from my body in an embarrassing drumroll. I bring my leg out and dip it into the new bath. For an indelicate moment I straddle the two tubs, only to glance up and spy the curious head of the mamma-san poking through the curtain. Catching her eye with my most unwelcoming scowl, the floating head disappears in a hasty poof. I lower myself down into the foam confection— an all-together foreign, but not unpleasant, sensation. Beneath the bubbles, the water is warm and inviting. It feels good. She turns her head just enough to confirm my descent and then unties her sash. The dressing gown falls to the ground and she stands there, her backside in full view—two perfect pears perched between her waist and unblemished thighs. Reaching between her legs, she grabs the lip of the tub and steps backward into the water, her innermost recesses peeking out among her curves. She sinks below the surface—all the way up to her shoulders— and finally spins to face me. As she comes to a stop, a little girl's giggle jumps from her lips, bringing forth a boyish laugh of my own at the comic sweetness of our proximity. Two peas in a pod.

"Well, hello there," I say. Pei-Pei responds by pawing beneath the bubbles for my leg, which she finds and brings above the surface. She rests my ankle on her shoulder and sets about caressing my calf and knee. Bringing a handful of the foamy confection to my skin, she begins to rub it in and I realize its purpose. "Soap. How 'bout that?"

Her soft touch drains away the troubles of the day in an instant. I lean back against the tub and let her fingers work down my ankle toward the heel. "You don't speak a word, do you?" The deep, circular motions send a charge up my leg while serving a greater purpose of removing any fugitive dirt. "That's all right by me. Heard more talking today than any man ought have to suffer in a lifetime. And I'll be jimmed if it don't leave me puzzled with more questions than what I started with. You ever been on a train?" She lays into my toes, working with meticulous precision until it is clear beyond all doubt that no part of my person has ever been so clean. Yet to punctuate the thoroughness of her handiwork, she spreads my toes with her fingers and slides one of them into her mouth. I melt into the water. So numbing is the sensation that the room goes dark as my eyes roll back into my head. She suckles as if each toe was a member all its own, only moving on to the next after such time that any man would have found satisfaction. As the double-barrel blow of her touch and the dizzying liquor take root, anesthetizing my brain into submission, I start up babbling again without the slightest care who overhears me.

"See, I find myself uncertain as to the proper comportment when it comes to high-hat travel. Should my name be required during the course of whatever all is they do, I am not convinced it would be in my interest, or that of my stallion, to offer it. The redness of my skin, what there is that can be detected, along with the knee-jerk response triggered by my last name, have, this day, caused me nothing but grief. I cannot wonder but would it be more prudent to travel free of such a burden. Although I am discomforted by how such a ruse would make me feel about my history, of which I bear no such shame or embarrassment." She slides my right leg back into the water and fishes below the surface for my left, kneading her fingers along the ankle and back behind the heel. Then her mouth finds my toes again, attending to all five soldiers with equal enthusiasm. "Still, now is not the time to let pride stand for foolishness. I have a need to press westward without delay. What do you call this drink, by the way? It has a powerful effect."

Pei-Pei's answer is to draw a circle in the air, a gesture identical to that what I issued to make her turn around. I float my leg down from her shoulder and rotate in the tub, my back now facing her, my knees scrunched up in front of me. The awkward maneuver does little to stem the river of unchecked thought. "I see your point," I say. "There is a difference between my name, what as I know it to be in my heart, and that what I offer to others as a matter of convenience." Pei-Pei lathers up my back, using both hands in firm, soothing motions. She starts with the tired muscles around the neck and works her way down the spine until her fingers are below the water line, where, out of plain view, they lose any trace of inhibition. She grabs my member and slides herself up tight against me, so close that her thighs straddle me and I feel the bushiness of her sex tickling the base of my spine. "That settles it, then."

She sticks her other hand down past my balls, lower than no woman ever touched, and then squeezes hard with her pecker hand and next thing I know I squirt right there in the water.

"Sorry," I say, leaning back into her. Here I was with the grand design of plowing the soil and instead spout off like a schoolboy playing doctor behind the barn.

I come to, face down on the table, and start to understand why it is set so high off the ground. I am naked as the morning and Pei-Pei, equally undone, stands beside me, working a sharp-scented liniment deep into the aching muscles of my legs. She must see my eyes flutter open, because she says, "MA-ssadge." She repeats the word and holds the bottle of yellowed oil close for my inspection. "MA-ssadge."

I don't know about any ma-ssadge, I think to myself, but it sure feels good after a month of bouncing 'cross the brush. Some mighty strong hands on that little girl. She knuckles her way up the backs of my thighs, and, with nowhere to stare but down at the floor, I see her tiny feet get off the ground as she lays her weight into mine. But then all at once her touch is gentle as a bird again and her soft fingers brush against an exposed bit of manhood. That is all it takes for the blood to start flowing a second time and I have to adjust my hips to let the thing land in a pose that won't snap it in half. Pei-Pei uses her forearms on my shoulders, kneading my back like she's rolling out biscuits. It feels good. My body lets go, sinking, dissolving into the table. Her strong hands make their way up my neck to the scalp. She presses and rubs and does a fine job of mussing up my hair, but all the while she finds an excuse to scurry her fingers down between my thighs just to keep things moving. Her finger appears in my vision, swirling in that circular motion again, and I marvel at how well we have learned to communicate.

"Turn over? All right," I say, starting to roll. I make no pretense to cover up or hide the obvious. But the girl is already climbing up the table. She sets about fiddling with the drapery that hangs over us. She pulls back the fabric, revealing a coil of velvet rope as thick as a man's wrist. "What you fixin' to do with that?"

Pei-Pei mutters some Chi-nee and sets her face in intense concentration. Straddling over me, her girly bits in full glory, she twists the rope around itself from the center and then wraps each end around both her arms from elbow to shoulder. She takes a deep breath and then lifts her legs off the table, sticking them straight out into the air—a full open-split. Then her body begins to rotate, the rope uncoiling itself as she gains momentum. Lower and lower, she twirls. A brief moment of panic grips me as her spinning legs close in—a pinwheel of stunning nakedness. A smarter man might roll off the table in the interest of self-preservation but I hold still, dumfounded, and I'll be damned if her business don't meet up with mine in perfect union. By the third revolution I shoot off again, and after one more spin, she comes to a stop on top of me, buried to the hilt.

"Goo-time?" she says.

"*Hozho.*"

CHAPTER SEVEN

My pockets lightened an extra ten dollars for Pei-Pei, I make my way back down the alley, accompanied by the sporadic sound of scraping metal. I realize it is the barrel of the Spencer, careening against the rough adobe walls, courtesy of my own unsteady footing. The combined efforts of drink, smoke and Oriental acrobatics have tilted the ground just enough to pepper my stride with a dash of comedic rubberiness. But in the confines of the narrow passage, I remain blessedly unobserved and—sucking the fresh air deep into my lungs—manage to rectify myself more with every step. By the time I negotiate the chicken obstacle and emerge back on the dead-end street, I possess my faculties in their full correctness.

The big eye shows only a pale yellow sliver of itself in the slot of blue sky overhead, lengthening the shadows before me in the stillness of late afternoon. I see a man walking toward me down the street, his eyes cast upward at the inscrutable signage. His unfocused meandering tells me he is at sea in a foreign land, and from the gentlemanly cut of his fine, Eastern suit, I know he is a white man—long before his trimmed, gray whiskers and ruddy complexion come into view.

His gaze fixes on the movement of my approach and then widens, relieved, to find a fellow white man—white enough for this alleyway, at least. A breath inhales across his lips, expanding the ample chest mounted atop a protruding, prosperous belly. But before he can unload his query, the full sight of me— heavily armed and outfitted for rugged country— registers on his face. The memory of the day's events crawl up my spine, bringing with it a defensive shield of armor that I wish to remain unused. I hold my eyes stern, focused beyond him, offering little invitation for engagement. But as I pass, I detect a courtliness—a resolve of both authority and good humor—emanating from his person that earns from me a slight, but respectful, nod. The man brightens at the gesture, melting into an air of avuncular disarm. The voice that follows drips like honey with the slow, easy drawl of impeccable Dixie aristocracy.

"I beg dearest pardon for the intrusion, sir," he says, leaving no trace of the r-sound in his languid *suhh*. "But I find myself dreadfully adrift. It appears I have disembarked from my hotel with faulty information designed to circumnavigate the globe rather than to my destination." He holds up a slip of paper with writing on it as evidence. "I believe the desk clerk was describing a locality with which he himself held not even a passing familiarity."

"Where you aiming to get to?"

"Well," he says, lowering his voice as if to invite me into a shared and secret conspiracy. "As you strike

me as a young man of well-tended virility, I hope
I proffer no Christian offense when I admit that I
find myself in possession of a certain . . . Oriental
appetite."

"Can't say I know much about Chi-nee chow. I
reckon I smelt some pig frying up back the way you
come."

"No, not food, sir. Allow me to speak plain that my
desires are of a manlier nature."

"Ain't my business what a fella sets his mind to, but
if you're looking for the Chi-nee whores you just
ought shimmy down that alley yonder," I say, thumbing toward the narrow passage from where I came.
"And mind yourself the chickens 'bout halfway
down."

"Much obliged," the man says, with a genteel dip
of his head.

I carry on for a step and then turn back. "Say."

"Yes, sir? How may I be of assistance?"

"You know where a regular fella can slap up some
grub?"

"Ah, well if it's hearty fare you require, you can
hardly do better than the El Dorado. Clean beds as
well, if that's your intention. Although their staff
could use a primer in orienteering," with a throaty
chuckle, slapping the useless hotel paper to make his
point. "Left at the first street, then down about a
quarter mile." I am about to thank him when he
pauses. His eyes drop to take in the sorry state of my
clothes. "However, if you're desirous of something
more reasonable . . ."

"No. El Dorado sound just fine," turning away with
a nod. All at once the steps I need to take and the
order to which I must make them fall into place like

fresh bullets in a six-shooter. Hungry as I am, the pangs in my belly will have to wait. There will be no supper, no hotel, no tea and cake aboard the Santa Fe—until I have first paid a call to the best tailor I can find.

"They call it an ascot," the tailor says, working his fingers along the wide swath of silk. He stands before me, tying the fabric into a knot, his gray, balding head no higher than my shoulders. "All the rage on the Continent this season."

"What continent?"

"Europe," he says, pushing the wire frames of his spectacles back up his nose. He gave his name as Josiah Cullen, adding that he was the proprietor and founder of Cullen and Sons, Fine Fashion and Tailoring. So far, the latest fashion trends of the continent of Europe have me trussed up like a braided Maypole and feel as fit for riding horseback as a clapboard box, only stiffer. Cullen checks his pocket watch and takes a step back, surveying my reflection in the mirror. "Excellent. Very fine indeed." The impenetrable scowl on my face fails to diminish the high regard the tailor holds for his own aesthetic. The heavy fabric of the dinner jacket and trousers makes every breath a battle my ribcage would eventually lose and binds so tight across the shoulders that I can hardly lift my arms up past my chest, much less draw a pistol. And the color, a pinkish tan watered with a hint of gutless white, leaves the unmistakable impression of raw chicken.

"What do you call this color?"

"Navajo white," he says, pleased with the sound of it.

Navajo white. I let the sound bounce unsettled across my ears. *If ever there were two words that ought never be hitched together, I stand here as living proof that—*

"Come again, sir?" Cullen says.

"Nothing," I say. He checks his watch again, and I wonder for a moment if he has forgotten the glimpse of gold coin I let flash when he had me swap my denims for the monkey get-up being entertained presently. "Am I keeping you?"

"Not in the slightest, sir. My attention is dedicated to your being smartly attired. Now let's see it with the waistcoat fastened." Despite his insistent fawning, the impatience bubbling beneath the surface says otherwise.

"Dad, you need to get going." I turn to the voice behind me and see a young man step out of the small office. I put him about my age, with angular features brought to light by an absence of facial hair that makes him seem much younger. His sandy hair— neatly combed and slicked with pomade—frames the deep blue eyes he must have inherited from his mother. But the impeccable tailoring of his dark suit shows he has well learned his father's business, developing, along the way, a style far more becoming and approachable than the stodgy tastes of Cullen senior. "You'll have to forgive my father," he says, turning his eyes in my direction and letting a hint of a smile reveal the white teeth of a man deliberate with his morning ablutions. "If he doesn't have the Duffman girl's wedding dress out to the church by five o'clock, Mrs. Duffman will have both our heads for Sunday dinner."

"I have some time yet, Peter," Cullen says. "As you can see, I am assisting the gentleman."

"Well, perhaps if the gentleman wouldn't mind," Peter says, "I could take over from here." Considering the two of them: the father, nervous about tomorrow, his mind stuck in yesteryear—and young Peter, firmly planted in the here and now—the decision makes itself.

"Fine by me."

Cullen senior blows a sigh of relief, pivoting on his heels toward a headless female mannequin festooned with an overwrought assemblage of frills and lacework. "The woman is an unabashed tyrant," he says, husking the frock from the breasted torso and laying it hurriedly into a velvet-lined trunk. "Four times I've had to let this dress out. If she wants her daughter to wear my creation down the aisle, she ought to worry less about the length of the sleeves and more about keeping her gluttonous child away from the egg custard." He slams the trunk shut and snaps the buckles.

"Mind your back, dad," Peter says, coming around to help his father.

"I've got it," Cullen says, hoisting the trunk with two hands over his shoulder as he finds his footing. "You see? Perfectly balanced."

"I'll get the door, then," Peter says. "Calpernia is yoked up to the hansom. She's right outside." Peter opens the door, revealing the street and an ancient bay mare harnessed to a wagon that has seen better days. "And I'll take care of closing up. You just worry about Calpernia and the wagon. The road is torn to pieces, what with all the rain last week."

"Thank you, son. And good day to you, sir," Cullen says.

"You as well," I say.

"Don't fight me, Calpernia," Cullen says warily as he approaches the animal. "One stubborn nag per day is quite enough."

The last image of Cullen before his son closes the door is the older man sliding the trunk into the back of the hansom and then climbing up the step to the driving bench. Peter produces a key and, shaking his head with a smile, locks the door from the inside.

"It was not too long ago," Peter says, "that he used to worry about *me* when *I* took the wagon. Funny how that gets turned around before you know it." Outside, Calpernia's neighing protest at being called into action resolves into a steady clomping that soon fades as the wagon disappears from earshot.

"We look after them what raise us, best we can," I say. "It's how we honor them."

"Yours still alive?"

"Nope. Dead for sure, or dead most likely."

"You don't know for certain?"

"Mamma's dead. Nearly ten years now. And the man and wife what brought me up after, buried them more recent."

"Sorry to hear that," he says.

"It's the way of things." Something about the younger Cullen puts me at ease, and I tell him more. "Him that sired me, I never met. Heard he worked the mines, so dead is a good guess as any. Not a job for living long."

"For heaven's sake, where are my manners?" Peter walks toward me and extends his hand. "Here I am sticking my nose in your affairs and we haven't been properly introduced. Pete Cullen."

"Harlan," I say, taking his hand in mine with a firm pump. He holds my gaze a hair longer than he should, waiting for the rest of it. Something about the way he called himself Pete, and not Peter, creaks open the door of trust, and for me to leave the mystery dangling would slam it wrong. In the mixed company of his father, I should have no problem keeping my business my own—money has that effect—but here, alone with Pete, I catch an unguarded honesty that, among white men, is new to me. "Harlan Two-Trees."

"Two-Trees. That's a strong name. Let me see, now. Oglala?"

"I been called a lot of things, but never Sioux."

"Sorry, I took a course last term in native ethnography, but when it comes to the names, it appears I was getting ahead of myself. I hope I didn't cause offense."

"My father was white, name of Harlan. Mamma was Navajo. Two-Trees come from her line."

"Navajo? Huh. I apologize that I never would've guessed that. Strikes me more like a name from a Plains tribe."

Because it is. Because mamma was stolen by the Navajo, taken from her people when she was a girl and didn't start using her birth name until I came along. But those facts I keep to myself.

Pete Cullen crosses to the window and turns the open sign around to closed. "Most of the Navajo names I know are either Spanish or Navajo," he says, reaching up to grab the draw-cord of the blinds and easing it down. The late-day sun seeps through the thick parchment, bathing the shop in muted amber.

"You know a lot of Navajos?" I ask.

"Tell you the truth, not a one, now that I think of it."

"Not many around. Not here anyway. Not anymore."

"No," he says.

I catch a glimpse of the wall clock. Ten minutes till five. He is closing early.

Pete turns and starts back toward me, his eyes combing up and down in a slow, deliberate study of my person. He shakes his head, disapproving. And then he stops, his mouth pursing with exasperation. "What the hell was Pop thinking?"

A sudden pulse of laughter escapes me as Pete's face breaks into a wide smile, followed by a laugh of his own. Then our heads turn toward the mirror, where the absurdity of the costume flares our laughter until, red-faced, we catch enough breath to speak.

"You have to forgive Dad," Pete says. "He believes all men should dress like they're headed for a night at the opera."

"Tough way to stay in business around these parts," I say.

"That's why I'm here. I was halfway through the fall term at Northwestern when Mother wrote, begging me to come home. It's not Dad's fault. It's how his father taught him. But times change. And we're not in Saint Louis anymore. This is the West. Not an opera house for a thousand miles."

"Or a circus tent, neither."

"Here, take that thing off."

I unbutton the coat and slide it off into Pete's awaiting arms. I expect him to cradle it gingerly—like his father had—instead he flings it crumpled onto the nearby table. Pete marches toward a rack of suits hanging in the corner, his mind gearing into practical contemplation. "Now, what do you need this for, exactly?"

"What do you mean?"

"The suit, what are you doing in it?"

Never had a stranger question occurred to me, as anything I had ever draped onto my frame had but the utmost, singular utility—to be for any and all purpose called upon by life in high desert. But in thinking about how to answer him, I saw the benefit in such an inquiry.

"I'm fixing to get on the train."

"Okay, that's a good place to start. What else?"

"Well," and here I feel myself pause, as I was about to confess the true reason for my visit. "I want to look like I belong."

Pete's eyes brighten. "Now we're getting somewhere. You can't board the Santa Fe looking like a Kansas clodhopper." He turns to the rack, making quick work of each selection as he paws through them. "You thinking new money or old?"

I fix on him puzzled and he elaborates of his own accord. "There's different kinds of rich, different ways to wear it. New money is you just struck your claim. Old money? You struck your claim twenty years ago and it's still paying off. Better yet, your *granddaddy* struck a claim."

I think back on the men I've known, the wealthy—and those pretending to be—or those who were, but wouldn't be for long. "Rich enough where nobody ask questions."

Pete nods, thoughtful. "Old money it is. But with vision." He keys open a special cabinet beneath the work table, and spreading the doors, reveals a cache of carefully folded clothes—trousers and waistcoats in the alluring colors of Earth and sky. Deep browns, lush greens, and the full spectrums of blue and gray.

I know by the way he navigates the contents that what exists in that cabinet is a world entirely independent of his father's.

"Secret stash?"

"Some projects I'm working on. Go ahead and shuck off that shirt, 'less you feel like trying out some coffins." Pete turns back to the cabinet and I peel off the old shirt, standing there, bare-chested.

"Union suit didn't make it," though not sure why I feel the need to explain.

Pete shrugs. "We may have one in the back. I can check, but honestly, you can get them cheaper at the Five and Dime."

"Ain't the first time I gone without."

"No, I suspect not," Pete nodding, turning his attention back to the cabinet. "You got a nice pair of boots there, once you get them shined up. I want to start from there and build up. So let's try . . . this." He rises, unfurling a pair of mahogany-colored trousers. Smoothing out the folds, he nods to the corner. "Screen's behind you, you're feeling modest. But no one can see in." Being rid of the last of his father's touches can't come fast enough, and I let the scratchy wool leggings drop to the floor.

Since boyhood, I have run beneath the sun and stars without stitch or hide hanging from my bones more times than I can count. But confined indoors, a true state of nature always strikes me strange, unless lying horizontal in the company of another. Yet here I am, naked as the day is long, in a foreign room, for the second time in as many hours. Such is the drunkening power of the city—with its money and sex and blood. Even sharp as I feel of eye and ear, two bare feet firm against a cold plank floor, my head swims like a butterfly in the wind.

Pete offers me the trousers and I take them from his hand. Sliding in, one leg and then the other, the fabric passes easy against my skin. "Nice, isn't it?" Pete allowing a grin. "Flannel-lined, but on the outside, best wool a man can buy."

Buttoning up, I turn to the mirror, taken at once by the color, the elongating cut of the trousers. Pete moves to catch me in the mirror, his brow furrowed in deep concentration, like a fiddle player working out a tune, circling the notes he hears in his head, and then, after much sawing about, landing in a place of unexpected possibilities.

"I think we're on to something," Pete stepping in with a soft cotton shirt set in light tan.

"Thought shirts were supposed to be white."

"Who told you that?"

"Don't know exactly."

"Mine's not white," pulling back his jacket. "It's got a hint of blue, but I'll bet you didn't notice till I showed you."

"You're right. I didn't."

"That's the idea. There's white and then there's, well, not as white."

"Navajo white."

"Oh, golly. Don't remind me," Pete blushing for an instant. Then he blinks, fixing those blues straight at me. "This whole thing is about drawing the eye to what works, and steering it from what doesn't. Take me, if my eyes were green, I might weave a little kelly in somewhere, maybe even slate gray. But they're not, they're blue, so . . ."

"So a bit of brown might do the same for me."

"Precisely. That and letting your build shine through. You cut a good line, no sense in hiding it." I slip into the shirt and do up the buttons, the only sound the cloth through my fingers. Pete takes off his jacket, drapes it over a stool. From the pocket of his waistcoat he finds a measuring tape and falls in behind me, all four eyes on the mirror ahead.

"How do you want this to fit?" Pete now the blue-ribbon champion of asking questions I never knew existed. But spotting the sharp angle of his shoulders, the waistcoat holding his frame with compact efficiency, he works his way around me like a bobcat up a tree.

"Like yours."

"Okay, then," Pete nodding, tugging the sleeves. I bring one knee up to my chest then switch to the other. "Trousers too tight?"

He steps back to let me move and I drop to a squat. Rising, I remember Storm.

"I need to be able to ride."

"A horse? Won't be much call for that on the Santa Fe."

"I don't put on clothes what I can't ride in. Don't care what I'm doing."

"I respect that," Pete says, thoughtful. "A well-made suit should serve a man for any eventuality. I'll see to it your trousers don't rip should they find themself in a saddle. Anything else I should know?"

"One more thing." I snatch up my denims from the floor and dig out the stubby thirty-two. "This stays with me. On the quiet."

Pete opens his hand for the pistol and I place it in his palm. He hefts it, shaking hands with the gun for what may very well be the first time. He shows some instinct for iron, but there is a touch of boyish fantasy behind his eyes as he aims and guns down an imaginary bandit against the far wall, adding a "pe-CHAW, pe-CHAW" with every overly pantomimed recoil.

"You every fire one of those?"

"Only at tin cans. I hit 'em, though. How 'bout you?"

"Usually hit what I'm aiming at too." Holding out my hand for the gun. Pete returns it.

"Something this small, I prefer a cross-draw," I say, showing him the motion.

"Okay," Pete's mind already at work on the puzzle. "What if you stuck it here?" He slips his hand into his own waistband just above the left hip. I tuck the pistol accordingly on my own trousers, the handle peeking out enough to grab clean, but plenty visible. "Don't worry, a good waistcoat will cover that," Pete shaking a finger as he returns to the cabinet, his brain plunking out the melody again, "but if we let it out just so," now adjusting the rear buckle of the vest as he brings it toward me, a patterned velvet textured in deep scarlet and darkest brown, "you should find your draw unencumbered if things turn sour." He helps me into the waistcoat as he talks, giving the back buckle the slightest tweak, but he'd pretty much eyeballed it dead-on. Rehearsing the draw again, my hand retrieves the pistol from its snug burrow every time without fail or fumble, my sense of awe—not just at the sheer invisibility of weapon, but how the stark addition of such a vibrant color choice enhances the earthiness of the rest of the creation—is audible.

"Ain't that something."

"Little splash of color," Pete's confidence never in

doubt. When he plucks an umber necktie from his private cache and hands it to me, I fix to tying it without hesitation.

"Now on the jacket . . . Don't expect them to match the trousers exactly. You're not a sofa. The idea is to complement. But if my eye is right," his gaze lingering on me as he walks to the back of the store, "you're a forty-two long, which means this is our lucky day." Pete disappears in the stock room and comes back a moment later, a proud glint in his eye, holding in his hands a ditto coat, sharply peaked at the lapels, the outer color like that of a rusted nail. Without a word, I turn and extend an arm, the silk-lined sleeve gliding over my elbow, up my shoulder. And then the other arm. The jacket falls into place like it was born there. Rotating toward the mirror, our eyes take the sight in unison—how perfectly the shades and fabrics work as one. A completed picture. The melody found. Pete's verdict is simple.

"Yes."

I tug on the sleeves, expecting an overflow of shirt cuff, but there is only a half-inch sliver, like icing on a cake. I shrug my shoulders, raise my arms, even throw a punch, all with freedom of movement that belies sculpted tailoring. "Feel like you got all the sizing dang near perfect."

"Harlan, you happen to have the exact stature of the best-selling mannequin in the entire Montgomery Ward catalogue. I knew there was something special about you. The prototypical male."

"The what?"

"It means when a tailor dreams up a suit, it's your body he builds it for."

Just then a clap of thunder splits my ears like a

hammer blow. Glaring back at me in the reflected glass is a vision, bleak and violent—the fine suit a tattered version of itself, streaked with char and blood and shredded here and about to the bare skin. And the wearer, a hollowed ghost of man I don't know. I turn away from the mirror, all this self-gazing and preening getting the better of me.

"What a man dreams up ain't always pretty."

"Eh, for some, I guess. But what's the point of dreaming otherwise?"

I leave his thought unanswered and set down in the chair to pull on my boots. "How much I owe you?"

"You wearing it out of here?"

"Don't see why not."

Pete finds a pad and starts scribbling, his brow furrowed, as if the tabulation of cost was more annoyance to his higher goal. But his mind is not finished. "You'll need a couple more shirts."

"White, not so white," I add, Pete laughing.

"They'll come in handy, I promise. And I'll put in maybe three or four different ties, and a second waistcoat, black probably. All those combinations, it's like an entire new wardrobe."

"Not like. Is."

"For everything," Peter tallying the numbers, "comes to one hundred twenty. I need to cut the shirts, but I'll do that tonight and drop them off at your hotel first thing. Where are you staying?"

"Across the street at El Dorado, I'm hoping, if they got room."

"You walk in the door wearing that, head held high, they'll make room. Shoot, old man Rawlings will be falling over himself to put you up."

There's a doe-eyed innocence in the young tailor's view, coupled with a healthy confidence in the power of his creation—two things in scarce supply around the Territory, but I find no heart to correct him, offering only, "My history has at times proved otherwise." I parcel out a hundred in gold and find his hand, holding back the last two coins, but sure he sees them. "A hundred now. The rest on delivery." Striding to the corner, boot heels clomping the plank floor, I ball the denims into a fist and stuff them into the saddlebag. These weathered bags—chapped and faded as my boots—look like they have been run over by a train. Here it is, the brushwork still damp on Pete's canvas—the oils unset—and my two meager adornments dishonor it like a cheap, ungilded frame. I hoist the bags up, careful not to further sully the pristine jacket with a coating of desert dust, and loop my other arm through the strap of the Spencer—doubly mindful of dripping gun oil.

"Harlan," his clear voice breaking the silence. Turning back, I am soaked in the watery blue spill of his gaze. "Your history is whoever you say you are. So is your present. Don't ever forget that."

"I won't."

We part ways, tethered by something unspoken. I step out into the street, straight across the muddy wagon tracks and toward the warm gaslight of the El Dorado, where a tinkling piano beckons like birdsong. Night has fallen, blanketing, in its veil of darkness, the sorry state of my leather along with any reminders of my former self. Grateful for the masquerade, emboldened by its power, I see no reason to represent otherwise. I feel right duded up and square my Stetson accordingly. With every stride my spine lengthens until my head seems high as a lamppost, perched atop the broad shoulders of privilege.

I am hardly to the spill of lamp light when a negro bellman, slouched against a podium, spies my arrival and perks to attention. "G'd evenin', sir. Let me help you with those . . ." The paint is not dry on his words when I pass him the saddlebags, my eyes fixed beyond him to the lobby. A dollar flows from my palm to his, effortless. The Spencer I make no attempt to hide at all, hitching it, in fact, as I enter the hotel, the door before me held open by a second bellman, conjured from the ether.

Moving with purpose, and yet unhurried by any man or notion, my presence elicits one of two disparate behaviors—one of avoidance, which sends ordinary patrons scuttling like roaches from the light, or that of attraction, as seen from the employees, who acknowledge my entrance with either a differential nod or a respectful "Good evening, sir." Such is the case from the lowly shine-boy, his cherubic face brightening as I pass, to the owner himself, the aforementioned Rawlings, who gently pushes aside the attending desk clerk to service my arrival personally. "Never mind the ledger," Rawlings says under his breath to the clerk, closing the leatherbound volume containing the names and addresses and room rates of those commoners whose lives would tolerate such aggravation. "A very good evening to you, sir. William Rawlings, hotelier, at your disposal. I see our bellman has your bags, how may we accommodate you this evening?"

"A room with a hard bed and a good breeze. I don't want to be disturbed."

"Certainly, sir," Rawlings turning to the clerk. "The Garden Suite, please, James." A key in his hand almost instantly. Rawlings now stepping toward the grand staircase, gesturing to me to join him. "Please consider El Dorado your home, sir. Mister . . . ?" He holds out his hand, waiting expectantly for a name. For any name.

"Harlan."

He bows approvingly as we start up the stairs. "Right this way, Mister Harlan."

CHAPTER EIGHT

"I see you're a hunter," Rawlings half-looking back as we reach the top of the stairs. "Excellent year for game, I'm told. Do let us put together an excursion, all-inclusive, of course: gear, horses, picnic lunches. And you won't find better guides in the Territory. They're natives, obviously, mostly Navajo, a few Apache, but docile. All vouched for and properly tagged."

"Tagged, with what?"

"Permission to leave the reservation. Can't be too careful." The third floor landing levels out and we start down a long, windowless corridor lighted by flickering wall lamps spaced too far apart to keep a consistent glow. "It's better now than it used to be, but there's still the occasional troublemaker wants to break for the border, or go celestial on one of the guests. Can't have that, no. We weed out all but the best and most agreeable."

"Must be a chore," I say, dipping the brim just enough to keep his eyes from mine as we pass from light to dimness and back to light again.

"The trick, we have learned, is to not give them whiskey, even though it is their preferred method of payment. The sportsmen who chose to share their bottles with the Red Man invariably return empty-handed and deeply disappointed."

"If they return at all."

Rawlings snorts a laugh, wagging a finger in triumph. "We haven't lost a guest yet, touch wood. And I don't intend to start." As we pass the other rooms I notice a curious sight—pairs of boots and shoes, placed neatly outside each of the doors, just like I'd seen the Chi-nee do.

"You take a lot of Chinamen, here?"

"Not a one, sir." Rawlings appalled at the suggestion. "You'll find the clientele most upstanding, I assure you." Reaching a double door at the end of the hall, he slips the key into the lock and pushes through.

The air in the room carries the scent of cut flowers—roses, from a glass vase on the table by the entry—masking the smell of fresh paint and cleaning soap. The walls split between bright whitewash and a striped wallpaper of gold and turquoise. A breeze caresses the gauzy drapes of the open window, bringing, on its creosote air, the livening sound of traffic as it shifts from the day's clattering wagons to the liquored merriment of evening.

"Your bags will be here momentarily . . . ah, thank you, Moses." The black bellman trundles in with the saddlebags and flops them on a folding stand near the wardrobe. "Will anyone be joining you this evening?" Rawlings clasping his hands before him, as if in prayer.

"Ask me in the morning."

"Very good, sir." Behind him, Moses fends off a smile and turns away to light the table lamp. "The restaurant serves supper until eleven and the bar is open until midnight."

"Tailor fella ought show up here with a mess of shirts for me. Ain't sure when, exact."

"Any deliveries, we'll have brought up for you."

"Funny about people touching my clothes."

"Of course. We'll send the gentleman to your room, straightaway, sir."

"I want not to be disturbed otherwise."

I fish a five-dollar piece from my pocket and offer it to him. Rawlings holds his palms up, demurring.

"I couldn't possibly, Mister Harlan. It's my pleasure." With that he bows his head and backs out the door, shutting it soft behind him. Moses gets the lamp going and puffs out the match.

"Moses, you ever see man say no to five dollars?"

"What I seen up and outta these rooms don't mean I ain't left rubbing my eyeballs raw tryin' to make heads or tails of it."

"More for you then." I hold the coin his way and he takes it with a grateful nod.

"Thank you, suh."

"I guess the man figures he'll get the money out of me one way or another, no sense gutting me on the first hand."

"That he do, suh."

I sit on the bed and start to pull off my boots. "I probably should have asked what this room cost."

"I've seen high-cotton guests like yourself stay two weeks never so much as look at a bill, and that's drinking French champagne at breakfast. They don't ask, Mister Rawlings ain't offerin'."

"If you have to ask . . ."

"Yes, suh."

My boots fall heavy on the floor and I lean back on the bed. The mattress is hard and squeaks from the weight, but it feels good. And I remember why sleeping on the ground suits most regular folks disagreeably.

"Be anything else, suh?"

"Where's a fella like me go *after* midnight?"

Moses must see a flash of devil in my eye, because he tilts his head to the window. "'fore midnight or after, don't hardly matter. I reckon you'll find all you can handle down the Blue Duck. Just up the way yonder. You head out the door, your ears do the rest." Moses goes out and I pull my hat down over my eyes.

When I open them again the room is dark, save for the orange spill of the lamp. Blackness fills the windows, and out on the street, men's voices shout to be heard over competing pianos and ripples of unguarded laughter. I rise from the bed, my mouth thick with sleep, and pour a glass of water from a pitcher left on the table. I drink deeply, emptying the glass, and set it down to refill again when I catch the suited reflection in the mirror. The image freezes me—a foreign, costumed intruder—as my mind uncouples from the dreamless void and regains its bearings. The man upstanding before me strikes an imposing figure, brimming with the easy grace of grandeur. He looks equally game to answer the seductive call of the city. The clothes, even slept in, hold true their shape and character. A little tug of the necktie, a smoothing of the lone crease in the jacket sleeve, nearly return the design to full potency. I drop the hat into place, square it, and the effect is complete.

I head downstairs—the small pistol hidden against my waist—and take a table in the restaurant. Rawlings seats me himself, brushing the cushion with his bare hand as I sink into a small banquet facing the window. I order a beefsteak, charred and rare, and when he proposes a dry sherry to wash it down, I decline— rejecting his first suggestion as a matter of course. I wave off the idea of whiskey as well—although the mention of it uncovers an itch I'll be looking to scratch in short order—finally allowing him to bring me a dark, German stout shipped in from Bavaria at considerable expense. The steak arrives, thick and sizzling beside a golden mound of roasted potatoes. My backside facing the staff, I take a discreet moment to reacquaint myself with the proper pageantry of fork, spoon and napkin, anticipating that in the company of my fellow riders aboard the palace car, nothing would call me out as a trussed-up alfalfa faster than slurping up beef stew with an eight-inch Bowie knife. I chew the meat slow, savoring my first meal in a month not cooked on a stick, and witness the parade of the city unfold out the window.

At first glance, the citizenry of Santa Fe, what there is of it, appears nearly devoid of women, at least any what venture out after dark. And the scant few passing by at this hour reside in the close company of grim-faced husbands who dare not slow their wagons. Only once does a female stroll past on foot—a proper lady in full dress—guided with both hands by a gentleman husband who steers her into the hotel. Within seconds the couple appears at Rawlings's podium, at home in his obsequious attention as he ushers them to a round table set for five in the center of the room. A bottle of tawny port sits waiting for them, Rawlings receiving an instruction from the woman as he fills their glasses. He relays the order to a male waiter, who spins on his heels and disappears out the restaurant and into the hotel in hasty execution of the directive. The woman removes her gloves with an exhausted sigh as her husband sheds his bowler and hands it, without acknowledgment, to Rawlings, who carries it to a hat rack behind the podium. Their manner rings of Eastern breeding, with the gentleman, through the travel of business, having gathered a workable familiarity with the rough edges of the frontier. But the wife wears the shocked disbelief of a boy soldier pinned down by enemy cannon fire. And for that her husband keeps a reassuring hand about her shoulder, tethering her in the tempest until the port wine takes effect. She looks all of thirty, a good fifteen years younger than her husband, whose receding hair is peppered gray above the ears.

Only when her children arrive does the woman find cause to smile, although the children do not. Trailing a young nanny and the male waiter, the children arrive combed and scrubbed for a supper that is far past their usual bedtime. The girl looks about twelve, fairing better with the hour than her young brother, who climbs groggily into his mother's lap. The family settles into a tableau of such unguarded domesticity that to continue my observation would constitute an intrusion.

Across the street, behind the drawn blinds of Cullen & Sons Fine Clothing, a lantern's glow betrays the presence of late-night labor. I imagine Pete, at his workbench, stitching with care and purpose, and doubt if he would consider it labor at all. A gust of piano music rattles the window, accompanied by a rising chorus of voices that overtakes the instrument in both fervor and volume. The song ends, devolving into an exultation of hoots and whistles that I take as my cue to further investigate the evening. I march to Rawlings's podium, his eyes meeting mine with a dose of apprehension.

"Mister Harlan, is everything satisfactory?"

"Time to be getting on."

"Yes, of course, I'll simply add your dinner to your final bill—"

"Let's have a look-see, long as I'm standing here."

"But of course, sir . . ." he says, drawing his note-pad and scribbling in some numbers. He pauses at a calculation, makes quick work of it, and fills in the total. Passing the slip to me for review, he adds, "I hope the meal was to your liking?"

I take a long stare down at the numbers, affecting a facility for figures to rival his own and, pausing at a number selected at random, turn my gaze pointedly at Rawlings. I tap the number, my lips formulating a question I am certain he will beat me to. "We add the gratuity for your convenience, Mister Harlan. Ten percent, as is customary. Did you wish to alter it in . . . either direction?"

"Ten'll do," I shrug, scratching my mark at the

bottom of the paper, confident that I'll have no creative arithmetic or phantom charges for the remainder of my stay at the El Dorado.

"Our pleasure to serve you, sir," Rawlings bowing his head. I depart without a word, crossing through the lobby, where Moses changes direction to reach the heavy brass door handle before I do. The only metal I touch is the dollar I flip him for opening the door. "You enjoy yourself, Mister Harlan," he says as I head out into the night.

"Clear the stool for a paying gentleman, you feckin' derelict," the Irish barman swatting the drunk from his perch like a pestilent fly. He had me spotted, the Irishman, the moment I stepped foot into the hard gas-lamp glow, and judged me worthy of his finest bottle, from which he began to pour before the warmth of the previously rousted occupant had dissipated from the padded leather seat. "Get you a taste of this, sir. Compliments of the Blue Duck."

"Obliged," rapping a knuckle against the dark lacquered bar to punctuate, but not overstate, my gratitude. Funny thing about whiskey—the amber liquid fanning the bottom of the glass and rising like a dry creek bed in summer rain—that first assault upon the senses, no matter how long its absence, settles as right and natural as a woman's kiss. The Irishman nods and backs away, keeping an appraising eye how well the shot goes down. I drank whiskey every night out-country—two fingers with supper, a quick pull before bed—and when the bottle ran out,

I poured from the bottle of memory. And now, as the trilling cascade of the piano seems, in a single swallow, to magically brighten, as the feverish limelight trained on the stage betrays, all at once, the true age of the woman gyrating beneath an overworked corset and glazing cosmetics, I am assured of how accurate I remembered the liquor's promise.

Even with the peaty richness luxuriating through my nose and palate, none of the saloon's competing aromas escape my detection—not the dogfight of stale-versus-fresh beer, or the unwashed rankness of too many patrons, nor the perfumed adornment of too few. All senses stand on heightened alert. My skin tingles alive. From sheer periphery I catch the Irishman nod to himself, pleased that his instinct about me proved correct and his largesse unsquandered. He holds the bottle down by his side, as if setting it in plain view would inspire more controversy than convenience, and with his other hand fills two beer glasses at the far end of the bar. When I turn to catch his eye, I need hardly raise an eyebrow toward my empty glass to engage his return.

"You appreciate a fine whiskey, sir," and then lowering his voice, "I'd know better than to serve our usual rotgut to the likes of a proper gentleman. My private reserve, of course. Two dollars a go, but if I charged any less this lot would use it as aftershave."

"I'll take what's left."

"Why, there's near a quarter bottle," his eyes widening.

"Well, no sense in making you dance about one-handed just to prolong the inevitable." I thumb out an eagle and an extra five for his trouble. He sets the bottle down in front of me and slides the coins into his palm.

"You need a fresh glass or anything a'tall, you give old Seamus a holler."

"Hey, I'd try a drop of that," says the beer-drinker at the far end, his mouth barely visible beneath a bushelled gray beard.

"Kep Wilder, the day I'd waste a drop of fine Dublin mash across your diseased tongue is the day I dance a cancan with me own dead mother, God rest her soul."

"Aye, Seamus, you don't have to get downright nasty about it," Kep Wilder turning upon his stool to offer Seamus his affronted backside.

"You see what I'm dealing with, here?" Seamus says, pocketing the coins.

The piano slides back into a final chorus as the dancing girl spins to the front of the riser, one of her hair barrettes having given up entirely. She exhales deep to shoot the offending strand of hair from her sweated brow, and with a coquettish sneer, flashes a biscuit of bare ankle flesh to the indifferent crowd before vanishing behind the curtain as the music pounds to a stop. A ripple of applause seems to convey more gratitude that she is finished than genuine appreciation at being entertained. Had this been the amusement-starved Bend, every unwashed poke in attendance would've clawed that curtain to shreds and caved in the skull of his own brother to get to that woman. But here in the city, an uninspiring female is bottom-of-the-bill. The piano player tips his straw hat and tells the tables closest to him that he'll return after a short break. That wouldn't play in the Bend either. Merle once tried a fiddler

player down at the Jewel. When the fella attempted
to go out for a smoke, a couple of toe-tapping
gamblers—itchy triggers, both of them—got him to
rethink his position. The fiddling start up again
straight away. Finally after about eight hours, Merle
had to escort the man out back under shotgun
protection before his bladder exploded.

I pour another whiskey and feel the closeness
of bodies tightening around me. In the absence of
music, a handful of patrons who had been seated
near the stage find cause to descend on the bar.
Seamus fields the onslaught with unruffled grace,
collecting two or three orders at a time and then
completing them all at once. He places a glass beneath the tap and pulls the handle, letting the glass
fill unattended as he works down the row, making
change for one customer and topping off another
before returning to the rising beer just as the foamy
head draws even with the rim—all without spilling a
drop. The artistry of the town burns bright, even
within her over-lighted halls of debauchery.

A hand comes down on my shoulder and the
thirty-two is out of my waistband and half way into my
palm before I turn, meeting the eyes of an older
white man. His clever gaze rings familiar, but I am
unable to place it at first. Sensing his overstep, he follows straight away with a mellifluous declaration that
recalls our meeting this very day upon my exit from
the madam's. "It would appear, since our previous in-
teraction, you and I both have scrubbed up into what
might pass as gentlemen." I return the pistol to its
hiding place and reply to the overture with as few
words as possible.

"Evening."

"And a fine good evening to you, sir," the man enveloping the stool next to mine, his sturdy frame bedecked neck-to-ankle in a tailored suit of brilliant white. "You will forgive my impertinence in addressing you so forward, but as you may have gathered, I am not native species to frontier country. Hence I find myself underserved on both custom and camaraderie."

"Well, for starters, most fellas 'round here don't much care for being touched, least of all by strangers."

"Yes, point taken, sir. By and large the men of this territory have exuded about as much warmth as a stone at the bottom of a river. But allow me to remove the word 'stranger' from your appraisal. Shelby J. Ballentine, Esquire, at your service."

"Name's Harlan. Good to meet you, Mister Squire." I take the hand offered to me beneath his blank stare. Then he shakes his head, and I know I have said something foolish.

"No, es-quire, I'm an attorney. We needn't fuss with titles. My friends back home call me Spooner."

"Spooner?"

"That's the South for you, Mister Harlan. A name gets to sticking and folks don't much dwell on the origin."

"All right, then. Spooner it is."

"Except in matters of jurisprudence, mind you. Then propriety requires 'Mister Ballentine' to make himself known. But I can't say I see any judges in this establishment."

"No, different kind of law out here."

"My observation as well, Mister Harlan. Such creative application of the law would not hold in the Commonwealth of Virginia. But I must say, for every perilous lapse in legality I have encountered on the frontier there are a dozen more I will admit to enjoying. Although it took half an hour to scrub a red ring of Chinese lip rouge off my John Thomas." And right then I know the madam had laid the painted-up laundress on him and he had not complained.

I flash a deuce with two fingers toward the Irishman. A second little glass appears in an instant. "It's the good stuff. Keep it quiet," I say, pouring a proper slug for the Southern gentleman. Any man who would confide what he just shared can drink from my bottle anytime.

"A well-met accommodation." I watch him slide the liquor down his throat, the quality of it registering in his eyes as he swallows. "Sweet mother Mary. My heartiest gratitude, dear friend."

Somehow his overstating our acquaintance does not bother me. In truth, I have found friends in short supply these last few months, and how better to begin anew than with one who only knows what he sees in front of him. I pour us two more. "To Santa Fe," he says, touching glass. "May we escape in one piece."

"Sound about right." The soft warmth of the whiskey settles my brain as the piano begins up again, less urgent than before, as if to offer a setting of conversational mood in the calm before the next wiggling songbird returns attention to the stage. The throng of patrons, now laden with fresh drinks, filters back to previous tables and benches along the far wall.

"Ah, Owens!" Spooner says, flagging a new arrival at the door. The stranger removes his bowler, and I recognize Owens as the very gentleman I witnessed dining with his family at the hotel restaurant. He finds Spooner's eye and proceeds toward us. "You'll like Owens," the lawyer tells me. "A mining man, but dry-witted like a shot of vermouth, and his wife is a vision."

"I've seen her."

"Owens, this here is Harlan," Spooner says as the arriving man extends his hand. "Come join our contingent of the washed."

"An elite group in this locality," Owens's tense upper lip barely moving. "I saw you at the El Dorado," his eyes landing on me. "That Rawlings got a heavy pen for arithmetic, don't he?"

"Tends to lighten when he knows you're looking," I say.

"You can bet your ass I'm looking."

"There's no getting one past Owens," Spooner says. "Man does figures for a living. Then he packs it with TNT and blows it all to hell. He's an engineer, you see, with particular emphasis on explosives."

"I put that together," I say.

"Well, ain't the Southerner the dull knife in this drawer," Spooner says.

"You lawyering types ought to be used to that," Owens says. A snort busts out of me and I make no effort to conceal it. Spooner laughs so hard he nearly pops a button.

"That earns a drink," raising my finger for the Irishman to bring a glass. I start pouring for Spooner and me and the third glass appears without breaking the stream.

"Obliged," Owens clicking his into mine before killing it in a single go.

"Savor it, Owens," admonishes the lawyer. "You're drinking like you left a kettle boiling."

"What I left, squire, is a wife and two smalls in a backwater hotel suite." Owens taps a metal key onto the bar. "Provided the city does not burn to the ground in the next ten minutes, they should be right where I left them. And anyone tries getting in that door besides me's gonna get a belly full of lead courtesy of Clara May." Here is a man who, even with beautiful children and pretty wife waiting in her bedclothes, needed a breath, and a drink, in the company of other men. Unburdened by children myself, I can understand his motive entirely. But he is no fool about it. A locked door in the best hotel in town offers protection for only so long on the frontier. He taps out every last drop of nectar and upturns the empty onto the bar.

"Well, friend, that's a finer whiskey than I'll find aboard that bag of bolts, I'm sure. But you'll have to forgive me for not sticking around to return the hospitality."

"A man don't need to explain his business," I say. "Good to know you."

"At least let me buy you a beer chaser, as that bottle is nearly killed and I helped kill it."

"You save your money. I'm plenty drunk as is."

"Well, when our paths cross again, then. Although I believe three days in Santa Fe has been one too many for me, and three too many for my wife."

"Owens and his family migrate westward, on to the golden hills and fortunes of California, as do I," Spooner twirling his glass in reflection. "Astonishing how quickly two nomads learn one another's story when watering from the same brook."

"Company needs me out California, what see if there's any gold left in those hills at all. And if there ain't, I'll turn them inside out and shake out any other colors they got," Owens pushing back from the bar now. "All right, then. Ballentine, I'll see you in the palace car. G'night, gentlemen." Owens doffs his hat and heads out, unaware our paths will cross in the palace car as well, where I hope to take him up on that drink. I think of telling the lawyer that I'm on the train too, but even with the liquor, I check myself, remembering my resolve to keep my private details just that.

I notice the Irishman fix his gaze out toward the street, where a patch of Appaloosa hindquarter has come to be parked just outside the door. Seamus nods thoughtful to himself and starts two mugs of beer beneath the tap. The doors swing open and in walks the army captain and his regular, the same pair who stood witness to my fracas in the street this morning. The Irishman sets the two mugs on the counter and waits to receive the soldiers, clearing a spot for their easy approach. The officer takes a step toward the bar, but then stops and surveys the room, his eyes scanning, first at the far corner and then working slowly, face by face, until he has clocked all in attendance. His gaze falls upon me, blank, and then moves on, only to snap straight back with doubled intensity. I do not turn away, but hold his gaze and offer a slight dip of the hat brim—careful to temper the act not as a challenge, but a simple act of respect for the stars and bars represented by his station. A thin wrinkle of bemusement crosses his eye and then vanishes quick as it came, along with his attention. Whomever the object of his search, I am grateful to not be it. All I know in this moment is that the captain's earlier suggestion that I leave town had not been open to interpretation, the least of which would entail—not only defying his order—but dressing up in the White Man's clothes, taking a room at his best hotel and ingesting his finest liquor in the presence of underdressed White Women. I have no indication from the officer's inscrutable stare if he simply does not believe me to be the same person, or if more pressing matters supersede, such that he cannot be bothered to care one way or the other. A third scenario, flashing through my mind like a thunder crack, figures that he knows damn well who I am, and having given me a fair warning to vacate, washes his hands of the foolhardy Indian who thought this all a game.

"Those boys appear to be on the hunt." An uneasiness in the lawyer's voice sends it low. "You're not a deserter, are you?"

"Can't say I've had much use for the U.S. Army."

"I can assure you, I've had far less use for it." Looking over at Spooner, sweat now beads on his neck where there was only redness. He breathing grows shallow.

"You all right?"

"Let's just say there's a particular shade of blue I shall never find welcoming." Spooner leaves it at that. I reckon even twenty-odd years on from the War's end, his distaste at the sight of uniformed Yankee aggression burns as hot as it does for the Diné, the Inde and all the displaced peoples of the plains. The officer utters something short to Seamus, who brings his mouth up to the captain's ear and offers some length of explanation. Through all of it, the officer's eyes never stop their investigation of the room.

"Right in front of you!" a voice calling out from some darkened corner, barely distinguishable over the general din of piano and revelry. I question if the liquor is playing tricks on me. The captain appears not to have heard it at all, what with Seamus yarning his ear. Behind him, the grim-faced army regular grips his rifle, keeping an eye on the patrons, but never allowing his commander to stray from his periphery. Then the piano kick up, the player's clear voice demanding attention as he introduces the next girl. I turn toward the back corner just as the sodium light flares bright again and I am unable to discern any faces beyond the stage.

"That's the one you want, Cap'n!" This time I have no doubt I hear it, the voice more brazen in its drunkenness. The Irishman finishes his piece, his hands open in apology and the captain nods, accepting whatever accommodation has been offered.

The graybeard, Kep Wilder, seated, by pure coincidence, in nearest proximity to the conference, blurts out his own unsolicited appraisal. "No Dazers in here, Captain. Beer's too pricey."

"And if the gentleman needs your opinion he'll seek it out, you wet-brained bastard," Seamus spanking him down quick. The officer glances in the general direction of Kep and grimaces like a fly just landed in his coffee. He picks up one of the beers, takes a short sip and then replaces the glass on the bar. The second drink sits untouched. Then he tosses down a gold piece to pay for both and heads out the exit, the regular not budging until his officer has cleared the door.

"You missed one, Cap'n!" the voice drunker now, but unmistakable in its clarity—a high, screechy tenor drenched in churlish entitlement. I pivot in my seat and make out through the glare a silhouette of a man's face—dark, greasy hair framing a scraggly attempt at whiskers. Offsetting the shadowed figure, behind the right ear, sits a white square—a bandage—and I make him as the one called Lem, his neck no doubt smarting and in need of the dulling effects of liquor, thanks to Storm's well-placed bite. Lem sits with his chair tilted back, his shoulders resting against the wall. Two men flank him on either side. One strikes a resemblance to my assailant, Kirby, but that would be impossible. I saw that leg break sure as the sun will rise. And the red-bearded Kirby at this moment lies in a bed somewhere cursing my name and immobile, without the aide of cast or crutch. Yet this man's fiery coloring and broad shoulders ring even more recent in my memory. Then the new girl on stage, prettier than the last, but of poorer voice—a trend I am sure will continue as the evening progresses—removes a silk glove and steps out into the audience, to the approving whistles of men. The sodium light follows her, killing my view of the heckler and them seated with him.

"What's the rumpus, Seamus?" a rail-thin man in spectacles asking over his beer suds. "Those fellas lose the way to Fort Wingate?"

"Captain Oliver's got a job to do, same as the rest of us, Marvin."

"Well, drinking's part of soldiering, but he didn't

seem too interested in that, so what's he up to, I wonder?" Marvin not letting it drift.

"Some Dazers run off. A whole squad of 'em!" Kep Wilder unable to contain his newfound gossip.

"Dammit to hell, Kep. I swear if ya don't stop your muckraking that's the last pint you'll get out of me and you can do your drinking down with the Norwegians."

"Jeez, Seamus. It ain't like it's a secret. Man said the squad's been on the loose nearly two weeks now. I don't see why we gotta be all tight-lipped."

"Two weeks, you say?" Marvin producing from his jacket a nickel tablet and pencil stub that reveal him for that most meddlesome creature, a newspaper man.

"Now here you go, trying to get your name in the papers based on privileged information."

"Well, it ain't privileged to me, now Seamus. I can't help what happens to cross my own ears just by sitting here on the by and by."

"Point of order, he's correct on that," Spooner muttering for my benefit alone, the lawyer justifiably wary of jumping into an argument so far removed— in miles and mentality—from the cozy sanity of a Virginia courthouse. Still, I would come to learn that a man who enjoys hearing his own voice as much as Shelby J. Ballentine, can hardly contain himself at the first opportunity for oration.

"That captain's a good man," Seamus says. "I needn't be getting on his bad side on account of your gabbing like me granny."

"Y'all talkin' 'bout that missing regiment?" says another man, an ironworker, judging by his scorched fingers, jumping into this conversation, now that the sharp thinness of the singer's voice has squandered any goodwill her womanly curves might have earned her.

"We were just deciding there's nothing to be talking about, Tom," Seamus says firm.

"Not what I hear," the man continuing. "My wife's sister's husband works down at the Western Union. Says the wires been buzzing all day about the regiment gone rogue. Bunch of Hundred Dazers, they was."

"It weren't a regiment," Kep correcting him. "It were a squad. That's about a dozen or so. And the prevailing perception is they have probably run off for Mexico, based on the direction of their tracks."

"They were out of Fort Defiance, then?" Marvin asks.

"No, Fort Wingate, hence the assumption of Mexico." Kep Wilder, his chest puffed like a peacock, enjoys being the man with the knowledge.

"Oh, the hell with it, then," Seamus giving up on attempt at secrecy. "The cat's so far outta the bag, you might well as hang a feckin' sign on the door."

"It's certainly nothing new," the newspaper man editorializing now; it didn't take long for him to get there. "Historically the Dazers have not proved the most reliable soldiers by a long shot."

I feel Spooner's elbow nudge my arm. "I suppose I should know what a Dazer is, but I confess my ignorance."

The newspaper man overhears and wastes no time in launching into an explanation, but I turn my attention inward. I knew what the Hundred

Dazers were. Everyone on the frontier did—men who conscript themselves to the army for a hundred days, the briefest term of enlistment currently available. Some consider it that last desperate measure of employment. Other men seek out the short-term duty until something better comes along, like a cattle drive, or farm that's hiring up for harvest. But the majority of Dazers are running from something— women, the law, hungry children, or sometimes just boredom. Although this particular quest for adventure usually snakebites the pursuer, as the true meaning of boredom takes on new, unfathomable depths among the garrisoned regiments of the U.S. Army. With the Indians mostly crushed and reservationed, there proves little diversion for the young soldier, beyond rotgut whiskey and endless drilling back and forth upon the parade ground. The monotony has driven many men to madness. And those unfortunate enough to come across an infected whore soon share their boredom with the agony of pissing fire and the lunacy of a worm-eaten brain.

Upon digesting the information, the lawyer scrunches his face in wonder. "I would imagine buckling oneself into a wooly blue blouse every morning would make even Mexico seem like a viable alternative." It is a straight dig at the U.S. Army and I bite my lip to keep from smiling, but none of the others appear to catch it.

"Well, you can never predict what a bunch of crazy Dazers will get themselves up to," Kep says.

"The *Crazy Dazers*," the newspaperman repeating, sucking the marrow out of every word. "Now that's got quite a ring to it."

"There you go, Kep, gone and got your name

quoted in papers," Seamus snapping his towel onto the bar. "And you, Marvin, got yourself a headline for the afternoon edition."

"It's Kep, with an E," Kep wagging a finger toward Marvin, "and Wilder. W-I-L-D—"

A man's shoulder brushes against my own. Enough weight propels the shove to know that it is no accident. Turning, I catch only a wide-shouldered figure lumbering slow away from me. His head cocks, revealing the reddish whiskers similar to that what has plagued me all day. "No Bluecoat's gonna save you this time, Injun." I feel my hand going toward the thirty-two as the man twists his neck back to make sure his words landed. Rising, the thirty-two palmed for easy use, I watch him filter through the crowd and back toward the far wall where he reclaims his seat next to Lem. I could kill them both from where I stand and have four bullets left for any comers who objected. The fire of the whiskey—already in full flame—stokes up against the newfound rage at this man's spineless threat.

And what would happen, if I acted? Drink has taken down far nobler men than me in a flutter of vengeance. I am leaving town in the morning with a first-class ticket and the finest stallion in the Territory. Santa Fe can have the rest.

I stow the pistol, square my hat and leave without saying a word.

CHAPTER NINE

Cross let himself through the picket gate on Palace Street, Van Zant a step behind him. The two men took note of the well-tended garden, but forewent discussion as they glided silently up the front steps and made their way to the door. Cross raised a hand to knock, and as his gloved knuckle touched wood, the door creaked open. Then he saw gouged bits of exposed wood along the edge. Three heavy locks jutted from the door, their bolts extending out into nothingness. The men drew their weapons.

"Somebody pushed in," Van Zant clutching the stubbier of the two shotguns he carried. "Them locks held up. It's the wood that give out."

Cross concurred with a nod and stepped inside, his pistol leading the way. On the floor of the foyer, a discarded crowbar confirmed the forced entry. The trail of blood leading to Garber's body confirmed murder.

* * *

Van Zant fell in behind him as Cross looked to his right. There, in the office, lay Milton Garber, flat on his back in a pool of thickening crimson, his torso cratered with rifle shot. The door of his empty safe hung open above him, like a laughing maw. Cross felt Van Zant press forward.

"No," blocking him with an arm. "Don't foul the blood." Cross reached down, undid his boots, and slipped out of them. Van Zant watched as the little man entered the office, his stocking feet so light upon the ground he nearly floated. A deep, trance-like calm overtook Cross, but his eyes fired with simmering energy. Van Zant had seen this before— he never got tired of seeing it—Cross transporting himself to the exact moment of confrontation.

"They knew he kept money here," Cross waving his hand over the safe. "Even though this Christ-killer pretended otherwise." Cross knelt down and inspected Garber's left temple, where a reddened lump had swollen over his eye. "A rifle butt to the forehead, that got his attention. And even then, the Jew held tight to his money." Cross moved down to Garber's hand, two of the digits broken at unnatural angles. "They had to break his fingers." His eyes combing further, Cross discovered the Derringer, half submerged in the congealing puddle of blood around Garber's body. He picked up the tiny pistol and brought it—dripping—to his nose. He sniffed both barrels separately.

"Wrong sort of iron for a rifle fight," Van Zant said.

"Yes, but effective at close range. He managed to get off both rounds, didn't he?" Cross's eyes danced about the room and then settled, locking on a spot on the wall behind Van Zant. "There." He pointed at a small hole in the wallpaper. "A clean miss." Van Zant turned and squinted at the bullet hole.

"What about the second shot? You think it hit the robber?"

Cross considered it. "If it did, it just made him angry."

"Way the Shylock's been worked over, I reckon the man who shot him showed up angry."

"Two men," Cross correcting. He stepped to the window and drew back the curtain. Light filled the room. He turned his attention to the floor and studied the patchwork of bloody smears—fragments of footprints—crisscrossing in some unintelligible hieroglyph that Cross deciphered with his eyes. He began nodding to himself, confident of the narrative forming in his mind. The floor told a story. "Two large men, nearly equal in size. Brothers, perhaps? The first one stood here and wore ordinary flat soles—indoor shoes—mostly likely a clerk or an office worker. But the second man wore riding boots." Cross followed the markings toward the body, then stopped abruptly, his brow furrowed. "No, riding *boot.*"

"You telling me the sum'bitch come in here to rob the joint with only one shoe?"

"Indeed I am, his right shoe, to be exact. Because if my hypothesis is correct, Mister Van Zant, our killer . . ." Cross eased himself down on all fours and stared back at the trail, his eyes only inches above the floor, "is *hobbled.* His left leg resides in some sort of cast." Cross pointed to a series of wide, square-like patterns that appeared every few feet.

"Well, I'll be dipped in donkey shit."

"I'd prefer you weren't. And if I'm not mistaken . . .

yes." Cross rose and waved his finger at a small, circular splotch, no wider than a half dollar. "Our man gets about with the aid of a crutch, or cane."

Van Zant's mouth hung open. Yet his amazement was cut short by the approach of rapid footsteps up the front porch. A man bounded into the house. Van Zant leveled his shotgun at the office door, Cross's forty poised similar. And then the arriving man turned the corner and saw the guns pointed at him. He screamed, his feet flying from under him as he fell backward onto the seat of his pants.

"Don't shoot! I'm the law!" his voice was young and wracked with fear.

"What is your business here, constable?" Cross flashed his credential and stowed it again, before the boy had time to make sense of it. The young lawman wore a city constable's uniform, void of any rank or commendation. Cross pegged him as a recent hire.

"Well, we know there was a shooting. Folks heard it."

"Why are you here alone?"

"Captain's on his way. And the others. Who are you fellas?"

"Who we are is, we're the ones who don't need to fucking explain ourselves." Van Zant growled.

"Deputy, every paper in the office is to be boxed and labeled for my personal inspection. Is that understood?" Cross stowed his pistol.

"Y-yes, sir."

"But first, tell your captain to round up every doctor in the city. Somewhere in Santa Fe there's a surgeon who recently set a broken left leg." Cross stamped his way back into his boots, and was about to admonish the constable for not yet departing when a heavy thud echoed from an upper floor. The men looked to the ceiling.

Cross's pistol was out again. He took the stairs two at a time, followed by Van Zant. The boy policeman fumbled out his revolver and brought up the rear. At the second floor landing Cross stopped—motioning the others to do the same—and listened. A door at the end of the hall stood partly open, and on the floor leading to it, the faintest whisper of blood-stained footprints told Cross all he needed to know. The men crept down the hall, the occasional groan of a floorboard the only betrayal of their advance. The constable—terrified beyond his wits—noticed how the two strangers communicated with only their eyes or a hand signal or a slight nod of the head. At the door, he observed the larger man slip ahead of his partner, taking point with the twelve gauge, as Cross pushed open the door and scanned the room.

It was a bedroom—Garber's—Cross gathered. A man's suit hung next to the four-poster. A twist of bedding lay in violent disarray atop the mattress. Van Zant stood in the center of the room, rotating with the shotgun toward all four corners. Then he checked behind the bed. And then under it. But there was nothing. Cross inhaled deeply from the doorway. The air sat heavy with sweat and sex. By the looks of the bed, the sex had been taken, not given. And then Cross's eyes fell on a second door. A closet.

Three guns turned in unison, leveling at the closet, as if a cornered shooter hiding within might, at any moment, decide to go out blazing. Cross issued silent instruction—he would aim high, Van Zant center. The young constable was to shoot low. He was now part of it, whether he liked it or not. Despite the pounding in his chest, he liked it very much. And it was a hell of a lot better than being the man in the closet. The boy dropped to one knee and rested the barrel on his crossed forearm, like he'd been taught. Cross sidestepped to the near wall and brought up the pistol. He raised his left hand and held up three fingers. Then two. Then one. Then—

A sob. A weak, little cry—and then a sniffle—eked from the closet. It was no sound of a killer. Cross slinked forward and yanked open the door.

Xenia—Garber's maid—knelt trembling on the closet floor, naked and violated. Her attackers had not been gentle. She clutched at her throat, and with tears streaking her swollen face, tried to speak, but her face contorted with pain and no sound came from her.

"Out of the way," Cross leaping to his feet. He shucked the folded quilt from the bed board and, unfurling it, brought it softly down around the woman. He knelt down and took her in his arms. She slackened in his embrace, her hand coming away from her throat and opening. A small crucifix—noting more than a pair of sticks crudely wrapped with twine—fell from her fingers. Cross saw it. His eyes filled with tears.

"Dear child," Cross wiping the sweat from her brow. "It's all right now." She lay back into him, her breath labored from exhaustion and from the damage to her windpipe. The man's choking fingers had left deep contusions on her throat, blood-shotting her eyes. Her dark skin had blued to near blackness from the beating. And there was blood around her mouth and seeping through the quilt on both sides of her below the waist. The boy turned away, unable to watch. Even Van Zant looked down. "Fetch that surgeon, boy. Tell him to bring laudanum."

The policeman bounded from the room and down the stairs. Cross cradled the girl's head and she closed her eyes. "Fear not, child. The men who did this cannot hide from God. Nor can they hide from me."

CHAPTER TEN

The clattering jolts me awake, wagons on the street below, the city alive and getting about its business. Late morning light invades unfettered through the naked window, turning the room impossibly bright—far brighter than when I last saw it—in the gray twilight just past dawn, when Pete showed up with the rest of the clothes and left an hour later. The whiskey's wrath had not yet settled in then, but now, lifting my head from the pillow, blinding white shards needle the skull like screws through soft wood. I paw at the small clock on the table and pull it close through a field of faulty vision until the hands take on some angle of meaning. The clock face pressed against my forehead, the incessant tick-tock obliterating the shallow calm of my hearing, and still I do not want to believe what I see.

"Shit."

I roll from the wrecked bed and stumble, stark naked, across the hard floor to the pot and empty my bladder and use the time to figure out what happens next. My union suit lays crumpled in a ball and

somehow I sort myself into it and, still buttoning, cross
to the door and open it. A familiar figure bends over
at the far end of the hall, lifting a tray of silver dishes.

"Moses."

"Mornin', Mister Harlan."

Moses walks toward me, his eyes settling into a
steady level of concern as he gets a better look at the
damage. "Everything all right, sir?"

"Come inside." I step away from the door for him
to follow and he enters, closing the door behind him.
"That clock right?" I ask.

"Yes, sir. Quarter past ten. I set it myself to the
church bell."

"Well. The state of things, I got a train to catch and
the train ain't waiting."

His brow releases, shifting his demeanor into one
of vigilant serenity. He has heard this ballad before.
"Mister Harlan. All you need do, get yourself dressed,
square up with Mister Rawlings and meet me out
front. Moses take care the rest."

I nod my thanks and set to searching about the
floor for my trousers, only to discover them properly
folded, along with the suit coat, across the back of a
chair where Pete must have hung them. And there
on the desk is the second outfit that he stayed up
all night finishing and took the time to wrap up in
brown paper for tidier transport.

"Smart lookin' jacket," Moses helping me through
the sleeves of last night's coat.

"Pete knows what he's doing."

"What I hear, sir." Moses goes back to packing up
the bags while I scan for my boots and come up empty.
"Your boots outside, Mister Harlan."

"The hell they doing there?" I open the door and

find the boots just outside, sheened to chocolate luster.

"Gettin' polished where you left 'em, sir."

"I never—" I stop myself because it weren't me, but Pete again. I stamp into the boots, grab the money and the thirty-two and stuff them into my trousers as I head downstairs.

Rawlings glances up from his ledger book, gold wire-frames resting low on his nose.

"Surely you're not leaving before you've had breakfast? Mirabel's made her ham and biscuits."

"I need be getting on. What's the reckoning, if you please?"

"Well," returning his eyes to the ledger. "With the charge from the restaurant, that comes to . . ." I feel my chest expand as I inch closer, casting him in shadow. His lips start to say one thing, and then halt and say, "Twenty-seven and fifty."

I pick out a twenty piece and another ten and slap them on the podium. "Maybe I'll see you again, if I don't get properly tagged."

"Sir?" his nose crinkling.

I walk away and bust out the front door, the bright sun resuming its assault on my pounding head. Moses is nowhere to be seen and I figure he and my guns are a mile out of town by now. But then a horse emerges from behind the building, towing a light-weight hansom. Moses sits atop the wagon and kicks up the horse at the sight of me. As the wagon approaches he extends a hand, but I pull myself up and plop down next to Moses. The saddlebags and the Spencer sit tucked up against the back of the bench.

"Halvorson's stable."

"Hold on tight, Mister Harlan."

* * *

Moses fires up that old draft bay and sets about navigating the pitted, churned-up roads of Santa Fe like a dog after a jackrabbit. I grip the bench and use my legs to steady myself as the hansom corners and zigzags and dodges around wagons coming at us from all directions until the split-rail of Halvorson's fence rolls into view and I ease my grip enough to let a little blood back into my fingers. Moses steers the bay up toward the gate and yanks back hard on the reins.

"Your pistol belt, just inside your smaller bag yonder," Moses says, the bay clomping to an abrupt stop. "Might suggest you keep it put among them fancy train folk. Ain't like it is out-country."

"Ticket fella done suggested the same thing." I hop down into a dry space among the puddles mudding the road's edge.

"And I snatched you up a couple Mirabel's ham biscuits on the way out. They's wrapped up in your other bag. And you take this here." He reaches down behind the seat and comes back with a soldier's canteen. "This here's your coffee. I told you Moses take care everything."

Hoisting the bags with one arm, I dig through my coin pocket with the other and stop at the first coin I come to. I press the quarter-eagle into his palm. He nods thanks, but his eyes grow serious. "You mind yourself, Mister Harlan. Ain't like it used to be. Things is changing out there faster than the weather."

"I reckon they're changing round here, too. You take care."

"Yessah." Moses gets the bay moving again and clatters off.

I sling the bags high on the shoulder and head into the office. Finding the small room empty I press on through the back door and out toward the barn. Human voices argue from the stables, Halvorson barking instruction and receiving an earful of back-sass in Spanish, from which he derives little amusement. The stable boy emerges from the barn carrying a hammer and a bucket of nails. A broken stall gate from the barn sits in splintered pieces between two pommels. A long, satisfied whinny lows from the paddock, and I know from the sound of it that Storm has enjoyed his visit, which means no one else did. Then he catches scent of me and whinnies again—my whinny—as if I didn't see him over there all alone, cut from the other horses. I whistle back short and settle him down as Halverson steps out of the barn, hands on hips. He sees me coming and starts right in.

"I'll bake a birthday cake for Satan himself before I let that cursed stallion stable here again. He destroyed the door to his stall."

"Door must've done something wrong."

"Only its job! Keeping them horses separated what have no business mingling. Like, for instance, a randy, hell-bit stallion and one of my mares what had the misfortune to be in-season."

"Did he get her?"

Halverson spits again, annoyed, and points over at the busted door.

"Does that door appear to be in one piece to you?"

"Well then, I hope she had a good time."

"Your animal is not fit to board with other horses and you ought have disclosed as much."

"He doesn't act like that when I'm around. He likes to test is all, see what he can get away with."

"Well, my options, far as controlling him, was limited, as I don't think you would've want me taking a stick to him."

"No. *You* wouldn't want that," I correct him. A trickle of fear bubbles behind his eyes, softening the boil of his anger. "I apologize about the gate, and for your trouble."

"I reckon you should."

I remember a train that won't wait and a seventeen-mile stretch that needs covering. All I need do is slap some gold in Halvorson's paw and be done with this. If the city has taught me anything, it is that a problem you can fix with money ain't a real problem. But something about the way he spits gets my dander up, and I dig in for the sake of it.

"Your mare got some valuable seed in her," I say. "She foals out, I got a mind to come back, collect my half."

"You're saying you would want to collect on *half* a *foal*?"

"Seems only fair. Minus the stud fee."

"Stu—Stud fee? Now hang on just dang minute."

"Tell you what. You eat the door and the stabling cost, I'll waive the stud fee. We call it square."

"Well this is all supposin' that the mare has conceived."

"Storm don't miss when he puts it in. Look, we gotta go. Either I pay you now and come back in twelve months, take what's mine, or we call it square and you just might get yourself a racehorse. I ain't fussed one way or the other." I pull a stack of coins from my pocket and let them clap together in my hand, back and forth, as the gears turn slow in the old man's brain. He spits again and turns to the boy.

"Berto, fetch the man's saddle. They got to be getting' on."

The boy called Berto drops the tools, relieved to be liberated from the unfamiliar world of carpentry, and darts into the tack room. He returns with my saddle. I hardly recognize it—oiled and polished to a dark shade unseen since it was new.

"Mind your ass don't slip out of it," Halvorson says.

The boy treads cautious as he nears the stallion, but Storm allows the approach and I soon learn why as Berto pulls a fistful of oats from his pocket. Storm devours it in two bites, but it is enough for the boy to place the saddle, cinch it secure and get himself clear.

"You know the way to his heart," I say, pressing two dollars into the boy's hand as he passes. The boy smiles, but a powerful weariness colors the gratitude.

"*Gracias, señor. El caballo es un diablo, pero un diablo hambre.*"

"Hungry devil. That 'bout describes him." I tie on the saddlebags and pull myself up.

"Good thing that horse don't speak Spanish," Halvorson adding between spits. "He strikes me as the type to be easily offended."

"Reckon he speaks a little bit of everything." I give Storm a nudge and ease him toward the gate. "If he ain't offended, must be 'cause he agrees." Storm feels the boot heel tap him again and that is all he needs to show them his shoes.

* * *

About a mile out of town, the ground drops off quick and Santa Fe recedes above us, taking with it all the distractions and heady poisons that pester a young man, until the last adobe hut has faded in the distance. I take the country air deep in my lungs and, for the first time in two days, feel like a man who understands where he belongs.

We pick up a little mule trail that winds down toward the valley floor and after about fifteen minutes I catch sight of the spur track that will lead us out to the junction. The sun has burned off the last of the morning haze, clearing the line of sight in all directions. I comb the track for any trace of steam, but finding none, imagine that Virginia lawyer, as well as Owens and his family, all crammed into that two-car shuttle, getting ready to push off from the depot in town to make the same trip I'm making, only in less comfort.

Storm dances his way down the slope, head forward, eyes on ground ahead. But his ears twitch lively and content, that horse brain of his chewing on the cud of last night's exploits.

"If you can navigate this hill without getting us kilt, I might just have a minute to eat this here biscuit." The stallion nickers low and picks up the pace a beat, his signal that I am free to eat my breakfast. "I saw that boy stuffing them oats in your face," I add, digging the warm, wrapped bundle from the saddlebag. "I'll bet you was working that poor squirt for grub the second I left." I peel back the paper—steam rising from the golden crust—and take a bite. The buttered biscuit and salty ham explode across the tongue.

"I don't know who Mirabel is, but she knows her way 'round a biscuit."

I like town. Town is good.

"Don't get used to it. The way you and me ate and drank and screwed our way through that place, I 'spect we was about two seconds from both our butts getting kicked to the boneyard in the heap they deserve. I reckon we're bustin' out just in time." Another grunt from the stallion confirms the obvious and we leave it at that. I lick the butter off my fingers and open up the canteen and take a long pull of the coffee while it still holds what little heat it has left. Then I replace the cap as the ground starts to level out and put my glove back on and pick up the reins in earnest. "All right, amigo, let's show this valley how we cut."

The trail dumps us out fifty yards from the tracks. We work through a run of low bushes and cross a dry arroyo and fall in right beneath the berm that holds the track. A swath, five yards wide and stretching as far as the eye can see, has been cleared on both sides of the rail of any obstruction—plant or mineral—and replaced with gravel to discourage further life from taking root. Heat rises from the road in shimmering waves. The air sits thick with creosote. Storm sees open space unfurl before him and within a couple of strides settles into the steady canter he can hold for an hour.

There is nothing natural about a steel road. The arrow-tip of White Man's ingenuity fires westward in a monument of speed and profit, leaving the bodies that fell to build it as the only echoes of its humanity, and their song—if heard at all—will soon drift into the ether like the fleeting breath of a locomotive. So it is that this Big Idea of metal and boiling water travels with such efficiency that even to run along-side it—as we do now—gives a false sense of one's ability. Storm and I burn through the miles as if pushed forward by a mechanical hand. We make up so much time that after three-quarters of an hour I am convinced we have not only atoned my sin of tardiness, but have gained sufficient edge to ensure an arrival well ahead of the shuttle. And as it is on the back of the stallion that my carelessness has found absolution, when we come upon a water tower I decide to stop and let Storm have a well-deserved drink.

I pull back and Storm blows to a halt in the shadow of the tower. "Figure this must be the mid-point. Though I 'spect a train can't make seventeen miles without stopping for water, it's a bad day to begin with." I swing down near the hand pump that stands next to the tower. A half-barrel receptacle sits off to the side. I kick it underneath the pump and get the pump primed and soon have warm desert water flowing into the barrel. The water is clear and the new barrel has not yet had time to rust.

"Good thing somebody had the forethought to consider them dullards what would think it a bright idea to cross this stretch on foot." Storm shoots me the blue eye and moseys over toward the barrel. "Yes. I am aware I speak of present company. I don't need you to tell me as much." Storm begins to lap at the water in the barrel, then decides he would rather drink it straight from the pump. I uncap the canteen and suck down the last of the cold coffee and go to the pump to fill it with water before Storm slobbers it all to tarnation.

"Mind if I get in there too?" He minds plenty, but lets me in enough to fill the canteen an inch or two, then nudges me aside again. "Think the country will look the same in California?" I fix out at the valley and its gentle shift from red to tan as the long, gradual slope down from Santa Fe seems to finally have an end to it. "I don't know why it would," answering my own question. "Country is country and I can't imagine any reason for things to be otherwise. I heard talk that out East a fella can gaze out in any direction and see nothing but green, but until I witness such event I will consider it hearsay."

Storm flaps his tail at a fly as he drinks, not much caring one way or the other as to my observation. The breeze bottoms out, leaving a silence disturbed only by the lapping of Storm's greedy tongue at the water. But there is something else—a pitch so high it skirts beyond the edge of what humans are supposed to hear. I look back at Storm and see his ears dancing, trying to make sense of it, and I know it is out there. It swells just a hair and draws my attention downward, toward the rails. I drop to my knees and press an ear against the warm steel. The train's song zings through my skull and down through the spine.

"Train's on the move," I say, still kneeling. If a little two-car spur generates that much disturbance, I can only wonder the noise preceding the Santa Fe when it gets to full speed. "Break's over."

I am about to rise when I notice the dirt beneath Storm, matted and scarred with the hard, arcing patterns of horseshoes. The markings are faint, but wholly different from those of the stallion.

"Somebody been through here today." Then the wind picks up sharp, snapping in from the east. Storm pulls up from the water, his top lip flaring. I know what is coming but I can't stop him. All at once the stallion breaks hard, charging into the wind and by now I catch scent of the mare as well. "No, Storm!"

His tail waves good-bye as he bounds up and over the berm. I give chase, narrowly missing the reins as they flap hopeless through the air. Rising to the top of the berm I see a mare—a chestnut star, unsaddled, way out here in the middle of nowhere. I call again, this time with the weight of the devil himself behind my voice.

"Whooooa!"

I'll be dammed if the stallion don't stop where he stands, halfway to the mare. And I know it is only by the dumb luck that he cooled his fire last night with that other mare that he is not presently atop the chestnut, or at least giving chase with hell's fury.

"Easy boy. Come on." I see in his eyes the battle raging between allegiance to my command and the maddening drive to conquer the estrus female. "Easy back now." He ponders my order and not much more. He turns. I need his bridle, but mostly, I need that Spencer. Trouble hangs so heavy in the air I can taste it, but cannot yet locate its origin. The whole thing is wrong. Dead wrong. And then I see the rope dangling from the mare. She has been ground-tied— left there on purpose.

A rifle chambers behind me. "Hold it right there, Injun."

CHAPTER ELEVEN

I could pick out Lem's needling voice across a windy canyon. But this time he is close, ten yards at most. "You step back from that stallion, real slow."

The stallion. Yes. He wants the horse, but fears that he might miss. Otherwise just shoot me in the back, you dang fool. I turn slow and catch his slight frame at the edge of my vision. "Hold it there! You get them mitts up."

I do as I'm told. He does not know that he has already lost. I cluck a soft breath from my lips, but it is enough for Storm to hear. The stallion tightens up closer to me.

"I said, get away from the damn horse."

"I can't help if he follows me." Lem straightens up, dust covering his face, his limbs moving stiff from the cramped hiding place on the backside of the berm. A Remington rifle jitters in his arms, shoulder height.

"You think you're smart? Showing me up like you done. Well, who's smart now? I'mma be taking that horse. I'll stud him. Then I'll gut him. And ain't a damn thing your dead red body gonna say about it neither. And that money too."

"I ain't got the money. I spent it all."

"Hell, you did. I seen you at the Duck. You stashing your coin right in them trousers."

"Quit yakking and shoot him!" The frustrated voice barks from my left. I just make out a dagger of rock jutting from the ground in my periphery.

"You want me to shoot up what we come all this way for?" Lem yelling toward the boulder. I keep my eyes on the Remington, but now detect movement stirring to my left. "This gut-eater ain't going nowhere. Ain't got his Spencer, neither. And all dolled in that pretty suit—got himself so citified he done forgot his holster."

"I'll shoot him then." The second man walking toward me, his margin for error shrinking with every step.

"Hell, you will," Lem's eyes narrowing. He steadies the rifle and aims at my belly. "I'mma watch this gut-eater squirm. You'll be begging me for a head shot."

"Fine. Take the money." I reach for my waistband.

"Slow," Lem tightens his grip on the rifle.

I creep my hand inside my trousers, finger the pistol and snap my arm up, falling left as I fire. The shot catches Lem in the face, through his bandage. I roll to the ground. A shotgun booms behind me and I roll again and come up shooting. A torso in checkered flannel turns my way, bringing with it the double twelve and its last unfired barrel. I squeeze again, this time finding his sternum. His arms bend, the shotgun blasting upward. The man reels back on his heels and stumbles backward. I see a beard now—reddish and heaving—and a hard face softened by pain. His hate-filled eyes, still defiant, narrow in a final push to turn the tables. He paws for his holster and I shoot him again, upper lungs, and he falls back flat. I cross to him, kick the twelve away and stomp on his arm. He struggles to move and then gives up on that and gurgles for air, his lungs filling with blood.

"You put that mare out yonder, try to draw out my horse?"

"Ain't no stallion say no to a wet mare."

"Storm ain't just any stallion."

"Ain't no horse worth dying for."

"Guess your life ain't worth much, then."

"Lem got the horse. I get the money. That's the deal."

"Who says I got money?"

"Lem said you was splashing it outside the Jew's house."

"Lem says too much."

"That he do. He dead?"

I look back over at Lem. "Blew out his skull. Most of his jaw. Looks like your scattergun got a piece too."

"Well, shit," the man says, a twisted smile parting his strawberry whiskers. "Plan-wise, this was not our finest hour."

"Nope. That it weren't." I take my foot off his arm and let the shadow of the pistol block the sun from his eyes.

"Make it quick, ya bastard." I set the hammer back and when he hears it his mouth tightens, but I stop, my mind chewing on a nut that won't crack.

"Thing is, one bit I can't figure is how come you knew I'd be out here."

"That's on Lem. I just bought into it."

"Yeah, but Lem ain't got your coloring."

The man's face turns sour. "Hell you talking 'bout?"

"See, there was people what knew I had a good horse, and there's people what knew I'd be taking the train, but there ain't but one who knows I'd be passing along this stretch at this very hour, and that's the fella what sold me my train ticket."

"Well, you best take it up with him, then."

"Thing is, looking down at your sorry mug I feel like I'm talking to him right now, what with both of you sporting a red beard on the same luggy frame. That ain't no coincidence. And the both of you could be twin to that sum'bitch Kirby who started all this."

"That ain't the way Kirby tell it!"

"Three fat red-heads. You think I can't put that together that ya'll is kin?"

"Burn in Hell, gut-eater."

I lower the gun to his leg. "Reckon I'll start at your ankle, work up to your knee, let the coyotes do the rest." The chugging rattle of the shuttle train rises from the north. I squeeze the trigger and blow a hole in his boot. He screams, his back arching, but there is no wind left in his lungs.

"All right, we's kin. Got the same daddy, the three of us."

"Thought so." I put the kill shot through his forehead and the coming train don't give me much time to feel bad about it.

A plume of billowy steam coughs skyward a half mile down rail. I grab the dead man's collar and drag him behind the boulder where he started. Storm lopes a circle around us, wanting to be close to the action and I catch a rein and ease him behind the boulder as well. He ain't much hidden, but it will have to do. I drop his rope to the ground and tell him to stay put. Then I sprint for the mare, whooping it up with my arms as I get closer. She says to hell with her ground tie and scampers off, away from the tracks, just like I want her to. Then I double back hard as I can run and grab hold of Lem's shirt and drag his messed-up corpse behind the bolder and collapse to my knees, sucking air as the shuttle train creaks past.

I look up and am taken by just how slow it moves. Only three cars, you'd think a straight downhill shot would get that thing going, but instead it rumbles along at what Storm would do in an easy canter. A thought comes to me, that if the mighty Santa Fe herself rolls that slow, we might not see California by wintertime.

Then the little train is gone and in the quiet that remains, the nervous energy that comes with killing a man shudders forth from my stomach and I vomit up breakfast. Taking a life—even them two what laid in wait to kill me—sits wrong in the heart, and I hope it always will. Storm turns his head and locks that blue eye on me like he does when he sees the world different.

You've killed many.

"Yeah, well, that don't mean it's a natural state for a man, and him what says it is ain't right in the head. Come on, let's get cleaned up. We're back to running late again."

I draw my knife and slice open the dead men's shirts and down the side of their trousers, leaving the flesh exposed. "Only ones we need finding these two are condors and coyotes. Anybody else is trouble we don't want."

I leave Storm behind the rocks and head back toward the water tower, reloading the thirty-two as I go. The little pistol pulled its weight and then some, but rolling across the ground left my new suit dusty and smudged all over. Could be worse, though. No torn fabric to speak of, just some spattered blood below the knee and streaks of dirty blood on the boots. Most of the dust feels like it landed on my face. I get to the water barrel and bend over it, studying the face mirrored back in the clear water of the half-filled barrel. That first reflection after bloodshed always seems to age a man ten years.

The water tower blocks the sun, leaving a cool circle of shade around the pump and barrel. I reach down to bring a handful of water to my mouth when I see, reflected in the surface, a pistol. The blue steel extends over the top ledge of the tower and aims down in my direction. Pivoting from the shoulders, I spin and fire the thirty-two upward as I duck underneath the tower. Blind shots rain down from above, thrashing the water in the barrel and pinging off the pump. I crouch low, retreating to the dead center of the ground directly beneath the tower, out of reach of the haphazard firing of the long-barreled Smith & Wesson. Then the shooting stops and I can hear him listening.

He shimmies—repositioning himself—his every move reverberating through the water tank, betraying his location while mine is obscured by the wind playing tricks on his ears some twenty feet off the ground. The roof of the tower extends beyond the width of the massive water tank in a three-foot overhang. He slides to the edge to get a better listen. I take silent aim at the overhang supporting him.

Slowly a hand creeps over the edge, showing all the knuckle I need as it angles the pistol down beneath the tower. I fire once and hear a scream as the pistol falls.

"Ah, shit!" He is young and unaccustomed to fearing for his life. Frantic scrambling as he tries to get back from the edge. I fire up at the overhang, blasting the boards where I know his body to be. But the wood planks are thick and absorb the small caliber. He knows it and I know it. "I got a rifle up here, mister. And your pistol ain't shooting through, so just leave me be. We'll forget this whole thing ever happened." I step around the base of the tower and can see his silhouette lying prone against the shadow of the sloped roof.

"You had a rifle, you'd a shot me already."

"All right, then. You just stick your head out from under there and see what's what."

I float back under the tower to the far side, closest to the way I came. I cup my hands around my mouth and whistle once, hard and quick. Over the top of the boulder I see the tips of Storm's ears perk to attention. His long gray snout dips around the corner, his neck turning just enough to let both eyes catch me head on. I hold my arm out straight, and Storm understands and breaks into a run dead at me.

"What is that?" The boy yelling now, panic in his voice. "Mister, I swear. I will shoot that horse dead."

I step to the side and grab the Spencer from the scabbard and try to halt Storm as he lopes past, but his momentum carries him underneath the shade of the tower and back out into the sunlight on the other side, exposed. Somewhere above me a hammer cocks. I chamber a round, turning from the waist, and bring the Spencer up in a single motion. I fire. The half-inch bullet craters the wood and leaves a hole ringed wet with blood. The boy makes a new sound, something mortal, and then, summoning all strength, slithers toward the center of the roof. I chamber-fire, obliterating the overhang in his wake until he has found the protection of the tank and the thousand gallons that stand between him and my rifle.

"Look, it ain't gotta be like this, mister." His young voice labors with each shallow breath.

"You shoot at my horse, I'll kill your whole family."

"I ain't gonna shoot nobody. That's plain enough by now ain't it? Hell I had you dead to rights. So that's gotta be worth something."

"Well, if nothing is something than I guess it means that."

"You got me good, through the belly. But I 'spect I can make it back to town. I don't know you. You don't know me. What say we just forget this whole thing ever happened."

I take a step back and blow a hole in the bottom of the tank, water geysering out and soaking the ground. A second shot punctures lower, causing a deluge and leaving my Coffeyvilles ankle high in water that ain't done rising. I wonder if the boy understands that in less than a minute the impenetrable shield he staked his life on will be nothing but a hollow shell of soggy lumber. Then I hear him scrape to his feet, his boot heels clambering across the tin roof. I slosh back toward the ladder that runs up the side and peek out and don't see anything. Then my foot gets stuck in the mud and I bend down to free it and when I look upward again the sky goes black as he crashes into me, boots first. His weight carries downward and strips the Spencer from my hands. I grab onto his legs and twist and we splash into the water, the pain of impact just starting to bloom in my back and shoulder. His gun must have gone flying too because I feel him pawing though the mud.

I crawl up his body, reaching for control of his arms as he flails through the black water in a desperate search for the first gun he can find. He is lighter than I am, but more scared of dying, but the two don't quite balance out. We struggle there for a bit and then I get a full grip of his young man's hair and push his head down in the water and into the mud. He starts to kick, his spurred heels slashing at my legs. I work my way up his back and wrench his left arm behind his back and center all my weight down into his hips, pinning him beneath me in the shallow foot of water. A panicked, high-pitched squeal bubbles up through the water and then the sound gets low and gurgling as he starts to take water into his lungs. I crank on his shoulder and something pops inside him and the shoulder bends like it shouldn't and then his legs stop kicking. I stay there, muscles tensed—I don't know how long, maybe a minute—until his whole body goes soft and his ribs stop moving and no sound comes from him at all.

I unravel my arm from his and roll off him. His body floats to the surface, and I sit back onto my tail, right there in the water. He driftwoods away from me, facedown, across the sudden pond. Storm doubles back, curious, and then bends down and laps up a little of the water. I get to my feet, my neck and shoulder throbbing where he landed on me. I run my finger along my collarbone and feel for a break, but it seems only the birthplace of a horrendous bruise.

Behind me, the gutted tank has slowed to a steady drip. The stallion finishes his drink, unimpressed, and then blows once and skips over toward me, steering clear of the widening puddle. He scratches impatient at the ground.

"I am aware of the hour. I'll be with you directly." I think about leaving the boy where he lay, but it don't feel right. The ruined suit—sogged through and heavier than a buffalo hide—clings to my skin as I slosh over to him. I grab the back of his collar and drag him out of the water and turn him over. Brown water dibbles from his open mouth and beads up on the straggly hairs a boy his age would proudly call a beard. There is some stature to him, but otherwise he lay caught between hay and grass young enough to have a momma who expects him home for supper. Best she never knows her boy begged for his life at the end and died—eyes open—in a foot of dirty water. He may have lost his nerve for killing as soon as he saw me, but that don't mean he didn't ride out here with murder in his heart. Sometimes that's enough. Other times it don't even take that much.

I take the rope from the saddle and tie the boy's ankles together and loop the other end around the saddle horn. Then I grab Storm's bridle and we drag him toward the boulder where the others are. "He shoulda chose better friends," I say. Storm throws me the wall-eye and blows long and hard, but I don't much care for his opinion at the moment. "Anyone finds his body, it's the same as if he made it back into town. Now point that blasted eye straight ahead. We got us a train to catch."

* * *

Ten minutes later, with Storm throwing down a hard canter, we catch up to the shuttle train as it plods along. I ride in my shirtsleeves, exposing as much of my sodden clothes to the wind and sun as I can. The shirt is nearly dry, but the trousers stick plenty damp against the saddle. The suit coat I have draped over the Spencer and it flaps beside me like a war flag.

A lone figure steps out the back door of the last car and wraps his meaty palms around the railing to steady himself. I must be quite a sight because his mouth drops open and he slumps against the pillar, gut-punched. His thick, red beard glows even redder against pallid skin that drains of color as the full meaning of my arrival dawns on him. Looking at him now, the ticket agent could be Kirby's twin. Half-brother be damned. I urge Storm forward until the train is close enough to touch, close enough so I can see the fear in the ticket man's gob-smacked eyes and he can see in mine, with no uncertainty, that his brother, and them who rode with him, are dead and their little plan foiled. Then when our eyes have said all of this I tip my hat to him and kick Storm on past the train, on to a life beyond this place.

CHAPTER TWELVE

Archbishop Lamy had hardly time to get cold in his grave before they slapped his name on the little depot and called it a town. The shuttle train sits nearly butted up against the backside of the depot, where the spur track dead-ends at a sharp angle. The only other building, set back a hundred yards from the main line, is a saloon called the Legal Tender, where the passengers from the spur—or them what got here on their own—can tie on one last cheap whiskey before paying double on the big momma herself. Sound of things, the Tender does a hearty business in the minutes leading up to departure. Every time the door bangs open, a gust of lively voices sweeps across the empty space between the buildings and echoes off the broad, open platform skirting the track.

A serpentine trail of trunks and travel cases winds down the middle of the platform—from the shuttle door all the way to the white-painted warning line guarding the main track. The red-bearded ticket agent stands at the end of it, distracted, no doubt wishing he were bellied up at the Tender bar, instead of ruminating how a simple plan of robbery and murder skittered so far off the rails. A black man in a porter's uniform wanders too close to Redbeard and gets a scorching earful for no discernable reason other than proximity.

"I 'spect we ought just stay where we be," I say, peering out from our shady perch, just east of the platform, beneath a stand of cottonwoods. Storm swats at a fly by way of agreement. Two more negroes unload crated provisions from a hand cart and stack them at the far end of the platform to await the train. A boy of about twelve—decked smartly in short pants, blue uniform jacket and matching cap—bounds between the two men like he owns the place. In one hand he balances a tower of cigar boxes taller than he is and with the other arm drags a small wagon piled high with apples, peanuts and what looks like every type of candy ever confected. Otherwise the platform is mostly empty, save for a few sullen families who couldn't find two pennies to rub together, most of them with small children and a few gunny sacks overstuffed with kettles, blankets and anything else they own. Tight-mouthed women keep the young ones close while the men folk peer down the track, anxious, or glance back at the saloon, wondering what a few extra dollars might taste like.

On the saloon porch, the lawyer, Ballentine, stretches his legs, stabbing the air with his whiskey glass as he clarifies some point or another to Owens, who mostly stares thoughtful out at the low mountains and offers the occasional nod between puffs on his cigar.

"I reckon that lawyer fella falls asleep asking one question and wakes up answering another." A beer would slide down glorious right about now—I admit—but there will be time for drinking once I see country rolling by through the fogged window of a moving train. Best we keep our distance from Redbeard. Three dead bodies and the muddy destruction of railroad property—no matter how warranted—dictate more caution than comfort. "Besides," I say, buttoning up the jacket and dusting it best I can, "this here suit of mine looks like it cleaned out the inside of a cannon. Once I get you situated, I reckon I ought to swap into my best bib and tucker 'fore mingling with the parlor crowd."

And then a trickle of sound, low and sweet, cries a mournful wail miles in the distance—like a mirage— so faint I wonder if I hear it at all. The people on the platform carry on as if nothing had happened.

"You hear that?" I ask. Storm's ears twitch—one forward, one back—daring the sound to return once more. It comes again, sure as the dawn, rising in strength and duration—a long, unbroken clarion that fills my heart with promise. All at once Redbeard straightens, the sound reaching the ears of White Men. He whistles sharply to the boy, who springs to his feet and sprints to the saloon.

"Train's coming, folks! Cut the gab and pay your tabs!" The boy's patter, well-worn as it is, gets an appreciative smile from the lawyer, whose idea of moving quick does plenty to explain why the South lost the war.

"Come on, amigo," I go to swing up and Storm lets out a snort, dancing away from me. "What, you throw a shoe? Let me have a look-see." The stallion lets me step in underneath and pull each leg back from the knee. His left rear shows a nail bent half an inch toward the hoof, but well clear of the tender part that would cause him pain. "Dang it, Berto used too long a nail. I 'spect that hard run didn't help none either. I know it's annoying, but it ain't like it quicked you. So don't you be carrying on like it did. We'll get you sorted out soon as we can. Come on." What really happened, I'm sure, is that Berto was too scared to be crawling back under Storm to fix his mistake and then was too scared again to tell me about it.

"I'm sure they got a decent farrier somewhere in California. Even though it is the end of the world." I throw the saddlebags over my own shoulder to lessen the weight and then take his bridle and walk him out toward the platform. The Legal Tender empties out, casting forth a sudden wave of expectant travelers that descends upon the snaking line of luggage, attacking it from all sides, until only a carcass of the heaviest cases remain. In no time the platform crawls with bodies migrating in a steady crush toward the painted stripe at the edge of the track. The whistle blows again, and what was once a whisper now cuts the air like a cannonball, bringing with it the pounding rattle and hissing valves of the Santa Fe herself.

Storm and I make our way down the near edge of the platform, steering clear of most of the crowd. Despite the excitement, those who drift our way manage to keep enough of their senses to allow the anxious stallion ample berth in all directions. When the Santa Fe unleashes her whistle a third time, from less than a quarter mile out, sound loses all meaning. It becomes a physical, punishing thing. Every bone in my body shudders. My balls want to shrink up and hide.

We stop short of the line. I turn my head down-track and behold the arrival of a breathing, snarl-tooth dragon. The gleaming cowcatcher curls into a fiendish grin beneath the perfect roundness of her forged and blackened face. A single, white eye glows in the middle, and all about her steam seeps and hisses from every orifice. A thick plume of smoke—fat as a tree trunk—rises from her blowhole, choking the air in her wake before dissipating skyward. Then her iron head passes, revealing a body that stretches for half a mile and counting, as segment after segment emerges from around the last bend of road.

The tender car sails by in a blur, followed by a stout, windowless coach and then begins a procession of identical coaches—the famous Pullmans—marching in unbroken formation before giving way to an assortment of box cars. As the train slows, I make out human forms hanging from the sides and a few more braving roofs. Their faces are uniformly dark, either negro by birth, or blackened by the unending trail of smoke that plagues brakemen.

I keep my eyes peeled for the stock car, and as the squealing whine of the brakes slows the Santa Fe to a crawl, I catch sight of a slatted car, ventilated, as if for animals. A few errant strands of hay jut from the slats. The smell of cattle leads me toward it, just as a door opens and a young man in boots hops onto the platform. The train has not yet come to a full stop when he turns back to the car and pulls free a wooden plank that slaps against the ground, forming a ramp up to the car. Cows low from inside. Then the train stops completely and a chorus of braking mechanisms sing out in defiant unison. Spontaneous applause breaks out from the crowd. The train, at rest, dwarfs the depot and surrounding bushes. The shuttle looks like a child's toy next to it.

"I 'spect you're the fella I'm looking for," I say. The young man's eyes brighten at the sight of us, although I don't think I'm much the one he notices.

"Blimey, ain't he a right corker." The young man stops cold, and with his head high and shoulders relaxed, brings his hand up slow into Storm's vision and scratches the crook between throat and jaw. I take comfort in his good horse-sense, and Storm, dipping his head to get the most out of the affection, is long past sold.

"Usually takes a fistful of carrots to get that close."

"He's in bloody good hands with Charlie, sir." Charlie's accent reminds me of a gambler came through the Bend once, name of London Joe, only not as fancy. "Born in the stables, me-self. Breaking thoroughbreds since I was wee, but none as fine as this one. What's he called, sir?"

"This here is Storm."

"Storm, 'course he is. Be a thrill to see what this one here could do 'round the turf at Dorchester. Those punters wouldn't know what hit 'em."

"Reckon you'll be needing these." I hand over the tariff receipt. He frowns and takes a look, his eyes making clear that paper-pushing is the part of his job he favors least. "You got any mares on board?"

"Nothing but forty head of angus. There's one bull, but I got him secured down at the far end. That leaves this end all for his lordship."

"Let's have a look-see."

Charlie takes hold of the bridle and, with a sure hand, leads Storm up the ramp and into an empty stall lined thick with fresh hay. A sack of oats lay in the corner and Storm sets straight to work on it. I care mostly about the construction of the walls, which are heavy slabs of oak that look sturdy enough for the job of keeping Storm in. As far as keeping a bull out, there ain't much that can be done to stop a bull from doing what he sets his mind to, but the walls are built high enough to keep all parties from eyeing each other and that should do the trick. The stall itself is a tight fit, but not unreasonable, with room enough for Storm to turn around, or lay down in the hay if so inclined. Charlie reaches for the door and starts to exit the stall when all at once a wave of trepidation knots up in the pit of my stomach. I bound up the ramp and inform Charlie about the bent nail. He tells me not to fret about it and then I list off a couple of treats he ought to keep handy if Storm gets to kicking, and after that I tell him don't bother trying to put a bag over Storm's head to quiet him because he don't like it and it'll just make things worse.

Charlie nods to all of it, but there's a little smile he's fighting off, and then he says, "Mister Harlan, sir. Might be best if I give you two a minute, but I shouldn't be taking much longer than that. She'll be pushing off soon." And with that Charlie hops down the ramp, gets on with his business. I give Storm a rub on his flank.

"Now listen here, amigo. Charlie's got you fixed up like a king, so I don't want you giving that boy no trouble, hear?" Storm rolls his wall-eye over toward me to say he's thinking about listening, but otherwise he stays facedown in his oats. "Ain't either one of us comfortable acting like gentlemen, but that's what we got to do. Just for three days. Ain't nothing we can't do for three days." I splash my hand into the water bin so he knows it's there if he wants it. "Hell, I'd squeeze into a ball gown if that's what it took to get your ornery hide to California." Then the lump in my stomach tries to move up to my throat and I figure I better go. "First stop, I'll come back and check on you."

Don't forget to wear your ball gown.

"Keep up that jokering, first stop'll be the glue factory."

"What's that, sir?" Charlie asking as I jump down from the car.

"Nothing." I press a gold piece into his hand. "Here's five dollars and there's five more when we get where we're going."

"Very much obliged, Mister Harlan. Are you all right, sir?"

"This thing do kick up some dust, don't it?"

"That it do, sir. And plenty of hot ash to go with it. Let's be getting you squared away yourself, then. Mister Burke!" Charlie hails a porter moving down the platform. With the bulk of the passengers already aboard, the platform is nearly empty again, a fact not lost on the consternated face of the man called Burke.

"Would you be Mister Harlan, sir?" Burke says, finding me through eyes as coffee brown as his skin, with a generous sprinkling of gray in the cropped, dark hair peeking beneath his porter's cap. I nod in the affirmative as Charlie hands me over. Burke's face relaxes, but maintains a ripple of irritation. "That would be everyone accounted for, then," Burke marking something down in a manifest, which he rolls up and stuffs in his uniform. "I don't much care to lose a passenger 'for we even shove off."

"I apologize. Had to secure my horse."

"Usually it's the women need securing. Let me help you with those." He takes the satchel and one of the saddlebags onto his shoulder and leads me back toward the nearest Pullman. Farther down the platform, a conductor blows long and hard into his whistle.

"All aboard! Last call, all aboard." The conductor does a final turn and ducks up into the engine well. Burke climbs up the steps of the Pullman and I follow, now certain that his carrying my bags has little to do with earning a tip and everything to do with ensuring a speedy departure.

"Y'all don't mess around."

"That we don't, sir," Burke looking back at me to drive it home. His gaze catches on the butt of the Spencer poking out over my shoulder, and he is about to say something, but then stops. We pass compartments when men stow the last of the luggage and women settle squirming children into their seats, many of whom press their small faces against the glass and wave to the scattered well-wishers on the platform. Then the brakes release, the whistle peals, and through a sliver of window I see the depot start to move. A moment later I feel the motion of the train and the track undulating underfoot.

As the Santa Fe builds her speed, I trudge behind Burke, still searching for my train legs. Burke simply puts a slight forward lean into his stride to counteract the train's momentum. Despite his age—which I put near sixty—the facility with which he negotiates his domain speaks to the surefootedness of a railroadman. The other employees we pass—conductors, apprentices and porters—display similar aptitude. To a man, they move with the breezy confidence of sailors on the high seas.

We reach the first of the coaches, and I will admit that the onslaught of noise, heat and general commotion—not to mention the assaultive odors of competing cuisines—assures me the overpriced ticket in my pocket was well worth the splash. Coach after coach blends into the next in a thickening cloud of tobacco smoke, Burke banging open the door at each new car and giving it just enough fling to allow me to pass through before it slams shut behind me. A narrow hallway skirts us around what smells like the galley car and another that smells like the WC. Finally we cross into the Pullmans, the noise and smoke and heat plummeting to a tolerable, even comfortable, level the moment the door opens.

"I would have you all the way down on the end, wouldn't I?" fatigue barely coloring the astuteness of Burke's voice.

"Can't say I mind the walk."

"Yes, sir," Burke minding considerable more than I do. The individual berths—most of them with drawn privacy curtains covering the portals—line the left side of the corridor. The right side is dedicated to a row of windows, where the landscape rolls by at full gallop. A man approaches from behind us, the urgency of his footfalls conveying a priority of mission to supersede that of any traveler or employee. I step aside, Burke doing the same, and as I turn spot a grim-faced man decked in black ditto coat that sends a ripple of cold recognition down my spine. The Pinkerton man does not slow as he passes. Rather, he scowls, his eyes seeming to appraise my entire person—rifle included—with singular irritation.

"Thought your company quit running the buffalo train."

"That's correct, sir," Burke offering with some apology. "There's no hunting or shooting permitted from the Santa Fe."

"Good. Fool's folly anyway," the black coat heading for the door at the far end of the car. "We've wasted enough time as it is."

"Yes, sir," Burke relieved as the Pinkerton bangs out of the Pullman and jams a key into the windowless, steel door of the next car. The heavy door slams shut behind him.

"What's a Pinkerton doing here?"

"He's the expressman," Burke resuming his walk. "You won't see him again till California."

"What about the WC?"

"They got everything they need in that express car. Even cook they own meals."

"What'd he come out for then?"

"Well, sir, most likely to see what the delay was." Burke shrugs, sheepish, and comes to a stop outside the last berth. He opens the door and shows me where I'll be living. At first glance—despite the silk upholstery of the lone chair and the dark, stained wood of the folding table—between the two of us,

Storm come out far ahead in usable square footage. "It may look a might cozy, but it's a marvel of engineering." Burke sets the luggage down on the narrow bed and pulls back the curtains, the bright midday glare filling the compartment. Just outside, the sagebrush zooms by too fast to make out individual plants, instead creating the effect of a dusky blue stream skirting the patchy golden country that sweeps upward toward what appears to be Placer Mountain. I ponder that, within the hour, every peak and formation passing beyond the glass will be something new and unfamiliar. Burke bends down and reveals an empty cabinet beneath the bed. "This here's your storage. And you got some more drawers over here," the porter sliding out a drawer and closing it again. "You want me to unpack you, sir?"

"No, I need to get myself correct." I flop the saddlebag into the chair and dig down for the other suit, still wrapped in brown paper. Burke walks over, scratching his chin.

"If I may, sir. That there Spencer won't fit in the cupboard, even with that short barrel, but I know just the place where it'll be out of the way."

"I'd be obliged," removing the rifle and handing it to him, stock first. "Unless you think we'll come up on some buffalo." Burke hefts it in his hands and I detect a hint of a smile.

"No, sir. The hunting trains proved a little too popular."

"Not with the buffalo."

"No, sir. I 'spect they objected mightily." Burke takes the rifle to the foot of the bed and gently tugs at the thin mattress, revealing a hidden recess along the sideboard. He slides the rifle into it and replaces the mattress good as new, with nary a bulge or indication of anything amiss.

"Anyone busts in while I'm sleeping, I don't even have to roll outta bed. They build it like that on purpose?"

"More like a happy accident."

"Somebody had to be the first to figure it out."

"Well sir, let's just say there ain't a inch of this train that can't be used for something other than what it was built for. Everything got a second purpose."

"Even this chair?"

"Sir, that chair fold out flat to a bed, though a man wouldn't know by looking at it."

"Well, ain't I the dunderhead."

"Sir, I hope I don't offend. I was simply making conversation." The porter's eye hitches, his palms spread in apology, as if he's overstepped—and to a White Man, I'm sure he had.

"You don't offend, Burke. I was being a wiseacre. What I get, trying to question a man on his own trade."

"Thank you, sir."

"I only laid out the one bed, seeing as you have the berth to yourself, but I'm happy to make it up when we stop for supper at the Harvey House."

"Harvey, who's that?" Burke scratches his head and I know I stepped into one of those clodhopper questions that a man with a double berth ought be knowing. But I figure, better to ask it now then to bust it out in the bar car with the cake-eaters.

"Well, now, Mister Harvey is a businessman, got himself a string of restaurants all along the line that done near put our galleys out of business. But truth be told, no one 'round here put up much of a fuss on that. Save us the trouble of cooking up a bunch of meals. Now we just wire the orders on up ahead, and the hot food's waiting when you get there."

"Model of engineering."

"That it be, sir." I peel out of the mud-stained ditto coat and set to unfastening the shirt buttons. "Was that a yes on making up the second bed, Mister Harlan?"

"Not unless you got someone soft to put in it."

Burke buries a smile and says, "Afraid it's not that kind of train, either, sir."

"Well, in that case, you better point me toward the bar car." I palm a dollar into his hand before he can answer.

Turns out the gray suit Pete made fits even better than the brown one. I splash some water on my face, square my hat, and bound down to the parlor car feeling like a new man.

"Ah, Harlan." I am not surprised that Spooner Ballentine found the bar before I did. He sits across from Owens, both of them on high-backed velvet chairs that rotate toward me as I push through the door into the plush comfort of the parlor.

"Mister Owens," I say, removing my hat. "I believe I'll have that drink now."

CHAPTER THIRTEEN

Hard country rolls past, brown and gold in the lengthening shadows. Each mile that ticks off—putting distance between me and a swirl of trouble—unclenches a knot in my gut just a little more, although the whiskey has a dog in that fight too. I spin my chair and, before it comes to rest, the waiter sees my empty glass and heads over with the bottle on a silver tray. He lowers the tray and I set the glass on it and he pours a healthy slug and holds the tray steady while I take my glass again. Then he goes back to the sideboard and marks the purchase of my third whiskey down in his little book—the reckoning to be settled later. Such is the privilege of wealth. The richer you get, the more conversation has a way of becoming unnecessary. I reckon if she set a mind to it, the Queen of England could navigate a whole day's worth of royal business flapping nothing but her eyebrows. Good thing too. All the air coming out of Spooner right now, the Queen would have to busy herself with breathing just to dispose of it.

The lawyer had switched subjects from the war to

politics and back to the war again and there were a few minutes in there where somebody, just to button him up, tried to corral him to the unfamiliar territory of hog farming. But Spooner just shifted on a dime into a formal oration on the merits of crossbreeding a Berkshire shoat with a Tamworth sow. At that point, with the smooth timbre of his voice harmonizing the train's hypnotic rhythms, I closed my eyes and had nearly drifted off when I felt my glass sliding off my knee and it brought me back again. The waiter spotted the empty and approached with the bottle.

"Despite the popular sentiment of my heritage," Ballentine says, "I find no repugnancy in miscegenation, whether it be swine or Homo sapiens. Why, even my own mother developed a predilection for a certain house negro, light skinned as he was. And I assure you, daddy was no stranger to the charms of Nubian pulchritude. Lord knows how many coffee-colored siblings trying to sharecrop their way out of penury could call me half-brother and not be lying."

"Would get 'em strung up, though. Wouldn't it?" Owens lighting his second cigar.

"In the wrong company, it just might," Ballentine says, conceding a fact that disappoints him. He stares out the window in a rare moment of reflection.

"That why you come west," Owens asks. "To get away from all that?"

Spooner's gaze softens and he gestures his empty glass toward the waiter. The car has cleared out, save the four of us, with most of the passengers taking their drinks elsewhere, blaming either Spooner's diatribe or the thickening raft of tobacco smoke as the likely reason.

"Who's to say why any of us make the migration?" Spooner, in one of his more confounding habits, answering a question with another question. Owens shrugs, holding his glass directly as the waiter pours, skipping the tray all together.

"For me the question's easy. To get rich. Soon as I shake the color from the ground, it's back to Philadelphia. My wife finds the West a bit too rugged."

"Well, you would not be the first to cross the Divide in search of fortune. I suppose for me, the motivation is rebirth." Spooner goes back to looking out the window and I can see there is more to his story, but I let it go and suspect Owens does the same.

The waiter takes the quiet to swap out the ashtray, asking, "Would you object if I opened a window, sir?"

"Object?" Spooner lighting up, even though the question was aimed at Owens. "My good man, I sustain most heartily. This compartment could use a rebirth of its own." The waiter lifts a pair of latches on the window and brings the top pane down a few inches. He lingers there, stealing gulps of fresh air before returning to the sideboard. Spooner turns in his chair and looks at me. "What about you, Harlan? What brings you beyond the frontier?"

I take a sip of whiskey and feel the burn in my throat and the eyes of the room upon me. I have no idea what I am going to say. And then I open my mouth.

"Rebirth, is it?"

"That's right."

"That'll do fine." Spooner smiles a sly grin, acknowledging a connection of secrets left unsaid. But Owens, normally a man of circumspection and reserve, can't help but stick his toe in the water.

"Hell, a young fella like you's hardly past his first birth. You musta scorched some bridges, be on number two." I hold no ill will toward Owens and attribute his poking about to boredom, and a desire to hear the voice of someone other than Shelby J. Ballentine. But I have no mind to elaborate and have no sooner evaded the cloud of expectation when the door bursts open and two sturdy young bucks—nineteen if they're a day—fill the doorway. Stuffed uncomfortably into their suits and neckties, they look like Protestant farmboys who can't wait to strip off their church clothes and break for the nearest swimming hole. But they carry enough size and muscle to warrant caution. And there's two of them. I feel my spine straighten, boots flat to the floor. Neither man cares to remove his cap when he enters, their eyes combing the car, as if unsure of its purpose. The blond works something small and white in his fingers as he steps toward the three of us.

The darker one, an inch taller than his tow-haired friend, rests on his broad shoulder a heavy, wooden club. I sit up in the chair, the pistol pressing hard and reassuring against my hip.

The smaller man finds his throat and says, "We in the right place to get a couple sarsaparillas?"

The waiter nods and motions them toward the vacant chairs next to Ballentine, the lawyer watching the boys with delighted interest. I let drift any thought that this corn-fed pair would mean me harm. Despite their physical attributes, the awkwardness they show in a civilized setting cancels out any threat of their being hired muscle. Still, the wooden club I can't figure until Spooner weighs in.

"I say, if you boys are looking to bat for the White Stockings, you'll be needing the eastbound train to Chicago."

The blond lights up and shows the white object in his hand to be some kind of ball, which he slaps from one hand to the other.

"No sir, we're headed out to the California Leagues. Hear they're paying top dollar for boys what can play."

"Well, that's fine. Fine indeed," Spooner says. "Make yourselves at home."

"Not too at home," Owens interjecting, "Best keep your shirts and shoes on."

"I'm fixing to try out for the San Francisco Emersons, hear they're hurting for infielders. My cousin George, here, he's got his eye on the Pioneers, on account of everybody needs a hard-slugging catcher."

"So you know how to swing that thing, son?" Spooner pointing toward the lumber on George's shoulder.

"Ain't a pitcher in Nebraska I can't take deep," George hefting the club, his hands choking around the thinner end. "Ain't that right, Skip?"

"From both sides of the plate too," his cousin adding. "Here, show 'em." Skip takes a step back and George retreats to the farthest end of the car, widening his stance as he raises the club with both hands over his right shoulder. Skip lofts the ball underhand, and as it arcs upward, the room breaks into a panic. The waiter drops the silver tray, his black skin ashes white in horror. Ballentine spins his chair toward the window, hoisting a meager newspaper for protection as his whiskey and cigar tumble to the floor. I stare in amazement as George locks eyes on the ball, and I feel a sudden dread at what is about to happen. But all at once Owens springs from his chair, leaping across the room and snatches the ball before it descends into certain disaster.

"Whoa, boys," Owens never losing his cigar. "Save it for the supper break, will ya?"

"Aw, we was just messing around," Skip waving him off. "Weren't we, George?"

"I can lay down a bunt, drop that pill right between your shoes, fella. You don't need to be jumping in."

"Settle down, friend. I ain't taking your toys away," Owens offering the ball to the reddening George. "But who wants to see a slugger playing small ball?" George holds a heavy stare on Owens, not yet sure if he's being made fun of. And Owens, for his part, seems ready to go whichever way George decides to play it. That's when Spooner regains his knack for interjection.

"How 'bout those sarsaparillas? Put 'em on my tab," Ballentine wagging a finger at the waiter, who only now collects his tray and what's left of his nerves. "Let's all have a seat and discuss America's game. Now, how about that collapse of the Knickerbockers last fall? Faded down the stretch like a two-dollar nag."

"Well, they ain't got no pitchin'," Skip chiming in. The waiter searches through a cabinet and comes out with two dusty brown bottles, which he wipes off in a hurry and pops open.

"True," Ballentine considering, "but their batters went colder than a witch's broom handle." The waiter thrusts a bottle into George's hand, stealing his attention enough to break the standoff. Owens turns away and starts for his seat again. He catches my eye as he passes, whispering, "I doubt the state of Nebraska shed a tear at their departure."

"Appreciate the sody pop, sir," Skip finding his manners for the first time since arriving. His cousin's search continues.

"Pleasure is mine, gentlemen." Spooner bends to retrieve his glass—empty, but unbroken—from the carpet. But the waiter beats him to it and retreats to the sideboard to fetch a clean replacement. Spooner's cigar, orange-tipped and glowing, has already returned to its place of importance.

The door opens, noisier this time—as the Santa Fe has built her speed—and the butcher boy enters, spots the lawyer, and says, "Who ever heard of drinking whiskey without salted peanuts? Brings out the flavor."

"Ah, a bag of peanuts would do nicely, my boy."

"Five cents, sir." The boy reaches into a pail, retrieves a small burlap bundle—the peanuts preapportioned for easy commerce—and hurls the sack across the car to the unsuspecting Ballentine who traps it, ham-fisted, against his ample chest.

"Kid's got an arm. We ought see if he can hurl a screwball," Skip says.

"You keep any sandwiches in there?" George rubbing his belly.

"Yessir. Ten cents apiece and fresh made in Lamy. I got hamsteak and hard cheese, or corned beef with pickle relish." George crinkles his nose at the options. "If that don't sound good, I'll make you a jelly fold-over."

"Gimme the corned beef," George fishing out a dime.

"What kind of jelly on them fold-overs?" Owens wandering closer.

"Apricot preserves. Straight from my daddy's orchard."

"I'll bet it is," Owens scoffs, flicking a dime from his thumb. The boy snags it with a grin.

"Born salesman," Spooner says.

The door opens again and Burke enters, notepad in hand. He sees the boy and frowns.

"Now don't you be spoiling everyone's nice supper with your candy." The boy just grins like a puppy that knows he's too cute to spank.

"No one goes hungry on my train, Mister Burke."

"Oh, it's your train now is it, Master Reginald?" Burke says.

"It will be someday," Owens answering. "I can guarantee that." Burke pulls a stub of pencil from behind his ear.

"Dining room or the counter, Mister Harlan?"

"Huh?"

"Your supper, sir. Got you a choice at the Harvey House. Dining room or standing at the counter. They's awful fancy in the dining room. Truth be told, it's all coming from the same kitchen no matter which way you go."

"Counter's fine, I reckon."

"Nonsense, my boy," Spooner frowning. "No friend of mine eats standing up like a horse. Put him at my table, Burke. He's my guest."

"Much obliged."

"I extend the invitation to all present, of course."

"Hey, that's swell of ya, sir." Skip beaming. George raises his bottle, tacks on a nod.

"Thank you, Ballentine, but I got the family." Owens says. "You don't want them monsters messing up a nice meal."

"Tallywhack, children add color to any meal."

"Oh, they add color, all right. Usually all over their faces. But thank you, Spooner, be our pleasure."

"Pleasure is mine."

"That'll be eight for supper, then, Mister Ballentine."

The lawyer beams wide and says, "Like Sunday dinner at my grandmamma's."

Burke turns to me, his notepad rife with fresh scribbling. "In that case, Mister Harlan. All you need do is decide what you're having so the kitchen can get it firing. Choices tonight are Cornish hen or salmon croquettes." He lowers his voice and adds, "Truth be told again, that's the choice every night."

"Which is better?"

"There's about as many salmon in the Territory as there is buffalo, if you catch my drift."

"I'll have the hen."

CHAPTER FOURTEEN

Ten minutes past Coolidge, the Santa Fe uncorks her whistle and begins the grand pageant of her arrival at the Harvey House. I join Ballentine and the others on the observation platform as the low, widespread building comes into view. Modeled after one of the great Spanish missions, the Harvey House sits protected by a pair of rolling hills at the mouth of a green valley and carries all the stateliness of a centuries-old casita—the kind that might anchor some venerable ranch or homestead—but the freshlaid stonework, still unsullied by the elements, betrays a construction newer than the railroad itself. The train commands all the attention she can muster as she brakes and steams and wails—sending Owens's children into dizzy circles of excitement until the young boy, overwhelmed by the noise, bursts into tears and flies upward into his father's arms. The little girl clutches her mother's hand.

"Can I have another chocolate, mother?"

"Of course you may not." Owens's wife wipes a

smudge of chocolate from the little girl's mouth. "I shall look forward to a proper supper," she says, turning to her husband, "before our children completely forget what it's like to sit at table."

"They sat at table last night," Owens says. "If that weren't proper, I got a bill from the 'Dorado says otherwise."

"Please don't confuse a lack of alternatives as justification for overpriced pig slop. I am not entirely unfamiliar with economics."

"That you are not, my dear."

"A pitiful excuse for pheasant. I've a good mind to pen a stiff note to the odious Mister Rawlings and let him know I shall be warning the Presbyterian Sisters to steer clear—"

"All right, Clara May, don't get yourself all twisted up." Owens slips his arm around her waist and pulls her close—the move settling her anger in an instant. She gazes up at him, doe-eyed, her mouth softening. Owens shakes his head, a smile forming, and all at once they wear the easy love of teenagers. Then the little girl tugs at Clara May's dress, delighted by the sight of uniformed young women assembled into formation at the main entrance of the Harvey House.

Skip elbows George. "Holy cow, it's true," jamming a finger toward the women. "The Harvey Girls. I thought they was just a story."

"Oh, the Harvey Girls are most real," Spooner says, "but I have read that the young ingénues reside under heavily chaperoned stewardship that leaves little room for dalliances."

"What's that mean?" Skip asks.

"What it means, son," Owens chomping his cigar,

"is that them cubs don't take a step sideways without mamma bear slapping them back in line."

"I'm up for the sport of it," George says, flat-voiced. His eyes comb the women with the coldness of a circling hawk.

"Now don't go getting some young lass in trouble," Spooner says. "One infraction can get a girl sent back home."

"Yeah, and since Spooner's the one splashing out, you boys keep your peckers in your pants."

"James Owens!" Clara May driving a soft fist to his bicep. "Please forgive my husband, gentlemen. The West has turned him into a pirate."

I bend Ballentine's ear and let him know I'll join the party in the dining room directly, after a brief check on the stallion. I slip under the guard rail and jump onto the landing while the train is still moving, aiming to reach the stock car before hungry third-class passengers impede my progress. The afternoon sun burns hot on my neck and the heat bakes upward from the dark, unfaded boards of the new platform. I make it to the stock ahead of Charlie, and find Storm bedded down in his stall on a mountain of fresh hay. His tail swats idly as a lazy dog's, and I can tell he has been well-fed, but he feigns near starvation at the sight of me.

"You ain't fooling me, chump." I fish out the sugar cubes I bought from the butcher boy and press them flat-palmed up to the space between the slats. He blows hard and lolls his head over as he manages to suck up every cube, despite the weakened state of his

obvious neglect. "I'd track down Charlie and see
about giving you a stretch, but I'd say you're too fat
and happy to think about moving. I'll check back
on you."

By the time I double back across the platform, a
line of people winnows from the side entrance of
the Harvey House all the way down the platform to
the train and then curls back on itself and is still
growing by the minute from those dawdlers who
couldn't get off the train in time. I spy Burke di-
recting traffic up ahead through a cloud of greasy
smoke that wafts down from the kitchen chimney.

"This here's the line for the counter, Mister
Harlan," Burke removing a handkerchief to dab the
sweat beading his upper lip. "Your people's on up
in the dining room." He points toward the main
entrance, where the squadron of uniformed women
has broken up—their duties now calling them inside.
Only a lone matron remains at the doorway, and
next to her a stick-and-bones girl of indeterminate
youth. Both wear black, ankle-length dresses and
white aprons. Although hardly flattering under any
circumstances, the get-up has a way of accentuating
the older woman's fatness and, in equal measure,
the unfortunate lack of curves on her beak-nosed
apprentice. I figure George's leering has been all
for naught, as the famous Harvey Girls turn infa-
mous upon close inspection.

"May I help you?" the matron's cruel lips twisting
the words out.

"I'm with the party, name of Ballentine."

"Ballentine," her eyes furrowing and she draws a sausage finger down a list of names. "And your name?"

"Harlan."

"Harlan?" the name falling on her ears like a foreign tongue. I look past her into the dining room, where Spooner's laugh draws my eye to a round table in the back corner. "Would Mister Ballentine be expecting you?"

"I don't reckon he's got that empty chair next to him for his hat."

The woman's mouth tightens, the fat in her neck shuddering with disapproval. The beak-nose girl goes wide-eyed, a wave of terror flickering behind them. Then I am certain she bites a ribbon of lip to keep from smiling.

"Agnes, if you would show this man to table six. He's already missed the soup course."

"Right this way, sir," the beak-girl composing herself as she steps forward. I am about to follow when I stop and turn back to the matron.

"What kind of soup I miss out on?"

"Barley porridge," the matron says, in a tone meant to sting. But the words have the opposite effect, thickening in the back of my throat as the thought of porridge—barley or otherwise—produces a reflex of revulsion.

"Well, more for you then, ma'am." I nod to Agnes and she leads me into the pink dining room as I add, "I reckon there ain't a speck goes unattended in her soup bowl." A sound comes out of Agnes like a cat sneeze, flushing her skin plum red. She weaves through a row of white-clothed tables on buckled knees, burying her face in her hand to stifle a laugh that would surely plant her on the first train home, but the din of conversation and tinkling silverware provides suitable cover. Harvey Girls whisk about in all directions, trucking in covered silver dishes and clearing half-filled bowls before the steam has left the barley.

"Ah, Harlan," Spooner jabbing a fork toward the empty chair next to him. I remove my hat and fix to plop it on the table, but the beak-girl takes it from me and heads for the wall rack, not yet fully recovered from our episode.

"Sorry I'm late," sliding into my chair. All at once the three whiskeys and the heat rear up together in a wave of tiredness. An empty coffee cup, crying out to be filled, reminds me that I have not eaten since the ham biscuit that seems a lifetime ago. The Nebraska boys sit to my left, napkins tucked into collars. Owen's family occupies the seats across, the boy plunked into a tall chair with its own little table that he can fuss about with. Clara May spoon-feeds him porridge, which he mostly spits out, causing her to frown and wipe his mouth with a napkin that never comes to rest.

"We were discussing the weather," Spooner says. "I was telling the boys how the dryness of the Western air wreaks havoc on my digestion. A little humidity helps lubricate the system."

"So does whiskey," Owens downing the last of his and raising the empty to the nearest serving girl.

"I think Mister Ballentine's point," Clara May grimacing, "is that the Eastern climate is more suitable to one's health. I must say I agree."

"Oh, I remember as a boy," Spooner launching in, "we'd take supper on the porch well into October. Daddy had the field hands working till nine, sometimes ten o'clock. We'd watch them haul their bales from the fields over a slice of Tituba's strawberry pie. Of course things are different now. Your man Sherman made sure of that."

"Must be nice," Skip says, "the way you Rebs have it. Waiters like this every meal, smoking a pipe of tobacker what got picked right off your own land. Hell, who wouldn't want to fish all day if the chores is getting done by someone else?" A rare silence falls over the table. Even George looks embarrassed. "What? What'd I say?"

Spooner's eyes, weighted with gentle pity, land on Skip.

"You are aware, son, that the South did not emerge victorious from the conflagration?"

"Sure," his voice uncertain. "I'm just saying, is all."

A plain-looking girl approaches with a bottle of whiskey and fills Owens's glass. I catch George as he tilts his head to view the entirety of her figure. He makes an unenthused appraisal and goes back to his soup, which he scrapes the last of onto his spoon and slurps up.

"Something to drink, sir?" A lilting voice flutters behind me. A different girl. I start my turn and feel the word "coffee" pass my lips before seeing to whom I have directed it.

"Right away, sir." Her face shielded in mystery, a young woman turns from me. The silly, bat-winged bonnet obscures any view of skin, but an errant wisp of hair—straw-colored—pokes beneath the corner. She glides off in the straight line of a cat, and with the same feline surprise, bolts sharply left, heading for a curtain. At the last moment, a pale hand emerges from her sleeve and tucks the stray hair into place, as if she could feel my eyes upon her—perhaps she can—and then she hits the curtain and is gone.

No amount of staring brings her back. "Your chicken's gettin' cold." Spooner's voice turns me center. Plated before me is a small bird, sadly under-roasted, fighting for space beside a mountain of mashed yams and an admirable scoop of succotash. Harvey Girls of every shape and size attend presently to our table, shucking off covered dishes, revealing main courses, all of which—fish and fowl alike—are subjected to a ladle of gravy from a large pot handled by the matron herself. The heftiness of the urn, I gather, requires arm strength that she alone—and none of the young ladies—possesses.

"Gravy," she announces, not waiting for an answer as she drowns Spooner's supper and moves down to me, bringing with her a scent entirely her own—a collective of sweat, liniment and bacon fat. I am presented with the quick dilemma of waving her off or holding my breath to avoid inhaling more of her. I make my decision and soon my plate is swimming like the others. A plain, but handsome, young woman reaches in front of George and uncovers his plate.

"You pull you up a chair, darling. There's enough for both." George flashes a crocodile grin. "Hell, you can sit right on my lap." The girl swallows a polite smile, but it gets no further before the matron has wedged herself between them, shutting George down with a withering scowl and a tightened grip on the ladle. I doubt his head would be the first to get a crack upside from her weapon of choice. And then as quick as the swarm had landed, the girls are gone and reconfigured elsewhere at another table.

"You know," Spooner stabbing at his meat, "I believe Mister Harvey could not have chosen a more unattractive garment if he had wrapped his young ladies in burlap sacks he drug out of a barn."

"Well, it ain't the Blue Duck," I say. Spooner blasts out a laugh that he cuts short for decency, but it is too late. Clara May has a counter opinion.

"Perhaps, gentlemen, the intention is to minimize distraction. He has a business to run, not a bordello."

"Bordello's a business, pet. Profitable one to boot."

"You know what I mean, James."

"I do, but if Harvey'd shorten them skirts a bit, he'd pull down a lot more coin that what he's getting slinging hash. No offense, Ballentine. This is swell."

"None taken. I'm inclined to agree."

"Lift those hemlines a single inch," Clara May raising a finger, "and not one train would leave here with the headcount with which it came."

"Some with more. Some less," George says.

"A disaster either way."

The silver spout of a coffee pot spears in from the left. Without thought I snatch up the empty cup with saucer and pivot from the waist to intercept the pourer. My attempt proves misguided, as cup and pitcher meet halfway in an awkward coupling that leaves neither party certain of the next move. Her bonnet brushes my shoulder, blocking my sight of the transaction and leaving to faith the steadiness of both our hands. Her face, still unseen, radiates furrowed concentration up through the starched wings of the infernal headdress. Feeling the weight of the liquid as it pours, all the assistance I can offer is to slow my quickening pulse and try to ensure that the thin little china cup stays level in my hand. The bonnet begins to move, clearing the line of sight to the cup and its rising contents.

Confident of her pour, the girl starts to straighten. Only then do I allow my eyes to move up her sleeve, past a gentle flare of breast and around the curved shoulder to the neckline—where skin the color of almond cream disappears beneath the starched collar and reemerges, descending into the divot of her neck and up to a sculpted chin. The coffee cup fills. All sense tells me to pull away, but I scroll upward. A band of freckles stretch above her cheekbones. I picture a belt of stars in the night sky. And then my eyes connect with hers and in a burst of light, a piece of something out of place corrects itself. I stare into puddles of pale, icy green—the winter water beneath a frozen mountain stream.

Our eyes widen—a secret transferring, its power too great—we recoil in unison. The spout of the coffeepot snags the lip of overflowing cup, pulling it off the saucer and upending it. My free hand shoots up, snaring the cup, but the hot liquid has no patience for my grasp and splashes through my fingers, down my suit front and into my lap. Still more coffee tumbles from the spout as she rears the pot back. My instinct, as the heat finds its way through the fabric to my skin, is to act as if nothing at all is the matter, sparing her—and the eyes surely upon us—any hint of my discomfort, which would further her embarrassment. A chorus of gasps from the others at the table undermines my subterfuge and sends the poor girl into near panic.

She slams the pitcher down hard with a clank, and

producing a wash cloth from her apron, begins to blot at the wetness in my lap. I become a statue. She touches the cloth to my thigh, and then, as if struck by a bolt of lighting at the inappropriateness of what she has done—rips her hands away. The cloth flops in my lap. Her hands flutter to her face, trembling.

"I'm terribly sorry, sir," her voice sick with worry.

"I messed you up. You had it in hand and I messed you up. I'm the one ought be apologizing." I hold her gaze and can see a jackrabbit of an idea bouncing back and forth behind those busy green marbles.

Then her brows furrow and she says, "Come with me." She grabs my hand and is already turning away when I feel myself rising, the cloth pressed against the wettest part with my other hand. She lets go of my hand and marches a good clip to the nearest curtain and ducks through. I have to double-time my stride to cut the distance. I slap through the curtain and she grabs my hand again and leads me down a dark corridor with curtains on all sides. Harvey Girls whiz past, this way and that, balancing trays and chirping orders—not a one giving more than a quick look at a fellow sister half-dragging a coffee-soaked dude through the inner workings of their domain.

The girl pushes through a swinging double at the end of the hall and we come into a laundry room with piles of clean, folded towels. She snatches one up and hands it to me.

"I got you all down the front of your nice suit. I am so sorry."

"I told you the error is mine. I have no cause to be interfering in your profession."

The sharp smell of lye rises from steaming tubs

behind her. Adobe walls drip with moisture and I feel the heat building beneath my jacket.

"It's hardly a profession. Your jacket seems all right. It's the trousers and shirt that are the problem. Take them off."

"What?"

"Please. We'll get them cleaned straight away. But if Packer sees that mess, I'll get sacked for sure."

"Ain't no way in tarnation that's going to happen." I peel off my jacket and she steps forward to take it from me. A patch of her skin brushes my hand. She hangs the jacket on a nail behind me. I snap off my tie and start to unbutton my shirt.

A round-faced young woman, a few years older than the green eyes in front of me, appears like a floating head above the swinging door and gawks at the sight of us.

"Hannah, what are you doing? Your table's nearly done with second course."

"I'll be right there. Cover me, will you? Start clearing plates."

"All right. And I'll get your desserts out. But hurry, girl. Packer's roaming the floor."

"Thanks, Gertie." The one called Gertie ducks out and Hannah—my girl's name is Hannah—says, "My cousin, Gertrude. We came out together. Missus Packer has it in for both of us."

"Packer. She that hefty crone out front."

"That's the one. Has a grudge against Presbyterians, says we're all just 'Baptists who can read.'"

I undo the last of my shirt buttons and hitch a pause as I touch my belt. The girl blushes, then turns around to face the wall.

"So it's Hannah." I unbuckle the belt and all at once remember the pistol in my trousers.

"Yes, that's right." I palm the pistol free and, turning backward, slip it into the inner pocket of the jacket hanging behind me. "Hannah Clinkscale. And whom do I have the pleasure of addressing?"

"Name's Harlan." There I stand in my union suit, with my trousers down to my knees and the shirt slung over my shoulder.

Then a biting voice snaps from the corridor. "Hannah? What's going on back here?"

"It's Packer," Hannah's whisper rife with panic. I see the matron's oversized bonnet bounding toward the swinging doors. Combing the room, my eyes fall upon an ash can. I grab it and, turning away from the door, bend over the can and commence to retching into it like my guts are seizing up on me. The door squeaks behind me.

"What's the meaning of this—"

"Can a man have some privacy!" the words come out of me like whip crack. I hear the large woman hold up at the doorway. I bury my face in the can and let loose another long retch, pausing only to shout out, "That hen was rancid! I think I'm dyin'."

"Rancid?" Packer aghast. "No one else has complained—"

"It's true, ma'am." Hannah running to my aid. She falls in next to me and holds my forehead, just like a dutiful nurse.

"Why are his pants down?"

"'Cause I puked myself."

"Hannah, better let me tend to him—" Packer says.

"Get the hell out of here," my viciousness halting

her. "Fetch the doctor. The *train* doctor. And be quick 'fore I tear my lungs out."

Packer hesitates, unsure of it. Then Hannah says, "It's spraying everywhere, ma'am. Best stay back."

"I'll collect the doctor. Hannah, you stay with the gentleman." Packer's girth sends the doors clambering against each other as she hustles out. We hold over the can until her steps fade and the two of us bust apart laughing.

"How did you know to do that?" Her smile beaming like the moon.

"I ain't got the foggiest. I seen enough fellas puke for real, I figure can't be much trick pretending."

The door to the outside opens and a negro woman, round as a berry, steps in from the harsh sunlight, carrying an armload of tablecloths, fresh from the line. She squints to adjust her eyes and then, seeing me there half-dressed, throws down her load and lays into Hannah something awful.

"Girl, what trouble you getting into? I don't need no carrying on in here!"

"It's all right, Livonia. This gentleman—"

"Spilled all over himself like a palsy case," I say, Livonia's eyes not yet satisfied with the explanation.

"We sure could use some help getting him laundered straight away."

"Before his train pull out? Miss Hannah, I can't be working no miracles, not with all the washing I got piled up already. Ya'll girls can't hardly keep your own selves presentable, what for I gotta be scrubbing up the customers?"

"It's just the shirt and trousers. They won't take but a plunge or two," Hannah countering.

"You an expert now?" Livonia's hands planted firm on hips.

"No, I would never assume—"

"That train pulling outta here in fifteen minutes. And how you expect this nice gentleman get back on that fancy train with soaking wet shirt and trousers? Ain't Miss Hannah gonna get in trouble for that. It's Livonia. And Livonia ain't having no trouble."

"Perhaps, ma'am, we could hang them by the kitchen chimney," I say, pulling off my trousers entirely. Livona's mouth hangs open, her eyes wide as saucers. I extract all the money from the pocket and transfer it to the coat, save for a shiny quarter-eagle that I present to her. She looks at the coin, then back at me, her face unchanged. "As for the washing, perhaps you could let me do that myself, if I promise not to get in your way." Livonia takes the coin. I move past her and drop my trousers into the steaming tub.

"Them nice clothes gonna smell all smoky," Livonia frowning.

"They'll catch the air in time. Don't reckon I have much choice. Besides, that train's so smoky, a little mesquite ought be an improvement." I ball up my shirt and throw that in on top of the trousers.

"What you gonna put on in the meantime?" Livonia vanquishing the coin to some hidden fold. "Because I can't be in here with no white man in his union suit. Mister Harvey himself would comb them hills looking for a tree limb sturdy enough to string up Livonia." Hannah springs to life and bounds to the far wall, where she plucks a workman's biball from a hook.

"Put these on," flashing a smile of well-kept teeth. I feel something stir and step into the biball. Then I turn for the basin, but Livonia waves me off.

"Oh, I ain't having you mess yourself up any more than you done already. Miss Hannah, you take him, find elsewhere to be."

"I ain't fit to sit at table, piecemeal as I am," I say, taking my jacket from the nail and sliding it on over the biball.

"I know just the place," Hannah collecting my hand as she strides for the door that leads outside.

CHAPTER FIFTEEN

Hannah guides me out the side door and into the smothering gold of afternoon sun. Her small hand squeezes mine, every tiny bone in perfect union beneath the silk of her skin. She banks a hard right and we slink along the rear of the building, hugging close to the adobe wall. We come up on a spot where the two sloping roofs that divide the house east and west converge in a low dip, just a few feet off the ground.

"What are you up to?" But she doesn't answer, quieting me with a finger to her lips. I am struggling to determine her plan when all at once a flash of mischief fires behind those eyes. She plants one foot on an upturned bucket and, rising upward, her other upon the lip of a rain barrel. She falters a moment—wavering—and quickly regains her balance, but I have already stepped in and lifted her up onto the lowest point of the roof. She accepts my help without looking back and launches into a series of carefully orchestrated maneuvers that carry her up past the first gabled window. She ascends in silence, that concentration from earlier returning in full effect, but the rote precision of her motions conveys a high familiarity with not only this particular gauntlet, but the complexities of climbing in general. Every feline has its hiding places and a mastery of how to get to them. She pauses, her head turning toward me with a baffled frown. I feel the dagger of her disappointment pierce my heart. She wants me to follow, of course, and in all of three movements I forgo the barrel entirely and swing myself up onto the roof. Her eyes go wide with fear that I will crash in a thunderous clang, but when my feet find their lightness and deposit me upright upon the undulating red tiles with hardly more than a soft tap, her smile reappears, broad as ever.

I follow her up the roof, the clay roof tiles baking beneath our feet. She wears strapped, blockish work shoes—another indignity of Harvey's required dress code—but travels light, served by practice and slight frame. She reaches the apex of the roof and stops, peering over the edge toward the front of the building. The Santa Fe stretches out before us on an endless ribbon of road, and beyond that, a snow-covered peak that I figure to be Mount Powell, but can't say for sure, on account of now having ventured beyond the boundary of my lifelong travels. The foreground behind shows the clotheslines and work sheds of the kitchen, leading out to gardens of tended crops, a corral for sheep, and a gleaming new barn. A green valley meanders back for miles, around some unseen water source, but is soon swallowed up by the towering rock slabs of the Malpais.

"That Bluewater Lake out yonder?"

"I couldn't say."

"Heck of a view up here."

"I know, but we can't stay. All somebody has to do is look up and I'm cooked. Don't worry, we can see plenty where we're headed." She sits her backside on the roof's spine and spins her legs onto the opposing downslope, unaware that she flashes a square of bare ankle. "We have to be quick about this bit, but I think we're good. Come on." She scampers down the roof on the building's front side. I swing over the top and go traipsing after her, both of us running down the roof like a couple of squirrels. We are halfway to the edge when I see a gap up ahead behind the ornate façade that faces out toward the road. She slows as she reaches the opening and slides down onto a stone-laid floor a few feet below. I jump down next to her and watch her grin curl with the slyness of a house cat. We stand on a false patio, unserviced by any door or window. Our view stretches clear to the mountains and offers superior surveillance of the immediate vicinity, both rail and restaurant.

"Pretty keen, huh?"

"Reckon so. And no one can see us?"

"They can't see me, I know that much. But you're tall. Your head sticks over the top of the wall." I hunch my shoulders as she says it, keeping a flex in my knees till my head sits level with the top of the façade. "But like I said, folks would have to look up to see you. And my experience, most folks don't think to look up."

"No, they don't."

"I'll show you the best part." She walks to her right, to the side edge of the building and peeks over. The drop to the ground is no more than ten feet. A nearby door opens below and one of the train porters steps out from the building, buttoning his fly in what he thinks is a private moment. Hannah slinks back from the edge, her voice in a whisper. "That's the WC for the help and the railroad boys. Door stays pretty busy, but it's the fastest way out of here."

"Fastest way up, I reckon too. Better than climbing over the roof."

"It's too steep. I've tried, believe me. That's why we gotta come the long way around."

"What for's a girl like you need with a hideout?"

Hannah sits down on the floor and pulls out a cigarette. I have my answer. She fumbles for a match, but I beat her to it and figure why not light one of my own.

"You be careful now," I say, shaking out the match. "Plenty good hideouts been undid by the sight of smoke."

"I blow it out slow," she says, exhaling a stream of blue vapor. "The wind takes care of me."

"Me too."

"Getting caught with one of these in my hand is what landed me here."

"That's a might strict. There's worse things than a girl twisting up a smoke."

"Not when it's behind the church." I shrug it off. Then she adds, ". . . and your dad is the minister."

"Heh. I reckon that could do it then. My mamma smoked a pipe."

"You get out of here, Mister Harlan," her voice brightening.

"Every night. When she couldn't find a good cigar." I set down next to her in the cool shadow and ask her how she got here.

"Cousin Gerty had already been accepted as a Harvey Girl, and when daddy found out, he said, "It's a sign from God. A year under Fred Harvey's care will make a proper woman out of you."

"Did he?"

"Who, Mister Harvey?" She scoffs through a plume of smoke. "Never set foot in the place, not in the month I've been here. Mister Duquesne runs the day-to-day. He's the manager. Best if he never learns your name. Otherwise, it's just Packer and a bunch of crones like her. The girls are all right, though. We look out for each other."

"But they don't know about this place, do they?"

"A couple do. But they're all too scared to make the climb. Mother always says I'm a bit of a rambler."

"You're a natural scout, what you are." That earns another smile and then she stubs out the smoke and rises, brushing her dress.

"I better run back, check on your clothes and what not. Packer'll be roaming the halls." She eyeballs over the façade and grimaces at the sight of a portly man in black suit and bowtie, standing out by the engine. "Oh, shoot, there's Duquesne now." The manager listens as the head brakeman explains something, pointing down at the wheels and then up at the steam pipe. Some of the engine crew gathers off to the side, hands on hips. "What's he facing this way for? Turn around, you old coot."

"Hang on a sec." I peek over the side and see the coast clear around the door to the WC. "I'll lower you down. Hurry, while no one's looking." I half expect a protest or even a hint of hesitation. Instead that devil fires again in her eyes and she jumps into my arms. I lift her, turning—her full weight no heavier than a dog—and hang her over the edge. I lock my arms stiff and she shimmies down them of her own power until her hands grasp mine. Then I hold them tight and bend from the waist, lowering her down until her feet dangle no more than two feet from the pavement. She hooks her eyes to mine and nods, her trust in me assured.

"Okay," she says. I let go and she drops with hardly a ruffle. Another smoothing of the dress and she disappears into the door. I barely have a moment to consider the last five minutes when I see Burke marching up from the train, and with him is a gray-haired man with a doctor's bag.

"Burke, up here." Both men fix their gaze upward, the surprise at finding me there apparent on their faces.

"Mister Harlan, I was told to fetch Dr. Ward, here. Everything all right?"

"Whatever I ate passed through already. Sorry to trouble you, doc." I find a gold piece from the coat pocket and flip it out to him, grateful that wall between us blocks their view of the biball. The coin spins high in the air and just as it begins its decent the side door opens and out steps a wiry infantry soldier. The doc misses the coin and it pings off the ground, rolling to a stop at the feet of the young private. The soldier pushes his kepi back and plucks up the coin. Then he looks up at me and then to Burke and the doc and deduces that it must belong to one of the men in front of him. He takes all of a second to figure the suited white man is the likely owner.

"Here you are, sir," The soldier extending the coin to the doctor, who takes it.

"Much obliged, son."

Then the soldier gazes upward, spreading a grin

of brown teeth and says, "but if you're throwing it down, I'll take the next one."

His humor gets a laugh from the doc and a smile from Burke, but something about it rings off. Then the lad tips his kepi and shuffles off toward the train. I make him for one of the guards from the express-man's detail, but as the private trudges off, I notice the tattered coat and flopping leather of his worn-out shoes. I somehow doubt the hard-nosed Pinkerton man would tolerate a sloppy uniform in his outfit and figure the boy is more likely a third-class passenger, on leave to visit kin or a sweetheart.

"Well, if your troubles return, Burke knows where to find me," the sawbones doffing his hat. He heads back toward the train, but Burke lingers.

"Anything I can bring you from your bag, Mister Harlan? Maybe some trousers," his gaze unwavering from me, though not so as to come off prying. Smart man, Burke.

"I reckon it's nothing I can't see to on my own."

"You know you's on a roof, ain't ya?"

"Better than down there, everybody fussing over me. I got it on good authority I'll be on board with the trousers I come with, but I can't promise they won't be a tad damp."

"Well, you can rest easy on that." Burke nodding toward the engine. "We on a bit of delay."

"I figured all the brakemen bunched up together probably weren't good medicine."

"She's leaking steam is all. The fire crew get that tightened up no time. Shouldn't be more than half hour. I'm fixing to head in, tell the others they ain't got to rush through dessert." Burke's eyes fix on something moving behind me and I don't turn around. Hannah's descent down the roof needs no further attention than what it receives on its own. "All right, Mister Harlan. I'll trust you not to alter my headcount in either direction. Anything other than what I come with cause me a mess of paperwork."

"I ain't partial to scribbling myself. I'll make sure I don't cause you none." Burke takes me enough at my word to nod and excuse himself into the building, well before Hannah drops in next to me—having retraced the path that brought us here originally.

"That porter saw me slinking over the roof."

"He's looking to avoid trouble more than you and me put together." I turn to face her and see my hat cradled under her arm.

"Thought you might feel more yourself beneath your own brim."

"That's fine thinking." She uncorks a grin that reminds me of the beauty I was hoping would peter out on second viewing. A blasted fool I am for thinking that. She hands me the hat and I see that underneath it she has a plate from the dining room with another plate turned upside down on top.

"What is that?" Squaring the hat to my head and feeling better about myself already.

"You didn't get your supper. And as that was all you asked of this establishment upon arrival, I took it upon myself to fix you a plate." She pulls off the top dish, showing off a fresh-made sandwich of barbequed beef and a layer of shredded cabbage.

"That weren't on the menu," I say, picking up the warm bread and bringing it to my mouth.

"No, it's tomorrow's supper, but cook likes to get a test of which way his sauce is going ahead of time." I chew in silence, the smoky sauce working with the beef and the vinegary snap of cabbage. "I know," Hannah reading my face. She offers me a napkin. "Cook barbeques up a ferocious brisket." Two more bites go down before I stop to dab at the corner of my mouth.

"Miss Hannah, you ain't got to wait here and watch me eat."

"I'm a waitress. Waiting is in the name."

"Never thought of that. But you must have chores need seeing to. I ain't looking to get you in any more trouble."

"Gerty's got me covered downstairs. I'll be doing her side duties for a week, but I don't mind."

A man's voice rings from the main entrance of the Harvey House, and I peek over the wall to see Skip jogging side-step out across the front lawn. His eyes stay fixed on the front door, until rising upward, tracking the white ball as it flies out over the grass in a long, gentle arc that gets Skip's arms churning and lolls the tongue from his mouth in concentration. He picks up speed—sprinting now—and with a boyish grin reels in George's throw over his shoulder, arms outstretched to full extension. Then he let's his momentum carry him outward into a dive. He tucks into a summersault over the manicured lawn and comes up beaming, the ball raised in victory, much to the delight of female voices. He shouts something to George and then drops the ball on the ground before bounding up the steps of the train.

A pack of bodies, young and old, filters out the front door, George at the lead and three Harvey Girls close behind. He pulls a billed cap from his back pocket and smushes it onto his head. Owens lights a cigar and collects his wife's hand as they stroll out onto the grass, the little ones chasing each another in wonderment at the wide, roaming lawn. Some young men from third class—Irish by the red in their whiskers—fall in beside George. A quick discussion ensues with George pointing out to a spot near the lightpost. The men start to fan out in that direction, but then Spooner, slow-moving down the center path, barks a suggestion that gets the men altering their alignment and reconfiguring it to his eventual satisfaction.

"Looks like a game is forming," Hannah resting her fingers on the edge of the façade. "Who is that man, telling the others what to do?"

"That's Spooner Ballentine, lawyering fella. He's a square fella, but there ain't a penny in the world he don't add his two cents to."

"I can see that. Let me take that for you." Hannah eases the empty plate from my hand and sets it down on the roof. I made such quick work of the sandwich I hope I didn't embarrass myself.

"You tell that cook he ain't need to fiddle his sauce none."

"I'll let him know," she says, a smile coming to her.

Skip returns from inside the train, his arms loaded with half a dozen leather gloves that he flings about to the men and boys gathered around George, though most of the players seem content to carry on barehanded. The butcher boy appears behind Skip, enlisted into service lugging the heavy wooden club, which George promptly takes from him. I don't pretend to have much notion on how this base game gets played, though I reckon the open space of the lawn suits the playing better than the confines of the bar car, as some of the men drift back a hundred yards or more and seem downright lonely, so removed from the action.

"Surprised you're not down there joining them," Hannah says.

"I prefer to gather up the particulars on a game before jumping in with the playing." A current of surprise splashes behind her eyes before melting into sweetness.

"I suppose baseball is still a novelty on the frontier. Back home, the boys were always starting a game after church. But this is the first one I've ever seen break out here. They say all you need is a patch of dirt."

"Fine evening for it."

"That it is." I feel the closeness between our elbows shrink in the softening light. A breeze passes through, and in the corner of my vision I see her hand brush that same unruly strand of hair back into place.

"You bring any other men up here?" I don't know what compels me to ask that, but she turns and gazes up at me, her brow crinkling.

"Mister Harlan, I resent that question. I don't even bring the other girls up here."

"Why me then?"

She hesitates, the water beneath the ice swirling deep and green. "I knew you'd follow me."

"Men would follow you anywhere. You know that. The West ain't nothing but dogs and wolves."

"Dogs and wolves would not get an invitation." A wave of shame boils up my belly and leaves me feeling downright small and regretful.

"In that case, thank you for inviting me, Miss Clink-scale." I remove my hat and with a bowed head, offer my hand. "And for the considerable pleasure of your company." She stares down at my hand, not ready to give in just yet. She crunches her mouth up and after a long moment, takes my hand in hers.

"You are very welcome, Mister Harlan," adding a small curtsy. I feel the rest of my name forming on my lips. I want to tell her all about myself. But I hold back.

"You know I'm getting on that train in less than an hour and we'll never see each other again."

"Well, then, you'll just have to write a letter some-day to Miss Hannah Clinkscale, care of Fred Harvey, Harvey House, Coolidge, Territory of New Mexico."

"I reckon I will."

"And as for our remaining hour, perhaps you'll wisely spend it as my viewing companion for the base-ball contest. That is, if you can comport yourself not to say something else foolish." Her eyes turn outward again, taking in the game, and as she resettles against the ledge, she narrows the distance between our hands—close enough to charge the hairs on my arm with her electric proximity. The breeze shifts, searing the fullness of her scent into memory. A hint of lavender soap rides atop. Beneath it, competing for attention, lay a dozen other traces I will be forever unpacking.

Over the western mountains, the big yellow eye touches the summit, splitting the valley, half in shadow and half in the gleaming gold of a majestic spring evening. George hefts the wooden club, chok-ing his grip down toward the skinny end. He takes a few swipes, building in speed and power and, even to my unfamiliar eye, wields that particular tool as an extension of himself. Spooner has perched himself close behind George and off to the side, and by his ceaseless instruction to all involved, appears to have appointed himself the game's commissioner. In between them, a stocky young hayseed rolls up his shirtsleeves and squats down behind George, extending his glove outward to receive the ball.

Skip works the ball into his palms as he marches out about twenty paces and stops, surveying the positions of the other fellas who have fanned out across the field, and offering some modest suggestion on their alignment. Then he turns to face George and leans in. An expectant hush befalls the gathered crowd. Skip's smile fades, his arm hanging loose at his side, fingertips dancing on the ball. George taps the bat to the ground and, with his feet spread in the balanced posture of an athlete, cocks the slab of lumber over his shoulder like it were made of paper. A toothpick bounces from one corner of his mouth to the other. The fielding players crouch into readiness. Even Spooner, his grapefruit of a belly protruding over the belt line, bends at the knees and peers in, lightly touching the squatting man who serves as his shield.

Skip straightens, and then twisting up onto one leg, rears back and uncurls his body toward the batter. The ball flies through the air—George tensing, then slackening in an instant—and smacks the leather glove of the catcher with a resounding snap.

Spooner rises and proclaims, "The pitch is low!" in full judicial timbre. A muted applause breaks out anyway. Skip snags the throw-back and sets into his windup again. He comes over the top this time and when he lets fly, the ball digs downward in a steep curve. But George, bending with it, muscles an uppercut that nicks the ball and sends it high into the air behind them. The direction must not mean much because the only pursuers are some small boys who run giggling after it while the players hold their ground and spit tobacco juice into the dirt.

"That ball is foul," Spooner says. The catcher lobs the ball to Skip who snatches it, jawing to himself in disgust. George points off in the distance and says something back to him.

"I wonder what he's on about, that one," Hannah says.

"He said," and I recite it back to her word for word, "'hurl that junky curve again, I'll knock it out past the cow patties.'"

Hannah turns to me. "You heard all that?"

"Yep. But I ain't pretending to know what it means."

Skip brings his glove to his face, lets out a breath, and then coils up into his windup once more. He explodes outward, his arm coming straight down from the top again, only now the ball bites through the air at a ferocious angle. George, hesitates, fully relaxed, his head locked motionless on the ball. His movement starts with his back foot, like squishing a bug, and travels up the chain of his body to the hips, where a quick pivot explodes the full force of his power down through his arms and into a focused point—where bat and ball converge in perfect union. A sharp crack splits the air as the ball fires straight out in a blistering flash, to the aah-ing amazement of player and spectator alike. The deepest fielder, manning the outmost reaches of the property, about-faces and breaks into a dead run, his hat flying from his head, as the ball passes high above him, takes one mighty bounce on the hardpacked dirt beyond the lawn and then, finally, of its own accord, rolls to a stop on the other side of the corral fence.

George lopes easy around the lamppost and then continues in a square course that brings him back to where he started, his head high, amid the cooing delight of a half dozen Harvey Girls. But not one of them holds a candle to the vision turning before me.

"I'd say he got all of that," Hannah says.

"Take a look over yonder." She turns back toward the corral, and there in a lope all his own, is Storm. Charlie runs alongside, holding the rope as the stallion works out the stiffness from his legs. "That's Storm. He's with me."

"What a magnificent animal."

"Yeah, he'd be in agreement on that."

"Well, Mister Harlan, you certainly have an eye." Hannah leans against the ledge, the slope of her shoulder bending in tandem with the purpling hill behind her.

"I wish I could say I picked him out. Truth is, one day you look down and you got what you got." I hardly feel like I spit out what I meant to say, but just then the engineer lays into the whistle, scattering the game, and signaling the end of one thing and the beginning of another.

CHAPTER SIXTEEN

Kirby Farlow struck a match against the heavy cast and thought, *at least this damn hunk of plaster's good for something*. He sucked flame through a plug of fresh tobacco and, easing the chair back, deposited his busted leg onto a stool. It felt better to have the thing elevated; Old Doc Marbry had been right about that. As for the doctor's second directive—plenty of bed rest—Kirby had been less compliant. And now, throbbing pain boiled out from his femur, radiating up the spine and down through the ankle. But the pain had been worth it. Sweet mother lode, had it been worth it.

Tomorrow he would send for Doc and order up two shots of laudanum and maybe tip the old sawbones a twenty to let him hang on to the vial afterward. If Kirby couldn't ride out with the boys and square things with that half-breed Injun the way he wanted to, he could at least savor the image of the slippery Jew's lying face right before he drilled him full of lead—*There's no money here! Oh, THAT safe? There's only papers inside. It's been so long, I've forgotten the combination*. Funny how a couple of shattered fingers can jar a stubborn memory. As for the How's Your Uncle he laid on that tasty nigger bitch—that was just a bonus. After he'd worked her over, he was happy to let Linus have a crack. It seemed to calm his brother down, Linus not being a natural to this kind of business like Kirby was. If they were splitting fifty-fifty, it meant all the way down the line. Too bad his other brother, Deke, had decided to ride out with Lem. The three Farlow brothers could have chopped the Heeb's booty in thirds then passed that shine's cunny around like a peace pipe. Ah well, it meant more for Kirby this way. After all, he was the one gimping around in plaster.

"That there's two thousand," Linus said, only halfway through the pile of coins spread out before him. "And I ain't even got to the gold dust yet."

"Hell, if I'd known how much gold that snip-cock was hoarding, I'd have swiss-cheesed him years ago." Kirby drew smoke deep into his lungs and let it tumble slowly from his mouth in the low, orange glow of the fireplace. The light danced across the dirt floor and the stone walls and the table where Linus sat, counting. Kirby had won this little adobe hut in a card game a while back and it sure came in handy after a score—tucked out on the edge of town, like it was, and with no meddling neighbors to come poking around. The roof kept out the rain and there were two doors—Kirby liked that—in case he had to make a hasty exit.

"Grab the scale and help me weigh out this dust," Linus said, drawing the lantern closer. Kirby just smiled and closed his eyes.

"You're the bean counter, little brother." Kirby

didn't mean it as an insult, even though most things out of his mouth came off that way. In this case it was true. Linus punched tickets for the railroad and that made him the bookkeeper of the two. Kirby was the muscle and the idea man. Been that way since they were kids.

"It would just make it go faster, is all."

"Don't be so nervous. Ain't nothing tying us to that Jew. Besides, the only two bastards saw us go in that house is dead. She is dead, ain't she?"

"I told you I took care of it. Why you keep asking me about it?"

"'Cause choking a bitch out is unreliable, especially if killing ain't your strong suit. I'da blown her head off."

"Well that ain't my way, okay? But it don't mean I'm soft. That uppity cherry-nigger showed me up too. Sassing off like a White Man. Half this plan was my idea, remember."

"Yeah, I remember."

"You didn't see the way he stared me down, out there at Lamy. I'm tellin' ya. I don't think Deke and Lem's coming back."

"Give Deke some credit. He's got ice in his veins, same as I do."

"That Injun weren't glaring at me like there was survivors. I saw it in his eyes." Outside the adobe, a twig snapped.

"Shh!" Kirby silencing him. He cocked an ear toward the shuttered window. "You hear that?" Linus froze where he sat. Kirby grabbed the rifle and hoisted himself up, grimacing as he teetered to the door.

"You think it could be Deke?" Linus wondered,

still wanting to believe. He picked up a six-shooter off the table and tried to keep it steady as he stood behind his brother. Kirby opened the door and peered out into the dusk, the cool air alive and sparkling.

"Deke, that you?" Kirby aimed his rifle at the darkness. He took a step outside and listened for movement, Linus hugging so close behind him, Kirby could feel his breath. High in the treetops, an owl hooted. A pack of coyotes, far down in the arroyo, sounded off as it closed in on a meal. But there was no sign of humans. No horses. "Shit, brother, now you got me all squirrely."

"What was it?"

"Nothing. Nothing at all." Kirby lowered the rifle and slowly turned back to the hut. "Grab a couple logs, will ya?"

Linus went over to the woodpile and set the pistol on top of the stack and scooped up an armful of split cedar. He'd come back for the gun. Keeping the fire going meant they were going to stay up all night, which was fine with him, because he didn't think he could sleep if he tried. Kirby reached the door and slumped against it, the pain worse than ever. Linus hated seeing him like this.

"I'll get your crutch. You stay put." Linus slid in behind his brother and crossed to the fireplace and dumped the logs on the hearth. Then he grabbed the crutch and brought it to the door. "Here, trade ya," taking the rifle from Kirby and situating the crutch under his brother's shoulder. Linus dangled the rifle at his side and pulled the door closed behind him. He turned back to his help his brother, who stood motionless in the center of the room, staring at the far wall. Linus looked up and saw that the back door was wide open. He opened his mouth and, before he could speak, a brown figure stepped from the shadows.

"Arms high, gentlemen," Cross said. "Any strange movement otherwise will be your last." The forty-caliber perched unwavering in his steady hand. "You, Linus." Linus swallowed hard when he heard the man speak his name. "Place the rifle on the table, butt-end first. Do it slowly. Keep your left arm where it is." Linus set the stock onto the table and lowered the barrel down. "Now slide it to me. Easy does it." Cross kept Linus on the edge of his vision, but his gaze stayed unflinchingly on Kirby. Any trouble would come from him. Cross knew that, and Kirby knew that he knew. The stranger's predatory stare left no ambiguity. Cross saw Linus tense his arm to shove the rifle, but then hesitate. "Linus, discard that thought you are entertaining presently."

"It's all right, brother. Send it," Kirby meeting Cross's gaze with his own. The rifle sailed across the table—toppling stacks of carefully counted coins—and came to a stop against Cross's hip. A sachet of gold dust fell open, its priceless powder dribbling to the ground as the coins on the table rattled to rest.

"You're a sneaky sum'bitch, ain't you?" Kirby said. "That, or this cocksucking leg's got me off my mark. Hell with it. You got the drop, so take your damn money and leave."

"All money is damned. When will you people learn that?" Cross picked up the rifle and leaned it against the wall behind him. "On your knees."

"Fuck you," Kirby's mouth wet with spittle. "I'm

hobblin' on a crutch here. I ain't getting on the ground."

Cross angled the pistol an almost imperceptible degree downward. "When I blow out your other knee, you'll wish you'd gone down of your own accord."

"Just do what he says," Linus already sinking to the floor.

"You goddamned son of a whore." Kirby steadied the crutch in front of him and slowly grunted his way down. He rested on his good knee and left the cast extended straight outward. "Who the fuck are you?"

"My name is Jacob Cross."

"That supposed to mean something to me?"

"It means everything to you. Your life. Your death. Your suffering."

"Just do whatever you're going to do. I ain't got time for horseshit."

"My friend, time is all you have."

"Damn it all to hell." Kirby put his weight into the crutch, his muscles straining. Cross snatched up the scale from the table and cracked Kirby across the head as he tried to get up.

"The only damnation is your wretched soul!"

Kirby fell back, howling. "Jesus, fuck me. Jesus FUCK ME!"

Cross's face drained of all expression. He aimed the pistol at Kirby's cast and fired, exploding the plaster on the backside of the knee as the bullet exited. A scream came out of Kirby that shook the windows. His mouth stood open, fixed in agony as the sound bleated, unwavering. Cross picked up a small sachet of gold dust and shoved it into Kirby's mouth, muffling—but not silencing—the horror. Then he placed a boot into Kirby's chest and flattened him onto his back. Cross turned to Linus, who had wet himself, and was kneeling, arms raised, in a puddle of his own creation.

"Don't kill me, please. I'm begging you. Please, God!" Cross shot his left hand forward and throttled Linus by the throat.

"God is as deaf to your begging as you were to hers."

"Who?" Linus wailing through gritted teeth. "I don't know who you're taking about." As the ticket man pawed at Cross's wrist, Cross slammed the pistol butt down onto the bridge of his nose.

"God's creature, that's who!" Cross sailing another blow into the meat of his cheek—the skin splitting—and yet another into the orbital bone below his eye. He heard the bone crack. "Oh, yes, the negress *lives*. By God's merciful power, she lives." Cross released the pulpy mass from his clutch and Linus crumpled to the ground.

"Linus, I swear . . ." Kirby flinging the spit-coated bag of dust to the floor, his once ruddy face now ashen gray, but his voice steeled with measured certainty.

"Quite understandable, Mister Farlow," Cross said. "Why trust a killer's job to a ticket puncher. I doubt that's an oversight you'll repeat." Cross turned to face Kirby, and when he did, Kirby swung the crutch and hit him across the face. Kirby was up with a roar, firing on pure rage. He lowered his shoulder and barreled into Cross, sending them both hurtling into the wall. A breathy grunt escaped Cross as the weight of the heavier man knocked the wind from him, but still he held his pistol. Kirby's arm shot up, pinning

Cross's arm and gun against the wall. The two of them fought for control of it.

"Linus, shoot this cocksucker in the face!" Kirby hissing as he dug his heels into the table. His forearm crunched against Cross's neck, but the little man fumbled his free hand down toward his belt. Linus slapped at his own belt and then remembered—the woodpile. He leapt to his feet and ran to the door and opened it and saw a man with a shotgun standing there. Van Zant fired and blew Linus back across the room. Then he turned and took aim at Kirby but could not fire, as the spray of buckshot would kill Cross. Van Zant went for the pistol he kept on his hip.

Kirby wrested control of the forty, ripping it from Cross's hand as Cross yanked his free hand upward. Kirby stepped back and brought up the pistol and then felt the cold shock as his belly opened up and his intestines emptied onto the floor. Puzzled, he looked at Cross, and saw that the cord around the man's neck held only the top half of the crucifix he'd been wearing. The lower half jutted from Cross's hand, where a needle-point blade dripped red with blood. Then Van Zant fired and blew half of Kirby's skull onto the wall. Cross steadied himself on the table and rubbed his neck. He glared at Van Zant.

"Sorry," Van Zant said. "I cut that a little close."

Cross wiped the blade clean and gently reunited the two pieces that embodied his faith. He brought the assembled crucifix to his lips and kissed it, solemnly. Then he picked up his pistol, stepped over Kirby's body and walked to where Linus lay on his back. Linus ground his boot heels into the dirt, as if there were somewhere to go.

"The Indian, Harlan Two-Trees. Where is he?"
Cross standing over him.

Linus Farlow gazed up at the ceiling and wondered what was beyond. He thought about his
mother. Cross repeated the question, which he rarely
did, and saw Linus trying to speak.

"On . . . train." Blood bubbled from his mouth.
Cross nodded and leaned down and spoke in a clear
voice.

"Which way is he headed?"

CHAPTER SEVENTEEN

Skip slides down in the heavy upholstered chair across from mine, somehow convinced his encroachment will loosen my tongue. "At least say if you kissed her. She was the prettiest one."

"She was all right," George correcting over his whiskey glass. "She weren't the prettiest." George switched to whiskey as soon as we lit out from the Harvey House, unlike his friend who stays loyal to sarsaparilla. I had sobered up in my time with Hannah—what with scrambling over the rooftop after her and the newness of the adventure—and hadn't much thought about whiskey at all. And now to consider numbing away the image of Hannah's smile, or the way her finger traced an invisible line on the white adobe ledge, or the scent of her lavender essence, seems a disservice to her memory. And those memories, every precious one, are all I have left of her.

"Sure I can't get you something, Mister Harlan?" Burke passing behind me in the parlor car, a fresh, white waiter's uniform replacing his sweated-through porter's jacket for the hour or so he has charge of the bar. "Just till Ernie come back from restocking the pantry. I can't mix a drink like Ernie, but I can pour whiskey straight enough."

"When you get to rest?" I ask.

"Old Burke learn how to sleep standing up long time ago."

The door opens and Ballentine strolls in, followed by a red-faced Owens who has to steady himself against the wall, laughing hard at some previous joke as the train shudders around a turn.

"Keep 'em coming, Burke," Owens jabbing his empty to the ceiling. "Clara May's putting the kids down and I ain't drunk yet."

"Friend, you're drunker than a Yankee in Savannah," Spooner patting Owen's shoulder.

"I 'spose I am. Enjoy your bachelor years, boys. It's all downhill once you take the plunge." Owens collapses onto the settee, his legs stretched out.

Ballentine holds his liquor well, and shows no sign of intoxication beyond fatigue and a slight flushness to his already pink skin. He lowers gently into the seat next to me and lets out a sigh.

"I'd pay union money for a liniment rub. My back is stiff as a board."

"You had the easy part," George says, brooding.

"I assure you, there is nothing easy about adjudicating a curve ball." Spooner leans back in the chair and closes his eyes. The thinness of the high desert air has taken a wearying toll on the game's participants.

"Reckon I owe you an apology," I say. "Vanishing from supper like I done."

"Nonsense," his eyes opening again. "It is I should

be apologizing. I invite you as my guest and your fine
suit is soiled? I am deeply embarrassed."

"Don't be. They took care of me. Got some stiff
trousers is all. A little smoked, but clean otherwise."
I tug at my trousers to demonstrate but his eyes are
closed again.

"Glad to hear it. Truth be told, your mishap with
the coffeepot inspired Harvey's manager to discount
the final bill by half." I feel a smile blooming and
hope he hasn't seen it. "What is it? Why are you
smiling?" his one squinted eye unwavering.

"Hannah would find that funny. Knowing she
saved you a bundle."

"Indeed," closing his eyes again. "I hope she stiff-
ened more than your trousers," his voice lowering
with suggestion.

"Good luck getting a story outta him. I already
tried," Skip rising from his chair.

"You'd make a fine defendant on the stand,
Harlan. Too often a man talks his way to incrimina-
tion when the smart move is to leave the talking to
the professionals."

"Comes to talk, you must be top of the trade,"
George says.

"You could do worse than retaining my counsel,
young man. Although fair warning, I am discomfort-
ably expensive."

"Then here's to never being on neither side of the
courtroom from you," George toasting the air. Skip
sinks down next to him and they retreat into their
private nickering.

Spooner leans in my direction, and without opening his eyes, says in a low voice, "Those huskers save
all their talents for the ball diamond. Sparkling

conversationalists, they are not." Then Spooner sets back in the chair, hands folded across the belly, and—in a breath or two—is snoring louder than Owens.

"I guess he won't be needing this," Burke staring down at the poured whiskey, his eyes considering if he should funnel it back into the bottle. "Unless you care for it, Mister Harlan."

"Not just yet."

He glances over at the boys, who seem as content as George's moodiness will allow. "Well, if you gentlemen don't mind then," Burke pulling on his porter's jacket over the barman's uniform. "I'll see to getting the beds turned down. I'll send Ernie up to tend on you 'fore you need another round."

Burke marches out the door, and there I sit between two snores and pair of jealous farm boys. I close my eyes.

All at once, Hannah's smell comes to me. The total complexity of her day—her routine—laid bare as I tease from the scent another layer—*cinnamon*. I picture her, the sly housecat, pilfering a fresh roll—hot from the oven—on her way past the kitchen. And then come the spoils—nibbling away below the stairs, contented, no one the wiser to her subterfuge.

When I open my eyes, I am smiling. The window outside shows changing country—stark and thickening shadows against fire-red strips of gasping sunlight. The lamps from the bar reflect in the glass, spreading a harsh glare that obstructs the view, as now the train's interior light glows brighter than sunlight outside. And with present company less than engaging, I declare it a fine time for a stroll.

* * *

I come out of the parlor car and into the dark quiet of the corridor, where the long window stretches the full length of one side, offering a fine vista enjoyed by me, alone. *Butter and onions.* Her scent, once again—more layers intruding unannounced upon my brain. You can't hardly work in a restaurant what without its heavy odors traveling home with you. I see her—late at night—scrubbing herself with lavender soap, frustrated by the tenacity of the kitchen's clinging aroma. A cat licking itself clean and not stopping till it has done so. Then again, the strong lavender might be her way of masking those stolen minutes with a cigarette. I find myself smiling again, this time with eyes wide open.

A banging door turns my head to the far end of the corridor. The young infantryman emerges from the darkness—kepi pulled low and his face absent the good-natured kindness on display at the Harvey House. He startles at the sight of me, as if I don't belong, when it is the lowly stamp on his ticket that, if detected, would have Burke ushering him back to steerage by the scruff of the collar—long-rifle or not. The soldier's walk hitches a step—then tries to conceal the hiccup unnoticed—before resuming a hair faster than what it had been.

"Evening." I say.

He manages a nod, his lips moving but producing no sound. The oddness of the encounter lingers even after the parlor door closes, the soldier inside. I stare out at the country. The mountains give way to a stretch of lowlands where the falling sun, unobstructed, finds new strength. The ground glows flat and orange. A sandy berm begins to rise up just outside the window, cutting off the view of the dry riverbed that extends to the horizon. A dark figure skitters across the top of the berm, ducking down the backside, as the train approaches, in an attempt to avoid detection. He might have succeeded against an eye less attuned to movement as my own. Yet in the flash of his presence I recognize the unmistakable blue of a soldier's tunic—the same blue that just slinked past me in the corridor. But the man outside wears a cavalryman's hat, the eagle feather in its band betraying his position behind the berm.

A troubling unease takes root in my gut, like the ground dropping away. The Santa Fe shudders, the floor vibrating as she accepts the change beneath her wheels—a trestle. The berm vanishes from view as quick as the apparition hiding behind it. We rumble out on a low bridge, spanning the arroyo—and the unease I'm coddling drips into sickening, cold dread.

I feel a shallow breath suck inward across my lips, and then it is too late.

BOOOOM!

A thundering roar splinters the air, firing a dark cloud of debris and smoke out into the arroyo like a ship's cannon blast. The trestle—my mind knows it is the trestle exploding as the window cobwebs before my eyes and shatters inward, bathing every inch of me with shards of biting glass. I turn and cover my face, the shock wave slamming me against the wall. The floor below jumps off the track and crashes back down again into the bridge—and then through it— metal grinding and shifting as the wheels claw for rails that are sinking as fast as the train itself. I grab a handhold and swing my weight downward, lowering the center of gravity. But the crumbling bridge does that for me. Down, down we plummet. A full second of free fall that seems an eternity, until the impact—jarring beyond conception—hurls me down the corridor. I slam the far wall like a wet ragdoll, white stars pocking my vision as a salty spike of blood fills my mouth. I collapse to the ground, deafened by a roaring dragon of crunching—squealing—ripping metal.

And then come the screams. Human voices, choked with mortal panic, cut a high-pitched drone that makes no distinction of man, woman or child.

I struggle to my knees—nearly blinded by twirling stars—but the train has not stopped moving. We drag across the gritty sand—churning and scraping—until the din of crunched metal gives way to new sounds. A calamitous banging, like an iron drum, beats once, coupled with screams of horror. All at once the wall on the far side pushes toward me, the steel sides of the train car crumbling like a tin can. My legs fire to life as the walls close in. I scramble upward—or is it sideways—straight for the exploded window and dive through. I hit the rock-hard ground with an awkward crash but never stop running until I am clear of the twisted, splintering mass of metal and wood. The acrid stench of cordite weighs heavy in the bone-dry air, sucked of all moisture by the tremendous blast. Another heavy bang booms behind me, followed by more screaming.

Only then do I turn around and see. The train cars, one after another, hurtle off the elevation and into the chasm where seconds ago stood a bridge. Each car pulls the one behind it to a similar fate, piling up—twenty yards below—in a smoking heap of mangled steel and dust. An over-crowded Pullman coach, the riders' arms and faces pressed to the glass, juts out over the precipice and teeters there—suspended—until it releases from the track. The coach falls.

It hits the cars below and bursts into flames, fire engulfing the wood frame with unspeakable swiftness. Through the smoke I see the outlines of desperate brakemen—tiny as ants—straining into their brake levers atop the roofs of the cars still on the track. As a car goes over the ledge, the brakemen jump, some landing on high ground, others plummeting all to the way to the carnage below. With the fallen cars cluttering the arroyo and stacking upward in a tower of carnage, the back half of the train—Storm's half—in a fateful twist of mercy—has nowhere to fall. The mighty Santa Fe slows to a crawl and finally—by the grace of Heaven—groans to a halt.

But the fire rages. I watch in helpless horror, but find my legs propelling me forward, toward the train. With every step, a stinging pain stabs through my ears into the brain. A ringing wall of sound rises up, consuming all, and instinctively I understand that I am dynamite-deaf. The miner's curse. *It will pass. You know it will pass*, I tell myself—as it does for countless men in the mines—but still my heart panics at the maddening tranquility of false silence. The remains of the trestle flutter down from the blackened sky in a flurry of glowing ash and embers. Something heavy, like a tree branch, slams down in front to me, halting my progress. I look down at the branch and see a man's leg, severed mid-thigh.

Where once was a boot—or shoe—now smolders a foot sheathed in nothing but a sock in woeful need of darning. When the owner pulled them on this morning, he thought no one would notice, no doubt saving his last good pair for a long-awaited reunion with his girl. I am pulled from the guilty strangeness of the thought by the trembling ground beneath my feet.

Horses.

I turn around and behold a company of ghosts. They gallop out of the smoke—a motley band of army soldiers in a wild, undisciplined formation— tattered uniforms flapping beneath mean, dirty faces made crueler by the—yes, I see it, clear as day—by the twisted ripple of excitement in their eyes. These ghoulish barbarians—these monsters—caused this destruction. And they are enjoying it.

A long-haired Apache rides among them, unsaddled, steering his horse with his legs as he raises his rifle and fires. But—blind luck—not at me. I remember the pistol, my hand reaching for it. I turn, hoping to find cover—hoping to be invisible—but before I finish the move I feel someone behind me and I know I am anything but invisible. A second Apache bears down on me, his eyes indifferent, until he looms overhead and a flicker of recognition strips away our White Man's clothes, and I am laid bare— red-blooded—at his feet. Time grinds to a halt. Either there will be mercy, or there will not. The wind catches the heat from the fire and warms my back like a summer breeze. The Apache makes a decision. All at once, his face knots with rage. And then his club hits my skull and everything goes black.

PART 2
ARROYO RED

CHAPTER EIGHTEEN

The campfire burns strong and hot. I feel the heat all down my legs and the power of its brightness through closed eyelids that I don't want to open—not from this nap. Sleep's talons seduce me with the promise of warm and deepening blackness. Besides, upstairs I detect the rumblings of a fearsome hangover. Must have finished the bottle. I know when I snap my eyes open and try to move, daggers will pierce the brain like a hundred icepicks. Best keep them closed; no sense letting the pain get the drop on me. But whatever I'd been eating before dozing off, I made a right mess of, because the chili or beans—or was it honey and biscuits?—sits caked on one side of my face, drying in the fire's heat. And the last thing I need—if the flies and ants don't start picking at it—is Storm wandering over and thinking he can help himself to a couple of prime licks. I'll just brush the food off—just that little motion—and then grab a few more winks as the fire burns itself

out. I bring a hand to my cheek and a sudden bolt of
pain rips up the jaw and into my forehead.

"He's moving." A voice. A voice I recognize shatters the cocoon of my dream.

Ballentine.

Oh God.

Oh dear God. It comes flooding back, the unspeakable truth. There is no food on my face. No hangover.
No campfire. Slowly—the splitting agony between
my ears far worse than the harshest whiskey sick—I
open my eyes.

I lie on the sandy ground of the arroyo. A smoke-
filled sky brings an early dusk, but spears of sunlight
tell me I was not out for long. I see two legs, two dusty
boots. I will them to move and they move. *You ain't
crippled*, I tell myself. *And you sure as hell ain't deaf.*

The air lives thick with the sounds of war—
gunfire, horses, screaming.

No. Not war—the gunfire too methodical—but
what comes after war—butchery and desecration,
when the superior side has its way with the defeated.
I try to sit up, but a hand, sleeved in blackened
seersucker, presses me down.

"Best stay put, son. They ain't done yet," Ballentine again.

Close by, a child sobs and a woman offers comfort.
"Mamma's here, darling, and I'm not going away."
Owens's wife, I forget her name. The crying continues. To hell with the pain. I roll to my side and sit up,
the world spinning—and through double-visioned
eyes make out Owens to my left. He holds one of the
children, his wife rubbing the head of the other—
the girl—in her lap.

"You took a blow, Harlan. Easy now," Ballentine

says from my right. I see two of him and close one
eye, like a drunk, but it helps. He's aged ten years in
an hour.

"How'd I get here?"

"You staggered out yonder," Spooner nodding
toward the open expanse of the arroyo, "then col-
lapsed. Owens and I, we dragged you back here."

I glance toward Owens. He strokes the boy's hair
and keeps his head low, but his eyes are alert as he
clocks the whereabouts of the soldiers. Or whatever
they are. The eagle feather—I remember it from the
berm—perches from the cavalryman's hat. He stands
guard ten yards away, his back to us, but pivots at the
commotion and steps closer, brandishing a rifle.

"Y'all sit still. I ain't telling you again," barking in
a husky voice. The hat swims too large on his head,
flopping forward until, annoyed, he shoves it back
and mashes it down onto his skull. I can't figure how
it would stay put at any more than a trot, much less
crossing fifty miles of desert a day. He whistles loud
to a point above my head. I look up and see that they
have us corralled at the base of the berm. The train
must be just on the other side, because the smell of
charred wood and burnt stove oil is so thick I want to
gag. An army soldier, with sergeant's stripes on his
arm and a sawed-off four-ten in his hands, sits atop
the berm, eyeing me through bored, squinted eyes.

"I see him," he says to Eagle Feather. "Won't be
long now." Then he spits and turns the other way.

Another soldier, his infantry tunic unbuttoned
over a red-checkered work shirt, walks up to Eagle

Feather. They exchange words and the man looks over at us, frowning, and then marches off.

I hold stone still and with my mouth barely moving say, "What they got planned for us?"

"Not sure yet," Owens's voice low, but keenly attentive for a man passed out drunk half an hour ago. Besides the Owens clan and Spooner, a black waiter—Ernie, I reckon—crouches nearby, his head in his hands, weeping. A man and wife I recognize from first class huddle in each other's arms, the woman shaking her head in disbelief. Her gray-haired husband gnaws at his thumbnail to keep it from trembling. Another woman, round and sweating, kneels in the dust, her shredded parasol offering little protection from the elements. Two or three men, all smartly dressed, kneel beside her, holding hands, heads bowed in prayer. And then beyond them, I see George. He sits alone, arms tied behind his back. He wears nothing but his union suit. Even his shoes and socks are gone and his swollen face bears the aftereffects of a mighty dustup, but the scraped and bloodied knuckles say he gave as good as he got, if not better. He stares motionless out into the arroyo, his face set hard in an icy scowl.

My gaze follows his out to the arroyo, and with the faculties of my brain and vision returning slow, I have to blink a few times to make sure I see the bodies. But I see them, all right. A dozen dead, maybe twice that—passenger and crew alike—lay sprawled about the dry riverbed in every direction. They died where they fell, mostly, shot in the back as they tried to run. But some—as I look closer—show the mark of a finishing headshot, administered at close range once the body was down. Otherwise, the corpses look unmolested—to be picked over at a later time.

And time seems to be no issue for these men. I let my eyes continue on, surveying what I can of the particulars of this operation, and the intent of its perpetrators. Across the skeletal remains of the blown-out trestle, where the track picks up again on solid ground, a short stretch of telegraph poles lay flattened against the earth like felled trees, their magic wires stripped away. That's why these bandits take their time. No one is coming.

An explosion rips from over the berm, jarring bones and—once the shockwave dissipates—causing a chorus of shouts and whoops from marauders spread over a quarter mile. The men guarding our group turn left as a thick cloud shoots upward from the front of the train. I use the distraction to hop up and shuffle over to Owens, squatting down next to him. We don't look at each other.

"Jesus Christ, these morons don't know what the hell they're doing. That was enough ordnance to flatten half a mountain."

"TNT?"

"Yeah, can tell by the smoke. It's a miracle they didn't vaporize the whole train and us with it."

"They cut the wires," I say.

"I saw. Be hours 'fore anyone knows we're missing."

"You make out who they are?"

"Is there any doubt?" his chin turning toward me. "We landed headfirst into the Crazy Dazers."

The Dazers. Of course, we had. The tattered uniforms, the slack formations, and as far I can see, no tangible chain-of-command, bore all the signs of a

unit that had gone rogue before the rote habits of
soldiering had taken hold. That gives them an un-
predictability worth fearing. And the stolen dynamite
turns the fearsome into the Horsemen of the Apoc-
alypse. As for the Apaches—rogues in their own
right—they must serve as scouts, if not willing part-
ners.

I glance back and now have a better view of the
front of the train. The explosion came from the express car. A handful of Dazers crawl over the steel
carcass like maggots and several more stand around,
conversing and swigging from a shared bottle. A
Dazer on board hurls out something—looks like a
bale of hay—but when it lands at the feet of the
others I see it is the torso of a real soldier—one of
the Pinkerton's detail.

"You don't want to look at that," Owens says, his
voice unable to hide the sadness. I figure he means
the express car but when I see the Pullman coaches,
where most of the passengers had been riding, my
belly sinks.

The Pullman car burns with the steady intensity
of fire that has crested but still has work to do.
Gray-charred bodies lay crammed against unbroken
windows. Others had managed to break their windows, their corpses hanging from the waist, gutted by
the glass, or their heads blown apart by awaiting
guns. The unceasing gunfire alternates between a
rifle's snap and the soul-churning boom of a big caliber pistol. The long-haired Apache stands on the
boxcar above the burning Pullman, taking deliberate aim with the pistol and ending the misery of

anyone still moving. A bearded soldier patrols the other side, dispatching any survivors with the rifle.

"A slaughter," the word passing my lips with depleted breath. "Fish in a barrel."

"Fish in a *burning* barrel." Owens struggling to make sense, like his brain won't believe what his eyes tell him. "There just ain't no reason for that. No reason at all."

I can't argue with Owens. Sure, there's a reason, but not one any of us want to think about. Instead a question that will define the next few minutes slips from my mouth.

"Why the hell are we still alive?"

"I have no idea."

All at once, I remember the pistol, the metal pressing warm against my pelvis. One pistol. Six bullets. And what looks like near two-dozen armed madmen with no quarter for human life. The sound of lowing cattle turns me around. *Storm.* I forgot about Storm like I'd forgotten my own head. I see cattle roaming off to the right, near the upturned train. They appear disoriented, even agitated, but they're not crushed or burned, so I don't know what it means for the stallion. An injured heifer breaks into a run, limping, but hell bent on finding elsewhere to be. She runs toward us, one leg broken, a bloody trail of liquid drooling from her mouth.

Eagle Feather breaks into a laugh as the animal nears. But the solider in sergeant stripes breeches the four-ten, removes one shell and replaces it with another, no doubt swapping out buckshot for a

single lead slug. He raises the gun and fires—the
sudden noise dropping Spooner and the others flat
to the ground. The heifer shudders once, a loud
squeal escaping her, and then crashes face first into
the dirt. The sergeant Dazer cracks open the shotgun
again, flicks out the smoldering shell and replaces
the buckshot.

I am on my knees, palms turned skyward, and
close my eyes.

*Great Spirit, spare the stallion. Let his thunder ring an-
other day.*

"Oh dear God," Spooner's breaking voice pulls
me from the prayer. "They've got Skip."

I face out toward the arroyo and see the Apache
who clubbed me riding in, atop his paint pony. He
keeps a steady trot and that makes it hard for Skip.
The ball player runs behind the pony, struggling to
stay upright, his hands bound in front by a long
rope tied to the saddle. Skip is completely naked, his
face and blond hair matted with bloody dirt and
his bare feet shredded to pulp and bone.

Eagle Feather brings his fingers to his mouth and
peals out a sharp whistle, which is repeated by the
sergeant and then Red Flannel. The signal travels
haphazard down the line until it reaches Dazers gathered at the express car. Four men on horseback
break from the pack and ride full-bore up to where
the Apache stops, about thirty yards out into the
arroyo. At the front of the riders, a tall man in black
officer's Stetson reins up as they near the Apache,
and the others slow down with him. The man in

charge always shows himself eventually. One of the riders in back, a guidon, carries the Union flag on a pole, only the stars and stripes are inverted. An upside-down flag—usually a sign of distress—here I make it for just a perversion.

The Man in Charge says something to Skip and then points over to our group, and I get the sinking feeling that this spectacle unfolds for our benefit. Skip pleads with his bound hands. His desperate cries nearly reach my ears, but not quite. He stays on his feet, despite the exhaustion. I would too. The Man in Charge nods to the Apache, who gets off his pony and draws his club. Skip tries to run but the other men dismount and grab the rope and stand on it until the Apache is upon him. He hacks the club at Skip's legs, landing once above the knee. Skip screams and drops to the ground. The Apache moves in, letting the club fall and drawing a knife. He grabs Skip by the hair, and with a measured stroke, cuts the boy's throat. A collective gasp of horror rises from our group. Blood shoots out from the Skip's neck, the fight not yet left him, but soon he slackens. The Man in Charge turns his horse and walks it straight at us, the other riders following.

"Don't look, don't look, darling," Owens's wife repeating over and over. I hear someone vomit, a few more weeping. The rest stay silent.

The Man in Charge approaches, revealing the garish appointments of his costume. He wears the brass insignia of both major and colonel. I think of a magpie collecting and hoarding trinkets of shiny silver for which it has no understanding. But as he nears, I see his eyes beneath the shadow of the gold-banded Stetson, their callow cruelty. I behold no great intelligence behind those brown-flecked discs. They are stupid eyes—eyes for whom luck will run out. The colonel-major stops his horse and addresses the unwilling congregation assembled before him.

"Anybody else wanna run?"

CHAPTER NINETEEN

The three other riders fall in behind the colonel-major, and mixed in among their various garments of army dress are pieces of clothing I recognize—a brown linen jacket, a white collarless shirt, now splattered with blood, and sturdy field boots. The three of them have divided, and now wear, George's clothes. The bannerman revels in showing off his new boots, smiling at the ball player. But George remains unmoved, staring stone-faced, as he had been, out toward the horizon. A soldier comes running up from the direction of the train, waving to get the colonel-major's attention and pointing, very clearly, at me.

"That one's got money! I seen it." His kepi, dark with sweat, sits back on his head. The nervous face I encountered moments before the explosion has given way to fiendish delight at the chance to earn favor with the colonel-major. I step back and feel the barrel of the four-ten against my spine. The kepi scout runs over, the horseman advancing behind him—all attention on me now. "He was splashing coin all over the Harvey House. It's there, in them pockets," Kepi Scout jabbing a finger at my coat.

Eagle Feather closes in on my right, barrel leveled at my chest. I think about the pistol in my trousers—not drawing it—but keeping it safe, for the right moment, a moment that has not yet come.

"Search him," the colonel-major says. Eagle Feather pulls a knife and slashes at the fabric of the coat. I raise my hands and press my shoulder blades back and let the jacket slip off the shoulders. The sergeant does the rest, stripping it off my arms and flinging the jacket forward. Eagle Feather and Kepi tear at it like dogs after a bone. The lining rips from the inside and coins rain down from the pockets, until every penny I own—over a thousand dollars—shimmers on the ground.

"Whoa, daddy. Pay dirt!" Kepi drops to his knees, plucking the coins from the crystalline sand as Eagle Feather shakes the shredded jacket empty. Bandits appear from all sides and soon the ground crawls in a mass of stolen blue. "I told you it was smart to put me on board. Reconnoitered the whole dang lot of 'em, I did. That's right."

"Turn your pockets out," the colonel-major says. The four-ten digs a little deeper into my spine.

"And do it easy," the sergeant's breath blowing warm and sour down my neck, "less you looking to get cut half-sized." I move slow hands down to the trousers and gently pull out the front pockets. Kepi waddles over, still on his knees. He slaps my hands away and feels through the fabric with curious fingers. I catch sight of Spooner and only now do I see that his pockets lay inside out, already fleeced, like flags of surrender. Same with Owens and the rest. My inspection, I reckon, was only delayed by their thinking I was dead. I feel something fall.

"A dollar . . . stick of gum . . . and what's this here?" Kepi rising to his feet, a greasy pistol cartridge pinched in his grip.

"Check his boots," Colonel-Major says, irritation in his voice. "You shoulda done that already."

"Yeah, you shoulda done that," Kepi making the grievous error of echoing the reprimand at the sergeant standing to my rear. A fist shoots out from behind me and lands square against the young Kepi's nose, standing him upright. The sergeant moves around me and smashes the barrel of the four-ten down onto the young man's head. The Crazy Dazers, to a man, erupt in grotesque laughter as the young Kepi, teary-eyed, staggers backward, blood pouring from his nose.

"Boy, you take a tone with me again, I'll tie your guts 'round your neck and hang you from a tree."

"Jesus, Lon," the boy's voice quivering, "I was only repeating what Craw said."

The colonel-major hears this, all humor draining from his face. I know what's coming and have no faith that he won't miss, but if I break, the shotgun ends me. I tense and lower my weight into my legs, ready to spring. The colonel-major draws a long pistol just as the boy's eyes go wide, realizing what he's done.

"No!" the boy turning, arms raised, pleading. The colonel-major fires. A woman screams. The shot blows through the boy's hand before hitting his chest. He slumps to the ground, life already drained from him. The laughter stops.

"No names, I said."

But I heard the names, two of them, *Lon* shadowing me with the four-ten—*Lonnie* to his momma, I'll wager. And *Craw*—the colonel-major himself. What kind of name is Craw? I burn them both into my memory with a white-hot iron and vow to survive this day. I won't die by their hands, not after what I lived through in the Sangres. Or in the Bend, or even today on the grade. I will live to die a more noble death than what these marauding bastards can come up with. And if they kill Storm, if they harm the stallion in any way, I will track them down with the full-blooded skill of the Diné. But when I find them, it will be the White Man's vengeance—the kind with a long memory and no sense of proportion—that cuts them open and watches them bleed. Such is the benefit when white and red run together in the same vein.

"You," the sergeant—Lon—barking to a stray Dazer still on his knees, pilfering the last of my gold. "Get over here, finish checking him." The bandit crawls over and I gaze straight ahead as his hands wander down into my boots, kneading the leather, and then up each leg. He can't bring himself to lay his paws on my business and I betray nothing, just staring out into the arroyo until he relays the findings.

"He's clean."

Sergeant Lon shoves me downward, driving a knee into the back of my spine to hasten the descent. "Sit your ass down and keep it there. You know we ain't playing now." I go down without protest or catching the eye of anyone who might take it as a challenge. As Lon moves around me I catch from him the strong odor of burnt wood—not charred planks of trestle—but fresh-cut pine. The strangeness of it, out of place in the high desert, sits funny with me. The handful of Dazers picking over the money rise and carry what they've found over to the bannerman, who holds open a sack nearly half-stuffed already with cash and coin.

But even so, the size of the booty bears no proportion to the enormity of the caper. Nearly a hundred souls lay dead already, with four score or more entombed in the Pullman. Such carnage hardly seems worthwhile for a few thousand dollars. And considering the manpower of the team—I've counted twenty-two, so far—the final haul, per Dazer, wouldn't equal much more than a good night at the poker table. It just don't make sense.

"Here they come now," says the rider in George's coat. By his place on horseback, and his proximity to the leader, I make him for the colonel-major's second-in-command. I even detect a resemblance in their jawline and squarish features. Brothers again.

Always with the brothers. Good or bad, I have about run out of patience for *bilagáana* fraternity. I don't know what it is about the frontier that breeds trouble among male kinfolk. More than likely, the seeds of trouble were there to begin with, but then, once migrated to the frontier, flowered in its lawless opportunities. In the Sangres, I fought side-by-side with three brave Germans—Frey was the family name. But short of them, most sets of brothers I come across find a reason to have a problem with me, and those problems put many of them in the ground.

*** *** ***

A mule labors up from the front of the train, dragging a travois, accompanied by a handful of Dazers who take great pains to keep the animal from losing its cargo. As slow as the mule moves, an even slower parade lags behind. Two Dazers push a reluctant prisoner up along the wrecked train toward the awaiting colonel-major and his horsemen.

I find myself unattended during the distraction and shimmy over toward Owens and fall in between him and Ballentine, the three of us shielding our conspiracy by never looking directly at anyone or anything.

"I heard the name Craw," I say.

"I'm thinking short for Crawford, maybe," Owen picking up the thread.

"Back home, we had a Crawley, so I made that assumption," Spooner chiming in. "Although I'm starting to think the commander's commission is of spurious pedigree."

"They's phonies, all of them." Owens says. "They ain't army, least not anymore. No, it's the Crazy Dazers, stake my life on it."

"Don't say that!" Clara May's voice—her name coming to me—sizzles in admonition. "You trying to get yourselves killed?"

"It's all right, darling," Owens quieting her. "They don't want us dead."

"I'm inclined to agree," Spooner says, "But I wish I knew what it is they want."

I can see from here what they want. The answer's being drug behind that mule.

"Money," I say. The others turn and notice the

heavy black cube weighting down the travois. "In that safe, there."

"My. Not very big, is it?" Spooner taken by the object's diminutive size, no bigger than a steamer trunk.

"No," I say, remembering the riches confined to a small space in Garber's office. "But you stuff it with gold, you can fit half the army's pay in there."

"So that's it," Owens marveling. "All this for one lousy safe."

The Apache, standing over Skip's body, wipes the blood from his knife on the dead man's hair, then looks over at the approaching captive. Annoyed by the prisoner's slow progress, the Apache leaps onto his horse, bolts over and snatches him from his Dazer escorts. The once dignified Pinkerton expressman—dressed waist up in only his tattered shirtsleeves, hands bound behind his back—looks like a bomb went off in front of his face. His white hair stands straight up in all directions, giving the Apache an easy handle as he grabs a fistful and canters the man—feet struggling to keep him upright—over to the others. The Apache stops abruptly and flings the expressman down into the dirt at the colonel-major's feet.

The safe arrives atop the travois a few moments later.

"Children, you keep your eyes closed now," Owens voice soothing into prescience of things to come. "You too, Clara May." The men unload the safe from the travois and stand it upright, with the lock plate facing the Pinkerton.

"Here's what's gonna happen," Craw says to the expressman, but loud enough to make it a show for all in attendance—the luxury of time again. "You're gonna spit out the numbers for that there strongbox, or you're gonna spit out what's left of your teeth one by one."

The expressman can't shake the stunned look on his face and gives no assurance that he understands. Then I squint, and in the dying sun, make out the puddles of deep red pooling in his ears.

The second blast deafened him so hard his drums burst. The colonel-major might as well be speaking Diné, but that hardly matters. Any expressman standing against his will in front of the safe he's sworn to protect knows damn well what's being asked of him. The only variable is his tolerance for pain. The colonel-major nods to his second and the man in George's coat swings down and puts himself square in the face of the Pinkerton.

"Feed me them numbers," the second pointing to the dial, then back to the Pinkerton. "Feed me them numbers for the safe, I says."

"Feel you? I can't hear nothing. Feel you what?" The expressman yelling as if separated by the length of a barn.

"No, *feed* . . . aw, you blitherin' idjut. Just tell me the damn numbers." To make his point he spins the dial hard to the right. "Now you tell me where to stop."

"Never!" The Pinkerton defiant.

The Apache, his fuse ever shortening, jumps down from his horse and moves in behind the expressman. He raises his club and swings it down, over the top, onto the Pinkerton's collarbone, dropping him to his knees.

"Damn you to hell, ya bastard," the Pinkerton

howling. He collapses onto his side, trying to get past the worst of the pain.

"Too bad the 'pache don't believe in hell," the man in George's coat says. "If he did, he'd probably gut you for that. Now tell me where to stop." The Pinkerton rolls onto his knees again, steadying his breath. He manages a look and sees the second spinning the dial once more. He shakes his head.

"You can't do it. I gotta do it. The dial is . . . particular."

An uneasy quiet over the scene, the Dazers unsure of what comes next. But it won't be good. I learned a thing or two from the greatest safe man of all time, and even the Snowman himself would defer to the pointlessness of trying to work the dial on a time-lock safe—the kind that only spreads her legs once a day—at a preset hour—which I strongly doubt is now. The second in command looks to his brother. Craw thinks a moment, grimacing, then nods toward the Pinkerton.

"Cut him free."

The Apache, eager for any use of blade or club, steps in and slices the cord that binds the Pinkerton. I feel Owens's head inch toward mine.

"It's a time-lock."

"I know."

"Pinkerton damn well knows it too. All he's gonna do is get them angry, get us all killed."

I agree with Owens. Only thing opening that door is dynamite—a tool for which the Dazers have not shown much subtlety or precision. The Pinkerton expressman rolls his wrists, limbering the joints. His right arm stays mostly straight, down by his side. I suspect his collarbone is broke, rendering the arm useless as he shuffles up to the safe. The Apache and the second pull in close beside him, the second watching his turning hand, the Apache eyeing the rest.

"Get back from it," the second admonishing, "I need to see what you're doing."

"I ain't got my spectacles," the Pinkerton says, his face mere inches from the numbered dial. The colonel-major moves over on his horse, the whole scene shrinking to the tiniest of stages against the vast backdrop of the Malpais.

"Left thirty-seven," the second relaying what he sees. "Then around the right . . . twice around to the . . . what's that, twelve?"

The Pinkerton nods, hunched over the dial, his left hand fingering the dial from memory. He starts it back the other way, and the Apache looks up at the colonel-major, conveying something in broken English. The colonel-major nods, but there's an impatience, like the Apache hasn't said anything he didn't already know.

"I can't read that last," the second bringing his head closer to the dial, and when he does the Pinkerton expressman slides his dead arm into his boot and snaps upward, his dead arm all at once alive and armed with a short knife that plunges into the eye of the second in command. The second reels back, squealing in horror. The Apache springs into action. He swings the club and hits the Pinkerton on the head. The little expressman slumps and the Apache grapples him from behind and throws him to the ground. He stamps on his neck and pins him there, then the

Apache looks back at his commander, pleading for permission to kill.

Swift rage consumes the colonel-major. He flies off his horse, mouth agape, as if he can't comprehend what his own eyes just witnessed. Three Dazers run over and start at once kicking the prone expressman all over his body. The colonel-major glances over at his second, now on his knees in a spill of blood that can't mean more than a minute or two more among the living.

"You lost your mind?" Craw demanding, "You think you gonna change the way this goes, you black damned fool? Look at my brother. Look what you done. And for what? For what, huh? Let me see his face." He marches over to where the expressman lays on his belly, covering his head with his arms. The Dazers stop kicking him. "You think we ain't gonna get that money?"

"Hell with you. Hell with all you bastards!" The expressman, red-faced, shouting through a blood-filled mouth pocked with dark voids of missing teeth.

"Get him up." For all his anger, the man called Craw shows little regard for his dying brother's condition or even easing his pain. All his attention sits focused on the Pinkerton—and a different kind of suffering. "Lay him out, over the safe." The Dazers huddled over the Pinkerton reach down and get control of his arms and legs. A small man, the Pinkerton, but the fight not nearly out of him. He sets to flailing and kicking for his life and even shoots a hard boot heel into the knee of a young man half his age. The injured Dazer hops off, swearing a streak, and the two remaining Dazers and the Apache drop their knees into the Pinkerton's back, hoping to let him flap about to the point of exhaustion. But Craw incites a flurry of activity.

"Fetch my two-man," barking to the Dazer in red flannel. "It's with the mules." The Dazer races off toward a clutch of mules and horses back up the arroyo. Something about the order causes unrest among the more senior members of the colonel-major's gang. Sergeant Lon and Eagle Feather intercept him in front of the bannerman.

"You do it this way, he's gonna kick," Lon says.

"Four of you hold him down. Hell, use the whole team, let him kick all he wants. He'll stop kicking when he sees the two-man."

"What I'm saying," Lon making his case, "is if we hold him down, who's gonna watch them?" Lon jabs an elbow toward us and the colonel-major looks up, an idea flowering in his head.

"Even better," Craw says. "You." He points right at me. "And that one there," indicating Owens. Lon starts my way, Eagle Feather heading for Owens. Clara May sets to protesting before the plan has even formulated.

"No, no. Please."

"On your feet," Lon approaching, the four-ten steady. I stand up and step toward him as Eagle Feather rouses Owens.

"Go with mamma, now," Owens passing boy to his mother. "You be brave, son." The boy wails, liquid bubbling from nose and mouth as he reaches for his departing father with a small, outstretched hand. Owens—his entire family howling in tears—lets Eagle Feather push him toward the safe and we bump elbows as Lon steers me in similar fashion.

"Two more," Craw appraising the survivors in

earnest now. "That old timer's got some pluck, get him in here." I think he means Ballentine, but I can't be sure.

Red Flannel returns, winded, with a mule so loaded up with gear the animal seems near collapse. The Dazers get off the Pinkerton's back and bring him to his feet, but if they were to let go he'd drop straight back down again. Two Dazers escort a third into my periphery and I look over and see Ballentine, his ruddiness faded to an ashen gray.

"Need one more, boss," Lon using the four-ten barrel to guide me to a position at one corner of the safe.

"That young buck, there," Craw pointing to George. "He can hold a leg." Eagle Feather doesn't like the idea.

"That one's trouble, boss."

"He makes trouble, he's next," Craw speaking up so George hears him plain. "Come on, get him up." Eagle Feather leads a small contingent over to where George sits motionless.

"You hear that?" Eagle Feather warning him. "Any lick of trouble and it's over for you. Now on your feet." George complies as they pull him up and lead him over to the opposite corner of the safe. Only then does Eagle Feather cut the rope that binds him.

"Where's my mule?" Craw growling as he stomps toward his gear.

"All right, rest of you, get back to work," Eagle Feather commanding, but a ripple of nerves undercuts his voice. "Be dark soon. Every car's gotta be checked. Go on now." The bulk of the Dazers head off, grumbling, back to their duties of looting the rest of the train and, most likely, executing any survivors. I think about the stallion again. The fight in him might just get him killed, if he ain't dead already. But the thought that burns the most is—what if the shock of the last hour has rendered him bashful, even docile? After the strongbox, Storm is the most valuable thing on this train. And if he's in one piece it won't take a trained eye to recognize that. I don't like any of it, not at all. The four-ten jabs my kidney, pulling me back to now.

"Get that shirt off him," Craw yelling from behind his mule. I can't see what he's up to, but the rage in his voice shows no sign of letting up. The four of us stand around the safe, surrounding the Pinkerton, and behind each of us is an armed Dazer. The Apache makes the fifth wheel, the last word come trouble. The sound of cursing and gear being tossed about rises up from behind the mule, and in the window before the tempest Ballentine catches the eye of the Pinkerton.

"What's you name, friend?"

"Quiet," Lon says. The Apache steps in and cuts down the back of the expressman's shirt. The rest of it rips off easy, revealing a torso eaten up with bloody gashes. The beating he took already would kill most any man half his age, and here he stands, meeting Ballentine's eye through blue-black slits nearly swollen shut. Toughness to a fault—that's a Pinkerton, for you.

"McLeash." The man straightening with pride. "General Jeremiah McLeash, Army of the Cumberland."

"Jeremiah, give 'em what he wants. Ain't a man here think less of you."

"I said shut up," Lon slapping Ballentine across

the head. Spooner absorbs the blow and, with a shudder, comports himself. Even at gunpoint, his chin and dignity stay high as summer corn.

The big eye pulls the last of its fiery redness down behind the ridge above the arroyo, draping us in the cold shadow of dying day. So much dying. The colonel-major works his way back from the mule, something long and heavy slowing his approach. A Dazer moves behind him at the same speed, an unwavering distance between them.

And then I see the saw blade—six feet of steel, slightly bowed, like a grin—every tooth nearly two inches of razor sharp destruction. A thick, wood dowel juts up from each end, forming the pair of handles that leave no doubt how the "two-man" earned its name.

"Oh, dear God," Spooner reeling as the saw's full presence unfolds. "Jeremiah, ain't no number of Union dollars worth dying for. Help yourself, man."

"Listen to him, fool," Craw's voice coolly resigned in its meanness. "That flouncy reb's makin' sense. I'm asking for the last time. You tell me how to crack that box, or I'll saw you in half."

There lives, in the heart of every White Man, an expectation of privilege. And even staring down the barrel of death, sometimes the message that a dire situation has slipped from bad to worse falls on deaf ears. Now this small, broken old man thinks the color of his skin, or the company he works for, or some forgotten title from a fading war might pluck him from his predicament. But if a talker like Ballentine can't crack the code, then the cold sand of a dry arroyo swallows up another body.

"I give an oath to Mister Pinkerton himself. I

survived Andersonville. I survived Comanche. I can sure as hell survive the likes of you."

"Suit yourself. Lay him down."

"You four," Lon says, "each of you takes an arm, or a leg. You let go of that arm or leg, we shoot you dead."

George steps forward and shoves Jeremiah McLeash backward. He falls back over the safe, his chest facing the sky, and I reach down and grab one of his legs, George locking up the other leg.

"It ain't gotta be like this," Owens whispering as he secures the old man's arm in his own. "Just tell 'em you can't open it."

Ballentine is the last to wrap up his duty, having to sit flat on his backside instead of kneeling like the rest of us. He doesn't move well, but once he gets a good enough grip, Craw steps in with the saw. Lon stores the four-ten in his belt and picks up the opposite end. The two of them heft the blade up and let it hang there for the Pinkerton to see. I can't help but look up at it, the bluish light finding a sliver of shine on the dirty, crusted steel. That saw has been through the paces, whatever they are, but cutting men in two weren't part of its recent past. The sweet smell of pine sap—unmistakable—flavors the air, confusing every sense of the landscape. No pinyon tree takes root within a hundred miles of here.

"Now or never, old man," Craw says.

I feel McLeash tense as the teeth of the blade settle over his vision. What man wouldn't? And a breath more like a whimper slips out of him before he can stop.

"Okay," the Pinkerton's voice a shell of what it had

been. Craw leans in, listening, but otherwise fully committed to letting the saw speak. "I'll tell you."

"Get to it, then."

"Left thirty-seven."

"Yeah, we got that much."

"Right . . ." Jeremiah choking back a sob.

"No, no." Owens muttering, close to his ear.

"Right, twelve."

"Go on, what's after that?" Craw unimpressed.

"Left, ff—ff—."

Craw bends all the way forward, his face hovering over the Pinkerton's sputtering mouth. "Fuck your mother!" Then the Pinkerton busts into a laugh—a full, deep gut-buster.

"Cut him already," I hear George say. But Craw stands frozen, caught in a haymaker of disbelief, until he explodes.

"Turn him over. Turn him over!"

Lon scrunches his mouth, confused. "What?"

"Turn him over. We're going through the back, *so it hurts more!*" Craw cuffs Owens across the head, ordering him to let go. Owens slackens his grip, I and the others do the same. And in a fluid motion Craw himself grabs the laughing Pinkerton and flips him over like a slab of dough. "Hold this bastard tight," the four of us resuming our positions with the opposite limb. Craw snatches up his handle of the blade, Lon's already poised above the Pinkerton. They maneuver the center teeth over the midpoint of his spine, holding it there, a foot above him, until Craw's signal.

Then Craw nods. The blade drops straight down, of its own weight, and I clamp my eyes shut, Jeremiah's leg convulsing against my cheek. A sound like no other—the kind of agony that equalizes all men—rings out in a curdling shriek that shatters the twilight.

And then the blade begins to move. It takes less than a full swipe to crunch through the spine, and only half that to end the terrible screaming.

CHAPTER TWENTY

They pull the body of Jeremiah McLeash off the safe and one of the Dazers drags it a piece—until the little flap of muscle holding the torso to the legs tears off—and then the man says to hell with it and lets it drop. Vultures can do the rest. The Dazers take far greater care with the saw, wiping it down and leaning it against the berm to dry. The four of us get ordered back to sit with the others, while Lon sends Red Flannel to bring more rope. I suspect now they plan to tie us all up, at least the men, but for now George and I sit at Lon's feet, the four-ten swaying above our heads. Craw parlays with his inner cadre, near the horses, close enough that I hear the urgency in his voice.

"Be pitch dark in half hour. Hell if I want to be blasting a strong box by torch light. Fetch the gelignite."

Owens lifts his head, concern heavy on his brow. He sits with his family. Clara May paws at his shoulder to keep quiet, but something about the new plan has him all worked up. The bannerman fumbles through a satchel and comes out with a leather pouch and a small wooden box. He hands them to Craw, who opens the box and stares down, frowning, at a square of gray clay.

"How much, you think? All of it?"

"The fella sold it said half oughta do, for most things," Eagle Feather says.

"All right then," Craw opening up the pouch. His hand returns with a blasting cap, the kind we used to play with as kids.

"Excuse me, sir." Owens raises a finger to speak and Clara pulls it down, hissing in his ear.

"Sit your ass down," Lon stepping toward him. The second Lon moves, I glance up and meet George's eye looking straight into mine—an entire conspiracy passing between us without a word. *First chance we get, we fight. And fight heavy.* Half a dozen barrels swing onto Owens. He swallows hard, his arms raising, palms out.

"Sir, my name is James Owens."

"What do you want?" Craw says.

"I am a engineer of demolitions, in the employ of Anaconda Mining Company."

"Anaconda?" Eagle Feather says. "That's the Hearst outfit."

"That's right, sir. And I believe my talents can be of assistance to you. I see you got a batch of gelignite there."

"What of it?" Craw growing impatient.

"Well, sir. Thing is . . ." Owens choosing his words careful. "As I'm sure you know, a chunk like that's enough to blow us all to kingdom come. The gelignite's powerful material. State-of-the-art. Also prickly as all get-out. And if not laid just so, every inch of lead in that safe becomes a cannonball, shooting in all directions."

"That so?" Craw says. "Guess we'll need to watch ourselves, then. Quarter oughta do it."

"It'll also incinerate whatever's in that safe." Bull's-eye. Smart fella, Owens. Craw looks at him, greedy-eyed, the gears turning.

A horse cries out, far down the line, and a cold shudder drips down my spine. Wood splinters off in the distance, followed by shouting. The rest of the Dazers are cutting their way through the cars. But I know every sound Storm can muster, and that was not the stallion. Not yet, anyway. Craw confers with Eagle Feather, the flag-bearer listening and nodding, not much else.

I feel a presence slide in behind me and George. I don't dare turn around, but I catch a whiff of aftershave that I make for the older fella travelling with his wife. A man's voice, nearly inaudible and shaking with age, begins to speak.

"Now listen, boys. There's no need to do anything rash. I overheard these fellas talking and they aim to keeps us alive. See, the railroad company will pay to get us back. We're first-class. Rich even. The rail company can't let the respectable sort get kidnapped." I am not rich anymore, but I let him keep talking. "So the plan is, we go with these fellas, and at the appropriate time, they'll sell us back to the company."

"And if the company don't pay?" George says.

"Of course they'll pay. And if not, our families will." Through his whisper, the man sounds hopeful, even cheery.

I bit down on a wave of sadness, but don't have the luxury or time to debate the old fool. I have no doubt he heard what he says he heard. Whether it was spoken in truth to keep us calm, or a lie to mask some darker course, I cannot say. But no matter how many times I unfold it and look at it, I can't figure how any sensible outlaw—even a reckless outfit like this—allows twelve witnesses to walk back into civilization knowing the faces of their captors. What would more likely happen, if they don't slaughter us here, is we become the last-chance bargaining chips in case the army tracks the Dazers down before they get back to their hideout. Maybe the army strikes a deal, maybe not. But my value, rest assured, wouldn't amount to a pile of pennies once the rail barons sniff out the true color of my blood.

"Just thought I'd make you boys aware. It's all gonna be okay." I dip my head, letting him know I hear him clear. The gritty sand shuffles behind me and I feel the presence retreat back to its starting place.

"I ain't got no family's gonna pay to get me outta this," George says.

"Me neither." And our plan, what there is of it, remains unaltered.

"That your kin with you?" Craw pointing to Owens's family.

"Yes, sir. My wife and children."

"All right then," Craw says. He waves Owens forward, Clara May tugging on his shirt.

"No, James, don't. Please!"

"Darling," he cradles her trembling face, eyes full of love. "Let me give them what they want. It'll be all right." He kisses her, like he did on the train. She lets him go, sobbing into her hand. Owens bends down and hugs both children at once, and when he tries to break away they won't let go, screaming in his ear to stay.

"Let's get on with it," Craw says. Clara May pulls the children's arms—like stubborn vines—off their father. The old woman slides over to help with the children, who are inconsolable. Owens takes the wooden box from Craw and before handing him the detonators, Craw says, "You burn up my money, I'll roast your family and make you watch."

They move us back, over the top of the berm, into a tight line for easier guarding. We are in fact, twelve, counting Owens—the only survivors, far as I can see. But only the men have their hands bound behind the back. The thin rawhide cord digs into the skin, but when I stretch it, there is play in the knot. George pulls at his too, every chance he gets. Red Flannel tied it with a mix of grannies and overhand knots that no respectable cowpoke would use beyond the age of nine. These bandits aren't soldiers and they sure as hell ain't horsemen. So who are they?

Eyes of a hawk.
Ears of a buck.
Nose of a wolf.
They've already told me plenty.

Craw and his inner sanctum peer over the berm, same as we do, with a handful of soldiers—six by my count, all heavily ironed with shotguns and repeating rifles—minding the captives. The horses stand unattended at the base of the berm behind us, not far from the drying two-man. One of the horses meanders over and gives the saw a lick. All along the line of the gutted Santa Fe, the sounds of blasting and sawing and chopping continue unabated as the rest of Craw's men go about their pillage. Fires dot the bluing dusk, made blacker by the thick smoke of burning wood and the glowing coal of the tender car.

On the other side of the berm, at the edge of the arroyo, Owens makes for a lonely island. He sits cross-legged atop the safe, working upside down by the flickering light of two torches planted into the ground. The strongbox door faces away from us, out into the arroyo. We stare at Owens's backside, but such nervous anticipation hangs in the air, you'd think us a crowd of picnickers what had camped itself too close to the impending fireworks on the Fourth of July. Even for a robbery, the prospect of something blowing up proves too enticing to look away.

"He ain't gonna stay sitting there when it pop, is he?" Craw asks.

"Says it's the safest place to be," Eagle Feather shrugging.

"His funeral," Craw snorts, a chorus of laughter following. "How much longer?" yelling to Owens.

Owens doesn't look up from his work, and only answers because it's Craw asking. "Just another minute. These detonators are very old," his voice in deep concentration.

"I'll be sure and parlay that to the dead man what sold 'em to us."

Owens wipes his brow on his sleeve and breaks off a dab of gelignite, then he breaks off two pieces from that and stuffs them into his ears.

"Children," he says. "Plug up your ears and look away."

"When's it gonna blow?" Eagle Feather asks.

"Now."

Something fizzles on the front of the safe. Owens covers his ear and spins on his butt and has hardly moved at all when—

An explosion, almost elegant in its clean precision, BOOMS from beneath him. A minor panic spreads through the crowd, faces kissing the dirt. I keep one eye trained over the berm. The safe door shoots straight out, spinning like a top, a hundred yards into the arroyo. And when the smoke clears, James Owens, chief demolitions engineer of the Anaconda Mining Company, sits cross-legged atop an open safe that hasn't moved an inch.

"Hot damn!" Craw bounds over the berm and charges down the hill, the cadre stumbling after him in raucous exaltation. My first look is at George. He separates his wrists—just enough to show me his freedom—then pushes them together again, preserving the visual effect of his bondage.

"Y'all stay put," Lon and the four-ten remindful of their proximity. Owens climbs down off the safe and brushes off the dust.

"Oh, thank God," Clara May crumbling with relief. Craw and the others blow past Owens without so much as a pat on the back and Owens starts up the berm toward us.

Craw peers into the safe and more hoots and hollers come with it. He reaches inside and pulls out two solid gold bricks.

In triumph, he hoists them over his head, "Lord, ain't that a beautiful sight—SONOFABITCH THAT'S HOT!" and throws them down, hopscotching in pain, with seared fingertips. The other boys fall about themselves laughing, and even Craw is too rich and happy to fret the insult.

"Guess I shoulda warned 'em they'd be hot," Owens smirking as he crests the top of the berm. Clara May is there to meet him with a slap to the face, which he knows he had coming. She falls into his arm and they set about kissing again.

"You're an artist, Owens," Spooner says, slapping his back. A cloud of dust poofs from the fabric. "Most impressive. If the South had a few pounds of that stuff, Fort Sumter'd be sitting at the bottom of Charleston Harbor."

"Hey," Lon calling to Red Flannel, "Get him tied up again."

"Yeah, you ain't gotta turn my hands blue this time." Owens says.

"I'm out of cord," Red Flannel says. "You got any?"

"Idiot," Lon unable to hide his contempt.

"Where the hell am I gonna go?" Owens shrugging. Red Flannel edges closer, hefting a rifle.

Craw and his four most trusted men stand together, admiring their newfound riches. The guidon removes his hat and fans out the smoke from the safe, cooling whatever is inside.

Both the torches blew out in the blast and Eagle Feather uproots one of them and brings a match to it. The torch flares and he uses that one to light the other. The bannerman pulls up the second torch and brings it close to the safe.

"There must be twenty of 'em," the guidon marveling. "Twenty bricks. And a shitload of paper, too!"

Craw slaps his hands together—victorious—as the enormous effort of his caper yields a bounty far beyond his dreams. Eagle Feather, his broad, smiling face bathed in fiery orange light, puts his hand on Craw's shoulder and says, "We done it, boss. We done it."

Eagle Feather's head twists hard to the side, half of it blowing off in a trail of pink mist. The Dazer next to him staggers backward, a soupy, red hole erupting from his chest.

Two men lay dead before the sound of the rifle even hits us.

"Sniper!"

And then the real panic starts.

George pivots and explodes from the hips, throwing an uppercut that lands true on the belly of Red Flannel. I hear an expulsion of air, bodies scuffling. I turn and run straight at Lon, the shotgun rising toward me. I lower my shoulder and crash into his chest, both of us flying down the backside of the berm. The four-ten booms near my head, the shock wave rippling against my skin. We hit the ground hard, rolling now, knotted together, down the berm until we crash into something. Lon screams—a terrified shriek. I peel off him, rising to my knees.

Lon lays twisted against the two-man, the jagged teeth buried deep in his side. He paws for the shotgun. Without thinking, I throw myself into him, impaling him further against the saw. He coughs, blood spurting from his mouth. I rear back and throw my weight once more. The breath goes out of him and he stops fighting. In death, he looks like a boy. Like they always do.

Amid the pandemonium—screaming voices and counterfire—the report of the sniper's rifle echoes, unabated, through the darkening canyon. I flop onto my back and shimmy my bound arms down the back of legs, over the boots, and around the front. I scrape the rawhide cord against of the saw's teeth, shredding the hide in an instant. Something about that rifle fire—the comfort of the sound—slows my racing heart. I draw the pistol from my trousers, scoop up the four-ten and bandolier, and charge back up the hill, double-fisted.

Red Flannel flies down the berm, unable to protect his fall. He hits awkward and comes to stop near my feet, clutching what's left of his throat. George ripped the meat of it out with his bare hands. George stands high up the berm, his fists and forearms covered in blood.

"Down!" I shout, raising the shotgun.

George flattens to the ground and I empty the last barrel into the chest of a charging Dazer. He falls back. George picks up Flannel's fallen rifle and smashes the butt into his face, crushing the skull. He turns toward me with the rifle.

"I can't hit shit with this."

"Trade me," handing him the four-ten and the bandolier. He snaps it open and reloads.

"Like bird hunting," he says, nodding.

"Aim at the middle. Don't gotta be perfect. And steer clear of the Apaches."

I stow the pistol and check the rifle, the magazine nearly full. Three Dazers lie prone atop the berm, guns pointed up into the canyon, but not at any specific target.

"Where's it coming from?" one of them shouts.

"Up on the ridge," comes the reply from down in the arroyo. Craw.

"I ain't see no muzzle flash," another says, his voice trembling.

"Nah, he's cloaking it somehow," Craw annoyed. "Cinnamon! C'mon here, girl," followed by a sharp whistle. A mare below us hears her name and breaks up the berm. We slip in behind her and hide our approach until one of the three Dazers finally looks behind him. The dizzying effect of the sniper fire has caused such confusion the bandits have neglected their captives.

"Guns! They got guns!" the four-ten cuts him down, and as the two others roll over, I shoot them with the rifle. The mare charges over the top of the berm toward her master. He falls in with the dead Dazers and I peek over the edge. Craw crouches behind the safe, pinned down by the sniper, but as far as cover goes he could do a lot worse. No bullet is piercing the walls of that strongbox. The guidon huddles tight behind Craw, but Craw has the prime location, leaving the bannerman well aware of his exposure. Directly below us, the Dazer in George's coat hides behind a rock, his backside unprotected from my vantage. I settle in, using the berm as cover, and aim down the rifle.

"Don't mess up my coat," George says.

I shoot the Dazer in the head. Craw spins our way, blasting a pistol that kicks up dust into our faces. We hug the berm. George pulls the guns from the bodies behind us and distributes them with a toss to our fellow survivors.

"Take these, keep an eye out both ways. Them Dazers come sneaking up train-side to get out from that sniper."

"Much obliged." I know Ballentine's voice anywhere. Unknown if he has killing in him, but if he wants a chance to gun down a Union uniform, he won't get a better one.

"Who is it? Who's shooting?" Clara May asking. She and Owens form a barrier around the children, whom they have hunkered down so close to the berm they may as well be buried.

"Dunno," George says. But I know. I've known since the first shot rang out.

The mare called Cinnamon skips down the berm toward the safe and all at once three other horses come scampering over the berm, not wanting to get left behind. The horses swirl around Craw and the bannerman, weaving in and out of the pale light of the one remaining torch.

"Get the torch out, ya idiot. That's how they're seeing us." The bannerman grabs the torch from the ground and hurls it out into the arroyo where it lands in a patch of dry shrub.

The sniper shoots again and one of the horses falls, giving Craw and the guidon more cover. Craw snatches the saddlebags from Cinnamon and, in the low light, sets to emptying the safe.

"Why ain't that rifle shooting?" George says.

"He can't see anymore."

"We can."

We raise the guns and start firing, sending Craw and the bannerman to the dirt. The torch ignites the dry shrub that turns quick to a small inferno, giving the sniper more light to work with. The rifle shot rings out, and pings off the safe.

"Somebody's coming," Owens says. "On the right." I turn right and look down our side of the berm and make out two men in blue working their way up the wreckage toward our position. One crouches behind a train wheel and peers down a rifle.

"Everybody down," I shout, and then I see a muzzle flash and hear a bullet whistle overhead. A woman screams. The old woman.

"Chester. Oh dear God." I let my weight slide me down the hill, belly scraping over the sand and come to a stop in a dark shadow. The shooter abandons his position, and slinks along the boxcar to the edge of an upturned Pullman, close enough to see his unshaved cheekbones. I let out half a breath and squeeze the trigger. His face caves in on itself and he falls back, dead. That springs the second soldier into action. He rises from behind a pile of debris and fires his pistol in my direction. The sand explodes next to me. Three guns, all different, boom from atop the berm. The man lurches once and falls down. I look back and see George, Owens and Ballentine each with a smoldering gun in his hand.

"My kill, gentlemen," Ballentine says.

"Hell it is," George countering.
"Who gives a shit, he's dead," Owens says.

"Stop them others," I say, racing up the berm. My friends turn in unison and take cover at the top. The brush fire burns hot, the whole landscape glowing bright like a fallen sun. Craw works from a crouch, shielding himself from the sniper with a gelding. He hoists the saddlebags, laden with gold, onto the mare and runs alongside it, using every inch of cover until the last second, when he swings up into the saddle, heels her in the ribs, and steams off. The bannerman struggles with his horse and nearly falls off his saddle, but he gets him running. They all start blasting beneath the steady echo of the sniper's rifle. The guidon fires wildly at us, just enough to earn a pause from our weapons, but then his back arches and he drops his gun.

The rifle booms again and the horse squeals, but keeps running. It changes direction and heads straight for the burning scrub. Then the horse veers again, avoiding the fire, but the banner—the inverted Stars and Stripes—kisses the flame. Hungry fire consumes the Union flag—bars of red and white glowing orange and blue and then nothing, as the churning air of a horse at full gallop breaks the flag apart, piece by burning piece. Pounding hooves carry horse and rider deep into the darkening night, a fiery trail in their wake. Then the guidon slumps and falls to the ground. The horse never breaks stride. The flag burns, feeding on itself—sinking into blackness—and then it is gone.

CHAPTER TWENTY-ONE

"Looks like they're pulling out," George says. All down the line, the clarion call of Craw's escape—punctuated by a flaming standard that was hard to miss—makes its way through the remaining Dazers in the form of catcalls, whistles and shots fired into the air. The burning wreckage of the Santa Fe illuminates a haphazard exodus. Bandits in both directions break for the nearest horse with whatever pillage they can carry and light out across the desert in pursuit of their departed leader and the loot that brung them here in the first place. A few men ride two to a horse and something about that bothers me, but in the excitement I can't figure why.

We crouch down in the darkened shadow of the berm, guns ready, as the riders from the front of the train blow past at full gallop. I count no more than eight or nine in total, and while we're braced for a fight, the truth is they don't seem much fussed about us at all. George peers down a pistol, steadying his hand against the berm, and I reach over and ease the barrel down.

"Let 'em go."

"The hell's wrong with you," his eyes narrowing.

"If you miss, you give 'em reason to turn around."

"I weren't planning to miss."

"You ain't making that shot in a month of Sundays," Owens says.

"How 'bout you go blow yourself up, college boy. Less you need to help your friends."

"What's that supposed to mean?"

"Now fellas, settle down," Spooner stepping in, but more in front of Owens than George.

"I'm surprised you didn't bag the loot up for 'em, tie it in a bow."

"Put it through your head, kid," Owens holding his ground. "Getting them bastards their money is what got them gone. And nothing else."

"Didn't have to make such a damn show if it," George heaving, plenty of fight left in him and nowhere to put it. But I can't think about that now, one thought only crashes through my brain.

Storm.

"The point ain't to help them sons-a-bitches."

"The point is to stay alive," I say, grabbing George by the shoulder. "I have to check on the stallion."

"I'll go with you," George says.

"Need your muscle here, with the injured, case they gotta be moved. These fires could flare up."

Ballentine steps forward. "There's safety in numbers, Harlan. I'll come with you."

"I move faster alone."

"You don't know they're gone. You don't know what's out there."

"I know them Dazers ain't letting too much distance get between them and their share. No point to sticking around, unless they're hurt. If they're hurt, I'll deal with 'em."

"We should have some kind of signal," Owens says. "Case there's trouble."

"Two quick shots in the air, that outta do it." I swap a fresh magazine into the repeater and check the pistol again, remembering that I haven't needed it yet. The men nod their agreement and I head off down the berm, walking in measured paces, head on swivel. Then Storm pops into my head again and I start to jog, and by the time I hit flat ground, I find myself in a full run.

The boxcars, and what's left of the palace cars, smolder—black and ash-gray embers wheezing a thin, stinging smoke that hampers visibility. But the brushfire finds new life and showers the gutted Santa Fe with enough light for me to find my way and keep an eye out for an ambush. The cattle have stuck around in surprising numbers, optimistic that some human will point them toward water, at least until dawn, when they'll go off to find it themselves. A few weeks from now, this forgotten corner of desert will have its share of skinny cows and fat wolf pups.

I see the stock car up ahead, upturned and split down the middle like a melon. But it hasn't burned. Cows meander back and forth, blocking the path. I slap the hides and get them moving and make my way to the edge of the car. A bad feeling sinks in my gut. Two men to a horse. I know why it bothered me now. No spare horses. Enough cattle milling around to feed a regiment and not one unclaimed horse. It means the Dazers, for their lunacy, had the forethought to wrangle any stray mounts, like a sniper collecting his spent brass.

I whistle, hard and sharp, waiting for a sound that doesn't come. The stock car sits off to itself, hard to miss. Another bad sign. Something glimmers against the ground in the orange light, a twisted mass in shadow behind it. I cock the hammer on the rifle and step soft.

It is a man, the shimmer coming from the blood puddled around his head.

Charlie.

Shit.

The English horseman lays on his belly, his head busted open. An axe maybe, but the weapon is gone. Charlie's arms stretch out before him, fingers spread into the dirt. A trail of claw marks stretches from his hands to an open space beneath the car, big enough to hide in. But not quite. They dragged him—clawing the ground—out from under the car and killed him. Charlie died next to the creatures he'd sworn to protect.

You tried. I know you tried.

I move past him and climb up the side of the stock car.

"Storm." I hold still, tasting the air for any reply at all. Reaching the top, I lean over the side and peer into the empty cavern where the cattle had been. A few dead, broken cows—blood and manure and filth. Storm's hold lies farther down, and I walk along the top edge of the car until I am directly over it.

It is dark, but the fire light shines through the slats and I can see all the way down to the matted hay at the bottom. I keep staring, like it would somehow change the outcome and make Storm appear.

But the stallion is gone.

Yet all at once a bolt of hope shoots through my heart as I spot his saddle, upended in the far corner of his stall. His saddle is here. I know there is absolutely zero chance that Storm let one of those untrained hillbillies ride him off bareback. I could imagine one trying and getting so frustrated that I'd find Storm sprawled out with a bullet hole in his head. But that didn't happen. And he didn't die in the crash. This much I know.

"You got out, boy. That's a good horse, that's a damn good horse." I start figuring he might be close by. I stand upright and shoot a whistle out in all four cardinals, every sense of my being peeled to maximum alertness. "I'm here, amigo. And I ain't leaving."

Something moves, close behind me. I snap the rifle up, sighting on a pile of splintered boards. A solid sheet of lumber lay across the top, motionless. I stay locked on, trusting my eyes. The corner of the board dips, juts a hair, and then rises—the rhythm of breathing. I stay locked on, edging my way back down the lip of the stock car to where the ground is high and I can jump off without lowering the rifle. I land easy and start toward the pile, finger itching the trigger.

"Come outta there." I stop and wait. The board settles, the life beneath it holding its breath. "I know you're under there. I swear, you don't come out, I'll light you up."

A fragment of sound—a whimper—seeps from the pile and then swallows itself. I may just blast it anyway, but I creep forward, now wondering how any grown man could contort himself into such a small confinement. Maybe a rat or some other scavenger. More likely though—a trap—the last stand of some injured Dazer, fixed on taking one more out with him.

Better to shoot first. But shooting blind gives away my position, and if I don't kill him clean—and he's waiting with a scattergun—the advantage swings his way. No, I need to see.

I float forward, barely touching the ground, and swing my leg at the board. It flies off. I lean in—trigger half pulled—and meet the frightened gaze of a child. He makes no move to recoil, or even cover himself, at the sight of a rifle aimed at him. His only defense—an effective one—is a guileless faith in the protective instinct an adult feels when confronted by the innocence of children. I lower the rifle.

He wears a torn waistcoat, his face blackened with ash. A thick dusting of pale gray ash covers him head to toe, leaving no trace of his hair or skin color. Only when he blinks, and a tear fall from his pale blue eyes and cuts a pink trail down his cheek, can I make him for white.

"You speak English?"

He dips his head in the affirmative.

"You hurt?"

"No." The mouselike voice creeping out of him bears only a ghostly resemblance to when it last passed my ears, aboard the train, slinging candy and sandwiches with the engaging patter of a born showman. The butcher boy.

"You can come out now. Ain't no one gonna mess with you." I hold out my hand and he takes it, his grip small but strong. He climbs over the pile of scrap between us, and when he gets close enough I pick him up—light as a bird—and set him down on firm ground. I pat the front pocket of my waistcoat and somehow I still got my folded-up bandana in there, so I snap it open and hand it to him.

"Let's get you cleaned up."

The butcher boy wipes his face, the gray sloughing off him in a powdery cloud. I take a knee in front of him and brush off his shoulders and hair. He dabs the bandana on his forehead and down his arms and gets to looking almost pink again. Then he hands it back to me.

"Best you hang on to that for a bit. Fella don't want to get caught short with a sneeze in front of the ladies." The corners of his mouth rise, not a smile yet, but getting into smile territory. "My name's Harlan. What's yours?"

"Reggie."

"Well, Reggie. I reckon the Santa Fe Railroad owes you a big ol' pile a candy. Probably a pay raise and a new suit of clothes. Come to think of it, they owe me a new suit too."

"I just want to go home."

"Me too, pal." I nod back toward the scrap pile where he'd been hiding. "You been in there the whole time?"

"Yes, sir."

"That was good thinking."

"I climbed under there when I see them soldiers set fire to that car."

"They weren't soldiers. They was outlaws, pretending to be soldiers."

"Why would they do that?" The orange light frames the boy's face in frozen bafflement.

"Tell the truth, there ain't a lick of sense on most things they done."

"I'll never look at a solider same way again."

"I 'spect none of us will." We set to thinking about that, and as the breeze shifts, bringing the coolness of the desert night across winnowing fire, I say, "There was a horse in this stall, here. Did you see what happened to him?"

"He took it." A cold knot sinks in my belly.

"Who did, a soldier?"

The boys shakes no. "Injun."

My knees buckle, the ground below turning to quicksand, and I plant the rifle to steady myself. The Apaches. All at once the new reality crystalizes in my brain, the memory of the departing Dazers repeating over and over. There had been no Apaches among them. Of course not. No Apache trusts gold enough to go chasing after it, and the White Man's dollar means even less. His prize is what he can use—a woman, rifles, livestock.

"This Injun, he have long black hair, half down his back?"

"No. I saw that one. He come through too, but he ain't the one took the horse. That one had silver hair."

Silver hair. An old Apache. He probably saw the stock car, went right for it. And if he knows horses—and find me an Apache who don't—he'd have taken one peek through those slats and seen his prize. A prize so rare, he'd ignore the cattle that could feed his people and take off straight away.

"Which way did he go?" Reggie thinks a moment and points off to the south.

"You sure?"

The boy nods and I believe him, because it makes sense. Mexico.

Those other two Apaches, the younger ones, they might even be jealous and feel like they ain't got their fill yet. The thought hardly has time to settle when two quick shots ring out. The boy bristles at the gunshots and turns for the pile, but I scoop him up.

"Come with me," and I start running the way I came.

The Pullman gives good cover in the flats just short of the berm. I crouch behind the edge and see two horses headed toward us. Even through the darkness, I can spot the two Apaches by the way they ride. I put Reggie down and he scampers straight for the shadows beneath the wheels of the Pullman. The lead horse breaks up the berm, the rider holding something bulky and alive in his rein hand and firing backward with a pistol at his pursuers, who run on foot, shouting. But the second horse—weighted with a heavier load—struggles for purchase in the soft sand of the berm. I bring up the rifle and sight the lead rider as he passes through the orange glow of burning sage. The short-haired Apache has Owens's little boy clutched under his arm. If I miss, I'll hit the child, so I take aim at the horse and put him down hard with one shot.

The Apache hops off the horse before it hits the ground and runs up along the berm, using the boy as a shield and squeezing off a pistol shot that don't come close.

Behind him, the long-haired Apache urges on the second horse, his progress powerful slowed by the tug-o-war he finds himself in with Owens. Owen's little girl is the rope. She twists in midair—stretched taut as a board between her father and the Apache, screaming with red-faced fury. The Apache has Clara May's body—slack and unconscious—draped over his lap. He steers the horse with his legs while swinging the club at Owens's face with one hand and holding on to the little girl's ankles with the other. Owens pulls on his daughter's arms, absorbing countless grazing blows from the club but doing his best to stay upright and avoid a knockout blow.

Ballentine trudges up the rear, threatening a pistol, but far too afraid to shoot.

Short-hair Apache reaches the top of the berm, carrying the boy. All at once, George appears, charging over the top from the other side. He hefts the shotgun like a baseball bat, swinging the stock-end into the Apache's knee. Short-hair spins, falling back, the pistol coming up. George flips the shotgun around, but the pistol fires first. George howls, the impact twisting him sideways, clutching his side. The shotgun falls to the ground.

Short-hair gets to his feet, hopping on one leg, and the boy kicking and clawing to break free of his grip. But the Apache holds on, and with a busted leg hobbles toward the top of the berm to hook up with Long-hair. I have a feather of a shot and take it without thinking. The Apache never stops moving and I hit him under the shoulder—not where I wanted— but maybe enough for a drawn-out death.

Long-hair, nearly to the top, lands a decisive blow against the side of Owens's head. The mining man falls back, but keeps his grip locked on the little girl, and as he falls, she falls with him, slipping from the Apache's hand. The Apache lets her go and instead takes the boy from Short-hair as Short-hair throws himself onto the back of the horse. Then Long-hair kicks the horse up in earnest, and I try to sight a kill shot, but the horse—burdened with four bodies—crests the berm and vanishes down the other side.

I break from my cover and sprint up the hill—all the way to the top—and dive onto my belly, raising the rifle to shoot prone. Long-hair drives the horse hard down the back slope, gaining momentum. They hit the flat ground and the horse digs in, racing for the safety of darkness. Short-hair clings on for dear life, both arms bear-hugging his kinsman to stay aboard. I pull the trigger, the shot echoing up the arroyo. Short-hair arches his back, and then slumps, but still he holds on. The horse passes through the light of the fires and then disappears into black.

With Ballentine's help, I get George and Owens and Owens's little girl back to what's left of the group. The old woman's husband died, but she proves pretty good with a sewing needle and gets Owen's head stitched back up. Owens is so eaten up with anguish that the pain of the needle hardly earns a grimace. He just pets the little girl's hair and tells her we'll get mamma and Jimmy Junior back soon enough, until she finally falls asleep. As for George, the bullet passes clean through his side and by some miracle missed anything important. The wound, or its infection, might kill him, but I doubt it'll kill him tonight. Then Ballentine and I fetch little Reggie from his hiding place and Spooner has to lure him out with a stick of chewing gum. Before heading back I stop at the horse I had killed and ask his forgiveness and make a promise that I will bring him

oats and sugar when we meet again on the Spirit Side.
Then I lead Ballentine and Reggie back to the others.
The old woman weeps with delight at the discovery
of the boy and takes Reggie down the way to get him
cleaned off.

Owens sits up, testing his strength. "I'm going after
'em. Tonight."

"Don't be silly, Owens." Spooner handing him a
flask. "We'll get the army after them."

"And in the meantime, what you think those sav-
ages are doing to her, huh? And my boy. My sweet
boy." Owens takes a drink, then he looks at me.

"Them Apaches took your stallion. We'll go after
them together."

"We can't."

"Hell, we can't."

"There's no horses."

"What you mean, 'no horses'?"

"I been up and down the train, there's no more
horses. Half them Dazers was doubled up riding
outta here." Owens looks around, we all do. Dead
horses are as much part of the landscape as a burning sagebrush or a gutted Pullman.

All I want to do is go after Storm. The thought of
him under some strict Apache, biding his time,
confused—turns my stomach. I can track the
Apaches on foot. And I can track them at night. But
I can't track them on foot at night, not at the speed
they're going. As much as it kills me, I have to wait
until dawn to have any chance of seeing Storm again.

I say, "First light, I'm heading out on foot."

"I'll go with you," Owens handing me the flask.

"I can't say we're going the same direction. The

boy says Storm went south, but your Apaches headed north, same as the White Men."

"That may have just been convenience. Maybe them Apaches are all fixing to rendezvous else-where."

"Maybe, maybe not. But I travel better alone. You do like Spooner tells you."

"Ain't nobody tells a man I can't go after my own wife."

"I ain't telling you can't go." I look down and make sure the little girl is sleeping. "I'm telling you, sure as morning, they'll kill you. And that sweet girl there is an orphan. Let the army handle it. They don't take kindly to Indians running off with white women."

"The army ain't gonna do jackshit to find my wife and boy."

"Now hold on," Spooner says. "I'll go to my grave before I praise a Union soldier, but I'm inclined to agree with Harlan on this."

"And I'm telling you, the army is gonna go after one thing only. Their money."

"*Their* money?" Spooner crinkling his nose.

"You boys didn't see into that safe like I did. Them gold bars was wrapped up in bands that said 'U.S. Department of War' all over them. You see what I'm getting at?"

"Oh my God," Spooner realizing. "They stole the army's pay."

"That spy they had on board, that's how they knew which train it was," I say, all of us piecing it together now.

"Exactly. Bunch of pissed-off soliders looking to

get revenge on the army. Hell, that's how I'd do it. Rob it blind."

"Crazy Dazers," Spooner says. I finish his thought. "Not so crazy after all."

I get up from the others and head down toward the front of the train in search of supplies. I see a flash of movement out in the arroyo and make out a human figure climbing down from the hillside. In all the confusion with Apaches and the fires and the boy, I'd forgotten about the sniper. We all had. And yet without him, none of us would be alive. He walks out of the darkness, his jacket hanging open.

"You don't look surprised to see me," he says.

"You think I don't know the sound of my own rifle. You're the only one knew where it was."

"I didn't think you'd mind," Burke says.

"Mind? You're better with it than I am."

"I doubt that sincerely."

"Two shots, two kills. That's how you started off."

"True, but the first shot, I was aiming for a different fella." Burke smiles. "This Spencer of yours pulls strong to the left."

"That it does. And it took you all of one shot to make the adjustment."

Burke nods, staring out at the horizon of a distant, but powerful, memory.

"Second Regiment, South Carolina Volunteers." He hands over the rifle. A soldier's habits die hard, even twenty years removed. I made Burke for infantry the moment he picked up the Spencer aboard the train. But the way he shot it—the precise firing, the subterfuge at avoiding detection, and the maddening terror caused by such an unrelenting assault—that is another animal altogether.

My mind imagines a string of dead, Southern rebels—gray tunics stained with blood—who fell at the hands of a killer they never saw. Burke's facility as a sniper speaks of unheralded stories I'll bet rarely cross Burke's lips, except on long whiskey-soaked nights around the fire.

"I didn't have no clean shot to save the Pinkerton. Y'all was too close."

"Pinkerton could've saved himself."

"And I was already climbing down when this last tussle broke out. I couldn't see anything. Mrs. Owens, she all right?"

"They took her. And their boy. We got the little girl back."

"Lord have mercy." Burke shakes his head, his eyes grave.

"Burke, ain't nobody hold a grudge on anything you done. Weren't for you, we'd be dead." Burke looks up at the small campfire near the others and then back at me.

"What you out here looking for?"

"Supplies. Heading out at dawn. You go up to the fire, get yourself warm."

"All the same, Mister Harlan. I think I'll tag along with you for now."

CHAPTER TWENTY-TWO

The small hours of night creep forward in a maddening cycle of restless sleep and mind-numbing wakefulness, punctuated by crying fits from the injured and bouts of choking, eye-stinging coughs brought on by a smothering blanket of smoke. The fires have nearly burned themselves out a dozen times, only to kick back up in a gusting wind and by dawn, burn themselves out again. I lay on the ground, scouring the heavens, until the first streak of pale shatters the blackness of the eastern sky and then I get moving.

"You done looked over those provisions ten times already," Burke watching me through a half-closed eye from his perch against an upturned boxcar.

"Nothing else to do," brushing myself off. I managed to piece together a pretty good haul of supplies during the night. A couple of dead Dazers gave me a shotgun and a second pistol and all the ammunition I can carry, including plenty for the Spencer. Burke showed me how to get back to my berth. Most of the car had been obliterated, but somehow the fire missed it. One half of the compartment had been smashed like a tin can, yet the other half remained bizarrely intact. Just yesterday—stepping through that door the first time, handing my bags to Burke along with a good tip—it seems like a lifetime ago. I found my other suit still on its hanger and switched into it. The saddlebags were wedged so tight I could only get one of them out, but one will do fine.

Next I sniffed out the galley car and scrounged up some food—canned peaches, tomato juice, and in the icebox, an entire ham. I hacked off a chunk of the ham and folded it into a napkin and put it in the saddlebag with the canned goods and carried the rest of the ham over to the campfire for the others. The men tore into it while the old woman fed little bites to the children like baby birds.

"They got a ham up there," I say to Burke. "Going fast, though," the sky lightening behind us.

"I got some pork 'n' beans, some of them canned peaches. I'll be all right." Burke folds up his bedroll and stuffs it into the sack he'd been using as a pillow. He looks like a man fixing to light out, same as I do. "Mister Harlan, you tell those folks I was down here?"

"No. I got the impression you didn't want them to know."

"I appreciate that."

"Though I 'spect they're all itching to know who their sharpshooting angel is."

"Well, if they're already thinking 'twas an angel, far be it for me to step on the toes of God Almighty."

A sound turns my head—a high metallic zing—soft, but rising steady. I look upward, over my shoulder, at the pair of steel rails, jutting from the high ground of the track to the nothing space where the trestle once stood.

"Train coming," I say.

I look to the campfire. Reggie's young ears—well-tuned to the rails—are the first to hear it.

"Train's coming! Train's coming!" The boy leaps up, pointing at the high road. The zinging gets louder. A fat plume of gray billows upward against the pastel sky.

"I hear it now, small train." Burke cocks his head, his ear picking apart the subtlety. "It's barely crawling. He's riding the brake." Burke shakes his head, frowning.

"That means they know the road's out. Looking to stop."

"Time for me to go," Burke slinging the sack over his shoulder.

"Hold up a minute."

"Best I move along."

"What's eating you, Burke? You didn't do anything wrong."

Burke stops, turns back, his shoulders slumping. "I killed white people."

"You saved white people."

"That don't change the first part."

"They was killing whites too. A lot of them. Ain't nobody more deserving of death than them what done all this."

"You know that, I know that, but I ain't interested in seeing that fact get chopped up, and turned around, and twisted into something it ain't. You know how this go. Time goes by, the truth get interpretized, people hungry for justice that ain't there. Because the only fact that ain't never gonna change is that this here old nigger killed himself some white people."

"I'll stand in court and tell it square, exactly as it happened."

Burke blinks his big, brown eyes and stares straight through me. "Men like you and me got no business staking our lives to the minds of white people."

I never told Burke about me, but he knows. And by his face, he knows that I know that he knows. Any argument on the subject would insult us both.

"Where you headed?"

"West," Burke says, looking off to the horizon.

"Hard country, that way."

"I'll manage. If you're smart, you'll set out right now too."

"I'm right behind you. Just gonna help load the injured."

The brakes of the train squeal loud and hard behind us, the whistle pealing—tinny and sharp, nothing like the Santa Fe's mighty roar. Burke shakes his head.

"I got a bad feeling about that train." The moment Burke says it, I know I have a bad feeling too. Every instinct says to pick up my bag and start off South and don't look back. But I was raised that you don't leave people behind, not once you get to feeling responsible for them. Two days ago I didn't know Spooner Ballentine, or James Owens—and George, I didn't even like him—but once you've fought side-by-side with a man, against other men who are trying to kill you, a bond forges that don't break easy.

"I can't just leave," I say. Burke nods. He understands. Then I say, "You got a gun?"

"I'll scurry up an iron on the way out."

"Hang on." I pick up the Spencer and toss it through the air. Burke catches it, a stunned look on his face.

"You lost your mind?"

"Keep it. You need a good rifle."

"This your weapon, son. This here a part of you." I can't argue with Burke on that. That rifle seen as much with me as the stallion has.

"Tell you what, hang on to it for me. I might need it back someday."

"Oh sure, once old Burke fix that nasty pull you put in it, gets it working proper for a change. Listen here, I put the work in, I ain't likely to let it go."

"Then I'll know it'll be in good hands."

Burke tips his porter's cap. "That it be," he says. Then he disappears through the wreckage as the Big Eye breaks over the mountains.

Ballentine helps Owens to his feet, and George gets up on his own accord, using a thin wood plank as a crutch. He grimaces as he starts moving, the bandage around his lower ribcage soaked reddish brown.

"You should be lying down," I say.

"Hell with that." Once again, the pageantry of an arriving train—even one as small as this—proves too irresistible to miss. The children run up ahead, the old woman trying to keep up.

"Not too far ahead, Eleanor. Stay close to Mrs. Whitehurst," Owens calling to his daughter. "I can't see right. I see three of everything."

"If we have to shoot anybody, aim for the one in the middle," Ballentine says.

"Maybe let us do the shooting," I say. "Is everyone armed?"

Ballentine pats his coat pocket and I see Owens has a pistol stuck in the back of his trousers.

"I'll never be unarmed again as long as I live," George flashing me a knife in his boot and that sawed-off four-ten in his belt.

"Gentlemen," Spooner says, "I'm inclined to believe the need for firearms has passed."

I want to share in Spooner's optimism, but with every step the bad feeling grows a little stronger. We work our way up the slope toward the tracks. Reggie bounds up the rocks like a jackrabbit. Spooner looks back over his shoulder, the elevation giving a new-found perspective to the scope and calamity of the wreckage.

"Considering how far we fell, it's a miracle the crash didn't kill us all."

"We weren't meant to die here," George says. "That's the only reason we ain't dead."

We reach the high, flat ground where the road runs, sweat beading our necks, the sun now well clear of the mountains. Two hundred yards down-track, a locomotive crawls toward us, the engineer's head hanging from the side portal as he scrutinizes the condition of the rail. He waves his arm and the children wave back and then a crewman jumps down and runs along side, relaying the remaining distance back to the driver.

"Well, I may be punch-drunk," Owens shaking his head, "but I think I'm looking at the shortest train I've ever seen."

The engine hauls behind it a tender and a single caboose and nothing more. But as it draws near, the fineness of its lone passenger car—paneled in dark wood and fresh-painted with gold and green trim—makes clear that this train carries someone important, the man who hired it. A bright Union flag snaps crisp in the breeze. The caboose reminds me of a stagecoach I saw once—the stateliest and most fabulous vehicle to ever roll into the Bend. All it brought with it was a mess of trouble.

"You need to stop right there," Owens yells. "Are they as close as I think?"

"Halt your train!" Spooner amplifying the sentiment.

The young crewman sprints ahead in our direction, his eyes wide as saucers when his brain registers the ripped-apart rails and sudden drop where the trestle used to be. He spins and throws his hands up.

"Stop!"

Owens grabs hold of his daughter. The old woman—Whitehurst, her name—snags Reggie's wrist and detains the squirming boy as the lone brakeman lays into his lever. The train hisses to a halt.

"Good God," the young crewman says, "what happened to the bridge?"

"Son," Ballentine says, "you need to prepare yourself."

The crewman walks to the edge where the road ends and stares down at the view. His whole body slumps. The rest of the crew—the brakeman, a fireman and the engineer—disembark and tend to their immediate duties, but the looming spectacle tugs at their attention.

"How's it look, Teddy?" the engineer's face heavy with concern. The young crewman—Teddy—doesn't answer. He looks down at a quarter mile of tangled steel and smoking lumber and begins to weep. The fireman lays a two-step platform at the door of the caboose for the passengers and doesn't wait for the door to open. He runs to join Teddy. Our raggedy group holds its ground—disinclined to take in a vista that needs no reinforcement in our minds.

The engineer strides past us, "What happened here?" he says without stopping. None of us knows how to answer that, and we let him go see for himself. He reaches the end of the road and stops. A throaty sound—like he'd been gut-punched—comes out of him and he drops to his knees.

The brakeman cranks open the caboose door and steps aside, revealing a small man in a brown suit—brown head to toe—waiting there, impatient. The brown man's gaze falls—unwavering—upon our group, as though the attack of the Santa Fe, and the presentation of its aftermath, bore not the slightest curiosity for him. A second man, heavier, with a graying beard and a big-gauge—no, make that *two* shotguns—falls in behind the brown man and the two of them stride with determined purpose toward our position.

"Well, aren't we glad to see you," Ballentine says. "My name is Shelby J. Ballen—"

"Nobody move!" The bearded man snaps both shotguns up so fast Spooner nearly chokes on his own name.

"Take it easy," George says. "We got a woman and children here."

"Keep your hands regular, and yourselves at rest,"

the beard says. The brown man's draw was equally fast, a single pistol, held rock steady. The odds say four-against-two should favor our end. But none of the four—myself included—feels inclined to test the short money. We been outdrawn, plain and simple.

"What's the meaning of this?" Ballentine says, "We're the victims here."

The brown man raises a finger, and Spooner—a man not used to being silenced—stops talking.

"My name is Jacob Cross. I am a federal agent of the United States government. Any man impeding my authority is guilty of a crime and will be punished accordingly." His eyes trained on us, he calls to the engineer. "Mister Carter, if you please."

"Sir, all due respect, we got a situation down here."

"Mister Carter, I have deputized you and your crew, and until I release you of your duties, you will do as I say. Now come here this instant." Carter and the train crew stumble over, their grief raw as an open wound. "Disarm these men," Cross says.

"By all means, *sir*," Carter glowering. "You heard him, boys. Grab the guns." The crewmen, eyes wet with tears, their faces frozen in shock, descend our way. The graybeard jabs the ten-gauge toward George.

"Hold still, young'un." The brakeman takes the four-ten from George and turns my way, when Cross stops him.

"Check that man's boot. He has a weapon there." The brakeman turns back and, patting down George's boot, discovers the blade hidden within.

"Son of a gun. How'd you see that?" the brakeman wondering.

Cross doesn't answer, his rattlesnake eyes combing each man with a predator's gaze. This man Cross—

he observes what the average man overlooks. Eyes of a hawk. I have no reason to believe any of his other senses are any less attuned. His stare falls on me and remains there. And the bad feeling that had been just a droplet in the back of my throat, now rages like a cold river through every bone in my body. The brakeman lays George's weapons on the ground at Cross's feet, where the engineer deposits the revolver taken from Owens. Ballentine directs the fireman to the iron in his coat. The graybeard kicks the looted guns into a pile, all while maintaining control of his four barrels. Teddy and the fireman move in behind me and I feel the pistol—the one I found this morning—lifted from the waistband.

"That's all he's got," the fireman says.

Cross shakes his head. "Step away from him." Teddy and the fireman back off to the rear. Then Cross says to the fireman, "You, with the pistol. Point it at him."

"That ain't in my line, sir."

"He shovels coal for a livin'," Carter adds.

"And he will again, in short order. It's just a precaution."

The fireman has no training as a sentry—much less holding a man at gunpoint—but his unfamiliarity with a gun makes me feel worse, not better. With reluctance, he raises the pistol at the vicinity of my back.

"Sorry, fella. Nothing personal," his voice shaking.

"It's all right," I say. "I ain't gonna make a murderer out of you."

"I 'preciate that."

"Mister Van Zant?" Cross says.

"Got you covered." The graybeard called Van Zant

steps sideways to give himself a clear shot. "He moves strange, I'll cut him in two."

Cross holsters his pistol and strides up to me. He stops a foot in front of my face, close enough that I see the flecks of yellow in his eyes that break up the brownness, and the slender crucifix around his neck.

"I'm going to take the gun you've got hidden in your trousers now." He sticks his hand down the front of my waistband and retrieves the pistol. He clucks his tongue, emptying the bullets on the ground and tosses the pistol backward onto the pile. And now, with his subject of interest thoroughly disarmed—he starts to look at me for real. His head comes in close to mine and he sniffs the air. Stepping back, he lets a thin, satisfied grin curl his mouth.

"Yá'át'eeh Diné."

He addresses me in the way of the Navajo, with none of the warmth, but with cold and hateful accusation. I don't bite and that makes his smile vanish.

"Don't play games with me, boy. Surely your White Man charade hasn't wiped every word of your native tongue from that thieving Navajo mind of yours."

"What the hell are you talking about, sir?" Ballentine incredulous.

"Harlan ain't no Navajo," Owens protesting. But the damage is done. Cross's smile returns.

"Harlan. Har-lan," Cross dragging out the syllables. "Haven't you gotten cozy with these nice people? Defiling a good Christian name with your lies. Too bad they don't know you like I do."

"You don't know me."

A darkness flickers behind Cross's eyes. He moves—his knee flying up—straight into my balls. I drop to the ground, the air sucked out of me. His boot kicks me sideways. I rise, throwing a punch that grazes his temple, knocking that stupid bowler off his head. But Van Zant is there in a flash, the butt of the shotgun crashing hard into my skull, lighting bolts of pain charging through my spine. Everything goes twinkly. The sandy ground scrapes against my cheek, a boot heel pinning my neck to the dirt.

I come to a few seconds later, still on the ground, my wrists and ankles bound in iron.

"The railroad authorities are aware of your predicament. The army is en route to assist you. This man is the mongrel fugitive, Harlan Two-Trees, wanted in connection with the Sangre de Cristo Massacre."

"Get out of town," George says. "That's Harlan? You gotta be shittin' me."

"I assure, I am not," Cross bristling.

"Well I'll be dipped in heifer shit. You're famous, Harlan. Why didn't you say nothing?"

Cross answers for me. "Because he's a killer of white men. But he's not a threat to you anymore."

"Come now," Ballentine says. "Surely this can all get sorted out at a later time. Do you understand what has happened here? Hundreds are dead."

"If you will take the woman and children down off the ridge," Cross says, "we will conclude our business and be on our way. You can retrieve your weapons after we've gone."

"What are you talking about *business*? What are you getting at, Cross?"

"This man is a fugitive of the law."

"You said that," Owens, hands on hips. "Now what are you planning on doing?"

"They're fixing to kill me."

"Hell they are," George says.

"Beg your pardon, sir," Ballentine finger-wagging, "Every citizen is entitled to due process of the law."

"If he were a citizen, he would be," Cross countering. "Now sir, you will take the woman and the children back down below. This is nothing they should see."

"You ain't got the foggiest notion what them youngsters seen," Owen says. "Ain't you got your eyes open, fella? Take a look down yonder. This here's been a shit storm of a robbery."

"The fugitive Two-Trees at the heart of yet another bloodbath. And alive to tell about it. My, how fortune favors him. I have no doubt you gentlemen have been duped by his conspiracy, but I assure you, this is no coincidence. Now take the woman and children down."

"I will not," Ballentine firm.

"Neither will I," Owens agreeing.

Cross, over his shoulder, "Captain Carter, please escort—"

"We are not going anywhere," Mrs. Whitehurst erupting, the children clinging tall to her dress.

"Very well," Cross respecting the resolve. "You can watch him hang. Mister Van Zant."

A volley of dissent shatters from my friends. They move en masse toward Cross. He draws his pistol, the barrel leveled an inch from George's face.

"Advance and you die," Cross's challenge stopping them cold. "That goes for any of you," Van Zant comes in around from my leg. He grabs the iron and the back of my collar and pulls me up to my knees.

"On your feet, or I drag you."

I get up slow, the blood rushing from my head. Far off near the horizon, a swath of dust, miles across, rises from the desert floor and breaks up the clear morning sky. I squint to make it out and Van Zant jams the shotgun below the ribs and gets me shuffling toward the edge where the tracks stop.

"Up ahead oughta work," he says to Cross. Cross backs away slow from the others. We march in somber procession toward the precipice, where a splintered ghost of the trestle frames the remaining road, the heaviest wooden beams still bolted to their moorings beside the tracks. Van Zant and I lead the way, followed by Cross, alone, then the others. Carter and the trainmen bring up the rear. Every step brings more into view the grisly panorama of destruction, until the Santa Fe herself lies unobscured below like a discovered tomb.

Only then—with the ribbon of wood and steel, that a day before was America's monument to progress, now coiled and smoldering upon itself—does Jacob Cross permit the scale of the calamity to register on his face. He pushes past me, walking ahead to the edge, where he stops.

"Oh, dear God," touching the crucifix on his chest. He closes his eyes, muttering a prayer, and crosses himself. The engine crew, eager to share their grief with anyone who will hear it, fall in next to him.

"Those are our brothers down there," Carter's

voice finding strength. "We got to go down and look for survivors."

"We are the survivors, son," Ballentine consoling. "We're all that's left. And if it weren't for Harlan here," his voice pointed at Cross, "we'd be as dead as those bleeding hunks out yonder."

I think about breaking for the cliff and taking my chances with the fall. Van Zant doesn't catch me on his best day, and I have the jump on Cross. But they'd shoot me in the back. And with my arms and legs bound, the only change to my current situation would be crossing over to death with a bag of broken bones. That won't do.

My gaze drifts out to the horizon, the dust cloud swirling closer—horses that number in the hundreds. With the First People locked up on reservations and all the buffalo dead, there's only one thing left on the frontier covering that much ground that fast. And right now it's my best hope.

Van Zant pushes the back of my knees and they bend me to the ground. He comes around to the front, at the base of the trestle, and takes off his coat. He wears a thick rope, coiled across his torso like a sash. He slips the rope over his head and folds the end of it back on itself and then starts to count off the loops that complete the noose. Jumping seems like a good idea again.

If that old silver-haired Apache has patience, maybe Storm will warm to him over time. Apaches know horses. Hell, the stallion could do worse—a lot worse—and it ain't like I'm going to California without him. I hear Mexico has fine grazing, even up in the hills where the Apaches hide out. I sure would like to feed him a couple more apple slices, though. And see his tail flick up when he chews on them. That's as close he gets to saying thank you, but we got our way of talking. Maybe they got apples in Mexico. I know if they do, he'll sniff them out in no time.

"Harlan, you got to confess and ask for mercy or do something," Ballentine pleading.

"I can't confess to what I ain't done."

"Well, I believe these men intend to hang you."

"There ain't no doubt about that."

"Shut up," Van Zant losing count of his loops and starting over, annoyed.

George throws his crutch to the ground and gets Cross's attention. "I don't need no gun, mister. How 'bout you and me settle this 'tween us?"

"Young man," Cross turning away from the cliff, his eyes wet with sadness. "I choose to forgive you."

"I ain't ask for no forgiveness."

"'Keep far from false charge, and do not kill the innocent or the righteous, for I will not acquit the guilty.'"

"The hell's that mean?"

"Exodus twenty-three seven," Cross says. "It means open your mouth again and I'll kill you."

Van Zant throws the rope over a trestle crossbeam and looks back at me, measuring in his head. They mean to shove me off the edge of the cliff with enough rope to snap my neck, and leave me dangling over the arroyo until I stop kicking.

Cross and Van Zant confer among themselves.

I catch Spooner's eye and flick my head and he trots over, bending down to keep our voices low.

"You got to stall," I say. "Army's on the way. They're ten minutes out."

"I don't see anything," peering beyond my shoulder.

"They out there. Trust me."

"Harlan, I don't know how to reason with this man. Can't you tell him you're innocent?"

"I ain't talked more than twenty seconds straight in my life. Need you to get a good streak going, till the scouts get here."

Spooner's eyes dart side-to-side, his intellect alive and firing. "Retain me."

"What?"

"Retain my services, as your lawyer."

"I ain't got no money."

"I'm sure we can work out amicable arrangements at a later time."

"Get away from him," Van Zant snapping. He marches over, a piece of black cloth in his hands. Cross draws his pistol again. Van Zant aims to blindfold me. Spooner eyes me in the waning seconds of my vision, his tongue curled in anticipation.

"You're hired," I say.

"NOW SEE HERE, SIR!" Ballentine rising, his body emboldened, like he's slept twelve hours on a soft bed. "I am Shelby J. Ballentine, Esquire. I am licensed to the bar of the Commonwealth of Virginia, the District of Columbia and the Carolinas. This man is my client and I demand to be heard."

"You're a world away from the Carolinas, friend," Cross says. Van Zant ties the blindfold around my eyes, leaving a sliver of sight down at my feet the only scope of my vision. "You have no jurisdiction here."

"Point of order, sir, I have litigated in federal court and I have presented oral arguments before the Supreme Court of this land. And as this territory falls under federal provenance, it would be a vexatious miscarriage of justice to forgo the right of counsel."

I hear Cross sigh. "All right, say your piece then."

"I believe the first issue before us is one of national sovereignty. It was the case of Calhoon vs. the State of Delaware, 1841—"

"Mister Van Zant," Cross interrupting. "Proceed."

"I haven't finished my opening remarks."

"I'd be quick then," Cross says. "Unless your intent is to increase your client's suffering. "Go ahead, Mister Van Zant. Just enough to get him started."

All at once a sack hood swoops over my head, cutting all light. And then comes the rope. I hear Ballentine arguing, his voice strident, Owens and George shouting their protest. The noose fits snug under my chin, Van Zant giving it an extra tug and then walking off, satisfied. My pulse quickens, breath rising and blowing back against my face from the stale confinement of the cloth sack.

Still on my knees, a good ten yards from the drop, I feel the rope tightening. It goes taut, pulling me over, everyone screaming, their voices indistinct and muffled beneath the hood.

I suck in breath, the dry cloth filling my mouth as my lungs crave fresh air. The tightness around my neck grows unbearable, yet my hips and legs drag across the ground. So this is it—a slow strangulation, worse than a proper hanging. Fire rages in my lungs. My skull wants to burst. I suck in one last breath. Cigarette smoke, deep in the fabric of the hood. The vestige of a previous wearing, a condemned man's last smoke. The tobacco—Hannah's tobacco.

Hannah.

What is she doing here? And jasmine flowers, yes. She smelled of jasmine beneath her cigarettes. Exploding blooms of red fill my vision against a field of black. And then all that falls away, and I see that band of freckles, running like a constellation across the bridge of her nose. She smiles. And then everything in my world goes—

CHAPTER TWENTY-THREE

Jacob Cross began counting backward from one hundred, silently, in his mind. . . . 99 . . . 98 . . . 97. How long would it take, really, three minutes? He could endure a lecture from this traitorous, rebel blowhard for that long. Think of the good it would engender, letting this traumatized and concussed band of stragglers feel satisfaction that they had done all they could to save a life, even a life as wretched as that godless savage writhing at the end of a rope in a slow, agonizing chokehold. . . . 86 . . . 85 . . . 84. At zero he would carry out the sentence of death exactly as he planned, throwing the mongrel fugitive over the cliff just to hear his neck snap. Cross had earned that. And if Two-Trees happened to die in the meantime, while this Dixie barrister salted air with his infernal stalling, Cross was fine with that. Until then he would allow only passing snippets of the lawyer's diatribe to pierce his concentration.

"Furthermore, jurisprudence of the Territory would dictate the compelling principle of *ex injuria jus non oritur*." . . . 77 . . . 76 . . . 75.

As the greasy Southerner slung his words—my, could the fat man talk. And talk. And talk—Cross played a game with himself. *What put you on that train in the first place, fat man?*

Cross looked into Ballentine's eyes—even though the lawyer was doing everything he could not to return the gaze. (That right there told him plenty.) The eyes don't lie. Not to Cross, anyway. *You're too old and soft to find fortune with your hands,* Cross thought. *But you strike me as smart enough to know that turning a profit from the legal trade in the lawless caldron of the frontier would be tough going. Why walk away from the wealthy East, with its friendly courtrooms and clients who pay their bills on time? You're running from something,* Cross said to himself, *something that stinks. A scandal.* Cross knew he'd hit pay dirt. He had that feeling he gets—deep in his belly—when he's found the truth. Cross didn't have the whole picture yet. That would come later. But he knew for certain, that at the soiled, vulgar bottom of the story—Ballentine's cock had been the problem. . . . 49 . . . 48 . . . 47.

Cross looked over to Van Zant and was pleased that the Dutchman seemed to be getting the hang of the rope. *Hang of the rope.* Cross fought off a smile. He'd have to remember that one. Van Zant kept active tension on the rope, adjusting to the fugitive's gyrations, but not letting him choke out either, not just yet. Two-Trees slumped, exhausted. Van Zant let him rest a moment before tightening the rope ever so gingerly. Van Zant checked to see if his boss was watching and, receiving the approval that he wanted, kept the dance going. . . . 33 . . . 32 . . . 31.

Oh honestly, fat man. Do you think I'm this stupid? The

lawyer had steered off into an anecdote about fishing with the Attorney General.

"I said to Brewster, I said, 'Ben, if you're calling that a catfish, then I'm calling Atlanta the nation's capital.'"

Cross had heard enough, and upped the speed of his counting, blowing through the twenties in a single breath. . . . 19 . . . 18 . . . 17. But then something in the wind made the hairs on his neck stiffen. He stopped his count, spinning on his heels, and peered out, in disgust, at the broad plain to the south.

"Get him up!" Cross snapped, charging to the mongrel and lifting—by his own considerable power—the man to his feet.

"Sir, I have not yet reached my summation."

Cross ignored the lawyer and said to Van Zant, "The army. An entire bloody cavalry troop, looks like. Let's get this done now."

Van Zant looked out over the cliff and saw the formations, dark squares of horse and rider, advancing like thunderheads across the desert.

"The army's coming!" Reggie breaking from the old woman and dashing toward the edge.

"They're still off a ways," Van Zant dropping the rope and helping Cross get the half-breed into position. "A mile or more, I'd say."

"Say, how 'bout we see what the army's got to say 'bout this?" Owens stepping forward, his daughter in his arms.

"You're pulling a fast one, and you know it," George fuming.

Cross had no interest in opinions other than his own. All the authorization he required was folded in his pocket. What he did not want was delay, or bureaucracy, or the slow-drip of stilted thought that eked from the brain of the United States Army. He was above all that, beholden only to the highest authority there is.

"Tie it off!" Cross demanding. Van Zant cleated the tail end of the rope to the pylon.

"I got too much slack, hang on." Van Zant looped the excess around the base knot as fast as he could.

"Leave it," Cross hissing through gritted teeth. "Harlan Two-Trees, I sentence you to die. May God have mercy on your soul." Cross lowered his hips, ready to drive the prisoner back and over the edge.

"Don't do it—you can't—please stop," all protesting voices bled into one. Harlan pushed his weight back into Cross, fighting to the end, enraging the man in brown.

"I said die, you son of a bitch!"

A rifle boomed behind them—frightfully close— the civilians screaming as they dropped to the ground. The shot splintered the wood pylon inches above Van Zant's hands, the Dutchman stumbling backward, the knot unspooling itself as he falls on his backside. A horse nickers, hooves gobbling up the short distance as two riders—soldiers on horseback— arriving like phantoms from the train side—descend on Cross, rifles cocked and steady.

"Hands in the air," the corporal commanding. "Where I can see 'em."

Scouts, Cross thought. *Fucking scouts.*

The second soldier, a buck private, halted his horse next to Van Zant, covering the Dutchman, but also the handful of cowering civilians, arms held high.

"I am a federal officer. This man is my prisoner," Cross said.

"And I said get your hands off him and in the air."

Jacob Cross looked into the eyes of the low-ranking officer peering down a barrel at him and could smell the arrogance, the false sense of security the man-child took in his uniform.

He could taste strict adherence to orders and could feel in his bones that attempting to reason with the unreasonable would most certainly get him shot. Cross let go of the half-breed and raised his hands.

"This man is a murderer and a fugitive."

"So says you," Owens yelling from his belly. But even the hint of confusion was enough for the corporal. And Cross knew it.

"Ain't nobody hanging nobody 'less the captain say so."

Cross let out a sigh of frustration. He had no doubt that this would all work out in his favor. The half-breed will hang, and hang today, so help him God. No, the thing that really chaffed Jacob Cross was that two white soldiers—schoolboys—had managed to sneak up on him. There was just no way.

And then a third scout appeared from behind the train—dark-skinned, riding bareback—and Cross understood. *There we go, that makes sense.* Cross pegged him for Warm Spring Apache. The native was hanging back, as instructed, so as not to upset the White People, but no doubt it had been his talents that wended the path up the rocky hillside. The scout's cavalry uniform—a loose interpretation of army standards, supplemented with feathers—involved no trousers at all, only a breechcloth.

"I think you better get your captain, then," Cross said.

The corporal addressed the Apache in clear words. "Get Captain Oliver." The Warm Spring Apache nodded that he understood. He weaved his horse around and rode off.

Then Cross added, "And I hope all your scouts have proper documentation."

U.S. Army Captain Terrence Oliver wanted answers from one person at a time. Talking over one another, he made quite clear, was not an option. Oliver had driven his full troop—nearly two hundred men—over eighty miles of high desert through the night to get here. That meant travelling light and lean—something Oliver did better than any commander in the Plains Cavalry. No wagons, pack mules only. His orders were to locate the missing Santa Fe (he'd done that), appraise the situation, and act accordingly.

Appraisal and action.

This was the appraisal phase. And he wanted it over as quickly as possible. Because his course of action had been clear for the last hour—hunt down the deserting sonsabitches who did this and drop the hammer of justice. But this business with a hanging, this was a sideshow.

His first sergeant returned to him with a list of names and began to read. As Oliver listened, he matched each name with the face of the participant. The federal agent, Cross, checked out, as did his goon. The private train crew that brought them verified that that they'd shoved out from Lamy around four this morning.

"These folks here were passengers," the sergeant said, gesturing to the ragtag civilians being tended to by the troop's medical officer. "They claim they're the only survivors. So far our men ain't found nothing to say otherwise."

Oliver gazed out from the cliffside, surveying the scope of the wreckage. The entire landscape crawled with army blue—soldiers lining up and tagging the dead bodies as best they could.

"What about this sniper I keep hearing about?"

"Nothing yet, sir. But we got sharpshooters of our own fanned out across the ridge in case he shows himself. I have two recon teams working down from the top of the rim. Two more spiraling up from the bottom. If he's in this bowl, we'll find him."

"Captain, if I may have my identification and my sidearm back, please."

Oliver looked down at the heavy gold emblem in his hands. Special Agent–Department of Indian Affairs. This man Cross appeared to be who he says he is, but that didn't mean Oliver was going to let him run roughshod over his investigation. As far as Oliver was concerned, they both worked for the same government. The captain handed the badge to his first sergeant.

"Give him back his shield. Hold onto his gun for now."

"Yes, sir," the sergeant striding toward Cross. He came back holding an envelope.

"What's that?"

"It's a letter of authorization," Cross answering a

question not directed at him. Good hearing on Cross, Oliver noticed.

"Read it," Oliver said. The first sergeant removed the letter and unfolded the parchment.

"'To whom it may concern,'" he began. "'Please accord my special agent, Jacob Cross, every consideration and accommodation necessary in the execution of his duties to this office and to the United States of America.'"

"Unless it's signed by the Secretary of War, I don't see how it changes much."

"'Sincerely yours, Grover Cleveland, President of the States.'"

"Do mind your thumbprints, sergeant," Cross concerned about the letter's handing. "The president's ink tends to smudge."

"Who is this condemned man, anyway?" Oliver asked, and before the sergeant could speak, four people, including Cross, drew in breath to answer. Oliver shot up his gloved palm, silencing all but the man he had addressed.

"Apparently," the sergeant checking his notepad for accuracy, "he's a Navajo half-breed name of Harlan Two-Trees."

"How do I know that name?"

"Well, I can't verify this, sir. But what the lawyer Ballentine and that fella Owens are saying, this Two-Trees is the same Navajo what helped bring down the Snowman last summer."

"I'll be damned, that's it." Captain Oliver nudged his Appaloosa toward the prisoner, who sat on the ground, arms shackled behind him, but his hooded head held upright, like he'd been listening. "Remove his hood." Cross thought about protesting, but a solider whisked the hood off before he could get a word out. "And the blindfold," Oliver added. The man called Harlan Two-Trees—his flesh damp and red-faced from the close, hot air beneath the cloth— looked up at him and nodded, like they knew each other.

"Captain," Two-Trees said. Indeed they did know each other, at least by sight. Oliver recognized him immediately as the man who'd been accosted on the street outside that man's house in Santa Fe. He saw him again that night, at the Blue Duck.

"Well, I'll be. Trouble sure has a way of finding you, doesn't it, Two-Trees?"

"That it does," Cross answering again. "I'm sorry we've taken up your time, Captain. I know you have a lot of work to do. I'll conclude my business and get out of your way."

"You're just itching to swing that poor boy, aren't you? What he done, got you so hot under the collar?"

Cross turned, and for the first time, leveled a withering gaze on Captain Oliver. "Tell me your third general order, Captain?"

"What?" Oliver not sure he heard him right.

"Your third general order. Let's hear it."

"I don't need to explain military business to you, Cross."

"My point precisely, Captain. This is a matter of Indian Affairs. I have neither the time nor the liberty to divulge the particulars of this fugitive's case. I suggest you tend to your office and I'll tend to mine. Now if you'll please return my sidearm and release my deputy, we can all return to our sworn duties."

Captain Terrence Oliver did not normally care enough about strangers to hate them, but everything about Jacob Cross—from his rattlesnake eyes to his letter from Grover Fucking Cleveland—made his stomach turn.

"I pity you, Cross. You have no scope of what's really important out here. The resources you burned tracking down one sad kid, I could run my troop for a month. Go ahead and hang him if that's what you want. Do it, and get the hell out of my territory." Oliver turned his horse and eased it forward.

And that's when Harlan spoke.

"Your squad that went missing, they're dead. Tombed up in the cliffs about twenty miles north of Santa Fe, not far from the Grande."

"Quiet," Cross said.

The captain held up his hand. "How do you know?"

"I stumbled on it, two, three days ago."

"Why didn't you tell me in Santa Fe?"

"I didn't piece it all together till this morning. Sorry to tell you it weren't pretty. Your men got massacred good. Them what done it tried to make it look like Apaches, got it almost right too. Just missed a couple things that gave them away."

"What makes you an authority on the Apache, Diné?" Cross hissed.

"Same authority as you."

Cross's eyes narrowed. He slapped Two-Trees hard across the face.

"Cross, you touch that man again, my first sergeant has permission to shoot you dead. You hear that, First Sergeant?"

"Loud and clear, Captain."

"You're threatening a federal agent of the United States. I'll have you brought up on charges."

"Wouldn't be the first time I flirted with a court-martial," Oliver shrugged.

"Forget your commission. You'll die in prison."

Oliver ignored him. He wanted to hear from Two-Trees. He looked right at him and said, "What are you saying, exactly?"

"Men who robbed the train, they killed your missing squad, took everything—their uniforms, horses, rifles, even the standard—just so they could make this whole caper here look like it were them Dazers getting back at the army by stealing its pay."

"Huh." Oliver considered that a moment, his brow puzzled. "If their clothes were taken, how do you know they were my men?"

"Yes, do tell, Two-Trees," Cross incredulous now.

"Because I found this." Harlan swung his bound arms best he could. Something shiny flipped through the air and landed on the ground. The first sergeant picked it up.

"Brass belt buckle. Standard army issue. Could be anybody's."

"Flip it over."

The first sergeant examined the backside, unimpressed. "Wait a minute." He turned from the waist, letting the sunlight fall across the worn piece of metal in his hands. "Got something scratched into it, a name or something."

Captain Oliver held out one hand and with the other retrieved a pair of wire-frame spectacles from his vestment. He took the buckle from his sergeant and read what someone had etched into the metal.

"E.W. MT. 5C." The captain stared at it stone-faced. "M-Troop, Fifth Cav. That's us."

"E.W." The sergeant repeating. Then he snapped his fingers. "Why, I'll bet that's little Eddie Wyeth, he's one of the missing."

"The youngest," Oliver said. "Seventeen." He had committed to memory the names, ages and home-towns of each missing solider in his charge.

"This means nothing. He could've picked that up anywhere down there," Cross thumbing down into the arroyo.

"Maybe." Oliver flipped the buckle over, holding it more carefully than he had a minute ago. "Maybe not."

"You disappoint me, Oliver," Cross throwing up his hands in contempt, "entertaining the raving lies of a man who would say anything to save his neck." Cross squared his prisoner in front of him and prepared to march him into position. "I've indulged you long enough. You have your investigation. I have mine. Mine is a federal matter, trumping whatever constabulary authority you might have in the territory."

"I don't think you understand, Cross. Those robbers stole the army's pay."

"I'm sorry your salary is in the wind. I wish you every success in its retrieval."

"And I'm telling you that robbing the U. S. Department of War is about as federal as it gets. And this man here," pointing to Two-Trees, "is a material witness with valuable information and he will be interviewed to find out what he knows." Oliver then addressed Two-Trees directly. "You could find that spot in the cliffs where my men are buried?"

"I'll lead you to whatever's left of them."

"Well, Mister Cross, looks like your hanging party's going to have to wait, because Two-Trees stays with us."

"Absolutely not." Cross pulled out a pair of handcuffs, slapped one bracelet onto to the prisoner's wrist and the other onto his own. "Come morning this man would be gone with the breeze and neither of us would get what we want out of him. He is in my custody and will remain there."

"What're you proposing?" Oliver asked.

Jacob Cross, without admitting defeat, took solace that even though the serpent tongue of Two-Trees had staved off the hanging for a day or two at least, that inevitable death just got a little more painful, a little less clean. Piano wire, maybe, instead of rope. And now it would happen in the basement of jail, where no witnesses would complain.

"You will find Two-Trees in the Santa Fe Central Jail. If you haven't made your inquiries in forty-eight hours, I'll assume you've come to your senses."

"Two-Trees stays alive until he is interviewed. I don't care it takes me a month. And just to make sure you don't get squirrelly in the meantime, First Sergeant Daniels and one of my corporals will be escorting you to Santa Fe, at which time a proper military detail will be installed to guard him."

"I'm a busy man," Cross said. "You have a week."

Oliver correctly sensed he had pushed Cross as far as he would go.

"Fine. A week. And you're taking all of these people back with you," Oliver indicating the civilians. Cross glanced at the wretched assortment staring back at him.

"I'm not a cab service."

"Well, how about I just commandeer your whole fucking train? I assure you I have the manpower."

Cross flicked a bit of dust off his jacket sleeve and squared his bowler. Sharing his coach with injured men, and old women and filthy, whining children—that was about as appealing to him as a cup of cold puke.

"Mister Carter, prepare the train for our guests. I'll take my weapons now, Sergeant."

CHAPTER TWENTY-FOUR

A sharp turn in the track shatters the veil of thin sleep that for the better part of an hour has had me in and out of the twilight between dream and misery. At one point in the delirium, I was certain that Xenia—Milton Garber's negro housegirl—had emerged from the back of the caboose with a basin of water. She knelt beside me, her neck showing hints of dark bruising beneath a gauzy muffler of white bandage, and proceeded to dab the dust and dried blood from my face with a cool towel until Cross shooed her away. Such are the fever dreams that spring from the depths of exhaustion. I awaken on the floor, chained like a dog to the steel bracket where a seat once stood and has now been removed to accommodate Cross's petty humiliation. I roll my wrist and try to work out the stiffness in my shoulder. With no other cars to balance it, and choked up directly behind the clattering tender car, the caboose bangs along in a deafening racket, a far cry from the weighty smoothness of the Santa Fe.

Sunlight strobes through the windows, the shadows

short as the day stretches into afternoon. A blue-gray haze thickens against the rich paneled wood of the ceiling. At the far end of the car, cigar smoke plumes over the seat backs, where a man—his voice heated with emotion—shouts to make his case atop the clanging din of the engine. I recognize the voice as Owens. The crown of a brown bowler and the brim of an sergeant's cap place Cross and Daniels as the recipients of Owens's admonition.

The rest of the car sees little activity. The widow Whitehurst sleeps upright along a central bench, her neck tilted back, mouth slightly open. Both children—little Reggie and the Owens girl—lay sprawled on the bench, their heads resting peaceful in the old woman's lap. A young corporal occupies the seat across from me, his eyes arranged in the military paradox of looking both alert and bored. He sees me wake up, sniffs to himself, and goes back to cleaning his fingernails with the tip of his bayonet.

The seat back in front of me bulges under the weight of its resident. The entire chair creaks as the sitter stirs, his wide, ruddy face peeking around the side to meet my gaze.

"Ah, you're awake," Spooner says, leaving only one member of our party unaccounted for.

"I don't see George," I say.

"Enlisted. On the spot."

"The army took him? He's got a busted leg."

"Oh, they had the chief surgeon look at him. George of course downplaying the injury like it were hardly a flesh wound. I'd say even with George's bum pin, the army came out ahead in that transaction."

"He'll make a good soldier."

"That he will. Hard to say 'no' when a man of his

physical attributes is itching to kill." The corporal glances over, sniffs again. "I'm consulting with my client," Spooner challenging.

"What do I give a shit," the corporal returning to his manicure.

"What's Owens railing on about?" I say.

"He's demanding to be let off at the Harvey House."

The Harvey House. I'd forgotten we're going to pass right by it. By *her*. She won't leave me alone. The scent of her neck groans against the wall of memory and I push away the pain before the wall buckles and comes crashing down.

"Owens wants to stay close," Spooner continuing, "in case the army finds his wife and boy. He tried to stay on with the cavalry, but Captain Oliver wasn't interested, not with Owens seeing double and having a little girl counting on him."

"Owens ain't George."

"No, sir." Spooner looks me over, pity on his face, like he wishes he could do something, but I see the gears working behind his eyes. "Harlan, I want you to know, no matter what happens, you are still my client. The question of your ethnicity," and here his confidence wavers, "diminishes your rights somewhat. I won't be leaving Santa Fe until this whole thing is settled." I want to tell Spooner that in the end, whatever legality he can muster would only stave off the inevitable for so long. Jacob Cross wants me dead. Every day that I live opens a fresh wound in his belly. Even if by some miracle I earn my freedom, he'd put a bullet in my head before letting me go. He'd say I tried to escape or that I came at him with a knife that he'll drop at my feet. I can't imagine a man hating himself so much that the only solace he can find comes from the suffering of others. And that he does it all under the adopted mantle of the White Man's God speaks of a soul so blackened, vengeance is its only sustaining lifeblood.

"I know you're doing what you can. That was some first-class lawyerin' you was slinging back at the trestle."

A gracious grin curls his lip. "You should hear me when I've had my coffee."

The door to the water closet opens behind me and Van Zant steps out, buttoning his fly.

"Break it up," he growls.

"You're aware of attorney-client privilege?" Spooner says.

"You're gonna be aware of my foot in your ass. Back to your seat." Ballentine rises with contempt and strides back to the center of the car. Van Zant plops down where he'd been sitting. I close my eyes, hoping the jerky motion can find a rhythm to lull me back to sleep. Maybe there's time for another memory. Maybe time is all I have.

A short train sneaks up on its port of call without warning or fanfare. A long whistle blast and then a minute later we are full-stopped at the Harvey House. Cross announces we'll be underway in five minutes, just enough time to deposit Owens and let the widow and the children use the W.C.

"I'll grab you a sandwich," Ballentine over his shoulder as he disembarks, leaving me alone in the dreary gray of late afternoon. I look up through the window at a gunmetal sky. The clouds have moved in.

I hear Cross's voice on the platform, just outside

the window, as he joins two men in conversation. "What's the problem, Mister Carter?" Cross says.

"We've been ordered off the road, sir. Tracks need to stay clear for the repair crews. Company's got them heading out to the trestle all through the night."

Paper crinkles as it passes hands from Carter to Cross. Silence as Cross reads the directive. He scoffs his breath, dismissively.

"Send word that our train is to be allowed passage, by order of the federal government."

"They can't, sir. The repair trains are already on the line."

"And how long are we supposed to stand down? I have a prisoner aboard."

"The last crew should pass through around five in the morning." This third voice, pinched and officious, I take to be Duquesne, the manager of the Harvey House.

"That's twelve hours from now," Cross incredulous.

"Sir, it would be our pleasure to accommodate you and your guests here at the Harvey House tonight. We've got comfortable rooms, whatever you require."

"Unless you have a jail cell, I doubt that."

"Can't the prisoner stay where he is?" Carter asks.

Cross doesn't answer, his pause long and simmering. "This is entirely unacceptable," he says, finally. "Tell them to clear the track at once. "

"This is from company operations, sir. It's not a suggestion."

"I don't work for your company," Cross's voice rising.

"I *do*," Carter says. "I defy that order, and were something to happen to you or anyone else, I'm guilty of murder. And that *is* unacceptable. I'm sorry, sir. But I'm the captain of this rig and I say we're docked." Cross crunches the paper to a ball, furious, on the brink of cursing beneath his breath.

"We might have a suitable place for your prisoner," Duquesne brightening. "Our winter pantry. A heavy door, bolts from the outside. No windows. If it can keep animals out, I should think it could keep one man in for a night."

I hear Cross's measured breathing, a man collecting himself. "Send a telegraph, Mister Carter. This train will depart precisely at one minute past five, tomorrow morning. By order of the President of the United States."

"Yes, sir."

"First sergeant, please stay with the prisoner," Cross says, and then to the manager, "All right, Mister Duquesne, let's see this pantry of yours."

A few minutes later, Cross comes back onto the train with Van Zant and the two soldiers.

"Stand up," Van Zant says. I get to my feet and Van Zant places the musty hood back on my head.

"You're being moved," Cross says. Van Zant unlocks the chain from the bracket and cuffs my hands behind my back.

"If at any point you feel inclined to take off running, help yourself," Van Zant soft in my ear. "I been looking to clean out both barrels."

He shoves me forward, guiding with a hand to my shoulder. We start along the aisle and down the steps to the platform. The cool air swirls up my back and underneath the hood, bringing the sweet smell of impending rain. We cross the platform up the walk

toward the side entrance by the W.C. I see the spot in
my mind, from above, as I remember it, and wonder
if she is up there, watching from her secret vantage
on the roof. What would Hannah think, seeing me
escorted in like the condemned criminal these men
make me to be?

Voices and shuffling feet accompany our entrance
into the building. We move down a long hallway, the
sounds of the bustling kitchen slow to a crawl as our
parade passes by. A door opens, Van Zant's grip on
my shoulder tightening as we reach the top of a
staircase and begin a slow, measured descent into
the damp coolness of the cellar.

I am marched along a concrete floor until Van
Zant stops me and removes the hood. A thick wooden
door stands open before me, Ballentine beside it. He
holds something wrapped in paper.

"All right, in you go," Van Zant nudging me into
the small room.

"Now hold on minute, I insist you unbind his
hands."

"Fuck your mother," Van Zant says.

"See, here, a man has the right to relieve himself
without fouling his hands. We are not animals. Mister
Cross, I implore your compliance."

Cross strides up, inches from Ballentine's face, his
probing eyes dismantling the lawyer's veneer.

"Listen to me, fat man. I don't know what you're
running from, but I'll find out."

"You've no quarter to get personal, sir."

"Mm. My money says you either take it up the ass
or you were poking little girls. Whichever it is, you
didn't run far enough." Cross turns away, sneering,

his eyes combing the makeshift cell. He nods to Van Zant in the affirmative.

"What about the cans?" Van Zant thumbing to the back wall of the pantry, stacked floor to ceiling with canned goods—fruits and vegetables for the hard winter.

Cross shakes his head. "I've looked at them. He wants to chew through metal to eat a few peaches, what do I care?"

"Turn around," Van Zant says.

I face the side wall as he undoes the cuffs. A short plank bench, meant to serve as a bed, and a short stool comprise the only furnishings of the windowless cube. A thin, moth-eaten blanket roll sits on the edge of the bench. Van Zant sets a bucket inside the room before stepping out.

"There's your commode." He moves to shut the door when Ballentine, still rattled, holds up the object wrapped in paper. "Wait, I have a sandwich for him."

"Check it," Cross ordering.

Van Zant snatches it from him and tears back the paper. He lifts up the bread, his dirty fingers pawing through the meat. It looks like that barbequed brisket I remember. Again I wonder if Hannah might be behind it. Van Zant licks the sauce from his thumb, "Tasty," then smashes the messy glob of beef back onto the bread. He drops it into the bucket, glaring at me. "Bon appetite, asshole."

"Oh, well I never, sir," Spooner beside himself. Cross steps between them and closes the door himself, enveloping my small world in a curtain of blackness. The bolt slides home, followed by the solid click of a heavy lock. Some last minute discussion accompanies their footsteps back to the stairs. It is agreed that the corporal shall have the first watch, with Van Zant posted as second sentry in the hallway atop the steps—a position he deems more strategic, and I would imagine, more agreeable, with a steady current of young women passing before him.

The corporal returns minutes later, a lighted oil lamp shining his way. He scrapes a chair along the concrete, grumbling as he leans it against the door and flops into it. The pale wash of the lamp brightens the thin strip of dead space between the door and floor. That ribbon of light serves as my only relief from complete darkness. And yet after a while, my eyes adjust. I can make out the edges of the stool and bench, the wall of cans. My ears sharpen, along with the other senses. I eat the sandwich slow, absorbing the sounds and smells of the subterranean confinement.

After about an hour, dinner service begins upstairs, girls' voices eking through the floorboards as they clomp overhead in those awful block shoes. The memory of the first time I saw Hannah—the brush of her skin against mine, the furtive glance as we ducked behind the curtains—play again in my mind like a storybook. Dinner is quiet tonight. I hear the girls complaining about it, what with the train not running, only a few locals who arrive by buggy take advantage of cook's delectable barbeque.

The hours pass into night, the noise from above quieting as service stretches into cleanup and cleanup drifts into preparations for the next day. Hannah would be brushing her hair about now. The pain returns, the wall buckling to the point of breaking. I bury my head in my hands and try to drown out the curse of memory. Why did I have to be brought back here, why give me hope? The torment of that young woman's face, only yards above, floating like an angel.

I forgo the bench and lay on the cold ground. Such is my life—alone and dark, in its final days. Some twenty-one years I have lived on this Earth, loved by those who would then be taken away: Mamma, Sheriff and the missus Pardell, Maria, Storm, and now—a final torment—a spark so bright it burns with searing pain inside me. This woman I barely know, Hannah—her mouth unkissed by mine, our dearest secrets unshared—takes up residence in the forefront of both head and heart. Warm tears streak down my face.

"You okay in there?" the corporal timid and embarrassed to hear my blubbering.

I choke it down and roll onto my back and let my breath steady out.

"I'll be all right," I say.

And maybe that's it. Maybe this woman's gift to me is the memory of her, a gift I can take to my grave, as beautiful as I choose to make her. My present to Hannah, then—if I overstate the impression I made upon her, so be it—will be the image of a man in a well-made suit, enjoying a game of baseball in her company during the twilight of a fine spring day. I close my eyes, aware of my smile. Outside a gentle rain begins to fall, building in power, until the downpour drowns out all sounds from the other world.

I don't know how long I sleep. When I awake, the glow of the lantern enters at a new angle, as though its position has shifted. Then the loud snoring from the other side of the door rattles the wood.

The snoring of an older man.

Van Zant.

I put head to ground and peer under the door and see the butt of a shotgun resting by the chair. The rain has softened to a steady patter, allowing the force of the man's snoring to cut through like a steam shovel. Beneath the layers of sound, I detect a soft rustling, like that of a mouse. I suspect Mister Duquesne's attempt to secure his foodstuffs from the ambition of tiny varmints has fallen short. But I am glad to have the company.

The mouse flitters behind the lowest row of cans, at the base of the wall, tapping at, and I suspect failing, to pierce the tin fortress encasing the desired sardines or split pears. He taps again, a trio of steady pecks.

Odd.

And then three more taps, equally steady.

Not odd. Impossible.

I slide, on my knees, to the wall of cans and tilt my head toward the bottom row, ears open. It comes again. Tap . . . tap . . . tap.

I bring a fingernail to the nearest can and return the pattern, three taps, but a hair faster. *Tap, tap tap*. I pause, blocking out the rain to focus my hearing down into the floor. *Tap, tap, tap*, comes the rapid reply. My heart leaps.

Slow, with hands soft as butter, I begin dismantling the wall of cans, working down to the bottom, toward the source of the beckoning sound. Thunder rolls far in the distance. I freeze, ears tuned to the steady rhythm of Van Zant's snoring, scanning for any disturbance, a snort of disruption. Quiet as I can, I stand and move the bench so it blocks the wall of tin. I drape the bedroll over the bench, obscuring what I can of my handiwork as a last-ditch precaution. Returning to the cans, I create an opening down the center of the wall, straight over the point where the sound originates. Removing the can at the very bottom, I paw along the ground, seeing with my fingertips, searching for any change or imperfection. Something sharp, like the end of a wire, pokes my thumb.

On instinct I bring my thumb to my mouth, tasting the droplet of blood. Now with the back of my hand, I feel the floor again. Sure enough I find the offending wire, and determine I have uncovered a bit of metal screen—a deterrent against rodents—but covering what? I look down at the darkness, and to my shock see the faint flicker of candlelight.

All at once, a mighty crash of thunder explodes overhead—as if the Harvey House itself has birthed its own thunderstorm. In the fleeting sliver of time before the crescendo of thunder has reached its peak, I am sure I hear the startled gasp of a female.

The offender silences her gasp, which is quickly drowned by three seconds of the heavens' deafening anger, a sound no one could sleep through.

"What's going on in there?" Van Zant growls. His chair scrapes. Keys jangle. I throw myself onto the bench, making my body as big as I can. The door opens, the lantern's light invading the darkness. I howl, as if ripped from a horrific nightmare, recoiling at the lamplight like a scurrying cockroach.

"I had a dream. Please don't go!"

"Oh, God," Van Zant recoiling, his bearded face

appearing directly over my piss bucket. "Stinks to high hell in here." The door slams again, the bolt sliding into place.

"An Injun afraid of thunder," Van Zant grumbling, amused. "There's a campfire story."

I lay on the bench in silence, letting him settle. He chuckles to himself, his chair leaning back against the door. A thunderclap cracks again, but the storm is on the move, the worst of it speaking elsewhere. Soon a low vibration rumbles from him, mellowing into the familiar pattern of his snore.

I slink off the bench to the floor, groping to make out the corners of the screen. I move more cans, nesting their metal edges against the dirt without a sound. Peering straight down along the wall to where it meets the floor, I wait. My breath slows to near stillness. And then it returns—a faint flutter of light— the weak throw of a single candle, struggling to stay aflame in the drafty hollows below ground.

The light draws near, the softest patter of movement joining it. Slowly the patch of screen on the floor reveals its shape—a square iron grate, less than two feet across, with a dust-coated wire screen lashed across it to fend off small invaders.

But management hadn't planned on this cunning little creature.

A nubby candle appears beneath the grate, held by the most beautiful hand I've seen. The hand withdraws and I drop to my knees, my face suspended a foot above the grate. Her candle draws near the opening again, but instead of a hand pushing it through, a quarter of a head appears.

In the wavering light, I see a cheekbone, banded with freckles, and a single eye the color of green ice. A glorious tightness, like an eagle unfurling its wings inside my chest, beats against my ribs. I touch the screen. Her eye dances with recognition, with triumph.

Hannah.

Hannah.

CHAPTER TWENTY-FIVE

A thousand thoughts explode inside my head. I want to touch her, to feel her skin against mine. All at once, the injustice of my imprisonment—to which moments earlier I had resigned myself—compels me to freedom. And when I have it, what factors shall determine my first step? Incomplete as I am, in my present form, the answer comes in a shattering crack of thunder. This journey began with a team of two. And I was raised to leave no man behind, not when he calls himself your partner. My first order of business, therefore, announces itself this very moment— with the winds and rain and thunder—commanding us to harness its power. And then once free, I will find him—my partner—namesake of the tempest sky that howls from the heavens as loud as the stallion himself.

But what of Hannah? How far do I entangle an innocent girl in my trajectory? I could send her away right now—her service rendered—but would she go? I get ahead of myself. We have work to do.

And it must happen without speaking. I run my

fingers along the sides of the iron grate sunk into the floor, finding no grip or leverage to speak of. Hannah watches me through the screen, nodding, as if she understands my dilemma. Her face vanishes through the hole. I hear a tinkle of metal, and her hand reappears. Clutched in her fist, is a hammer. She turns it upside down, pressing the butt of the handle up against the center of the grate. I paw for the edges of the forged iron square. She strains to push the hammer upward, loosing the grate just enough for me to locate its corners and give purchase to my grip. I start to pull—and stop immediately—when the grinding clang of rusted iron spikes the silence. We freeze, my ears tuned to the doorway. Van Zant grunts, but keeps snoring. The grate feels like it will lift with our combined effort, but not without considerable noise.

Hannah pops her head in again, her eyes eager and attentive. We bring our faces as close as we can. Soundlessly I mouth a single word.

"Thunder."

Her eyes brighten. She pulls her head out, sticks in her hand and throws me an affirming thumbs-up. Clever girl. The hammer reappears, placed gingerly against the grate. I reclaim my grip on the corners and we wait.

And wait.

Unable to see each other's faces, we depend on our mutual intuition—a suitable thunderclap, and then we shove. We hold there—legs burning and starting to cramp, her arms twisted into the hole, supporting a heavy hammer. The heavens choose now to be uncooperative. Fitting, in that the stallion—

named as much for his tempestuous demeanor as the thunderhead coloring of his coat—made an art of doing things in his own time. A low, sustained grumbler rolls in through the walls, teasing us to make our move. But we both know to hold our line—when Storm speaks, he speaks loud.

I see her arms start to tire and hear the fatigue in her soft breath.

Hold on, girl. It won't be long. A weak, but shorter, clap barks outside and I get the sense the storm has another wave in it. Then, in a sudden, frightening crash, a mighty peal of thunder BOOOMS overhead. Hannah's arms tense. She shoves upward, I lift with my legs—the grate rising from its screws—the dry, grinding squeal all but lost in the din of colliding heavens. I stand up, nearly falling back into the tower of stacked cans, the grate clutched in my grasp. I steady my balance, heart pounding, and deftly set the heavy chunk of iron on the ground without a sound. I look down at the opening, Hannah lighting the way with the candle. A few pesky wires—remnants of the screen—jut into the mouth of the opening like jagged teeth. Surely, they will snag my clothes. Without thinking I pull off my boots. I yank off the shirt and shuck loose the trousers and shove them through the hole. Hannah dutifully takes them, no doubt confused that I am no longer in them. A thought occurs to me: I don't know what lies ahead, but I'll need strength. I grab a couple of the nearest cans and pass them down. And then, stark naked, I sit on the ground and feed my legs through—like I'm slithering through a hole in the ice. The sharp wire snares my hips, and I push through it, ignoring the pain, until my waist and belly and chest drag across the metal, scoring a long deep grove in the skin. White-hot agony courses down the spine. I nearly bite through my tongue suppressing the urge to cry out. But I don't, and with my eyes bleary with tears, I feel Hannah's hands on my naked hips, pulling me through.

I pass through the hole and spill out in a dark, damp passageway carved directly into the earth below the building. Hannah looks down at me, her face fixed in a battle of concern and readiness. Then, all at once, she bends down and brings her lips into mine. We kiss—our lips conveying the words of a hundred stories. Our arms enfold one another, her hands pressed into my naked back. And then we stop. She turns around, and in the tepid wash of the candle, I shimmy back into my clothes. Stomping in my last boot I touch her shoulder and she starts down the corridor. How many late-night explorations it took her to discover this place I can't hazard, but if anyone would know every crack and crevice of her landscape it would be the resourceful housecat leading me presently.

I follow her to the end, where a ladder—nothing more than shards of wood nailed to a post—leads up into a dark hole. She grabs ahold and starts to pull herself when I stop her. I turn her face to mine.

"The barn," I whisper, barely audible. Hannah nods, a grin forming, as if she'd known my destination before I had determined it. She waves me to follow and begins to climb. I let her get ahead of me, somehow compelled to catch her should she fall. But with the surefootedness of a goat, she ascends the tricky ladder, and I am watching her round, little backside rise upward, veiled in the thin fabric of her bedclothes. Once she reaches the top and crawls off the ladder into darkness, I grab hold and pull myself up. The slats creak against the nails as they absorb my weight, pausing my ascent as I listen for Van Zant. Free of the jail cell, I hear the patter of gentle rain outside, and with it, the tantalizing closeness of freedom.

The ladder ends beneath the floor of what I figure to be the kitchen. Hannah crouches on all fours, just off the ladder, in a dirt-lined crawlspace separating the cellar from the ground floor of the house. She wriggles along, toward the near wall. I follow, the earth beneath us dampening as we near the outside. A swirling draft blows over, extinguishing the candle, but now the blue-green hue of night air seeps through every crack and crevice in the boards that skirt the building. We reach the edge of the crawl-space, Hannah stopping at a rectangular panel that, I see now, sits just off its mooring. Beside her lay two folded lumps of fabric. She passes one to me. It is a man's coat. I feel like kissing her again, but instead I put it on, and transfer the canned food to the outer pockets. The other garment is a coat for her, which she dons. The loosened panel pops out without effort or hardly any sound. Rainwater from the roof splashes down into the mud outside. I've never been so happy to have my face splattered.

Hannah slithers through the opening and I go right behind her. I am barely standing upright when she takes off running across the backyard toward the barn. Wind and rain lash from all sides as I give chase. Compared to the pitch darkness of the pantry, the stormy night glows like a midday sun. We slosh toward the barn, our feet making more racket than I care to, but the howling storm provides ample cover. Hannah bounds across a short field toward the barn, circling around to the back side, where the double stable door bangs against the chain that holds it closed. But enough space appears between the doors and Hannah slips through without touching wood. She holds the doors apart for me and I slide through into the dry warmth of the barn. The smell of hay and horses charges my lungs with newfound energy, my heart pounding.

Hannah turns to me, soaked to the bone, her hair dripping and matted to her head and we fall into each other's arms, stifling our nervous laughter and rejoicing in victory. She wears a dark winter coat over her bedclothes and a pair of thin black slippers, good for padding around in silence and not much else. I notice that the coat she found for me looks familiar, in fact, I had seen it on the previous wearer just a few hours ago.

"I knew you'd need a coat," she whispers. She is right about that, but how she managed to get Ballentine's, I can't guess.

"Did he give it you?"

She shakes her head. "No, but I gathered, of all the men here, he's the one who wouldn't mind you having it." Right again. I feel something heavy in the pocket and reach inside. My hand returns holding a cold, black forty-four pistol. Hannah shrugs, sheepish.

"Figured you'd need that too." The pocket jingles with a good supply of bullets. Spooner took this coat off a dead passenger when it turned cold in the arroyo. The gun he found the next morning. I reckon he won't mind both getting put to good use.

I see horse blankets folded in the corner and I gesture to them. She follows me over and we sit down.

"I hate this is how you're seeing me, trussed in here like a criminal. I didn't do the things they're saying I done—"

She touches my lips. "I know you didn't. Because I know you're a good man."

"You don't know much about me."

"I know enough." And then she says. "Did you ever think about me?"

I want to tell her that, facing the moment of my death, it was her face that I saw. And that had told me everything I needed to know. But instead I take her hand and say, "I thought about you, even when I had no business doing so."

"Well, that settles it then. Because I never stopped thinking about you."

Indeed it is settled. But what it would look like— the two of us together—right now seems murkier than fog on lake.

"I ain't got much time to explain too much," I say. "You done good by me, better than a lot of fellas what break out of places for a living."

"We'll need a horse. I think we should take Queenie, she's the fastest."

"We?"

"I'm coming with you."

"No, you're not," watching her eyes jerk, like she'd been punched. "What I have to do is too dangerous for you. I'm not bringing you into that."

"I'm already into it." Again, she is right. But staying here, she at least has options.

"You remember that horse of mine?"

"Storm, of course."

"I need to go get him."

"You can't come back here after. I'll have to meet you."

I think about that a moment. "The train, that's the best bet. As soon as they start up again, you need to jump on and head west. Don't wait, you understand? And stay clear of that fella, Cross. Do you have money?"

"Almost two hundred dollars."

"That's good. I don't like you on a train by yourself, but I don't see any other way."

"I'll be all right. I'll find some older couple to sit next to, pretend to be their daughter."

"That's smart."

"You'll write me, care of Western Union, tell me where to meet you."

"No, I leave any trail like that, Cross will find it. We need to have a place picked out, a place only you and me knows about."

"In San Francisco, then."

"Neither one of us ever been there."

"All right," she says, with a calm far beyond her years, "every city has a central post office. I'll meet you on the steps of San Francisco Post Office. Twelve noon, every Sunday. For one hour, I'll wait for you. Or you for me, whoever gets there first."

"You're a born bank robber, girl." I kiss her again, our mouths hungrily entwined.

"Which way are you heading?" she asks, pulling away. I am about to answer when I realize the next thing I say could cause her problems. So I tell her some things I'd figured out, but leave off a few more she don't need to know about.

"Them men what robbed the train weren't soldiers, despite what you're gonna hear. They was logging men, come down from timber country. The way they killed, tools they used, even the smell of their clothes. That means from the north, out near Flag, or some such. I ain't shared that with no one. You keep that to yourself."

"I will."

What I don't tell her is that I'll be heading south, following Storm and the Apaches, who split from the Dazers and broke toward Mexico. What Hannah don't know can't hurt her.

"I need to go," I say, standing up.

"Queenie's down this way," she pulls me and I stop her.

"Hannah, I'm running because I ain't looking to die for something I ain't done. But if I steal a horse, it changes things. They'll hang me for that."

She bites her lip, seeming to understand. "What's a horse cost?"

"Oh, a decent mare, that's about fifty dollars."

"Hmm."

"Don't even think about paying for it. That wouldn't work anyway."

She nods, agreeing. "Well then, you'll just have to make sure you don't get caught with it. I'll leave the door open. They can think it blew open in the wind."

"I doubt your Mister Duquesne will buy that story."

Hannah looks at me, knowing. "You let me worry about Duquesne."

"All right then."

She leads me down the aisle to the stall, where a strong, chestnut mare sniffs at us. Queenie.

"She'll do fine," I say.

"You need a saddle."

"No, I don't." I touch her face, burning it into my memory, as if I'd ever forget such wonder.

"Tell me something," she says, the moment of our parting at hand. "Am I your girl?"

"If I die tonight, I die your man."

She steps back from me, behind her, a pile of fresh hay. Her coat falls to the ground and in a single motion, she peels off her nightgown, standing before me, naked.

"I ain't got a minute to spare," I say, lost in her curves.

"Well, then, you'd better be quick about it."

CHAPTER TWENTY-SIX

Xenia prepared the bath precisely as he had instructed—bringing the water to a boil and then allowing it to cool for exactly one minute. After a lifetime in service, she had drawn countless baths for men—first the cotton baron, his doughy, pimpled paunch seared forever in her memory, and then when he grew tired of her, for Garber, who at least was kind in his infantile baby talk. But Mister Cross was different. Never had she seen a man lower his naked body into a cold empty tub and have the water, scalding hot to the point of blistering, poured over his back.

And the story told on his back frightened her. The intricate arrangement of lines and geometric shapes, deeply inked and spanning the width of his smooth, brown canvas, looked to Xenia's untrained eye as if it had been scraped into his skin with some primitive implement—a bone or a shell—rather than a tattooist's needle. What did the markings signify? Only once had she asked him about the design—not with words—the pain of speech still too unbearable—but by running her finger down the central pattern. The lines reminded her of an arrowhead.

"A godless custom," he had said, almost ashamed. "Boys were taught to be hunters and fighters. But nothing of Christ's love."

She lifted the bucket and poured it over his neck and shoulders. Cross barely flinched, he only sucked the air in slightly though his teeth. As he leaned back, some of the water splashed out of the tub and onto the dark wood of the rented caboose. She froze, petrified. But he said, "It's all right, child. Water is God's tears." And then he raises his hand, as if gesturing to the falling rain outside.

Tonight she was more nervous than on previous bathing sessions. For one thing, the hour, the small clock on the table said it was not even three in the morning. But mostly she feared she had displeased him earlier by washing the bloody forehead of his "prisoner."

"Such a compassionate creature, you are," was all Cross had said on the matter.

It was her nature to clean things. Although the brush she used on his skin took some adjustment— for her, not for him. It was the kind of stiff bristled scrub brush meant for stone or tile, not the human body. And Cross demanded such force in her scrubbing that she though she would peel off his skin. Maybe that was the idea, she wondered. After a few days, she got used to it. But she would never understand why he required her to be naked as well. If he wanted to touch her—sure—that would make sense. But Cross never laid eyes, or a finger, on her when she bathed him. He only stared straight ahead. And when she came around in front to scrub chest and his sex, he kept his eyes tightly shut.

All at once his eyes popped open. He cocked his head to the side, listening. Sometimes he heard things that she could not hear. Cross drew his pistol from the chair where it hung, and twisting his naked torso, aimed at the door.

Someone knocked. "Mister Cross?"

Van Zant, his voice troubled.

"What's the matter?" Cross said.

"You'd better come quick, sir."

Shelby J. Ballentine awoke to the sound of shouting voices and needed a moment to figure out where he was. Blinking his eyes in the feminine, unfamiliar room—with its miniature bed and straw-filled pillow—it all came back to him. The Harvey House. The men's voices came from outside, where dawn's first light was breaking through the window. Ballentine rose, instinctively pawing for his glasses. Not finding them on the bedside table, he moved to the chair back where he'd hung his jacket. That was missing as well. The glasses, he remembered, had smashed in the arroyo.

The arroyo. Yes, that had all happened.

But his coat, no. He was quite certain he'd draped the suit jacket over the high-back chair because he'd deemed the room's only clothes hanger too flimsy.

And then he stood upright, straight as a board, a thought occurring to him. He went to the window, wiped off the dew, and peered out. Jacob Cross strode across the back of the property from the barn to the house. The manager, Duquesne, followed close behind, looking most distraught at the tongue-lashing Cross was giving him. The staff matron, Mrs. Packer, sloshed through the wet grass on the other side of Cross. She said something to him, and together, they both looked up at the windows.

Ballentine turned away from the glass. Could it be? A smile bloomed across Ballentine's face as he entertained the possibility. His coat was gone, most surely. As was—Ballentine gasping with delight—the pistol he'd hidden inside.

"Godspeed to you, son. Godspeed."

And then Spooner Ballentine flopped backward onto the bed, giggling like a schoolboy.

Jacob Cross bounded up the stairs to the second floor, two at a time.

"Second bed on the right, lower bunk," Packer said through labored breath as she stayed close behind him. Cross hit the landing, marched down the hall and threw open the door of the girls' dormitory. A chubby girl, half-dressed, gasped and covered herself. Cross ignored her, his eyes roving across the stacked twin beds. Second bed on the right.

A tuft of sandy blond hair blossomed from beneath the covers. *What frizzy hair you have*, Cross thought, *like you've been out in the rain.*

He crossed the room in two paces, the matron Packer grinning behind him. Cross sunk his hand deep into the roots of the girl's hair and yanked her from the bed.

Hannah screamed, half asleep, but waking quickly. She grabbed at his hands but it was no use, his grip too strong, his anger too powerful. Cross wrapped his other hand around the whore's nightgown, and in a violent motion, flung the girl across the room. Hannah sailed through the air, crashed hard into the far wall, and dropped to the ground like a sack of potatoes.

Even Mrs. Packer stopped smiling.

"Stop, don't." Hannah weakly as Cross went to her. He bent down and pulled from her nightgown a golden strand of hay.

"Well," he said.

"What do you want?' Hannah sobbing.

Cross put his hand on her neck and lifted her off the ground by her throat.

"Everything, my dear. I want all you have to give."

"I don't know anything," her airless voice choked with fear. Cross shook his head.

"Wrong answer." And then he punched her in the stomach and let her fall again.

CHAPTER TWENTY-SEVEN

I drive Queenie hard through the night, holding the mare to a steady canter as we head west. We make good time, keeping in sight of the tracks, but far enough removed to stay hidden from the trains carrying workers out to the arroyo. The rains blew north, leaving a dewy fog that clings low over the swollen country. But the sky above shows the promise of a clear and cloudless morning. An hour past dawn, with the rising sun warm at our backs, I start to read the ground for signs of life, and the heavens for signs of death.

A lone vulture patrols overhead, wings fixed for cruising. He banks slow to the left, letting the air take him, as much on the hunt as I am. I could follow him all day and come up empty. But he has a better vantage up there, and his nose is sharper than mine. I decide to give him ten minutes—his languid path pulling me offline—until he is little more than a speck against brightening blue. But then he circles back, curious, weaving a figure eight through the air, perhaps a whiff of something. All at once he beats his wings—an effort his kind don't undertake without good reason—and assumes a dead-straight course to the southwest.

"Think he's on to something, Queenie."

We work our way toward a cluster of low hills about twenty miles south of the tracks. A column of vultures spirals upward beyond the hilltops. Cresting the nearest mound, I see one of the birds swoop down and not return. Ten minutes later I edge Queenie down the final downslope before the ground flattens out again. An outcropping of rocks lay ahead, and gathered at the base of it, a black mass of scavengers, packed wing to wing, feast on the dead. The birds take mild interest in our approach, but not enough to stop eating, only parting like an oil-slicked ocean at the last moment, when the mare's hooves bring the threat of trampling.

Owens's little boy lies on the ground, his eyes pecked out and a hole in his belly where the vultures had punched through and begun to suck out his insides. I climb down from the horse and kneel down next to the body. The boy's skin, fair and pink, speaks of a recent death—this morning. I nudge the boy onto his front and see the hole in the back of his head where the bullet entered. At least the Apache had done it quick.

The soft ground after a rain leaves no secrets. One horse rode in from the west, disposed of the child, and returned along the same path. I go down on all fours and bring my face close to a stretch of hoof

prints, pristine in the damp sand. Three of the four
prints offer ordinary evidence: a well-shod horse, of
larger-than-average size, carrying a light load. But
the fourth print sends a current of electricity down
my spine and out through the toes. The bent shoe
nail—its impression cast unblemished into the soft
earth—glares back at me as if Storm himself were
nuzzling his head into mine.

The stallion was here. Recently.

I leap onto the mare and have her moving with
newfound purpose. We follow the horse trail south,
toward a range of barren hills that rise upward and
plateau into a jagged sculpture of cliffs and sandstone spires. As we ride, I try to piece together the
narrative of what happened. The silver-haired
Apache, who broke Storm from his berth, fled the
arroyo with the stallion, alone. Yet this morning,
whoever was riding Storm had the Owens boy with
him, which means the Apaches had all reconvened,
as I thought they might. A picture starts to emerge.
An elder—a seasoned horseman—his hair white
from decades of breaking and stealing horses, and
then restealing the horses stolen from him, took
Storm as his payment for helping the bandits rob the
train. A lifetime of being lied to and shot at by the
army would make any man seek his revenge. He's no
reservationed Apache. We're headed straight for
Mexico, which most likely means Chiricahua or
Tonto Apache. Good horsemen, brave and honor-
bound fighters.

From the spot where I found the boy, to the
arroyo, can't be more than thirty miles. Storm, beneath a good rider, should be half way to Mexico by
now. Something slows their progress. I suspect family

ties—the only reason that makes sense. The two younger Apaches, the long-locked executioner and his short-hared kinsman are probably related, if not brothers. And I'll wager the elder horseman will turn out to be their father. The long-hair son took the Owens woman as his prize, equally valuable as the stallion, but more of a hindrance to speedy travel. The other son got shot in the back, and if he still lives, would require frequent stops to rest and tend to his wounds. My best guess then, is that the two healthy Apaches—father and son—needed to lighten their load. So the father took Storm and the boy out to the rocks, shot the boy and headed back. He didn't want to kill the child in front of his mother. That means Clara May Owens is still alive. It also means that when I find Storm, I'll find her.

I wasn't preparing for that.

But so be it. Plans change. If she managed to survive this long—after all she's been through—she's earned all the help I can give her.

The ground dips to a depression that runs like a fast stream with all the rainwater. I see no tracks on the other side. The Apache walked in the water for a bit before cutting out. I've done my best to avoid detection and so far have felt like I was chasing someone who didn't know he was being followed. The distance between strides indicated Storm's business-like, but unhurried, gait. But a cagey old silver-hair doesn't stay free this many years without keeping an ear to the ground. He may stroll through running water at every opportunity simply out of habit. And why wouldn't you? It would be like passing a well without drinking. Or maybe he's on to me. When I find his tracks again, I'll have my answer. I lead the mare straight across and then canter along the edge, one minute in one direction and then two minutes back. If that old Apache hasn't seen me yet, this makes a good way to get spotted. But I have no choice.

I find Storm's trail a half-mile down, locating the exact spot where the Apache kicked him up into a hard gallop, which the stallion was happy to oblige. If the Apache didn't know he was being followed before, he does now.

Storm's tracks lay across the high desert floor like printed ink, at least to my eyes. When the ground turns hard, the Apache dismounts and tries walking the stallion to make the prints less noticeable. And I'm sure that works on White Men. But the walking slows him, and I gain ground. I come across the stallion's droppings, so fresh the flies haven't yet found it. But my heart warms that there's plenty of straw in it, and I know the Apache must've taken the effort to load up some straw from the Santa Fe. He knows that horse is special, all right, not the kind whose feeding you trust to sagebrush and milkweed.

The tracks grow faint as we climb up into the cliffs, the ground hardening into sun-baked caliche. And now, with the rock formations peaking from the surface like gravestones, I become the hunted—every cliff a sniper's perch, and every shadow an ambush. Soon I lose all sight of Storm's hoofprints. I pull back on the mare and listen, the breeze rolling clean and cool over the dampness of the sandstone. The wind shifts abruptly, and I draw the pistol from my coat.

Tobacco smoke.

No way would the elder allow his sons to burn tobacco right now. The smoke travels a mile or more in clean air. And this tobacco, no doubt another prize from the fallen Santa Fe, burns very nearby. The explanation hits me like a train. I've reached his sons before he has. And they don't know I'm coming.

I swing down from the mare and leave her, guided by my nose as I track the vapor up into the cliffs. I glance back at Queenie. The mare turns and trots off the way we came. I don't risk calling to her. Soon she shifts into a canter and vanishes over the nearest rise.

And here I thought we were friends.

But I can't help feeling some relief, as I catch a fleeting glimpse of her, now a hundred yards away. If she has any barn sense, she'll be home by nightfall. Who knows, her return might keep me from getting hanged as a horse thief someday. I've always believed horses know when they've been stolen. Some, like Queenie, just bide their time until they can make their break and head home. It makes me wonder what thoughts are running between Storm's ears right now.

I bring my mind back to focus and creep silent against a heavy slab of stone. The smoke odor gets stronger. After about a minute, I peek my head around a corner and can see the gray-blue tendrils of smoke rising from behind a boulder.

Mindful of my shadow, and floating on the balls of my feet, I sneak forward, couched at the knees, finger itching over the trigger. Then a heavy breeze picks up, and a lighted cigar, caught by the gust, rolls out from behind the boulder and skitters away across the rocks. I pause. What man lets his cigar blow away?

An injured man.

I reach the boulder, touching its coolness with my off hand, the gun cocked and ready in the other. I spin around the corner—the trigger half-pulled—and freeze. The short-haired Apache, the one I shot in the back at the arroyo, slumps against the rock. His eyes sit fixed in the glassy stare of the dead, but I'd wager five minutes ago he was still alive. The cigar, no doubt, was his comfort as he made his journey to the Spirit Plane. Fresh red blood re-stains his shirt and trousers, already soaked brown with stale, brown blood down to the tops of his thigh-high moccasins. I see now that he is Chiricahua, and no older than twenty.

I consider putting a bullet in his brain, finishing what I started, but I don't. He'll get to cross over unmolested, not because he deserves it, but I can't have the noise. Still, I won't pass in front of him. I double back and cross behind the boulder to the edge of the cliff. Peering out to the horizon, I hope to find some disruption that lays claim to the stallion. Then I look straight down at the landing below me and nearly drop the pistol.

A white woman, dressed in a thin white gown, lies on her side at the base of the rock wall, her nose pressed against the stone. I can tell from here it is Clara May Owens. Her hands move in unison to clear the long, unkempt hair from her face, her wrists bound together with cord. Tears forge a river through the dusty plain of her cheekbone, and the fair skin of her bare shoulders burns red from too much sun. Her clothes, unsuitable for travel or any semblance of propriety, offer no protection from the elements. I realize now that she wears only her undergarments—knickers and thin chemise—her dress long discarded, either as punishment, or to provide her captor easier access to her body.

I see no sign of the Chiricahuas, or the horses, but the long-haired son would be close by, most likely scrounging for food. Sinking to my knees, I reverse and hang down over the ledge and lower myself down. The drop is only a few feet and I land soft, but my shadow passes over Clara May's vision and she sits up, squinting into the sun over my shoulder as I approach. I bring my hand to my lips to keep her silent, but she just shakes her head, as if I am some silhouetted apparition.

"Clara May, it's all right," my voice in a whisper. I step out of the sunlight and let her see my face.

"It's you," her mind straining to work out my appearance or if I'm really here at all. Then, in a flash, her eyes go wide with terror. I see the shadow on the rocks and am already turning. "Behind you," she cries.

I bring the pistol up and see the shape of a man on the ledge where I just stood. A gunshot booms and I spin. Searing pain explodes in my left shoulder as I aim at the figure above me. And then he is in the air, spearing down from the cliff, feet first. I squeeze off two shots. His trajectory alters midair, but his feet land against my side and the two us crash backward against the rocks. The blow knocks the wind out of me. I roll to my knees and bring up the gun, but I don't have it. My left shoulder feels like it fell in a bear trap. The long-hair Chiricahua glares at me with hate-filled eyes and unleashes a pained war cry, blood pooling at his hip where the bullet caught him. He draws a double-edged skinning knife from his belt and leaps toward me. I pivot left and go with his weight back to the ground. The smoke and sweat from his body fill my lungs. I can taste the anger on his skin, and he grabs my neck and tries to thrust the knife into me. I drive forward with my legs and we slam into the rocks again, this time his bones taking the worst of it. He answers with the knife, jabbing at my legs, the blade slicing into muscle like a thousand hot needles. I smash his head into the rocks, but he holds on to the knife. Then all at once he centers his weight and shoves back into me, driving with his legs. We struggle backward, his torso turning to drive the knife home. I spin my arms as I stumble back. My boots catch the dirt and I go down. Long-hair's eyes narrow, the beginnings of a grin. I bring up my arms, prepared to lose them if I have to. I slither back, hungry for distance, and feel a large boulder halt my progress. Wedged against the boulder, I run out of options.

The Apache closes in. I brace for more pain.

A gunshot. Long-hair's eyes widen, his mouth agape, and then twisting into confusion as he turns around. Clara May holds the smoldering pistol with two hands. Long-hair drops the knife, but it doesn't matter. She shoots him again, square in the chest, and he falls on his ass. Clara May steps toward him, the gun steady in her hands.

He says something to her in his tongue.

"Fuck yourself," hissing through her teeth. And then she fires again. His head snaps back, the rear of his skull blowing out in a soupy splatter. She strides over to him—the rage in full force now—and squeezes off three more rounds, until his face and skull are pulpy memories and the gun clicks empty.

"You saved our lives," I say.

"What life?" She turns toward me. In one look I see the young girl Owens married and the unimaginable hell of the last two days waging full-scale war behind her eyes. She turns to the horizon and stares north.

"My son," her voice breaking.

"Your boy walks with the angels. I saw where they left him. There's nothing for you out there."

"My son will have a proper burial," she says, leaving no room for discussion.

"I need to get my horse. We don't find a horse, we're gonna die here."

And then she looks at me, as if a fog has lifted and she sees me plain. "Oh, Mister Harlan. My God, you're injured . . ." She takes one step and then a rifle shot cuts the air. A ball of crimson flowers her chemise and she crumbles where she stands.

The rifle is close.

I summon my strength and crawl toward her, belly to the ground. The pistol lay at her feet. I pick it up and roll onto my back to reload, pawing through the coat for the spare rounds. The rifle fires again, and I feel the air sizzle inches from my head. The shot pings off the rocks. I slam the cartridges into the cylinder, snap it shut, listening.

I hear a click as he chambers another round.

I grab the dead Apache's knife for good measure and lift my head and see him. The Chiricahua elder—his long, silver strands half-way down his back and tied with a red string—from his position behind a rock. The stallion stands behind him.

Storm.

My heart leaps. The stallion, his charcoal coat gleaming in the high sun, looks all right. Hell of a lot better than I do. My whole left side has gone from searing heat to feeling like it's buried in ice. And the joints are stiffening so fast, I fear soon I'll have no movement at all. I have to keep moving and I can't stay here. I come into a crouch and slink along, below the elder's line of sight, to an outcropping of stone about twenty yards closer to his position.

I realize, as I catch my breath, that Storm could cause trouble for himself. Any sensible man would think I'd come out here for the woman, not the stallion. That old Chiricahua has no clue as to Storm's provenance, and I don't need his vengeful mind getting any ideas. I peek around the edge of the rock. The Apache peers down his rifle, combing the ridgeline where Clara May fell. I have a shot, but it'd be tough with this pistol. But it might well be the only shot I get.

I swing out from the boulder and take aim. His back foot extends behind him at an angle. I lay the pistol over my forearm and try to steady my breath. I squeeze the trigger.

His foot snaps back behind the rock. I've hit him, so I charge the rock, my speed far below normal.

He pops up with the rifle, ready for me, and fires.

I drop and roll behind a low rock. Springing back up again, I fire the pistol, the shot skimming off the rock in front of him and funneling toward him. He falls back, hit again. I slink over to a large boulder, only ten yards separating us. As I move, I hear the familiar blow of the stallion and then it drifts into a low, long nicker—a sound a horse reserves only for those it loves.

No, you blasted fool—the thought blaring in my head. I spy around the rock. Maybe the Apache didn't catch it. The Chiricahua stands there, his mind turning. He looks to the stallion, then to me, then back at the horse.

Then he aims the rifle at Storm.

I rise up and peal out the loudest whistle I can muster. Storm's ears twitch as he rears up, excited. I aim the pistol at the Apache, but if I miss I hit Storm and if I hit the elder and the bullet passes through, I hit the horse as well.

"Don't shoot him," I say. "Don't shoot him."

The Apache turns to me, pointing the gun at me now. I stand there, out in the open. Storm dances at the sight of me, but the Apache raises a flat palm, his tone stern and soft—a born horseman—and Storm doesn't know what to do. He blows in frustration. The elder yells at me, pointing off to the side, then back at my gun.

"All right," I say, throwing the pistol. I throw it far and it thumps to the ground. "It's not his fault."

The elder admonishes me, waving his free hand, the rifle on Storm. I pick out the word "son" but not much else from his lecture. Slowly I move toward him. The Chiricahua reaches back and touches the stallion's neck, telling me something about the fire in the horse.

"Yeah, he got a mess of fire in him," I say.

But the elder hasn't stopped talking. He wants me to understand something. I nod my head, telling him I understand, both of us speaking over each other. Storm braces for whatever comes next. I raise my arms. It looks like surrender. Storm turns his wall-eye to me to get a better look. His ears flatten.

"Ya! YA!" All I at once I slash my arms downward. Storm sees the command and bolts left and back, away from the Apache, who spins from the waist, aiming the rifle up at a rapidly disappearing target. He fires, Storm jukes left and keeps running.

I pull out the skinning knife and charge at the man, oblivious to the pain. As I close the distance, he spins toward me and fires. It feels like a bull just kicked my femur. He cocks the rifle and I throw myself in the air.

He catches me, the blade slashing into his hand. We fall back, I on top of him. The blade slices off two of his fingers and still he struggles for the knife. We lock eyes, a hundred stories passing unspoken, every sinew of muscle straining for an inkling of advantage. Nervous strength pounds through my body, but behind it, I feel the weakness coming. I am losing blood.

Flat on his back now, the old man seems to age. His breath, like rancid meat, pours over me through his brown, gritted teeth. But his arms are starting to waver. The knife, suspended between us in a mass of bloody and stiffening arms, begins to move toward him. He makes one last thrust of his hips, trying to buck me, but I hold on. And then he stops fighting.

He looks at me and says, "I go, Diné. I go." He pulls his hands away from the knife and the force of my arms drives the point straight into his ribs. He lets out a breathy sigh, his eyes turning to glass. And then he is still. I collapse onto him, too tired to even gulp the air my lungs scream for.

I roll off him onto my side and then flatten out onto my back, staring up at a sky of perfect blue. As far as a last image to look at, I could do worse. Then I feel the ground start to vibrate, and I hear the stallion skipping over the ground. He blows when he gets close, and blows again, irritated when he sees I'm not standing up with a handful of apples. His giant head cuts into the blue sky and nearly blocks out the sun.

"Amigo" is all I can muster. He brings his head down and sniffs me and gives me a lick to make sure I'm really there. Then he waltzes back a step, eager to be getting out of here, and stamps the ground in case I wasn't listening.

"I ain't got it in me, pal. Can't feel my left side, or nothing below the waist." Storm squeals and rears back, and slams both front hooves down a few feet from me.

"You didn't think I was gonna let you go to Mexico, did you? I'd be following a trail of frustrated Apaches until I found you dead."

He kicks a little dirt on me and skips around to the other side so I can see him better.

"Looks like we both need a bath. Sorry I won't be able to give it to you, pal. But I can't mount up. My hip and leg and shoulder are bust up. Losing blood too. You're gonna have to go it alone."

Storm scratches at the ground and blows again.

"You got a better idea?" I ask.

Storm comes back around on my left. To my surprise, he bends down onto all four knees, his belly resting on the ground. He nudges his nose into my side. A laugh comes out of me that I can't help.

"Well, I didn't think of that." I try to move. With all my strength I roll over onto my side. The pain swallows up my legs and bites into my hip. A cry blurts from deep inside.

"I got no lift, amigo. No power. Even on your belly, I can't make the climb." Talking to him exhausts me, but it feels good to have my friend with me at the end. I sink down flat to the ground again, on my front this time, and just lie there, listening to him breathe.

Hannah's face comes to me.

Oh God, not her again. Let me die, please. I either say it or think it. I can't be sure which. I close my eyes and let the image wash over me. Storm nudges me all down the side. I barely feel a thing.

"We tried, amigo. It ain't meant to be." I open my eyes and he rolls that wall-eye over to me and gives me that look.

"Don't look at me like that. I can't get up there."

Storm blows one more time and then does the darndest thing I've ever seen. He flattens out on his side, all four legs extended outward.

"Oh, pal, I 'ppreciate the effort. But I can't do it. I got no feeling in my legs."

Storm cranes his neck and chomps his teeth down on my ankle.

"Ow, you broke the skin, you sonofabitch!" I bring myself up to one elbow just to make sure he heard me. His gaze holds me, unwavering.

Climb on.

I fall back. "I got a good mind to climb on and run you straight to the glue factory." But then Hannah is standing on the other side of him. She looks back at me, like she did at the baseball game, and smiles. She touches her hand to her belly.

I drop my head and sigh, resigned.

This is really going to hurt.

Forbidding the agony to stop me, I pull with arms, clawing at the dirt until I grab his front knee. Storm doesn't flinch. I draw myself up his body, sliding over his legs until I get a hand on his shoulder. I scooch my hips around and, with every last drop of power, will my leg over his flank.

The stallion, so as not to throw me, eases back onto his knees and then, feeling that I am centered, straightens his back end. I grab onto his neck with all I got. He extends his front legs, slow, and then he is standing upright.

"How 'bout that, amigo?"

I got you.

"Well, I hope you smelled a barn or some such because I ain't got much in me."

I GOT YOU.

I see the ground below me start to move. The

jarring motion of his trot nearly throws me. My arms burn like raging fire. But then his speed builds, first to a canter, the motion smoothing, like a boat on a lake. Until, finally, trusting that I will not let go, he hits his full stride.

And that's when we start to fly.

Connect with U s

Visit us online at
KensingtonBooks.com
to read more from your favorite authors, see books
by series, view reading group guides, and more.

Join us on social media

for sneak peeks, chances to win books and prize packs,
and to share your thoughts with other readers.

facebook.com/kensingtonpublishing
twitter.com/kensingtonbooks

Tell us what you think!

To share your thoughts, submit a review,
or sign up for our eNewsletters, please visit:
KensingtonBooks.com/TellUs.